Daughter in Exile

A Novel

Bisi Adjapon

HarperVia

An Imprint of HarperCollinsPublishers

DAUGHTER IN EXILE. Copyright © 2023 by Bisi Adjapon. All rights reserved. Printed in the United States of America. No part of this book may be used or reproduced in any manner whatsoever without written permission except in the case of brief quotations embodied in critical articles and reviews. For information, address HarperCollins Publishers, 195 Broadway, New York, NY 10007.

HarperCollins books may be purchased for educational, business, or sales promotional use. For information, please email the Special Markets Department at SPsales@harpercollins.com.

FIRST HARPERCOLLINS PAPERBACK PUBLISHED IN 2024

Designed by SBI Book Arts, LLC

Illustration on page 29 © ricochet64/Shutterstock

Library of Congress Cataloging-in-Publication Data is available upon request.

ISBN 978-0-06-308900-6

23 24 25 26 27 LBC 5 4 3 2 1

For Tolu and Tayo

Sesa Wo Suban

Change Your Character

May 2007

After the trial, I'll no longer be a woman without a country. I'll either live legally in America or be deported back to Ghana within six months. I welcome either choice. I'm weary of peripheral living.

I've never voted in my life. When I was growing up in Ghana, the voting age was twenty-one. By the time they changed it to eighteen, I had already left. In America, I pay taxes but can't vote. I'm a skeleton of a resident without the flesh of belonging.

I've been up since three a.m.

The letter my mother wrote a week ago lies unfolded on my bedside table. I've read it so many times that even when I close my eyes, I can still see the looping cursive swimming before me:

February 9, 2007

My dear Akua,

It is a pity that you have not seen fit to write to me, your mother, for such a long time. I hope you are doing well.

As for me, I am nearing the end of my life. Now my hair has hoary streaks. I am afraid you may never see me again. I don't know if you hold the nuggets of wisdom I tried to impart to you through those Adinkra symbols of our Akan people, but I cling to the hope that you're living a good life.

I pray that the almighty God takes care of you and keeps you safe when I am no longer here.

Your loving mother,
S. D.

Ten years. That's how long I've been away from home. Akua is what my family called me because I was a girl born on Wednesday. I used to hate it. What scant appreciation I had for our culture then.

I hated my Western name too: Olivia. My mother's obsession with the name felt like a nutmeg grater on my skin. I didn't care that it had belonged to her childhood best friend who died. My parents had given the name to my big sister who had died at age three or six, no one is sure exactly when. When I was born, they affixed the same name to me, which left me feeling that I was supposed to be a replacement for my dead sister. I felt no connection to her, no sense I'd been on earth before. The whole business kept me awake at night. I imagined my sister's ghost hissing, "You're not me!"

From the moment I entered university, I called myself Lola, a Nigerian name I loved. The idea that Yoruba names are shaven from sentences appealed to me. Lola derives from Omolola, which means the child is wealth, which made me feel precious. This fueled a letter from Mama about how I had hurt her, how much Olivia meant to her. Now in America, I yearn to hear her call me Akua, Olivia. Anything. Just to hear her voice. This was my response to her letter:

My dear Mama,

I'm so sorry for my silence. I know you think I've forgotten you, but I haven't. How could I forget the woman I trusted not to drown me when our car drifted off the road and ended up in the sea?

You've always insisted that, at age three, I was too young to remember, that someone must have told me. Mama, to this day, the scene swirls in my mind. I was sprawled on the backseat when the sound of men shouting and water splashing jolted me out of sleep. We were in water. Darkness covered us. Shadowy men surrounded the car, grunting, pushing, pushing. The water was so vast I couldn't tell where the sky ended and where the sea began. Somehow, I knew to be quiet as you hunched over, twisting and wrestling with the steering wheel. Right. Left. Like the windshield wipers. I didn't understand how you ended up in the driver's seat and why Dadda was slumped beside you, never to get up again.

The men pushed until the car turned around and we faced the sand, silhouettes of coconut trees rising to meet us. Then we were no longer rocking in water but on the steady sand. That's when you crumpled onto Dadda, shaking him, telling him to wake up, the scream ripping from inside me.

I don't know how, but you got us home.

You got us through the funeral. You got me through life. Because of you, I never felt the urge to dive under a blanket and remain there forever. You see, Mama, you are my safety.

Yes, I think of the Adinkra symbols, now more than ever. Do you remember when I came home from university after skipping Christmas and Easter? You pointed to the San kɔ fa swan symbol hanging on the wall and said, "Why do you think she arches her neck all the way back to pick up the egg she laid and left behind? That's because she realized it's the source of future life, the continuation of she. She doesn't fly forward while looking back like foreigners think. No. San kɔ fa. It simply means Return to take it. Her feet are grounded for a reason. Never forget where you come from or you will be lost." I used to snort and roll my eyes, but how well I understand, now that an ocean separates me from home. Oh, to be the San kɔ fa swan, reach over my back and pick up what I left behind! I live for that day.

Your daughter always,
Akua
Also known as Olivia

My hands tremble. I brush down my gray skirt suit. Breathe, I tell myself. I pick up my purse and sling it over my shoulder, car keys in hand. It's time to face the judge.

PART ONE

Ɛse Ne Tɛkrɛma

The Teeth and the Tongue

1995

You could say I entered America while living in Senegal, by way of my American friends, one evening, in a house near the sea, filled with the smell of salt, flowers, alcohol, perfume, tobacco breath, and pheromones. Americans had crossed my path, but never this many in one space.

Olga's house boomed with their loud conversations. They circulated, fixed smiles on their faces, clutching wineglasses, bending over to reach for crackers and cheese laid out on the wicker table in the center of the room. They didn't sit. They didn't break into merengue, despite the Congolese soukous music thumping in the background. At twenty-one, I was a fresh university graduate. Everyone else was above thirty and married. I was the only African, one of three Blacks. The other two were a couple whose masculine half was laughing louder than anyone else. Olga had

7

introduced him to me as Len George, or Lennard George, a man with a smile so broad his teeth seemed to begin at one ear and end at the other, strong and white. His wife, an oak-colored woman with green eyes and cotton-ball blond afro, formed part of a clump of people complaining about Senegal.

"Can you believe it? The houseboy was playing with my son's toy car!" This was delivered with round-eyed indignation by a blonde.

A collective "Nooooo!" arose from the group. They spurred one another on.

"They're so unbelievably lazy!"

"And the weather, talk about the heat!"

"I know, and then suddenly it gets cold and there's no way to keep warm!"

"No heat when it's cold. No AC when it's hot. Jesus Christ!"

"Get me out of here, that's what I say!"

"Back to D.C.!"

"Back to civilization!"

They groaned, avoiding my pointed stare. I had a good mind to retort, *Is life perfect where you come from?* But I was reluctant to ruin Olga's going-back-to-America party.

From behind me, a shrill voice announced, "*I* love it here!" That was Olga, striding toward the complainers. My heart warmed over. She stood tall above them, in a loose print dress and scarf tied over her head to form two cat ears. Her slanted, dark eyes flashed. "Gosh, I'm gonna miss it. Come on, you guys are so ungrateful." She spread out her arms. "I mean, look at this house. And listen to you all griping about servants. I'll give a hundred dollars to anyone who can point to houses like this and servants back in Kansas or wherever you came from."

No one spoke. A chill had settled over them. Then Len George guffawed and the voices bubbled up again. Olga's husband, Barry, appeared from nowhere and moved to the middle of the marble floor, clinking his fork against his wineglass. "Yoo hoo!"

The voices subsided as we all drew closer. He grinned, revealing his wolfish teeth. "I'd like to thank you all for coming to our goodbye party. It's been a wild three years, but it's time to head back to America."

"That's right," Lennard said. "Raise your glasses, y'all. To Olga and Barry!"

"To Olga and Barry!"

At that moment, someone's glass shattered on the floor. Wine splashed on my ankles. We gasped, sprang away from the watery shards. That was when, with a benevolent smile, Lennard George looked across at me and said, "Fatou, you go get rag and—" he made wiping motions "—mopez le floor."

I froze. Fatou was not my name. Before I could unglue my tongue, Olga said, "That's not the maid, she's my best friend. My best friend in Senegal." Either Len didn't hear her or wanted to cover up his embarrassment, because he persisted, "Get rag, mopez le floor, haha!"

"*YOU* mopez le floor." I pivoted away from him.

Olga called the maid while we spilled onto the veranda. Mindy, a blue-eyed lady, touched my arm, smiling as if to apologize for Lennard. Her husband, Ted, said, "Let me fill your glass. What are you drinking?"

"Sauvignon blanc."

"Sauvignon blanc it is."

I handed my glass to him, and away he went on sturdy legs, his shaggy black hair bouncing around his ears. I had the impression one could lean on him and not fall. Mindy tilted her head in Len George's direction. "What a fool."

"I don't want to talk about it."

"Yeah. Forget him. How are things going at the Thai embassy?"

This cheered me up. "I love it. They're really nice. Did you know they eat plantains just like Ghanaians?"

"Huh, I didn't know that. Last year, I visited Vietnam and they ate plantains too. I imagine most tropical countries have them."

"You went to Vietnam? How come?"

She laughed as though it wasn't a big deal. "Yeah, for my USAID project." I wondered if Ted had gone too, since he also worked for the same organization, but before I could ask her, he returned with my wine. I took a sip, savoring its chilled semisweetness.

He grinned through his glasses. "I take it you like it."

"I love it. Wine is the only alcohol I tolerate."

"So, you said you were writing a book. How is that going?"

"Not well. I wish I had more time to write."

Mindy mentioned a book she was reading titled the *Women's Room,* which she said was about women in various stages of problematic marriages. I was about to ask if she'd read Erica Jong's *Fear of Flying*, a book depicting a woman's sexual frustration, when Olga grabbed me from behind, wrapping me in a hug. Only she would breathe cigarette over me, mixed with a primal scent from her armpit. She eschewed perfume, deodorant, and underarm shaving. When I turned around, she kissed my cheek.

"I'm going to miss you, Lola." She teared up for an instant, then flashed a naughty smile, her voice throaty. "You could come with us, you know. In whatever capacity you want. Mistress to Barry. Whatever."

"Olga!" I whipped around to see if Mindy and Ted had heard her. They had drifted away and were now engaged in conversation with another couple.

Olga's slim shoulders went up in a careless shrug. "In some cultures, it's done, you know. I mean, Barry is always whooping about your breasts." She waved at her husband. "Hey, Barry! Tell Lola she must come with us."

He sidled over and pinched my butt. "You yummy thing," he said in a playful, raspy voice. I swatted his hand, whereupon he ouched and slipped away, chuckling to himself. For all his constant pinching of my butt, he was a toothless wolf. Whenever he found himself alone with me, he'd stammer, hands glued to his sides and eyes on the floor. Olga loved to goad him.

"Can you blame him? You've got the most beautiful body."

"You're crazy, Olga. I can't believe you're thirty-eight and a mother of three."

Her laughter was unrepentant. "Now, come on. Let's have it one last time."

I looked at her suspiciously. "Have what?" One never knew what percolated beneath her words.

"That song you taught us."

Ah, she was talking about a little ditty from *Treasure Island*. For reasons I didn't get, that song threw her into giggles each time I sang it. I didn't want those snobbish ears to hear me, but then I looked around and thought, why not give them one more thing to complain about? I lifted my chin and belted out the tune my mother made up:

> Fifteen men on a dead man's chest,
> Yo ho ho and a bottle of rum!

The room went silent. Olga threw her head back, a loud cackle erupting from her. A few guests giggled, then their conversations resumed their buzzing. Olga's eyes misted. "God, Lola, what am I going to do without you? There's no one like you for fun. Listen, don't pay attention to Len George. What he said. He means no harm."

It still stung, I wanted to tell her, but she was in no mood to listen.

"Let's just dance," she said, striding toward the boom box and turning up the volume.

Len's casual treatment of me as a maid cut deeply. And yet, weeks later, when we bumped into each other without the presence of an audience, he beamed at me as though he'd encountered a lost friend. "Lola! How *are* you? Good to *see* you! Why don't we grab a cup of coffee? Come on!" Reluctantly, I accepted, and was surprised to find him pulling out a chair for me, smiling at me, pressing pastries on me.

Typical, I thought, as I bit into a chocolate croissant. "How come you mocked me in the presence of Whites, but now you're pushing chocolate and croissant at me?"

His smile disappeared. "Mocked you? What are you talking about?"

"*Mopez le floor*, remember? Fatou?"

"Come on, Lola, you know I was only kidding."

"I don't know that. You called me Fatou. Olga had just introduced us, yet you called me Fatou. Fatou is what the French colonialists called their maids when they couldn't be bothered to know their names. A name isn't just a name. It's my family, my dignity. We have a whole ceremony, a whole day of feasting set aside just to give you your name after you're born. How could you dismiss mine like that?"

He grew quiet, his coffee untouched. "Gee, I'm sorry. I didn't know you were that upset."

"You don't understand. At my university in Ghana, I used to trace the faces of American Blacks in the *Ebony* magazines that traveled by mysterious ways to tables in our cafeteria. I wanted all you Blacks to come home to Ghana. Then I come to Senegal and discover you Black diplomats don't want to know us. Here, we live in this layer-cake society the French created: Whites frosting over deepening shades of brown, Blacks firmly packed at the bottom. I don't blame you for distancing yourself, but don't expect me to love you for it."

He reached over and grabbed my hand. "Whoa, whoa, hold it there, girl. You do get off on being an intellectual, don't you?"

I snatched back my hand and stood up, my chair scraping the concrete. "You know what, thanks for the croissant."

"Come on, Lola." He rushed around to block my way. "Look, I was only joking. That's what I do. When I'm embarrassed or something, I try to be goofy, you know, funny."

"I wanted to throw my wine in your face."

A childlike grin spread on his face. "You should have. I'm truly sorry. Truth is, I totally forgot your name and just said Fatou. I thought . . . I don't know what I was thinking. Look, sit down. Please. Let me make it up to you." He walked back to the table to hold out my chair. He looked so contrite I found myself relenting, dragging myself to the table and slouching down. He returned to his seat, picked up his coffee mug, set it down. "You're so lucky to be growing up in Africa. You've never walked into a room feeling like you had to prove you belonged, have you?"

"Why would I need to prove I belonged?"

He laughed softly. "Wait till you go to America. By the way, do you know the head of the UN Food and Agriculture Organization? He's also from Ghana."

I sat back, surprised. "Mr. Koranteng? Yes, his son is my friend. A true brother."

"Ouch. A true brother, eh? Well, Mr. Koranteng's my boss. I work for the FAO, you know. So, you see, I can't look down on you. You Ghanaians are so smart." He shook his head in disbelief. "Man, that guy is fit. I mean, he's sixty. I'm forty, but he beats me at tennis every time."

"Tennis?" It was hard to associate the game, which I thought of as a well-mannered sport, with this man who irritated me so much. "I didn't know you played tennis. I always wanted to learn. At university, I tried, but the coach shooed me away because I hit all the balls into the bushes."

He leaned forward eagerly. "I could teach you. Listen, let's start over. No more goofiness from me. I promise." I said nothing, which prompted another "Come on" until I yielded. "Aha! I see that smile. That's what I'm talking about. Now, are you ready for your lesson?"

"Right now? Isn't it dangerous to exercise after a meal?"

"You call a croissant and coffee a meal?" He pushed to his feet and held out his hand. "Come on, let's go. By the time you go home and get changed, what you ate will be long gone."

I allowed him to take me by the elbow. He ushered me into a white VW Beetle and zoomed away to my apartment building, which was only minutes away.

"Wow," he said, swiveling, taking in the gray three-story building. "So, this is where you live? Not bad at all. Wow, Plateau. Are you rich or something?"

That made me giggle. "No, I'm not. Ours is the plebian dwelling of the neighborhood." I pointed to a tall, aloof building in the distance. "Look at Immeuble Kébé, with its uniformed doormen and garbage chutes. That's where Mr. Koranteng lives. His son Kwaku, too, when he comes to Senegal. We don't even have an elevator. I have to climb to the third floor."

"Still. You're right across from the American Embassy. Wow."

"I'm within shouting distance. What of it?"

"I mean, I could stop by and say hello anytime I'm in the neighborhood. Pick you up for tennis. Whatever. Wow, Plateau. The neighborhood of the rich. You live alone?"

"No, I live with my friend Joana, also from Ghana."

"Awesome. Wow, you Ghanaians are something else." I felt suddenly shy and hoped he wouldn't follow me up to the flat. It was nothing unusual for married men to befriend single women and visit them. Sometimes the visit was innocent, sometimes not. It was important for me not to give him the wrong impression. As if guessing my thoughts, he leaned his elbows on the hood of the car. "I'll wait here while you get ready. You've got sneakers?"

"Yes."

I darted upstairs to get changed, feeling the budding of a friendship.

We had fun. He showed me how to hold a racket. He pulled two cans of yellow balls out of his bag and said, "These are yours. You're gonna hit them. Don't worry if they fly into the trees." He bounced the balls in front of me and showed me how to step, pivot, and swing the racquet to my shoulder. I kept hitting the ball out of the court, over the cage, but he never lost patience. "Keep trying. Just hit it over the net. There you go! You're a natural. Come on, hit it."

I loved the way the ball and racket connected with a resounding thwack. When I figured out how to hit the ball over the net without it sailing into the sky, he trotted to the opposite side and fed me more balls. I chased them down, laughing and swinging away, thrilled at my power.

An hour later, I couldn't believe how quickly I had gone from disliking him to sitting beside him on a bench, our sweaty skins touching, expelling air into the Senegalese breeze. It was the easy air of friendship. I wanted nothing more from a married man.

Bi Nka Bi

No One Bites the Other

I pushed into the studio to find Joana dancing, music blaring from the stereo, her copper-colored thighs straining through the rips in her jeans. She grinned and waved hello before closing her eyes, gyrating to the reggae. Normally, a constant troupe of visitors climbed up the stairs to see us every day, but this time she was alone. Half-Ghanaian and half-Jamaican, Joana loved to collect peddler friends and hard-up artists who sat on our floor penning poems about life's injustice.

"No visitors today?" I asked.

She opened her eyes, grinning. "Weird, eh?"

I sat in the big wicker chair and peeled off my tennis shoes and socks. "Let's go out. They're showing *Scarface* at the cinema. Do you want to see it?"

She stopped dancing. "*Scarface*? That film must be at least ten years old."

"Have you seen it?"

"No."

"Well, then. You know there's just one cinema house in all of Dakar. We watch whatever is showing. I just want to go out."

"Okay then, let's go." She looked me up and down and screwed up her face. "You're so sweaty."

"That's why I'm going to bathe."

"Good luck, ha. *She* is there."

She was our maid. Jobs were so scarce in Dakar that women routinely knocked on our door to ask if they could wash our clothes or sweep for us for a pittance. We'd ended up hiring Thérèse, who behaved more like our mother. *It's midi and you're still sleeping. Dancing every night until morning. You didn't eat my couscous and you say you're hungry.* I headed to the bathroom, where she was passing a ropy mop on the floor.

"Mademoiselle wants to take a bath?" she asked in grumpy French.

"Oui, Thérèse, ça va, non?"

For an answer, she picked up the bucket, mop stick tucked under her arm, and shut the door behind her. I giggled, filling the tub before sliding in and letting the cool water cover my body.

We were strolling by the Place de l'Indépendance, almost at the cinema, when Joana grabbed my arm. "That's Armand!" She pointed at a café to our right. Through the glass wall, a large man perched on a bar stool, a glass of foamy beer the color of tea in his hand. Joana had mentioned him weeks before as an American marine stationed at the U.S. Embassy, originally from Haiti.

"Lovely, Joana. Now, can we go on, please?" I knew that once she started a conversation with someone, I could say bye-bye to the cinema. I took her arm and began leading her away from the window. She brushed off my hand.

"Come on, Lolo, let's say hello to him." Lolo was the pet name she used whenever she wanted to coax me into doing something.

"I don't want to say hello."

She was already inside, leaning in to exchange French-style kisses with him. She turned to wave me closer. "This is my friend Lola. You bad boy, I haven't seen you in a long time. How have you been?"

"I've been doing fine." He rose to his feet, fixing grave eyes on me. I gave him a reserved smile and turned around to focus on the people strolling in the town square. I couldn't get over how beautiful the women were, their blue-black bodies in off-shoulder boubou that caressed their ankles and billowed in the wind.

Joana prattled away while I resisted the urge to tap my foot. Mercifully, she said we had to leave.

"Nice meeting you," Armand said to me.

"Nice to meet you, too," I lied, pushing out the door.

Joana clucked after me, "You know, Lola, I wish you wouldn't be so aloof with men."

She was right and she was wrong. I loved men, just not those sugar daddy, expat types who thought it fine to push their tongues into my mouth or avail themselves of my body without an invitation. Take the septuagenarian German dwelling in the apartment below us, who invited us to the beach and proceeded to insinuate his fingers into my bikini top. When he didn't grasp the word *no*, my palm left a scarlet imprint on his cheek. Or the Gambian diplomat, uncle to a university friend. A perfect papa whose benign smile barely illumined his face, who cornered me at a party and tried to pry my legs apart. I concluded it was something about me. Something in my smile. A mark on my forehead that bid old men to come hither, that said I wanted it so desperately they had to go at me. From that day, I steeled my face, determined to alter whatever signals I was emitting, doling out cautious smiles when the occasion demanded.

The minute we returned home from the cinema, our clothes flew off and the music came on. We each shimmied into a loose blouse and wrapped cloths around our waists. Then we danced like mad. That was our drug of choice: dancing, singing, and laughing ourselves into a stupor, Armand completely forgotten.

The day after the movie, we were doing our thing, practicing salsa, when someone knocked on the door. I opened it to find him standing there. I turned around to glare at Joana. She was bouncing on her heels, her teeth on full display. "Hello, Armand! Come in. Make yourself at home."

I picked up a book, fell backward onto the couch that also doubled as my bed, and fixed my eyes on a page. Armand strolled past me and sat forward on Joana's bed, facing me, his long arms dangling between his knees. I heaved away and turned my back to him. For two hours until he left, I read. Afterward, Joana lectured me some more. "You know, it doesn't take much to be friendly. Humans shouldn't bite other humans, as you yourself say. You don't treat Kwaku that way. You didn't even blink when he invited us to spend the night at Immeuble Kébé."

"Kwaku is a Ghanaian brother," I said with defiance.

"He was a stranger when we first met him."

"Yeah. Well. I know how to relate to Africans. I don't know about Black Americans. Len George was snobbish when I first met him." I pinched my lips together.

She shook her head slowly, as if to say I was hopeless.

Armand took to knocking on our door often. His visits were like a fly buzzing in my ear. Each time, I tuned him out and read. A couple of weeks later, when Joana left for the market to get us food for an overnight party, I was stuffing beachwear into a plastic bag when someone rapped on the door. I opened.

Dear God. Armand again, towering over me with his six-foot-plus frame, his hands buried in the pockets of his brown trousers.

"Joana is not here," I said, not moving back to let him step inside. His shoulders sagged with obvious disappointment. With Joana's last lecture ringing in my ears, I invited him in, wondering how I was going to entertain him.

"Would you like something to drink?"

"Yeah, thanks a lot."

I wished he wasn't so polite because it made it hard to be rude. I went outside to our kitchen, which was an enclosed balcony, and poured a glass of iced water.

"Here you go," I said briskly. He accepted the glass with his big hands. I didn't ask him to sit down. We stood in the middle of the room without talking. Only the hum of cars and conversation from the street below edged the silence. He seemed to fill the studio, sucking up the air. I cleared my throat. "Joana went to Sandaga Market to buy some food. We're going to Gorée Island for a party. Our friends have just graduated from medical school, so we're going to celebrate." He said nothing. I cast my eyes around the room and met his eyes again. He was looking at me with the intensity of a cat. I loathed cats, they scared me. I cleared my throat again. "Gorée Island is a lot of fun. It used to be a slave port."

"Sounds interesting."

Another uncomfortable silence. I studied the gray sand painting on the wall, a portrait of a Senegalese woman sucking on a pipe, black smoke spiraling upward, her arms folded under her bare breasts, an emblem of bold femaleness. Her eyes dared me, *Say something, you oaf.* "Actually, I have to get ready. We're meeting our friends at three p.m. at the docks to catch the ferry." I was hoping he'd take the hint and leave, but his eyes continued to burn into mine, so I added lamely, "You're welcome to come with us if you want." I fully expected him to understand I was just being polite and refuse. That was the Ghanaian way.

"I'd love to. I can get ready quickly and meet you at the docks. I just need to go to the Marine House and get my swimming trunks."

My jaw was still on my chest when he turned and dashed down the stairs.

When Joana returned from the market, I explained the invitation. "Now, remember, he is your guest. Not mine. You'd better entertain him." I hoped he would miss the ferry.

Around three p.m., we made our way to the docks and boarded, the sun heating our bodies. The ferry was full of tourists as well as locals and friends, some dripping with water from having jumped into the sea. I was laughing at a man who had slipped and fallen to the floor, when someone said, "Hi, Lola."

My stomach dropped. It was Armand in shorts and T-shirt, holding a duffel bag, a pleased smile on his face.

"Armand!" Joana said. "Oh, look, there's Chantal!" She dashed toward a biracial girl with tight curls. I expected Armand to follow her, but he stayed by my side. We stood without speaking, my eyes looking everywhere but at him. At length, the silence forced me to attempt a conversation.

"So, what does a marine do?"

He told me, and it sounded like a lot of hardship: little sleep and constant physical exercise.

"Do you feel homesick for your family?"

"Yeah, I miss them a lot, especially my two kid sisters. They love to jump on me and be like, 'give me a quarter.' They're good kids, you know." His father was a mechanic who worked hard to support his family. Armand admired his commitment to them.

22

Dad had left for America first, leaving them behind in Martinique for years—they'd moved from Haiti to Martinique. As soon as he'd saved enough money for an apartment and tickets, he sent for all of them: five kids plus Mummy. Oddly, I found myself wanting to stroke his cheek. There was something touching about this big man who talked so lovingly about his family. We stood at the bow of the boat, the wind on our faces, my skin tingling. The boat churned through the turquoise water, causing it to froth and arch away in symmetry. Armand wasn't watching the water, though. I felt his eyes on me. My cheeks heated.

I concentrated on the Senegalese boys leaping out of the water and diving like dolphins. When he wasn't looking, I sneaked peeks at his profile. He didn't look Black American to me. Those I had met seemed of mixed race. His skin was the color of mahogany. His nose had a broken bridge and lay flat as though someone had punched it. Huge shoulders. No one would call him pretty. He was pure maleness and, unlike Len, he was single. My underarm prickled.

The beach was crowded when we stepped off at Gorée, an island where slaves were packed tighter than tuna and shipped to America. Feet sinking into the baked white sand, we picked our way through sunbathing tourists and canoes painted in a riot of blues, reds— every color. The smell of sizzling meat rose off kebab stands. We dodged shrieking children playing catch-me with the waves. Turning into an alley, we ambled between moldy stone houses until we found the place, a gray two-story building. Then we creaked up the wooden steps to the deck where our hostess, a German diplomat called Heidi, bustled over a grill.

"God," Joana muttered, "isn't it awful, partying on an island previously owned by slave masters."

"I know." I hated the holdings where female slaves were washed before being hauled to the colonial governor, who raged inside their vaginas. I hated the rusty iron chains and cannons used to fire on would-be liberators or escapees. "Have you seen the castles in Ghana, though? Much worse."

"If you're trying to console me, it's not working."

I slipped my arm around her shoulders. "Look, today is different. I mean, we're celebrating our African brothers. What's the point of dwelling on the past? We are the kaleidoscopic future: all colors of people frolicking together. Jah and peace and all that good stuff you're always drumming in my ears."

Joana gave in to the smile. "Yeah. I suppose you're right."

It was a nice party. Heidi grilled shrimp, chicken, and fish. We had brought drinks, baguettes, cheeses, and grapes. Other guests stood in little groups, chatting and sipping from highballs. At some point, a half-Vietnamese man grabbed Joana by the waist and said, "Come on, let's party." Her head bobbed as she shook her head and hips, brown arms waving to Bob Marley's *Who the cap fits, doo doo doo, let them wear it, doo doo doo . . ."*

Armand leaned back against the wooden railing, studying me from narrowed eyes. On an impulse, I said, "Do you want to dance?"

He did his best to imitate the merengue. After a couple of numbers, I tried to catch Joana's eye for her to come and claim her guest, but she just smiled, raised her arms, and drew circles with her hips. When the sun turned orange and slid into the ocean, we drifted inside. It was a huge house, with rooms rambling from one to another. The air smelled damp. We settled into a large room whose Moroccan couches lined the stone walls. The music boomed.

Armand danced with me and no one else. His eyes followed me as I danced with a Senegalese guy. Around midnight, everybody decided to go for a walk on the beach. The moon was so bright you'd have thought it was day. Apart from our voices and the crunch of our feet on the sand, the only sounds came from birds cawing, and waves sneezing and spraying us with icy water.

I didn't mind the rocks that were slippery and sharp under my bare feet. Armand lagged behind. Wondering what was holding him up, I turned around to see this huge muscleman grimacing, like someone walking on live coals. The moment his foot touched a rock, he raised it. I bent over laughing. "Don't you ever walk barefoot?"

"In New York City? No way. I don't go anywhere with no shoes on. This hurts."

I decided I wouldn't love New York, a place where no one walked barefoot. I darted ahead of him, my arms wide, embracing the wind. The earth was mine. It was such an innocent time. My beliefs were still intact: faith in the world order, in the church, and in goodwill to all people.

At some point, Joana jumped into the water. "Come on, Lolo, get in with me."

"No way. I'm not swimming when I can see nothing but ink."

She splashed water in my direction. When I refused to budge, she shouted, "Hey, everyone, let's throw Lola into the water!"

Someone grabbed my arm and another grabbed my legs. I beat off hairy arms, protesting, "Stop! I don't want to swim!" Just then Armand's quietly authoritative voice cut through. "Leave her alone." He stepped forward and put an iron arm around my waist. They couldn't free me from him. I was ice cream in the sun, melting into him. My cheeks brushed against his hairless chest, which was so hard my fingers wanted to drum on it. The tangy scent of Old Spice entered me and I knew I had to pull away fast.

"Thanks for rescuing me." My voice sounded cracked.

"My pleasure."

Something caught in my throat and I couldn't speak another word.

After we meandered back to the house, we danced some more until people began dropping off. We girls piled up in rooms separate from the boys. This was what I loved. Great friends enjoying a grand time together. No old married men trying to sneak into our panties. I told Armand he could sleep in any of the rooms with the boys, but he said he wanted to sleep wherever I slept.

"There aren't enough beds," I said. "You would have to sleep on the floor." The stone floor was cold.

He shrugged. "I'm a marine. I've slept in worse places."

I averted my eyes and chose a bed in a corner for myself. He spread a blanket near the foot of the bed and lay down, a homage that made my face hot with embarrassment. I thanked God for my dark skin that didn't redden. From the bed next to mine, so close I could touch her, Joana leaned toward me, whispering, "He likes you."

"No, he doesn't," I hissed. "He is just being nice."

"Right," she said with a sly smile.

In the morning, I showed him where to shower. When he returned, dabbing at rivulets running down his temples, I explained that the group was leaving the island for another beach, about eighty kilometers away, to swim and ride horses. I told him he could go if he wanted.

He broke into a big smile. "That's great. I've always wanted to be John Wayne."

"Who is John Wayne?"

"He's an actor. Rides horses in cowboy movies. Usually a hero."

Well, I wasn't going with the group, I said. I had to return to the mainland because the ambassador of Zimbabwe had invited me to watch a soccer match between Senegal and his country.

26

"The ambassador himself? How do you know him?"

I shrugged. "It's a small city. As an employee of the Thai embassy, I get to meet people at receptions, you know."

"Wow, you speak Thai?"

I laughed. "No. I'm actually the ambassador's special assistant. He speaks English, not French. I translate or interpret for him."

"Very impressive. So, you say you're going back to the mainland?"

"Yes."

His smile faded. "In that case, I'll ride the ferry with you and go back to the Marine House."

"I thought you wanted to ride horses."

"I can do that another time." He started packing.

Joana, who had been listening, sidled up to me. "I told you he liked you."

"No, he doesn't. He's leaving because he's quiet, and I'm the only one that talked to him."

She gave me that knowing smile again.

Around noon, Armand and I boarded the ferry. We stood on the deck, watching the island recede behind the white foam, the wind lifting my skirt. He recounted how many of his marine friends frequented bars and prostitutes, which meant isolation on his off days when he'd rather visit the theater or see a bit of the country. As I watched his solid chin and calm face, I had a sudden urge to show him the lake whose water was pink, and Ngor Island, where Joana and I sat around a fire, eating grilled lobster. I told him about the inlet at a private beach where I lay on my back on a cool boulder, sipping champagne while tiny fish nibbled my feet.

"Wow," he said, "I had no idea there was so much to see."

I promised him a tour. When we got to the mainland, he hailed a taxi and took me to my building, telling the driver to wait while he carried my bag up to the studio. He kissed me on both cheeks before leaving. Living in a Francophone country, I was used to kisses as a way of greeting or saying goodbye, but Armand's lips burned my cheeks.

Dear Mama,

Thank you for your letter that I received this afternoon. You see how quickly I'm replying? I do miss you.

Dakar is such a lovely city! I am behaving myself, Mama. Yes, I will make sure not to stay out late at night. Please don't worry so much about me. I really want to go to church on Sundays, but this is a Muslim country. I know of just one Methodist Church with a congregation of fifteen, hardly any young people. It's so boring! But I do make sure to pray before sleeping.

Please greet everyone for me.

Love,
Your daughter, Akua

P.S. Could you kindly not put "Olivia" on the back of the envelope? It's so Shakespearean à la Twelfth Night, that play I read to you: "When mine eyes didst first see Olivia, methought she purged the air of pestilence . . ."

Bye again.

Menso Wo Kɛntɛn

I Don't Carry Your Basket

"I'm going back to America," Len George said. Having played tennis earlier, he sat on the couch sipping iced water, sweat trickling down his temples. From my cross-legged perch on the floor, I looked up at his face, surprised at how my stomach dipped at his news. We'd come a long way from the day he'd asked me to mopez le floor. He dropped in once in a while on his way to the American Embassy. Surprisingly, he'd turned out to be a decent friend, not the usual married man hoping for a squeeze.

"Who would have thought you'd be sitting here on the couch I sleep on? We didn't exactly get along the first time we met."

"I know, haha. Look at you now, a half-decent tennis player. Admit it, you love me now."

I scowled playfully. "No, I don't"

His head bobbed up and down. "Yeah, you do, I see that smile, haha. Boy, I tell you, I miss Olga. She was one heck of a lady."

"She brought so many people together, didn't she?"

"Yeah, she was real special. I'll go visit her when I get back to America." He grew quiet, as if his thoughts were far away. "So, ever thought about moving to America?"

"No! I mean, I've always wanted to see America. Who doesn't? But to live there? No."

"Really?" He had the look of someone who couldn't believe how a person could turn down diamonds.

I tried to explain, counting off on my fingers. "I have a good life here. I love my job. I love my flat. I'm only twenty-one, yet I have a maid who comes to clean, cook, and wash my clothes. I'm just a middle-class girl. Could I afford that in America?"

"Yeah! Well. Maybe not a maid, but you could earn some serious money. Work for the UN or something, you with your language skills." He set his glass on the floor and flipped his hands open. "You make what, four hundred dollars a month?"

I had to laugh. "It's funny how you Americans talk. Actually, I make the equivalent of six hundred dollars, but my flat costs two hundred a month. Okay, it's only a studio, but, as you yourself said, it's in the best neighborhood in town, with granite floors. I pay my maid twenty. Could I live like this in your America?"

"Well, not at the beginning. But you'd have more opportunities. Look, what do you really want?"

I stretched out on my belly, propping myself on my elbows, the granite cool under me. "I want to write. I'm always writing anyway, but it would be great to write for a living. Right now, I'm translating a book into French for Macmillan, besides my job at the embassy."

He nodded vigorously, pointing with his finger. "There you go. You can write in America. You can't make it here."

I was pulling my fingers, shaking my head. "I'm scared of snow. You people live in a deep freezer."

He threw his muscled arms out. "Aw, come on, it's not that bad. You put on a winter coat, gloves, boots, and you're fine. And you know, you're so pretty. You'll meet a nice guy and make pretty babies with him."

"I'm not keen to marry and give birth. But can I tell you something?"

"What?"

"I've always nursed a secret wish to adopt orphans." I told him about an orphanage I'd visited once in Ghana, where a boy ran crying after me as I was leaving. I could do something for kids like that. "I mean, you walk on the streets of Dakar and what do you see? Children poking through rubbish for a piece of baguette."

"True. Here's the thing, you can do more for the poor when you've got dollars coming out of your ears." I agreed and, with that, we drifted into a heated discussion about the merits and demerits of giving money to the poor, until he said something about taking his wife to dinner. He pushed to his feet, patting around his pockets. "Do you have a piece of paper?"

I fumbled around for one in the chest Joana kept in a corner. He scrawled down his address and number and held it out to me. "Anytime you want to come to America, just call me. I'll give you room and board. But," he wagged his finger, "only one boyfriend, okay? You have too many admirers, haha."

I gave him a teasing smile. "Look who is talking. Don't think I haven't noticed American wives turning red and acting hot and bothered around you. Especially Olga."

"Don't go there, Lola."

That was an Americanism to get used to, as though words were vehicles that could transport you to a dangerous location. After he left, I tossed the paper with his address and number into a drawer, convinced I would never need it. Everyone had to carry their own basket. I lay on my bed, a vague sense of loss niggling at me.

Joana struggled in, bearing a baguette under her arm and a bag of fruit, her slippers slapping the floor.

"I just met your friend Len," she said. "How come he never stays around to visit with me?"

"You know how Americans are, always rushing."

"Hmm." She strode onto the balcony and returned with a glass of milk and a piece of baguette. She held out the bread to me. "Have a bite?" I said no. She settled into the wicker chair, munching and talking with her mouth full. "Why not?"

"I want proper food. I hope Thérèse cooks us some mafé or something. How long does it take to hang clothes on the drying line?" I loved the peppery groundnut stew with chunks of cabbage, carrots, and eggplant lurking in it.

"You're so bourgeois."

"No, I'm not! And I'll have you know that during the French Revolution, the bourgeois were merely merchants, not upper class. Don't you roll your eyes at me."

"Fine, you're not bourgeois. Your mother is only a judge."

"And *your* father is only a university professor whose books are read everywhere in the world."

We glared at each other. Her lips twitched. I tried to maintain an angry face but tittered. We collapsed into laughter.

"Oh, Lolo, what a pair we are!" She got up and slouched beside me on the couch. I wiggled closer to rest my head on her lap, looking up at the ceiling as she stroked my hair. "Our parents did well, didn't they? Look at us, fresh out of university and into our own flat."

"You know this would never happen if we were in Ghana, right? We'd have to live at home."

"I know! No overnight parties with male friends, however innocent. Church every Sunday, everyone poking around to make sure we're not disgracing the sacred family name."

"So true, haha! Here, we get away with living on our own. Just because we aren't Senegalese or Muslims. My mother would die if she knew."

We fell silent. Islam in Senegal, Christianity in Ghana. Both powerful imprints on the mind. Closing my eyes, I saw myself, a child in my mother's bed, she whispering fierce prayers: *God, I beg you to watch over your daughter. Banish bad dreams from her. Keep poverty and disease from her. May her good name be untarnished.*

Tears rolled out of my eyes, tickling into my ears. "She worked so hard, my mother. Everyone clucked on about what a man-woman she was because she wouldn't marry after my father died. Sometimes I wish she had. Then she wouldn't have had her eyes so fixed on me. My sister, Awurama, had it easier because she was older, but me? Boarding school was the only time I got to be away from her protective eyes."

"I don't know, Lolo. What if you'd ended up with an abusive stepfather?"

"You have a point there."

We must have drifted off to sleep, because when I opened my eyes, the sky was black. Joana sat up, rubbing her eyes. There was no sign of Thérèse. I glided out to the balcony. There was no stew steaming on the stove. She had left without cooking.

I sighed. "She's still upset with us. No cooking today, too. I guess she wants us to eat the couscous."

"Let's go to the Marine House," Joana said.

At the Marine House, the place where English-speaking diplomats congregated on Friday nights, the smell of grilled meat and beer greeted us. It was a welcome change to hear English spoken around us as opposed to French.

"Look," Joana whispered as we entered the buzzing hall, "there's Armand."

He was standing near a couch, beer in hand as usual. Something warm spread through me. As soon as he saw us, he strode over to meet us, a broad smile on his face. "Hi, ladies, how are you doing?"

"Hungry. Thérèse is angry," I said.

"Say what?"

Joana explained. "Our maid didn't cook today."

He burst out laughing. "You have a maid? You girls are too much. Here, sit right here." He led us to a sitting area in a corner, decorated with two armchairs and a couch for two, beating the couch as though he wanted to soften it for me. "Is this okay?"

"Thank you. It is, really." I sank into the couch while Joana took the chair opposite me.

"What would you like to drink?" He was looking at me as if I might disappear. "Anything you want, it's on me."

I found my cheeks heating up. "Coke for me, please. Thanks."

"Just Coke?"

"Yes, for now. Maybe I'll have wine later."

"All right, then. Coke coming up." He turned to Joana. "What about you?"

"I want a beer." She grinned from Armand to me.

"How about something to eat?" He was looking at me.

"I don't know. Perhaps a burger?"

"You got it. Joana?"

"Grilled chicken."

"Be right back."

I wanted to smack the smile off Joana's face. "Stop it."

She arranged her face into innocence. "Have I said a word? I'm just sitting here enjoying the breeze."

I wagged my finger at her. "Don't say anything."

"Oh, come on, Lolo, why not? He likes you, and if you weren't so stuck up, you'd admit you like him, too."

I couldn't help smiling a little. "Well, he's actually nice, not snobbish like I thought he'd be."

"So . . . ?"

"So what?"

"Nothing, forget it," she said as Armand returned with the drinks.

"Here you go." He handed us a glass each and slid onto the couch beside me. "Your food should be ready in about five minutes."

We sat back sipping, Joana beaming at us as though she were our mother. I wished my leg were long enough to kick her. The Coke burned my throat. I turned to him, delight on my face. "You sprinkled pepper in my drink. How did you know I liked that?"

"That night on Gorée Island, you asked the German lady for pepper. You sprinkled it in your drink."

I was stunned. "You saw that?"

"I notice everything you do," he said softly. "I hear every word you say." Our eyes locked. It was as if Joana wasn't facing us, as if other people weren't milling around talking and laughing. I couldn't tear my eyes away, couldn't breathe. At length, he exhaled. "So, if I asked you to dinner, would you come? I just want to—"

"By myself? I wouldn't want Joana to feel left out." I wasn't sure why I said that.

An amused smile played about his lips. "Sure. Joana can come too."

I stole a look at Joana, who mouthed, *I don't need to come.* I looked away quickly. "Okay. We'll go out with you."

"As long as you're at the same table," he whispered.

The burger was delicious, I thought, licking the mustard oozing from its sides. Somehow Armand had known not to put ketchup on it. I smiled at him, with him looking happy, Joana giving me sly looks.

He took us to dinner the following Wednesday. Then Saturday. Each time, I centered the conversation on banalities like sports and the best beaches for swimming. On Saturday night, when we returned to the studio, Joana said, "Armand has been so nice to us. Why don't we invite him to dinner? I could cook."

"*You* cook?" She either burned everything she cooked or put too much salt in it. "No, I'm doing the cooking."

"Fine, then, you cook."

Since he was Caribbean, I made rice and peas in coconut milk, fried plantains, and meat stew. All my thirty-two teeth showed when I opened the door and saw him standing there.

This time he sat in the big wicker chair in the corner instead of on Joana's bed. She served and he took a mouthful. "This is delicious!"

"Lola cooked it," she said.

He looked up at me. "You cooked this?"

I nodded, my cheeks burning.

"I'm going to marry you."

Normally I would bristle at the thought of someone wanting to marry me for my cooking, but I knew that wasn't the case with him. My armpits prickled with heat. I forked some rice into my mouth. After dinner, Joana put on some music and we started dancing. Armand looked on, admiration on his face. "You girls are very liberated. That's not what I expected from African girls. Here you are, living on your own, doing your own thing. I like that."

Joana changed the music and the room vibrated with the drums and chanting for adowa, a traditional dance of the Asante. To perfect my skills, I had taken dance in an African studies class at university. With adowa, you move the right foot and arm at the same time, then the left foot and left arm. The whole time, your hips, chest, and shoulders undulate to the beat: taa ta taa ta, taa ta taa ta. Joana didn't know how to do it.

"Dance for us, Lolo," she said.

I was wearing a blouse over a cloth wrapped loosely around my waist. The marble floor felt oiled on my bare soles as my body snaked to the rhythm. Everything vanished save the pulse of the music vibrating through me. Not even Armand's camera setting off a series of flashes broke the trance. When the music stopped, I collapsed onto the couch and they both applauded.

At some point, Joana said, "Let's go to *Le Sahel,* oui?" It was a club where Youssou N'Dour performed regularly. I slipped on some pants and we piled into a taxi.

At the club, Armand slipped his arm around my waist and pressed me to his chest, the heat of his body matching my own. We danced until I could barely stand. When we finished dancing, we dropped onto a couch, side by side. I tilted my head back, my eyes closed. Then Youssou N'Dour and Super Etoile started another song, setting my torso swaying. I felt Armand's hand brush the hair away from my forehead, his breath hot on my cheek. "You don't even have to think about dancing, do you? It just comes naturally to you."

"Yes, dancing is the thing I love most." I felt him take strands of my fluffy hair and draw them out. Then he brushed them back repeatedly, and it felt right that he should touch me.

"How about we go for a walk, just you and me?"

I opened my eyes. "What about Joana?"

"I don't think she'll miss us, do you?" He was looking at me with more intensity than usual.

I glanced at the dance floor. Under the pink and purple strobe lights, Joana was dancing with an old friend she'd found, gyrating to the drums. I said okay, but not before I had walked over to let her know Armand and I were stepping outside.

The air was warm. Armand put his arm around my shoulders, and we strolled along the canal, looking at the shimmering waters. During the day, the canal was murky, trashed by traders who peddled groundnuts and bananas at the edge. But at two a.m., the streets were vacant. I could hear my heartbeat. When a taxi rolled toward us, Armand hailed it. This wasn't part of the plan, but I said nothing. It was as though an invisible force were nudging us toward something we both knew but were unwilling to name. We got in the back of the taxi, not saying a word. Electrons zigzagged between us.

"Marine House," he said to the driver.

Armand had once told me that women weren't allowed in marines' private rooms because of fears of espionage. Hostile intelligence agents could use women to seduce marines and cause them to betray codes. But it was tough going not to be allowed to get married while on embassy duty, so marines broke the rules all the time. The gunner, the marine in charge, turned a blind eye. The Senegalese guards merely shrugged.

With Armand's arm around my shoulders, we entered the huge recreational hall. We sailed past the bar and pool table, past the deep couches, and slipped through a door that opened onto a narrow corridor. In his room, the only furniture was a desk with a wooden chair, and a single bed made military style, covered with a lime-green blanket. My chest expanded with so much air I couldn't exhale.

"Please, sit down," he said. I sat on the bed, smoothing the blanket with my hands even though it was already smooth, anything to postpone what was now inevitable. "Would you like some wine?"

"Yes," I whispered. A glass of wine would give my hands something else to do. He poured some red into a goblet and gave it to me. The wine burned my throat. I lifted my eyes to his for a moment, and then I couldn't look at him anymore. I gulped more wine. Then he reached over and took the glass from my hand. Slowly, he lowered his head toward mine until I was breathing him in and he was breathing me. I lifted my chin and our lips met. I hesitated for a minute, then I melted into him.

He pulled away to look into my eyes. "I'm in love with you, you know that?"

I could only nod.

"You're okay with this?"

I silenced him with my finger on his lips. I rose from the bed, crossed my arms over my head, and pulled off my dress. I had nothing else underneath. I wrapped my arms around him, pulling him down with me, the mattress firm under me. Oh God, the feel of him. How I met him. How I moved, moved, moved, long after the tremors had shaken me down to my toes. Still I moved, a dancer possessed, unable to stop.

I didn't return to the studio until noon the next day. Joana was not amused. She met me at the door, serious as malaria. "I was worried, Lola."

"Sorry." I couldn't stop smiling.

"I waited and waited and waited for you!"

"I'm sorry." I tried to look serious. "Truly. I am."

The smile overcame her. "I forgive you. That's only because I like Armand. See, I knew he'd fall in love with you when I introduced you two!"

I hadn't known I would fall, too, and so quickly, so deeply into a love that would alter my life forever.

Nkyinkyim

Twisting

"What are you doing?" I asked Joana, who was folding clothes into a suitcase.

"Leaving Dakar, me dear."

The air thickened. I needed to process her words. Carefully, I closed the door behind me. I had just returned from spending another night with Armand, two months after he and I had disappeared from the club. Now she was leaving? She was humming a tune, smiling to herself, not looking at me.

"Why? Is it . . . is it because I'm always gone?"

"No, silly." She burst out laughing. "You should see your face!" The dress she was folding slid from her hand into the suitcase. It was a striped dress I had got her for her birthday. I failed to see the humor. She took my hand and walked me to the couch, patting the spot next to her. I remained standing. "Come on, Lolo. Sit down."

Slowly, I obeyed.

"Okay, maybe you do have something to do with it. You and

Armand are so happy. I had forgotten how it used to be. Remember my old boyfriend, Pete?"

"The one in Jordan? I thought you didn't want him. You haven't mentioned him in a long time!" She wasn't making any sense. As far as I knew, he was a bore who was better off with another bore.

"Well," she said with an embarrassed smile, "I had felt I needed space from him, but the truth is I miss him. I went to Télé-Senegal and called him, and now I want to be with him."

"You're going to Jordan? Joana, I can't see you covering yourself from head to toe and waiting for him to take you to market. This is insane!"

"Jordan isn't Saudi Arabia. It's not that bad. Look, he's only going to be there for another year. It's lonely for him, you know. And he's not a bore. He's just quiet. Like your Armand."

Nothing I said made a difference.

Things moved quickly after that. I remember the ad she placed in the British Embassy newsletter, selling the wicker chair and leaving me everything else, the boxes of clothes we crab-carried to a friend's flat. In a matter of ten days, we were at the airport, hugging and crying. What was I going to do without her? We had been sisters, cried over boys, braided and stroked each other's hair.

"I'll write," she said, wiping her tears with a handkerchief. "Every day."

"You'd better."

After Joana's departure, Armand filled the void she'd left. Because I loved to read, he brought me books by the carton from the American Embassy. In bed, we read to each other from Alex Haley, Erica Jong, and Maya Angelou novels. I also introduced him to African writers like Mariama Bâ, Ama Ata Aidoo, and Peter Abrahams. As well as not being allowed to entertain women in their rooms, marines on embassy duty weren't allowed to sleep outside the Marine House, but Gunny saw no evil and spoke no evil. Armand spent every night with me. He paid rent, paid the maid, and learned to cook. He did my laundry at the Marine House, where they had a washing machine. "I love to smell your clothes," he said. I hadn't got over my childhood fear of the dark. On nights he had graveyard duty, he curled his big body around me until I fell asleep, then he'd arrange pillows by me so I'd think he was still there. When that didn't work, he just left the lights on all night. But I would toss about because the lights were too bright. In the end, he bought a flashlight and left it on so the room wouldn't be too dark.

For all our happiness, something gnawed at Armand's innards. He wanted to be a millionaire. We'd be tearing off the claw of a lobster at a restaurant and he'd moan, "I'm sorry, Lola, but I've got to be rich. Not just comfortable, but rich rich. In America, you'd have to pay a lot to eat like this."

I had no idea what he meant. In my mind, America was a land flowing with dollars, where Michael Jackson and Diana Ross held street parties, and everyone could afford lobster and much more. My idea of poverty wasn't Armand. For me, poverty was a nursing mother opening her legs to a man for next to nothing. When I was at the University of Dakar, I had witnessed one such mother leave her baby on the cold concrete floor of a corridor at the male students' hostel, to service a student who couldn't have paid her more than enough money to buy a baguette and tea. The death in her sunken eyes made me want to cry, and I hated the student who had only done what was legal. Poverty was Thérèse knocking on my door, asking if she could clean my bathroom for money to feed her children because her husband had three other wives. Which was why I didn't have the heart not to pay her even when she skipped work yet showed up at the end of the month so she could collect. Poverty was not a hefty marine who was not permitted to use taxis (though he did) but could radio the embassy for chauffeur service anytime he needed to move.

"You're not poor," I said to him one night. We lay skin to skin facing the ceiling, a comfortable warmth flowing between us.

"No, I'm not, but I'm not rich. Not like I want to be. My parents had it rough, they came to America with five children and nothing else. In winter, I didn't even have gloves. I'd get so cold on the playground my fingers would hurt. But now, my parents are okay. You see, in America, long as you have a job, you can buy just about anything you want. A car, TV, you name it. It's not like here, where you have to pay cash for everything. You get to use credit cards. You know what those are?"

"I've read about them."

"Long as you have a job, you can buy stuff on credit. You can buy a house and you don't even have to put anything down. Maybe a thousand. The bank gives you a loan, it's called a mortgage. You can stay in it for thirty years before you finish paying."

"Wow, that's interesting." I rolled onto my side, propping my head on my elbow.

"Yeah. I mean, look at you. You've got a good job, but you can't afford a car. In America, you don't have to wait to enjoy life. Apart from mortgages, you can pay for anything with a card."

"I don't know. I love walking, and buses are easy. It seems weird to live on loans like that."

His voice picked up energy. "But you're not a slave to credit cards if you're rolling in money. That's why I don't wanna be just middle class. I want money falling out of my pockets. There's at least eight million people in New York City. All I need is a dollar from each person and I'd be a millionaire. I want to buy a big house for my parents. I want the good life for my kids."

I nestled my head in the space between his jaw and shoulder, stroking the smooth marble of his chest. "How many kids do you want?" I asked carelessly.

"A lot of kiddies. At least six." My fingers stopped moving. "But only after I've made a ton of money," he added quickly.

A lot of kiddies? Natural-born children? I had no intention, no desire to expand my waist with children. Ever. I wanted to adopt, but that was for later, when I was thirty or something. For now, I loved being on my own while my friends back in Ghana were already married or getting there. Which was strange, considering people dubbed me the Pied Piper of Dakar. At the beach, children called me "Histoire." The minute Joana and I settled on the sand, they'd surround us, clamoring for me to tell them a story, which I did with exaggerated enactments that left them gasping or laughing. Place me in any waiting room and a child would appear between my knees, poking me, asking me to open a bottle, read a book. But I dreaded the toll of motherhood on the body, especially after I saw my sister, Awurama, sit on a chamber pot of hot water to heal birth wounds, and bind her waist with cloth so tightly she couldn't eat. And her breasts, so swollen with milk that she moaned when the baby fastened her mouth on a nipple. No way did I desire to launch into that life. Perhaps I could persuade Armand to adopt orphans with me, all the kids he wanted. Many children needed the good father I knew he'd be. For no apparent reason, as I lay there nursing my thoughts, he flung himself to his side, causing me to slide down his back.

"What's wrong?"

He shook his head, his back to me.

"Talk to me."

He remained quiet and unmoving.

"Please."

He sighed, then rolled back, arms folded across his chest, staring at the ceiling before shooting me a cold look. "I heard what you said."

"What are you talking about?"

"When we went to the embassy picnic. The cultural attaché's wife asked you what would happen to me and you when I left Dakar. You said you didn't know."

"What? That was days ago. I didn't know you'd overheard us. Look, she caught me off guard, so I said the first thing that came into my head." All this time, he'd been bottling up his hurt? "I'm sorry. I mean, we have never talked about it."

"Fine. We're talking about it now." He flipped away again.

I leaned over his shoulder, stroking what little hair was left on his almost shaven head. "What do you want to see happen?"

He twisted around to face me. "Let me ask you this, do you think you could wait for me?"

I hedged. I didn't want the agony of a long-distance relationship. What if we couldn't communicate effectively? What if he met someone else? What if I did? I didn't want to be hurt, and I didn't want to hurt him. He looked into my eyes. "I know I can wait for you, so you tell me, could you wait for me?"

Without my knowing how, we'd become fused together. I couldn't imagine being sawed apart from him. "Yes, I'll wait for you."

"Just one thing—" his voice dropped to a hard whisper "—don't hurt me. Don't make me look like a fool."

My stomach knotted. "I won't." I wondered what would happen if I didn't measure up.

His body lost its rigidity as he gathered me into his arms, planting his lips on mine. "I'm crazy about you, Lola. I want to maintain you in this lifestyle you're used to." He took my hand. "Look at these little fingers. So smooth. I never want to see them chapped." He touched my chin. "And your small face. I don't want to see your smile fade. I wanna make you happy, Lola."

I rolled on top of him, my voice whiskery. "We'll make each other happy."

"Think about it, though." He was stroking my nipple absent-mindedly. I wished he'd stop talking and keep stroking. "Imagine being so rich nothing can touch you. You see, Lola, if you work for someone, you're like a piece of furniture. You're nothing. The boss can just get rid of you when he doesn't need you no more. If you've got *your* own money or *your* own business, no one can cut you out. I can't get that out of my head, Lola. We have to find a way to make money." In eighteen months, he would get out of the military and go to college, courtesy of the GI Bill, but he wanted a quicker way to make money.

I had heard how easy it was to get one's hands on gold in Ghana and sell it for ten times its cost in Europe. As he talked, the idea popped out of me. "We could get into the gold business, you know," I said. I possessed zero business acumen. If I tried to sell you something and you told me about your financial woes, I'd beg you not to buy. I had no business suggesting any moneymaking scheme whatsoever.

He brows shot up. "Gold? That sounds like serious money, Lola. You know how to get gold?"

"I'm sure I can figure it out." I took his nipple between my

47

teeth, causing his breath to quicken. He stopped obsessing over money and focused on what I wanted. He reached for my hips. I closed my eyes and sank deliciously onto him.

Over the next few days, we tossed the idea of selling gold back and forth between us. There was no time, however: he was leaving Dakar in three short weeks to be stationed in Barbados. The solution was for me to start the business with two thousand dollars he would deposit into a joint account. I would grow that to twenty thousand, a tidy sum that would give us a head start in the million-dollar sprint.

Returning from the bank in a creaky taxi, he pulled me to him so that my head rested under his chin. "Lola, two thousand dollars is a lot of money to me. Please don't lose it."

"I won't," I said with determination.

June 20, 1996

My dear Akua,

What is this nonsense about flying a man to Ghana to meet me? Does your head hurt you? It is a terrible idea to marry a foreigner, because a woman has to follow her husband to his country. America is far away. If something happens to you, how will we come and help you? There is a reason why our elders tell us not to engage in a distant marriage. Twisting and twisting in this world isn't good. Choose a simple path. Do not, I repeat, do not bring this man to Ghana to meet me. This is for your own good, believe me. Find yourself a nice Ghanaian man, not someone who lives so far you have to cross an ocean to get to his family.

What about your desire to write stories? I didn't give you everything for you to throw it away to marry a foreigner. You better come home quickly. I need to put some sense into your vacant head.

Your loving mother,
S. D.

Dear Mama,

I am very sad to read your words. Were you not the one who taught me that love was the most important thing in the world? Wasn't that why you never married after Dadda died, because you never found someone you loved the same way? Armand is good to me. If only you would open your mind, you would like him. Instead, you reject him because he is a foreigner. I love him, Mama. We have plans to build a great future together. I beg you to reconsider. Let me bring him to Ghana and you can see for yourself.

Lots of love,
Your daughter, Akua

Kɛtɛ Pa

A Good Mat to Sleep On

At Gorée Island, Armand and I sat on a towel, under the blue sky, his arm protective around me. We'd never been back there since the beach party that drew us close, so it seemed symbolic that we'd spend the day there, his last in Senegal. My mother never responded to my plea about taking him to Ghana, but we'd forged ahead with our plans. He was so confident about the future. His eyes were full of tenderness. "Don't worry, Lola. Believe me, I'll always write you and we'll be together when I get out. Only eighteen months. Time will fly by fast, you'll see. I'll be back for you. I promise."

When I looked at his determined jaw, I believed him. What a pity my mother had remained intransigent about not meeting him. We swam, we ate, we toasted each other from a bottle of chenin blanc. Later, we found a private spot behind rocks and peeled off our bathing suits. The water washed over us, leaving us tingling. I hadn't known it was possible to climax just from someone sucking your breast.

Back on the mainland, I sat in the tub washing myself, stroking my neck, the water lapping deliciously between my legs. After bathing, I slipped into the dress Armand liked me best in, a long, pinkish wine dress with minute purple polka dots, gathered loosely at the waist. I completed my dress with a kente strip tied loosely around the waist. After slipping on black roman sandals and combing my shoulder-length hair, I took a taxi that zoomed me along the corniche to the Marine House. There was a heaviness to my limbs, but I had never felt so loved. The way he slipped his mother's ring on my finger, a square ruby set in gold. It had been his talisman and he'd never taken it off. "I'll get you a proper engagement ring. Just hold on to this until the real thing." It fell off my finger, tinkled onto the stone floor. "I think we should put it on your necklace," he said. His fingers found the clasp on the back on my neck. He removed my necklace and buried his mouth on the nape of my neck. Then he threaded the ring on my beaded necklace and fastened it. "My mother's gonna love you, and you'll love her. We're gonna have a fantastic life in America, you'll see!"

By the time Gunny came to take him to the airport, Armand was all packed and dressed in a dark suit. We stood in the big hall and had our pictures taken, him pressing his lips to mine like we were at our reception. Except this was no wedding. This was a parting. We climbed into a station wagon, the chauffeur at the wheel. I sat in the back between Gunny and Armand, feeling the heat of Armand's muscled thigh against mine.

At the airport, he held me for a long time, kissing my brows, my cheeks, my chin, my neck, lingering on the corners of my mouth. When he let me go, he looked into my eyes, rubbed my lip with his thumb. "I'll be seeing you," he said, and tore himself away from me. Just before he got swallowed up by a bend in the corridor, he turned around and lifted his hand in a wave. I had held myself back from crying because I wanted him to walk away strong. But when he disappeared, my knees buckled. Gunny caught me and let me sob into his shirt.

In the station wagon, the chauffeur started the engine. When Gunny asked where he could drop me, I felt panic, amputated. How could I go back to that apartment whose bed bore Armand's imprint? I found myself blubbering, asking if he wanted to go somewhere for drinks, not realizing how ridiculous I sounded. He gave me a gentle but firm no. I had to return home to that empty space, where Armand was at the door, on my pillow, on my couch, in my bathroom, where the smell of Old Spice clung to my sheets.

Mmere Dane

Time Turns Over Itself

I took to showing up on people's doorsteps, overstaying my welcome, cackling loudly, eating too much, giving suffocating hugs. I found myself wanting to lay my head on men's shoulders, wanting to sleep in someone's bed. Any man could have taken advantage of me. Beyond one letter from Joana announcing her arrival and urging me to be happy, I'd heard nothing from her. Each morning when I opened my eyes, the silence in the flat clawed at me and pushed me outside. Time crawled this way until five weeks later when I visited a clinic.

"You are seven weeks pregnant," Mademoiselle Talar said, staring at me.

My limbs weakened. The walls of her office closed in on me. Outside, cars sped by. Horns blared. Vendors shouted. A woman in an off-shoulder white boubou drifted past the window. Surely the world could not be going about its business with such life-altering news.

Mademoiselle Talar's voice floated to me from afar. "Do you want to keep this baby?"

"I don't know." I was falling off a precipice.

"Are you and the father hoping to get married?" she asked encouragingly. She was in her late twenties, petite, with large, moist eyes.

"Yes." I wasn't sure what I meant. Yes, Armand and I wanted to get married. That was why he had given me his mother's ring and left me money to grow a business. But I couldn't forget his wanting children only after making at least a million dollars. On the other hand, he was a Catholic and didn't believe in abortion. He'd made that clear on more than one occasion. On another hand, I didn't want a child from my own body.

"Alors, perhaps you should keep this baby."

I swallowed hard. "I'm not sure."

She smiled with compassion and suggested I think about it. "But you have to decide by three weeks' time, because after that, an abortion would be dangerous."

Although the clinic was only two blocks from my studio, it took me nearly an hour to get home. I dragged myself along to the rhythm of *seven weeks pregnant*. Stop. *Seven weeks pregnant*. Stop. I swung from staring into nothing to wanting to punch Armand. Why did he have to leave for the Caribbean, where he could have fun with island girls while I was pregnant? They loomed before my eyes: half-naked, big-breasted girls languishing in the ocean, beckoning to him. Why wasn't he the one pregnant? He could physically walk away from a pregnancy, but this baby had planted its roots inside me. It was now an extension of my body. The only way to walk away was to have someone reach inside and cut it out, cut a piece of me. I shook my fist at the skies. How could God do this to me? I had a book to write, a business to start.

For two weeks, I bounced from anger to sadness to anger. One day, while puttering around the studio, I stumbled upon a pamphlet on aborted babies. I had no idea how it got there. It featured a write-up about a movie titled *The Silent Scream*. The article described a scene where instruments dug into an unborn baby while its mouth opened in a silent scream. Here I was, Mademoiselle Histoire, the Pied Piper of Dakar, about to gouge a baby into screaming silently. A ton of guilt dropped on me. I holed up in my apartment sobbing.

When I finally ventured outside, I walked for hours. If I had a miscarriage, that wouldn't be the same as having an abortion, would it? But, in defiance of my efforts, nothing happened. My womb held as solid as concrete. Each day, I exerted myself. One day, I labored up the stairs to the eighth floor of a friend's building, not pausing for breath. The next day, I doubled over as spasms seized me. All I could think was *Oh no. The baby. Oh no, please. God, don't let this baby die.*

The pain subsided and the knowledge stared me straight in the face: I wanted my baby alive and in my arms. It was irrational, considering I had forsworn motherhood until I was older. Perhaps it was some kind of hormonal switch, some primal need to protect what I was carrying. I couldn't explain it. Somehow, when I wasn't looking, some nesting instinct had kicked in and suddenly I had become protective. I picked up a pen and wrote to Armand. He replied, asking me to call him.

"You're pregnant?" he asked after we'd exchanged nervous hellos.

"Yes."

"Are you sure?"

My neck stiffened. "Yes, I'm sure."

"Are you okay?" His concern sounded genuine.

"Yes. Look, I want to keep this baby." I listened to his even breathing, wanting to catch the slightest hint of hesitation.

"Okay."

"You're okay with it?"

"Of course. I mean, I wish I wasn't stuck here and we'd already made a million bucks, but yeah, it's okay." Then he laughed. "You know I've always wanted lots of kiddies." I joined in his laughter. Oh, how it felt good to laugh.

As marines on embassy duty weren't allowed to get married, there was no question of a wedding before the baby was born. We fretted about its U.S. citizenship, if that would be compromised because of foreign birth. What if it was a boy who decided to run for election as president? He needed to be born on U.S. soil, didn't he? A Black man ruling America. We giggled. That would never happen. Still, we made plans. I would move to New York before my due date and wait for Armand to return from Barbados and get out of the marines. Then we'd get married.

"I'm going to talk to my best friend, Daniel," he breathed into the phone. "Daniel Roberts. He's like a brother to me. He's going to take care of you until I get back."

"How?" I would have thought he'd send me to his parents because of the baby. On the other hand, in Ghana, it would be nothing unusual for him to ask a friend to take care of his fiancée.

"Daniel is a great guy. Just enlisted in the military. I trust him completely. I'll have it all worked out by the time you're ready to travel. I'll write you with details, baby."

I felt giddy with excitement. We were planning a real future together, a future where he'd find a way to wheedle a dollar out of each New Yorker and become a millionaire, where I'd write a bestseller, where motherhood wouldn't be such a big deal after all. Before all that, though, I had to fly to Ghana, find someone to sell me two thousand dollars' worth of gold, find a way to send it to Europe and make ten times the profit. We would live happily ever after, and I'd show my mother how wrong she was about him. That simple.

Ananse Ntentan

Spider's Web

"You want to do what?" Binta's slit eyes were as wide as open zippers. An Air Afrique stewardess, she was one of the friends Joana had attracted into our lives. We were sitting on the floor of her apartment in one of those high-rise buildings that featured garbage chutes, courtesy of a rich admirer.

"Sell gold," I said. "My question is, if I got the gold, could you take it to Paris or Brussels and sell it? For a share in the profits?" I didn't know how to do any kind of business in either city, not to mention I had never stepped foot on European soil. Air stewards, on the other hand, were famous for engaging in trade to supplement their incomes. I filled her in on the cheapness of Ghanaian gold and watched her slanted eyes turn things over.

"I'll do it," she said after a long silence. "This will work, if the gold is as cheap as you say it is." I couldn't believe how easily she agreed. All I could think of was how rich we were going to be, how Armand was going to be so proud of me.

When I left her apartment, I was whistling Bob Marley's "Born to Win."

Three days later, I stepped into the arrival hall of Kotoka International Airport in Accra. My cousin Oforiwa was waiting for me, wearing a loose dress, her smile white against her blue-black face.

She looked happy to see me. "Pregnancy agrees with you, Lola! You look healthy." Although a Jehovah's Witness, she delivered no lecture about the consequences of a pregnancy without marriage, which is what I had expected, since her mother and sisters regularly knocked on doors to sermonize and coax copies of *The Watchtower* into people's hands.

"I hope Auntie Faustie agrees with you."

"Mummy?" She gave me a no-nonsense suck of her teeth before hefting my suitcase. "She's thrilled you're not aborting your baby. Besides, you're not a Jehovah's Witness, so no one can excommunicate you. She's at home waiting."

I slid into the backseat of the taxi with her beside me, inhaling rain-soaked earth, millet porridge, and fried bean paste from roadside sellers. At the intersection of Airport and Liberation Road, young men darted around us shouting, "Chewing gum! PK!" Women carrying doughnuts in glass cases balanced on their heads called to us. I waved to indicate we weren't buying.

"So," Oforiwa said as our taxi overtook a rusty minibus. "What is this about wanting to buy gold? Your letter was vague."

I explained, expecting a torrent of are-you-mad from her.

"Oh, that's easy. There's a woman staying with us, Auntie Peace. Her husband works in the mines and can easily get you gold. He's done it for a couple of people I know."

I could hardly breathe. It really was that simple. This was going to happen. Armand and I were about to become rich!

"You know," she laughed, "trading gold isn't such a big deal. This is Ghana. People do it all the time. I mean if you get caught, they make a big to-do about it. It's so hypocritical. Everyone does it, from government officials to the typist."

She was right. The only reason the police would make a big fuss about transporting gold out of the country was so they could either steal the gold for themselves or collect a hefty bribe.

Oforiwa's house sat on a corner lot in Airport Residential Area, a neighborhood featuring walled homes, hushed lawns, and gates with signs that warned people to beware of dogs. Auntie Faustie and a woman I took to be Auntie Peace were in the vinyl-tiled kitchen, a steaming pot on the stove. They hugged me. They rubbed my belly. They thanked Jehovah I was not like the bad girls of Accra who got their wombs scraped the minute a baby took root.

Auntie Faustie said in her deep voice, "Jehovah will bless you and your Armand."

I couldn't get over her youthfulness. She had the same blue-black skin as Oforiwa, smooth as sardine, and teeth so perfect they looked artificial. The other woman said to call her Auntie Peace. It occurred to me she was one of those people my uncle always complained about, Jehovah's Witnesses who laid claim to his house. As far as he was concerned, they were responsible for the insufferable wedge between him and my aunt.

"So where is Uncle Kwame?" I asked.

Auntie Faustie's voice took on a flippant tone. "He's gone to London. He'll be back tomorrow."

"Are you sure he'll come back tomorrow?" said Auntie Peace. "Since I arrived with my children, he seldom stays at home."

"My sister, stop talking so I can stop listening. Who is Kwame Agyare? He doesn't get to tell me who I can entertain and who I can't. My God Jehovah is the most important person to me. You are a Jehovah's witness, just like me, so we're supposed to share our belongings. If he doesn't understand, he can go burn the sea!"

I quickly declared I was hungry, whereupon they ceased talking about my uncle and clucked about the importance of feeding a pregnant woman.

After a breakfast of rice water and fried egg, Oforiwa left for town while I huddled in the kitchen with the two ladies. We sat on low wooden stools, sipping Milo from china teacups as I filled them in on my quest for gold.

"That's nothing," Auntie Peace said with the rounded body of one who ate well in my aunt's kitchen. "For two thousand dollars, my husband can get you ten pounds of gold. You just give me the money."

I swallowed, tried to breathe. Ten pounds of gold. Times two thousand. Twenty thousand. Twenty thousand dollars! I could re-invest it and turn it into two hundred thousand. We could be in the millions before Armand even got out of the Marines. We could buy one of those long cars with darkened windows. A big house some-where in New York. A beach house in Dakar. Four children scampering around the beach. All the lobster Armand could eat. I'd take my mother on trips to wherever she wanted. Sweet saliva oozed into my mouth. I put my cup down on the floor. "You're sure?"

Auntie Peace drew herself up and acquired two chins. "Ah, don't you trust me?"

"Ten pounds. You mean, ten pounds of gold?"

Auntie Faustie said, "What you'll get is real gold, not like some of the fake things they sell."

If anyone was honest, it was Auntie Faustie. People knew better than to cross her. Those foolish enough to try felt the sting of her palm across their cheeks. Even my uncle knew to maintain the peace. A broken door to their bedroom testified to her temper. Auntie Peace would not dare cheat me. Without further consideration, I raced upstairs, unzipped my suitcase, and returned with twenty crisp hundred-dollar bills. I handed them over to Auntie Peace, and she counted them twice. Then we pressed our bosoms together in a fond deal.

Auntie Peace dispatched her teenage son to the mines with my money, a bag slung across his shoulder and chest. A week later, he returned. With Oforiwa on a trip to Nigeria, the rest of us women hunkered down in the kitchen for the momentous occasion. Auntie Peace unwrapped a dark cloth to reveal the twenty-four-carat gold, so yellow and shiny. But that couldn't be all, could it? It had to be a sample, for the gold was no bigger than my middle finger. I looked up at her. "Where is the rest of it?"

"What do you mean, where is the rest of it?" she said, pointing at the gold. "It's all here."

I felt the rushing of wind in my ears. "But you said ten pounds. This isn't ten pounds."

Auntie Faustie took the gold from me and weighed it in her hand. "This *is* about ten pounds. A pound of gold is not the same as a regular pound, you know. "

Sweat prickled my armpit as I struggled to understand.

"A pound is actually an ounce," said the peaceful woman. "Miners just call it a pound."

I swallowed. "Do Europeans understand this? Do they use the same measure?"

"Oh yes, they do. Nothing to worry about." She patted my arm with plump hands, called me "beloved," and crooned more soothing words. I looked at Auntie Faustie, who nodded her agreement.

The price of gold at the time was between four and five hundred dollars an ounce, so Auntie Peace's price was fair. I just didn't know it. I wasn't one of those people who opened the newspapers to check stocks and the price of whatnot.

"Now, let's talk about your spiritual life," Auntie Faustie said.

I squirmed, wishing I were in Nigeria with Oforiwa. "My spiritual life? What do you mean?"

"Have you been reading the Jehovah's Witness literature I sent to you?"

"Yes, Auntie." I had yawned through a couple of pamphlets, but the rest found the bottom of my rubbish bin.

She wagged a warning finger. "You cannot become a Jehovah's Witness unless you complete your study, and you cannot be baptized until then."

"Yes, of course." I had no intention of becoming a Jehovah's Witness, but saying so would only invite more lectures.

"Being a Jehovah's Witness is such a good thing," Auntie Peace said. "Look at me, I am not family yet I live here." I thought it best not to point out her part in my uncle's self-imposed exile.

"We are all one," Auntie Faustie said. "Even if you're in America and you need a place to stay, you can just go to the Kingdom Hall and they will take you in. Just like that. Oh, do you remember my friend Yvonne, the Black American who stayed with us last year? She lives in New York. If you ever need anyone, just go to the Kingdom Hall and ask for her. Remind me to give you her number."

"Yes, Auntie." I had no intention of getting in touch with any Jehovah's Witness. The one time Mama caught me reading a copy of *The Watchtower* that Auntie Faustie had pressed into my palm, she said, *Have you cracked your madness open?*

I felt a twinge of guilt for not going home to see my mother. Because we lived in Kumasi, four hours' drive from Accra, I couldn't dash over for one day and return. I needed to get back to Dakar to catch Binta before her next flight to Brussels. Besides, Mama would know immediately that I was pregnant. I wasn't ready to face her. The pressing question was how to slip the gold past customs and make the flight back to Dakar. If I put it in my suitcase, they would catch me. I couldn't hide it on my body either, there was always a body search. I decided to hide it in plain sight: in my hand.

At the airport check-in, they rifled through my clothes, shaking out dresses. They found nothing. I proceeded to immigration. No problem. Then it was on to security. My temples throbbed. A stout female customs officer in a brown skirt and shirt blocked my way. Her big eyes probed me.

"Put your bag on the table."

I obeyed. Moisture formed around the gold in my left hand.

"Stretch out your arms. Feet apart."

I willed my heart to stop hammering. I inhaled as she palmed my breasts through my silk blouse. She reached behind me and swept her hands up and down my back. The gold felt slippery in my moist hand. I gripped it tightly. She bent and slid a hand between my legs. She straightened up and looked at me. Sweat meandered down my sides. I kept my face steady.

"Go on," she said.

I felt weak. I slid my hand into my trouser pocket and let go of the gold. As soon as I boarded the plane, I fished it out and dropped it into my handbag.

When Binta the stewardess flew to Belgium to sell the gold, I called Armand and panted excitedly into the handset. "Do you know how much we're making? Twenty thousand dollars!"

"Wow, baby!" he said. "You're magic, you know that? I love you. Now, just put the money into the account."

When Binta returned a week later, I rushed to her apartment. Too impatient for the elevator, I took the stairs, disregarding my doctor's advice against strenuous activities.

She glided over the marble floor in her leotard, revealing her curves, but her slanted eyes were empty. "I didn't sell it," she said before I even sat down. "It was ten ounces of gold, not ten pounds. I didn't want to sell it in case you thought I stole from you."

"What?"

She glided into the bedroom and returned with the gold. "Look, this doesn't even weigh half a pound. I think what they meant was ten ounces, not ten pounds."

"I know, I know. But she said 'pound' was mine vocabulary, that it was understood the world over."

"Whatever the case, this won't fetch you twenty thousand dollars."

I sank onto the couch, my hand over my mouth. I should have known it was too good to be true. There was no quick fortune to be made in the gold market. Oh, God.

If I had been less agitated, I could have sold the gold for a small profit, but I panicked. Back to Ghana I flew. Auntie Faustie and Auntie Peace and I huddled together in the sitting room. I thrust the gold finger into Auntie Peace's hand and told her to give me back my money. "They said it was only ten ounces."

"Ah, didn't you understand? Ten pounds, ten ounces. Same thing."

"It's not the same for the rest of the world. Only Ghanaian traders call an ounce a pound. It's not going to fetch any profit. I want my money back."

Auntie Faustie's eyes turned into stones. Her neck lengthened. "Peace, she says she doesn't want the gold. Return it and give her back her money. I don't want her to lose."

Auntie Peace's face twisted into someone aggrieved. "Oh, is that so?"

"That is so," I said.

She adjusted and readjusted her cloth. A series of sighs blew out of her. "Fine, I'll send my son back to the mines."

I closed my eyes with thanks. At least Armand could have his two thousand back.

A day passed.

Then another.

Auntie Peace's son remained gone. She sent her daughter after him. A week passed. Still no money. Each time I inquired, Auntie Peace would say, "Don't worry, these things take time. Look, I cooked fufu and light soup with goat meat." I would swallow her words and the delicious mounds and think she couldn't possibly be lying to me. Then she herself went to Kumasi and I never saw her again. For all anyone knew, the mines had swallowed up her entire family.

I wanted to die. I wanted not to be pregnant. "Two thousand dollars is a lot of money to me," Armand had said. Now I had lost it all.

That evening, Oforiwa found me languishing on the veranda, arms folded and wishing I were one of the moths hurtling themselves against the streetlight and dropping dead. She stood beside me, putting her hand on my shoulder. "What are you going to do, Akua?"

"I don't know. I just don't know."

"Are you going to tell Armand?"

"I can't. How do I tell him he has lost everything?"

"He has you."

"Yes, he has me." I laughed bitterly.

"Well, now that you're pregnant, you have no choice but to be with him."

"I know, I know. But can you imagine what would happen if things don't work out and I have to return to Ghana?"

"Shh! Close your mouth! Don't invite that shame at all. Please. Think of your mother. Your disgrace is hers as well. A pregnant woman without a husband? With a foreigner no one even knows? We would never hear the end of insults. Why would you even say that?"

I was twisting my braid between thumb and finger. "Did I tell you he is sending me to live with his best friend?"

"No, you didn't, but what's the big deal?"

"I wish he were sending me to his parents, our baby's grand-parents. I mean, that's the Ghanaian way. I don't even know this Daniel person. And renting a place for me, how could I live by myself?"

"Staying away from Armand's family isn't such a bad idea," she said in a quiet voice. "Because it will be better to wait for him to introduce you to his family. I'm sure his friend will take care of you. Cheer up, you're going to love America. Mummy says you're going to get excellent medical care in America. The midwives and doctors are going to pamper you. Not like here, where nurses shout at you to push and you should have thought about the pain when you were fucking your man."

"Yeah, I guess."

"But you've got to tell your mother. Quickly. Before Mummy tells her."

I tried to stay calm. "I'll go tomorrow. After I call Armand."

***

"I miss you a lot," Armand said, when I got through to him.

"I miss you, too. Did you receive the pictures?" I had sent him nude images of my blooming belly.

His voice caught. "They're beautiful. How's business?"

"Business is, uhm, okay. I'll tell you in person."

He grew quiet. "What's wrong, Lola?"

"Nothing." I forced a laugh. "Nothing. Really."

"Is the baby okay?"

"Oh yes, he keeps me up at night with his kicking."

"Lola, you know you can talk to me, don't you?"

"Yes," I whispered, feeling tears burn my eyes.

"I love you, you know that."

"Yes," I said quickly. "I hope to be in the U.S. in three weeks, I have to travel before the seventh month, you know."

"Yeah. Sure. Just let me know when you get your visa so I can tell Daniel. God, I miss you. I can't wait to kiss your belly."

"Me, too," I whispered.

"And listen, this baby is going to be fine. He's going to grow up in America and have every opportunity."

"He or *she* is also African. I want the baby to know my family."

"Sure thing. Our baby will be American and African. You're going to be American, too. We're gonna make it. If it's a girl, I hope she has your small face. And your laughter."

I laughed out loud.

"That's my baby. You take care of yourself, okay?"

"I will, darling," I said softly, a whisper of guilt, a spiderweb of lies.

Akɔkɔ Nan Akɔkɔ Nan

The Leg of a Hen

I climbed onto the State Transport Corporation bus bound for Kumasi. As my body sank into the cushioned seat, panic rose in my chest. Dakar was the farthest I had ever traveled from my mother and sister. Until now, home was an easy hop on a plane, a mere couple of hours' suspension in the air before landing. America lay on the other side of a vast ocean I had never crossed before. Add to that, a baby nestling inside me. How would Mama receive the news? I couldn't hide my stomach from her. Although I looked more like someone who had gained a little weight than a woman six and a half months pregnant, I knew her keen eyes would pick out the shape of my belly. But at least I was going to marry Armand. Even if she disapproved of him, surely, she had to be grateful for the legitimacy of the baby?

Three years earlier, when Awurama married the son of the chief justice of Ghana, in a ceremony attended by Ghana's elite, Mama couldn't stop smiling. I felt strangely weary when Awurama and her husband swept off in a white Mercedes tied with white silk ribbons. Mama had to tug at my arm to urge me into the back of our car so the driver could take us home. It was the first time we had returned from a wedding without Awurama. Later that night, I knocked on Mama's door, still wearing my ankle-length purple gown. We had moved from the small house of my childhood into a big, white colonial, the official residence of a judge.

When I entered the room, she greeted me with a huge smile. She had shed the silvery sequined attire for a cotton nightie.

"Akua," she said. Just my name and nothing more, as if she just wanted to assure herself that I was there.

I pointed at her dress laid carelessly on the bed. "Do you want me to hang this for you?"

"No. Just put it on the chair. Afia will tidy up tomorrow."

Afia was the maid. I draped the dress carefully over the chair. A dreamy smile was plastered on my mother's face. "Mama, do you worry about being alone one day?"

She propped up her pillows and leaned back on them. "What kind of question is that?"

"Awurama is gone now. I mean, they will remain in Kumasi, but she won't live here anymore."

Mama's eyes filled with such a softness that tears welled in my eyes. She knew me too well. "Come," she said. I sat so close I felt her warmth, the soothing expansion of body as she breathed. "You're feeling lost, aren't you?"

Tears rolled down my cheeks.

"My baby-last," she murmured. "You're such a homegirl." She snatched a handkerchief from her bedside table and dabbed at my cheeks.

"Mama, you will never be alone."

Her eyes widened. "You are worried about me?"

I nodded, unable to speak.

"With all the relatives who visit anytime they need money? And the house girls and houseboys who make me useless? I will never be alone."

"Maids like Afia can't replace your children."

"Stop, stop it." Her voice was firm. "Don't act like some of the characters in books written by Western people. Awurama may have left home, but she lives near and will visit regularly. Who do you think is going to bathe the baby and teach her things? I get to do it over again. So don't cry, you hear? It's unhealthy. By the way, I have something for you."

She took me by the hand and led me into the outer room that served as her study. I loved the picture of her in the black choir robe of a judge hanging on the wall above the desk, though I found the blond wig ugly and a reminder of colonialism. On the floor next to the desk, a lump pushed up, covered with a reddish wax-print cloth.

"Remove the cloth," she said.

I bent down and pulled the cloth off. I couldn't speak, couldn't move. On the floor was a new electric typewriter.

"Mama!" I turned to her in wonder.

She was smiling proudly. "You can now type your stories and stop stealing my notebooks."

I flew at her. "Thank you, thank you, thank you!"

Mama. She was everything to me. How would I get her to accept I was casting off the family blanket for Armand, the father of my baby, the man she had urged me to forget?

Getting off the bus at the transport station, I hailed a taxi to the University of Science and Technology. My sister and her professor husband lived in a large three-bedroom house on Ridge Road, a street housing university lecturers and senior civil servants. I needed her support in my endeavor to persuade Mama.

The garden boy, Kofi, was hoeing the flower bed in front of the house. When he saw me get out of the taxi, he dropped his hoe and ran to meet me.

"Welcome, miss," he said, wiping off his hands on his shorts before taking my bag.

"Is Madam in?"

"Yes, miss."

Awurama threw the front door open. "Akua!" She stopped, staring at my stomach. Her smile didn't reach her eyes.

"How are you, sister?" I asked.

"I should be asking you that," she said in a suspicious voice. She preceded me into the sitting room furnished with an orange settee and matching armchairs. From the kitchen, I could hear running water and plates clattering. "Adjoa!" she called to the house girl. "Bring a glass of water for Sister Akua."

"Thank you." I sat on the sofa. "Where's my niece?"

"Sleeping. Thank God. If she were awake, she would be begging you to tell her a story and we'd never be able to talk." She stood facing me, searching my face anxiously. "You're pregnant?"

I nodded into my lap.

"Have you told Mama?"

"No."

"The American?"

I nodded again.

She fell silent, just looking at me. Then she let out a long sigh, lowering herself into an armchair. "I guess you're going to marry him. You'd better, you can't have a bastard child. In your letter, you said you loved him." Her words were flat. "Have you thought about how you're going to tell Mama?"

"I'm hoping you'll come with me."

"Oh, don't worry, I will. Adjoa can take care of Nana when she wakes up. Her father will be home soon."

"I know Mama will be angry, but I hope she can see Armand isn't a bad person. And it's not as if I'm in secondary school. I've finished university. Surely that elevates me to the morality and responsibility department?"

"Yes, it does."

Our conversation felt broken. I said words, she agreed, followed by unspoken words, like missing links of a chain. She tried to press food on me, but everything tasted like cardboard.

The sun had left crimson streaks in the sky when we entered our home. Mama relaxed in a blue leather chair. My first thought was how much she looked like an older version of me, with her turquoise blouse and a cloth wrapped around her waist. I wanted to throw myself into her arms but she wasn't looking at me. That had never stopped me before. Now I hesitated, a nervous visitor. The white-and-blue tie-dye curtains behind her ballooned, hid her face for a minute. She swiped them away, beaming at my sister.

"Hello, firstborn," she said, and then she saw me.

"Hello, Mama," I said softly.

Her smile widened, she got up with her arms open, and then her eyes fell on my belly. Her arms dropped. The light froze in her eyes, then slowly dimmed. Those eyes bore the pain of someone stabbed by her best friend. Her gaze traveled up to my face and down to my belly again. Her mouth opened and closed. Her breath

BISI ADJAPON

came in small puffs, as if she was struggling to breathe. Slowly, she backed into the chair, steadying herself. I rushed and knelt before her.

"Mama? Is your body good?"

She shifted away from me, talking to the door. "She's going to have a baby." She looked at me, then at the door. "You bring a child into the world, give her the best education, dream the biggest dreams for her, and the minute she gets out of school, oh God. A man I don't know. A family I don't know."

"Mama, please."

She whipped her head to me, eyes blazing. "Please what?"

Our eyes locked on each other. I flashed back to the many times she'd call me into the sitting room after receiving my report card, telling me how proud she was of me. The typewriter she bought me that still sat on a desk she'd had a carpenter make for me so we could sit side by side in the study, she in her law books, me typing a story. Now a huge chasm yawned between us. We stared at each other, two people at opposite edges of a gulf, each unable to reach out and pull the other to her side.

My throat burned so I couldn't swallow. I had anticipated disappointment, but not this split-apart feeling. She rose to her feet and marched into her bedroom, that room where I used to exchange breaths with her. The door slammed. I sagged onto the floor. Awurama rubbed my back.

"She's upset now," she said, "but it will be well. I'll talk to her. You'll see. It will be well."

Mama remained in her room with the door shut, the door that had stayed open all my life, not even when she was naked. Awurama left with a promise to return the next day to take me to the bus station. In the morning, when Mama emerged from her puffy-

74

eyed sleep and I greeted her, she merely bit her lip. Sitting beside her to eat my breakfast, I began, "Mama," but she rose from the table. I followed her into the sitting room. "Mama, I'm going back to Dakar."

She looked steadily at me and marched into her study. Her lips were still pinched together when Awurama's car pulled into the driveway. I ran outside, wailing, "She won't talk to me."

"Give her time. Remember what she always says? The hen treads on her chicks with her legs, but she doesn't kill them. She'll come around. You wait and see."

We found Mama in her bedroom, sitting at the edge of the bed, her head in her hands. Awurama motioned for me to leave them alone, so I went back to the sitting room, pacing about. I couldn't hear their muffled conversation. When Awurama finally emerged, she looked drained. "You know how hard she held us together after Dadda died. Now she blames herself for not doing something right."

I pushed past her into the bedroom.

Mama's eyes burned into me. "Why are you disgracing me? No knocking-of-the-door ceremony for permission to marry you so that we can meet his people, research his family. Why are you even here, when you disregarded my advice and got pregnant? You have torn yourself out of the family and thrown us onto a rubbish heap. Are you going to move to America?" She looked up at the ceiling. "Oh, Lord."

"It won't be forever, Mama, I'll come back."

"I don't want to hear it."

"Please, Mama."

"You're already pregnant. There's nothing more to be said. Just go." Her face was turned toward the window, rigid.

"Mama, don't!"

"I have nothing to say to you." I knew from the twist of her neck to the window that nothing would turn her from her position. I clutched my belly from the pain that punched me so hard I wondered if the baby was coming out. My breath came out in hot puffs. How could I choose between two loves, one forever linked by a child who needed parents? I looked long at her, feeling I had only one choice. Using my last reserves of strength, I turned and stumbled out of the room.

Mmusuyideε

That Which Removes Bad Luck

Last day in Dakar, my last day on African soil. The strange thudding of my heart.

The U.S. embassy had given me a tourist visa valid for only six months, but Armand would take care of my resident visa later. I had bought my plane ticket, a round-trip fare to New York that would expire in two weeks, the cheapest I could find. But I was going to make a home in America and wouldn't need a return ticket for a long time. I tried to shut out Mama's stricken face, her cold voice. *Just go.* I swallowed hard and focused on my second family-to-be: Armand, his parents, five siblings, plus his brother-friend, Daniel, the one who would host me and play temporary Dadda for Armand.

I had bought a silvery bracelet for Daniel and had his name engraved on it. Silver was so cheap, even houseboys owned one. I figured it would be a relationship warmer. I planned to love him like the brother I'd never had. I was sure he would be a good uncle to the baby. I had already sent Armand a fax advising him of my arrival so he could tell Daniel. Just to be on the safe side, I went to Télé-Senegal and placed a call to Daniel himself at the number Armand had given me.

It was six a.m. in New York. Right away, from the sleepy, female voice that rasped a hello, I sniffed trouble. Doing my best to keep the tremor out of my voice, I said, "May I speak to Daniel Roberts, please?"

"I don' know, lemme see if he's in."

"Is he sleeping?"

"I don' know, maybe he come home, maybe he don't."

"Well, could you find out, please? This is a long-distance call from Senegal. My name is Lola."

"Whaas ya name?"

"Lola."

"Whaa?"

"Lola, L-O-L-A," I spelled, exasperated.

"Okay, you hold, I'm gonna see."

I waited, growing more doubtful by the minute. What sort of place did Daniel live in? Visions from Nicky Cruz's memoir, *Run Baby Run*, flashed before me. Cruz used to be the leader of the notorious Mau Mau gang of New York. Or was Daniel at a military base? Armand had said he was joining the army.

"Hello," a male voice broke abruptly onto the line.

"Oh, hello, is this Daniel Roberts?"

"Yes."

"Hi, this is Lola, Armand's fiancé." Silence. "Did I wake you up?"

"That's okay." It was obviously not okay.

"Well, I thought I'd let you know that I'll be arriving tomorrow. I sent a fax to Armand but I thought I would call to be sure."

More silence. Then, "He was supposed to call."

"Didn't he? Oh, well, maybe he received my fax late and—"

"But he was supposed to call me." He sounded agitated. "We talked yesterday. Said he had to dash off to get you a present before the shop closed. He was supposed to call me later."

"I don't know, but never mind, I'm arriving tomorrow on—"

"Look, give me a number where I can reach you."

"Well, you can't reach me. I don't have a phone in my studio. I'm calling from a phone booth."

"Give me Armand's number. I've never had to call him."

I gave it to him, as well as my flight details. He didn't sound too pleased, and as I hung up, I felt nauseated. That night, after packing and falling asleep, I dreamed about America. I saw a woman stumbling from street to street, looking for shelter from the snow. I sighed in pity, floating behind her like a spirit, unable to help. Other spirits floated with me and we hovered over her, moaning in unison until, utterly weary, she lay on the snow, her startled eyes open, like a doll's. I looked into her face and jerked awake, heart pounding. The eyes looking back at me were mine.

The dream dogged me as I completed my last-minute packing. I calmed myself as the driver drove me to the building manager's office to turn in my apartment keys. What stupid fears to have when Armand was taking care of things, when I had Olga and Len George ready to welcome me? Not forgetting Auntie Faustie's Jehovah's Witness friend, Yvonne somebody.

At the airport, I joined the line of passengers inching toward the check-in counter. I thought of scenes I would never see for a long time to come: the beaches of Dakar, the white sand, the pale blue sky, the heat. *I'm leaving.* A pair of hands reached from behind me and covered my eyes. I whipped around. It was Kwaku, son of Len's boss.

I shrieked, "Kwaku! You are here, in Dakar!"

"Yes, ooo, my sister." He brushed back his jerry-curled hair, which gleamed with oil. "I went to your studio but you weren't there."

"I've been in and out of Dakar. Ghana Airways has been chopping my money."

"Ei, you were in Ghana and you didn't come see me?"

Shame flooded my face. This was a man who never failed to take Joana and me to dinner whenever he flew in from Ghana. "I'm sorry I didn't call you. I've been, well, okay."

His eyes dropped to my stomach. "You're pregnant? Who is the lucky man?"

I told him about Armand and our plans for the future.

"Is that so?" He looked pleased. "I'm flying to London, but I visit America sometimes. My big sister lives there, you know. You've got to stay in touch so I can look you up." He pulled a tiny notebook from his pocket, scribbled his sister's address on a page, and gave it to me. I hugged him for a long time. There was little chance I would see him in America, but it felt good to know some things remained unchanged. His was the kind of friendship I could count on, whether we had been minutes apart or years.

From behind me, I could hear Americans talking in loud voices. *Did you watch the news last night? Did you see the snow? I hear schools are closing because it's gotten so bad out there.* Just hearing those words, I shivered.

A tall, muscular White American man in front of me turned around and smiled. Despite his blue eyes, I blinked at his tight blond curls, wondering if he had African blood lurking in him.

"Hi," I said brightly, eager to make friends.

"You going to New York?"

"Yes, and it's my first time."

"New York's pretty scary. I'm from Virginia. I'm only stopping in transit in New York."

"Well, you know, I don't even know if I'm going to be met. I spoke to this person on the phone who is supposed to meet me, but he seemed kind of out of it."

"I tell you, New York's a dangerous place. If you ever get lost or something, just talk to the police. Don't talk to anyone else."

"Gee, thanks. I'll remember that." I resisted the urge to grab my suitcases, hail a taxi back to the building, and beg the administrator for my key. My heart hammered with both fear and excitement, the kind an athlete would get before a race: feet to my marks, head raised, heart pounding, waiting for the gun to blast me off. My flight was called. I took a deep breath and walked to the plane.

It was January 1997. I was leaving behind friends, a job, my mother, my sister, and the security of a culture to which I had always belonged. Going to have a baby in a foreign land in the middle of the worst snowstorm of the year, with a fiancé in the Caribbean, to stay with a best friend I had never met. The plane took off.

It was too late to change my mind.

Boa Me Na Me Mboa Wo

Help Me, and I'll Help You

We had just begun our descent when I sat up and looked out the window.

"New York!" I gasped, staring at the blaze of lights like trillions of jewels, the shivering taffeta of water. My doubts vanished. I couldn't wait to get off the plane and dance on the streets, let American lights speckle my skin. America, here I come!

At immigration, we got separated: Americans in different lines and foreigners in others. I clutched my handbag tightly. I'd heard stories about immigration officials denying entry to pregnant women whose children would gain citizenship and populate America.

A uniformed Black woman faced us, chewing gum as if daring anyone to tell her not to. "Next!" she barked, pointing me to an immigration booth.

I breathed in as the man examined my passport, looked me up and down. After forever, he stamped it. "Enjoy your stay."

I let out the breath, but oh, the confidence of the people. The loudness of their voices, the rapid working of their jaws as they popped gum, their swagger, all made me drop my pen, fumble with my passport, and feel shrunken. How fearsome the clicking of shoes on the floors as uniformed men led dogs with big teeth. I took a deep breath to calm myself. Then I picked up my suitcases and, with Julie Andrews's *Sound of Music* bravado, walked out into America.

Daniel Roberts was not there.

The entrance to the waiting area teemed with people who had come to meet their loved ones. Some held placards bearing the names of people they didn't know. Others smiled with expectation, waved, or whooped in recognition. None of the signs bore my name. Maybe Daniel figured he could make me out by my pregnancy. I looked all over but there was no sign of whatever my mind conceived him to look like. I willed myself to breathe evenly. I stood there, my chest squeezing tighter and tighter.

A body pushed past me. It was the blond man from Virginia. "Hi there!" he said. "Are you okay?"

"The person who was supposed to meet me isn't here!"

He had a flight to catch, but he hesitated. "Do you have his number?"

"Yes."

He dug into his pocket. "Here," he said, and dropped silver coins into my palm. "You'll need this to make a phone call. But you can save yourself money by dialing zero and the number you want to call. You know, call collect. And remember, don't talk to any strangers. Only to the police. Just stay close to a policeman, okay? I'm sorry. I wish I could stay with you, but I've got to go."

"It's okay," I said bravely. "Thank you very much."

"You're welcome. What's your name?" he asked in a kind voice.

"Lola."

"Rob Morrison here. Sorry I have to leave you, Lola, but good luck, okay? Hang in there. I'm sure your friend is on his way." He was gone before I could beg him to stay.

I darted into the glass booth and pressed Daniel's number with trembling fingers. The same woman I'd spoken to when I called from Dakar answered the phone. I tried to keep the tremor out of my voice. "May I speak to Daniel?"

"No, he gone out."

"Do you have any idea where he went? He was supposed to meet me at the airport."

"He left with a friend. Said he was gonna meet some girl he don't know."

"It's me! He is not here, though."

"I think he's at the airport. Have him paged. If he comes home, then I'll tell him you called and I'll ask him to come git you."

"Oh, thank you. Thank you very much!" Brother-friend Daniel was coming to get me! I found the information booth and had him paged. Then I asked for a sheet of paper and printed "Daniel Roberts" in bold black letters on it. I held it against my bosom, smiling hopefully at any man who looked my way. Remembering Rob's advice, I found a policeman and stuck to him. If he moved two steps to the right, I moved two steps to the right. Once or twice, he reddened and stared at me quizzically. I smiled to reassure him I wasn't trying to pick a policeman's pocket, of all people.

I was so focused on the policeman I didn't notice the man approaching. The next thing I knew, I was looking into the bespectacled eyes of Daniel Roberts. They were cold. And he had a girlfriend in tow: a short, chubby copper-colored girl with straightened hair. She was not smiling either. His mouth opened. The voice was flat.

"You Armand's friend?"

"Yes," I replied, giving him a bright smile, hoping to inject some warmth into his eyes. They remained cold.

"This is my girlfriend, Nora." Nora gave me a reserved smile.

"Hi," I said in a voice gone an octave higher, not at all sure of myself. Daniel started to say something but changed his mind.

"Let's go." He grabbed my suitcase and Nora took my smaller bag.

As I followed them outside, the wind whipped my face. My cheeks suddenly had weight, and my breath was visible. Snow and ice covered the sidewalks and buildings. Daniel deposited my luggage in the trunk of a silvery Toyota. I remembered Armand telling me about credit cards and how they helped people buy cars. He'd also tried to explain mortgages to me, but I didn't understand. How could you own a house that really belonged to the bank?

The houses-on-loan sat like cakes with white icing, reminding me of the witch's house in "Hansel and Gretel," which I had read as a child. I wondered if I had catapulted myself into a land that could gobble me up.

"Listen," Daniel said, twisting around from the driver's seat and fixing his cold eyes on me. "I called Armand after I spoke to you yesterday. He'd asked us to look for an apartment for you, but we didn't know when you was coming, so we don't have the apartment yet. But he said to put you up in a hotel and not to worry about money, 'cos you got lots of currencies."

"A hotel," I stammered. And currencies. That had to be money.

"So, you got currencies, right?"

"Er, yes."

"How much you got?"

"Two hundred and fifty dollars."

Nora tittered. Daniel's mouth fell open. "What! You come to America to have a baby with two hundred and fifty dollars?"

"Wait a minute, I don't understand. Armand told me you already had a place for me to live. Look." I pulled out Armand's letter to me, and Daniel practically snatched it from my hand. He grew angrier as his eyes moved back and forth over Armand's scrawl.

"What! Holy shit, man! You think I own an apartment building or something? It takes weeks to find a place! Armand told me: Don't do nothing until you hear from me." He continued reading. "I never said I had a place for you! The whole thing's fucked up! And you travel with two hundred and fifty dollars. What were you thinking of doing, eh? Come over here, have the baby, and disappear? You got Armand's number?"

"Yes." I was shaking. In my entire life, no one had ever yelled at me that way.

"We're gonna go to my house and we're gonna talk to Armand!"

The car peeled off. Nora added her piece. "Here in America, you don't have money? You're nothing. No one will look at you. You don't have insurance, nothing. And you, a foreigner? The doctors won't touch you, because of all those foreigners coming here hoping to become Americans. You need money."

Daniel jumped in. "Man, we ain't talking a few hundred bucks! We're talking Gs!"

From underworld crime novels I had read, I deduced that G stood for "grand," which meant a thousand. He sounded very much like my impression of Al Capone. A wave of dizziness overwhelmed me. The bright lights of New York blurred. I wanted to be anywhere but in that car, listening to him yelling.

They continued their tag team of berating me until we pulled up to a small brick house. We spilled out of the car and went inside. My luggage remained in the car. Without a word, Daniel strode past a woman and two youths at a rectangular table in the living room. A low-hanging lamp cast a pale light over them. I felt the weight of their eyes on me as I hurried after Nora, who hurried after Daniel, who sprinted up the orange-carpeted stairs to the attic, his room.

"She needs to pee," Nora said.

"How you know that?" Daniel asked.

"When I was pregnant, I had to go lots of times." She turned to give me an encouraging smile. "I have a two-year-old, you know."

He turned to me. "Do you need to go?"

I felt like Nora's two-year-old, standing before two parents discussing her bladder. I was so eager to please that I went to the bathroom and obliged her. When I returned to the room that was half the size of our studio in Dakar, Daniel was on the phone, pacing, his brows furrowed together. "Man, the babe arrived, and she ain't got nothing but two fifty bucks. Shit, man! The whole thing's fucked up!" The curses flew on like a drill sergeant's. Armand must have asked to speak to me, because Daniel thrust the phone at me.

I failed at keeping the tremor out of my voice. "Hi-i."

"Lola, you came with only two hundred and fifty dollars?"

"Yes."

"What? God. I forgive you, Lola."

"What are you forgiving me for?" I hadn't even told him about the money I had lost.

"You don't know what you just did. How could you do a thing like that?" Now was not the time to tell him about the stolen money.

"Well, two fifty seemed okay as pocket money."

"My God, Lola. We're in the middle of our inspection."

"I didn't know that." I understood his panic. Once in a while, some big marine officer would arrive from Washington, and for days, it was a flurry of activities and tests and exercises and things I never understood. I just knew we couldn't see each other.

"Listen, we'll figure it out. Let me call you back, okay?"

"Okay." I hung up. I turned to Daniel. "He says he'll call back."

"What the hell?!" Daniel grabbed the phone. "SHIT! The whole thing is fucked! Damn!" He jabbed Armand's number with furious fingers. The phone fell out of his hands a couple of times and he had to jab again. "Man!" he shouted into the phone. "And she knew everything about me! You gave her my address, my mother's telephone number! She even called from the airport!" I felt like a criminal and burst into tears. "And now she's sitting here crying!" He raced downstairs, probably so I wouldn't hear what he was saying, the long cord snaking after him. I could hear him ranting but his words rushed out with such speed I couldn't separate them to understand.

I wiped my eyes and tried to compose myself. My mind flitted around mindless things until it settled on the bangle I had bought for Daniel. I fished it out with trembling hands, an incomplete circle with a round knob at each end, an unanswered puzzle. I don't know why, but I held it out to Nora, whispering, "This is for Daniel. I'm sorry. I didn't get you anything because I didn't know about you."

"That's a nice bracelet," she said sincerely, and laid it on the bedside table. She got up, stretched her arms, and padded catlike to face the full-length mirror by the window. She ran her fingers through her short hair. How easy she was in her skin. The confidence of belonging. I had filled my skin like that in Dakar. Now I had shrunk.

"My hair is growing," she said, fluffing it up. Through the mirror, she eyed my long hair. "I don't like long hair. I keep my daughter's hair long, but personally? I don't like long hair. My hair used to be real long, I tell you."

I was in no mood to discuss hair lengths. As she babbled on, my eyes fell on an open letter on the center table. The handwriting was Armand's. I knew it wasn't for my eyes, but I picked it up and scanned it quickly before she turned around.

Armand's parents didn't want to have anything to do with an African woman, he'd written. I remembered previous letters from his father, how he couldn't wait for Armand to leave "that Africa" and come home. This was after Armand had written touting Dakar as a city like any other in the world. I remembered feeling vaguely amused that Armand had needed to write that, and saddened by his father's response. I had never expected someone from Haiti, a country where Toussaint L'Ouverture fought Napoleon and won independence, where they celebrated Black freedom, to look down on Africans. The letter slipped from my hands onto the carpet. Why hadn't Armand told me? I never would have left Ghana if I had known his Caribbean family wanted nothing to do with an African. Then again, I had concealed the state of our finances from him.

Daniel returned, subdued. When Nora showed him the bangle, his granite face softened.

"Gee, thanks," he said in a gentle voice I didn't know he possessed. "You didn't have to do that."

I forced a smile. "That's okay."

"No. You didn't have to. That's sweet of you." The shadow of a smile lit his coffee face for an instant before disappearing. In the silence that followed, I could almost hear everybody's heartbeat, every pulse. Finally, he said, "Listen, do you know anybody around who can help you? You see, God, this place is too small, and Nora and me, you know . . ."

He seemed to be waiting for me to say something, but all I could think of was Armand. Yes, he had an inspection, but surely, he would call back later with a solution? Why was Daniel in such a hurry to be rid of me?

"So, what we gonna do?" Daniel asked.

"What about Armand's family?" I asked, even though I now knew how they felt.

Daniel bristled. "His brother lives right around the corner in his own apartment, but . . ." The incomplete sentence said it all.

I took a deep breath. "Well, I have the telephone number of a friend." With Olga in Maryland, Len was the only one not out of immediate reach. He'd said he lived in Brooklyn.

I called the number, but there was no answer. It was after midnight, four long hours since the plane had touched down in New York. He was probably asleep. My body ached. I cast a longing look at Daniel's bed.

"Well," he said with determination, "let's drive over there. I'll drive you to Canada if I have to. I'll drive you anywhere you want."

I didn't see the use of driving there, but I figured that if I cooperated and there were no other options left, at least he would let me stay for the night, by which time, Armand would hopefully have a break from his inspection. We drove past unlit houses shrouding the streets with dark shadows. The leafless branches were fat and gray with snow, the warm beaches of Dakar far away.

"She shouldn't be alone in the city," Nora said.

Daniel nodded at the windshield. "Yeah. You know, you're real lucky you met Nora and me. There's not many people in New York like us. Yeah, I know, cuz Armand told me. You people are real kind, you take in strangers and share your all and all. But this ain't Africa. This is New York. Here, no one gives a damn."

A flicker of hope leaped within me, that I wouldn't be alone until Armand returned, because there weren't many people like him and Nora in New York, where no one gave a damn.

"You hungry?" Nora asked in a kind voice.

I shook my head.

"You gotta eat something."

Daniel stopped the car at the yellow-and-red glow of a McDonald's. He rolled down the window and talked to some box on a stake, and the box said something loudly back. Then we drove up a narrow lane and a man handed him a paper bag from a window. I didn't understand how the food got to us so quickly. I accepted the burger, but my throat was so tight I couldn't swallow a bite.

It was a wasted effort driving around for an hour. I had only Len's building address and there were no names on the mailboxes. Daniel parked on a curb and threw up his hands. "Man, he gave you the number of the building but not the apartment number!" He twisted around to look at me, his head cocked to one side, his chin lifting. "And you got two fifty dollars. That won't get you even a week's rent, God!" He thrust his face at me. "So, tell me, what d'ya suggest we do now, eh? Tell me."

"I don't know," I answered quietly, "but I don't want to make trouble for anyone."

"Shit," he said softly, then turned to Nora with a slight shake of his head. "And she so sweet, she don't wanna make no trouble for nobody. What you suggest we do, hun?"

"I wanna go home." Her voice had turned sullen, her head low, arms folded across her chest, eyes staring at a spot on her lap.

"You wanna come spend the night with me?"

"No, I just wanna go home."

We drove in an uneasy silence. When we got to her gray building, she scrambled out of the car before Daniel came to a complete stop. She slammed the door without looking at him, walking away with rapid steps. He jumped out and caught up with her under a streetlight. Their mouths moved rapidly. Nora's arms remained folded and her head shook a lot. I wished I had the gumption to rush and fold her in a hug, tell her she would never lose her man to me. Daniel threw his arms up and down. They agitated for a long time before their bodies grew quiet. Then Nora turned decisively and stomped into the building. Daniel stood looking after her. He seemed to call her but she didn't look back. Then he looked in my direction. His shoulders sagged. Shaking his head, he shoved his hands into his pockets and walked heavily back.

He plunked himself into the driver's seat, staring through the windshield. At length, he twisted around to look at me, blinking rapidly. "Look, I don't know what to tell you. I just enlisted in the army. I'm supposed to be deployed soon. Nora and me, we wanna get married before I'm deployed. I'm really sorry, but I can't risk it. I mean, you know." He blinked some more. "Listen, I'm gonna drive you to a hospital. You'll be safe there." After that, his voice gained strength. "I'll advise you, call Armand in the morning. If you don't get him, then you call the police, okay?" I heard the words, but they didn't register. Or they registered but I disbelieved them because he was spinning before me. A wave of nausea rose within me. He started the engine. "Just tell the police someone was supposed to meet you at the airport but didn't show. And if they ask you how you got there, just say someone gave you a ride, okay? Don't mention my name."

I found myself stuttering. "But what, what will I do at the hospital?"

He kept blinking. "Don't worry about it," he said, pulling onto the road. "They'll give you a bed to sleep and all that."

When the reality of what was happening sank in, I pushed back the tears and looked out the window, a haze in my eyes.

The neon letters at the top of the large building read "Kings County Hospital." I said nothing as he took my suitcases out of the trunk. Nothing as I followed him into the lobby. Nothing as he indicated a wooden bench near a phone booth and said, "Sit here."

Slowly, I sank down, not taking my eyes off him. He placed my suitcases on the floor, next to me. His eyes met mine and held. I hated the way my voice faltered despite my fight for control. "You are leaving me here. Armand said you were like his brother."

"I'm sorry, sweetheart," he said mournfully. "I tried. You know I tried, don't you? I really tried. Look, tomorrow, on my way out, I'll stop by and see if you're okay."

We both knew he wouldn't. He was running away. I held myself rigid so as to conceal my wretchedness. I looked at him steadily, not trusting myself to speak. I turned my face away, refusing to look at him, not even when his slow steps faded into the distance.

Dame-Dame

Game of Drafts

It was two thirty in the morning. Back in Dakar, it would be six thirty. The baby pressed down. My abdomen was on fire and my back ached. How I longed to stretch out on a bed, sleep, and forget this nightmare. I looked around me. The lobby was filled with shadowy figures seeking shelter, I assumed, from the biting cold outside. Most slept slumped in chairs. Others simply sat and stared into space. They had a frightful air of belonging, people who roamed the streets during the day and dragged themselves in at night for shelter, people I dared not become. I was the newcomer in a fancy red coat and pumps. The cold finger of fear pushed into my throat and pushed down into my belly. I was terrified of this dangerous, unpredictable city I had heard about, where a fight could erupt at any moment. I forced down the bile rising to my throat.

A plump woman wrapped in a mud-colored shawl walked over and slid beside me, staring at my face with a loony smile. I fixed my eyes on the floor and prayed her away. My eyes traveled up and down the tiles, wondering how many there were, why a man in overalls was running a mop over the floor at three a.m. To my knowledge, no one in Ghana worked this late unless he was a nurse, a thief, or a security man. The idyllic beaches of Dakar were so far away. I tried to picture the bikini girl laughing with friends but didn't recognize her as me. Who was this person in my body, sitting in the lobby of a hospital in America, terrified of even the walls around her? It wasn't me. I was neither here nor in Dakar. I was a phantom.

Loud American voices bounced around me. Behind me, two men's voices rose above the others. I raised my eyes and turned to look. Two policemen stood at the entrance to the ward, one middle-aged, the other young. Their eyes kept cutting to me.

"I don't like the look of this," the older one said. I could tell that what he didn't like had to do with me because he was walking in my direction. I pulled my coat tighter around me. *I've done nothing wrong. You won't arrest me for crowding the lobby with two suitcases?*

He looked at my baggage and leaned toward me. "Are you from the airport, sweetheart?"

"Yes." I willed myself not to cry. Every vein in my head and throat hurt with trapped tears. "Someone was supposed to meet me at the airport but didn't come."

"How did you get here?"

"Someone was kind enough to drive me."

He studied me for a moment. "Come with me. I'll introduce you to someone who can help you."

Instant relief washed over me, though I had no idea what help the someone would offer. I didn't know what to do with my suitcases.

The woman with the loony smile was still staring, but the police-man was already walking away, so I left them behind and followed him into a large reception area where more homeless people, mostly men in dark clothes and stocking hats, sat or slumbered in rows of chairs. We entered an office labeled Female Crisis Center.

A young Black American lady with honey skin and ripe cheeks sat behind a small desk attending to a woman in a chair across from her.

"This is Annie Brady" the policeman said to me. "Miss Brady, this lady here needs help. She'll help you, honey." Then he left, clicking the door shut behind him.

I gave Miss Brady an uncertain smile.

"Hi," she said with a not-unkind look in her almond eyes. I watched her jaws clench and unclench with gum-chewing. I won-dered how she could do that when, growing up, I had been taught that chewing gum in public was vulgar, something only prosti-tutes or bush people did. Even with the pink rubber in her mouth, she spoke in that quick, confident American manner. "I have to finish with this client, then I'll attend to you. Please wait outside."

I closed the door behind me, and rather than sit with the home-less people, I stood facing them. Men stared. Some whistled at me. I looked at the floor and tried to keep the fear out of my face. It was a long time before Annie came out and asked me to step into her office. Before I sat down, I asked if I could get my suitcases.

"Sure. How many you got?"

"Two."

"I'll give you a hand."

Despite my fears, the suitcases were still there. So was Loony Woman. Annie took one suitcase while I took the other back to her office.

"So," she said, once we had settled down, "what brings you here?"

Again, I repeated what Daniel had told me to say. She leaned back in her chair and fixed her gaze on me. "D'you have a return ticket?"

"Yes."

"Then your best option is to get on that plane and go back home. Trust me. You'll be better off with your family."

"But I don't want to go back home." How could I when I hadn't even spoken to Armand? We were going to be a family. This situation was just an obstacle to overcome.

Annie's brows were raised high, but I kept quiet. She sighed, resting chubby elbows on her desk. "Well, another option would be to send you to a shelter."

I imagined a lovely little room with a private bathroom and kitchen from where I could call Armand in the morning. Still, I dreaded leaving for the unknown. I felt safer in the hospital, the devil I knew.

"Couldn't I stay here? I'm almost seven months pregnant."

"You don't look that big. Besides, to be admitted to the hospital, you'd have to be sick, you know. Look, why don't you call your fiancé in Barbados and see what he says? Here." She fumbled in her drawer and came up with some quarters. "There's a phone booth in the lobby. Call him."

I went back to the lobby, less afraid now. A crisp male voice answered the phone.

"Sorry, ma'am, Armand isn't available."

"This is urgent, please."

"Very sorry, ma'am." The line went dead.

On wobbly legs, I returned to Annie's office, sank into the chair.

"What did your fiancé say?"

"Well . . . he couldn't come to the phone."

She gave a discreet nod and changed the topic. "What did you do before you came here?"

"I worked for the Thai embassy."

"Doing what, exactly?"

"Preparing documents in French for the ambassador, that sort of thing."

Her eyes widened. "You speak French?"

"Yes. Senegal is a French-speaking country."

I didn't understand why she blinked in astonishment. After all, in Africa, most English-speakers could butcher their way through French and vice versa, plus speak at least two other languages.

"You finished college?" Her eyes were the size of saucers.

"Yes, I have a BA in international relations."

"A BA in international relations?" She snapped her fingers. "You could get a job just like that! I mean, I'm still in college."

That surprised me. Here was a nondegreed person holding what appeared to be an important position. I was thinking things weren't so bleak after all when, suddenly, an idea popped into my head: Jehovah's Witnesses. Why, that scoundrel Auntie Peace had lived with my aunt because Jehovah's Witnesses always helped one another. Yvonne. The woman Auntie Faustie had said to call if I ever came to the U.S. and was in trouble. Yes, Yvonne! But what was her surname? I knew she lived in Queens.

"Do you know the Kingdom Hall of Jehovah's Witnesses?" I asked.

"Which one? There's so many Kingdom Halls of Jehovah's Witnesses in Queens. You have to know the address."

"There's more than one?" I had no idea how big Queens alone was. "I am trying to reach a lady. Her name is Yvonne."

Her eyes narrowed. "Are you a Jehovah's Witness?"

"No, but I'm, uh, studying to become one." Surely, God would forgive me for the lie.

"Oh, that's neat! I'm also studying to become one." She brightened, as though hit with an inspiration. "I'm not gonna send you to a shelter. You don't wanna go there, trust me. There's a policeman here whose mother is a Jehovah's Witness. They're from Dominica. I'm gonna talk to him and see what he says. Come with me."

I followed her staccato steps across the hall, amid staring eyes from the dead faces of homeless people. We walked past the policemen guarding the section where the hospital staff operated, where the smell of disinfectant rose off shiny floors. She introduced me to a tall, cinnamon-colored policeman. "This is Jerry Barnes."

"Hello, Jerry," I said, shaking hands.

Annie explained my predicament to him. He looked at me the way a priest looks at a parishioner before placing a communion wafer on her tongue. When Annie finished, he withdrew into an office and picked up a phone. She whispered that he was calling his mother. Then he said something to Annie that I didn't catch. She turned to me. "His mother wants you to come home."

I wanted to sink onto the floor and weep.

"I get off in an hour," she said, "so I'll get you a taxi. They'll pay for the taxi when you get there. His mother's name is Mrs. Summer."

At last. A bed. My body felt as if I was already falling into one.

"You shoulda told me you were studying to become a Jehovah's Witness. You'da been outta here hours ago."

At eight in the morning, I stepped into the crisp morning air. The cold bit into my nose and made it run. I couldn't believe the sun was shining and it was so cold. The soft snow had hardened into white ice, which was beginning to look dirty brown in places. Annie hailed a yellow taxi and sent me off to Jerry's mother, who also lived in Brooklyn. I hadn't slept in nearly twenty-four hours.

The driver pulled out my bags and placed them on the curb. I paid him so Mrs. Summer wouldn't have to pay for my taxi in addition to taking me in. The street was deathly quiet, as if the row of ghostly houses stuck together held secrets. Snow shrouded the roofs in white, and the brick walls were the color of rust. For all I knew, thieves with knives and guns lurked in the shadows, ready to jump on me. I mounted the concrete steps to the front door and knocked frantically.

It took a few minutes before the wooden door creaked open and a woman appeared. She was plump, with the fair skin Nigerians call yellow, wrapped in cloth from chest to calves like an African woman. She rubbed the sleep from her eyes.

"Is Mrs. Summer in?"

She nodded, took one suitcase from me, and I followed up the narrow wooden flight of steps to an apartment. A tall, slim woman, also yellow, stood in the tiny living room with worn-out red carpeting. Her eyes were dark, as if someone had reached inside her and switched off the lights, and the deep lines cut between her brows and around her mouth were those of a woman who had suffered. I couldn't help thinking Winter might have been a more apt surname for her.

"Hello, I'm Jerry's mother," she said in a subdued, dignified voice.

"Thank you for taking me in, Mrs. Summer." The tiny kitchenette, dining table, and frayed couch told me this was not a well-to-do family, and yet they had reached out to help me. I wanted to hug her, but I didn't because she was so grave.

Without a word, she turned to the kitchenette and scrambled eggs, toasted bread, and brewed herb tea. I sat at the table for two and inhaled the food while the two women watched me.

"Have you had enough?" the plump woman asked.

"Yes," I whispered. "Thank you very much. Are you also from Dominica?"

"No. I'm from Martinique." Her voice, soft as a feather, matched her soft body and relaxed me. She didn't tell me her name, so I thought of her as Ms. Martinique.

"Would you like to lie down?"

I didn't need to be asked twice. My stomach was full and I was warm. In a flash, I was sprawled on the couch and dead to the world, still wearing my winter coat and shoes.

Nyame Biribi Wɔ Soro

God's Essence Is in Heaven

I floated on an ocean, the sun on my face. Every now and then, snatches of female voices touched my ears but I brushed them off. Then I heard them having lunch or some meal at the dining table. A peppery smell tickled my nostrils. Jerry, the policeman, was back. I recognized his gentle voice saying something about letting me sleep. A voice asked, "What are we going to do with her?" I shut my ears and went back to sleep on the sea. I wanted to sail away to distant shores, forget I was in New York, forget Daniel, forget I couldn't reach Armand, forget . . . the waves rocked me, faster and faster. I was no longer on the sea but on the couch in a tenement in Brooklyn.

I opened my eyes. Ms. Martinique was shaking my shoulders gently. She smiled. "Sorry to wake you up, but we have to work something out before it gets dark. You see, we don't have any room at all."

Oh, no. Though her eyes shone with compassion, her words pelted me.

"Even the couch is taken. There is another daughter who has gone to work. You know, nowadays, no one wants to help anybody. The other day, one woman from our church took a man in, and the next day, he made off with half of her belongings."

What could I say to that? They didn't know me and had no way of judging my character. I had already learned something of the American culture: you don't take strangers into your home. I remembered how Mama even took in a woman claiming to be a witch, how when we had parties, the poor gathered outside to receive food . . . oh God, I had to stop thinking about home. "I understand," I said.

Mrs. Summer said nothing.

"You say you're studying to become a Jehovah's Witness, but you're not yet a member. You haven't been baptized, so we can't vouch for you." That made sense, but the flood of tears threatened anyway. "This man who was supposed to meet you, what's his name?"

"Daniel Roberts," I said, adding quickly, "but I don't want to get in touch with him. I guess he didn't want to have anything to do with me. That's why he didn't show up in the first place."

She let that slide. "What is the name of that Jehovah's Witness friend of yours?"

Why had I even brought her up? I gulped, "Yvonne. Her name is Yvonne."

"Yvonne what?"

"Yvonne Lester." It was a guess, but Lester sounded good to my ear, close to what I remembered.

"And she lives in Queens?"

"Yes." My ears grew hot.

Mrs. Summer fished out a Queens telephone directory from a cupboard. Ms. Martinique pored through the pages beginning with L, tracing names with her finger. They searched and searched but there was no Lester with the first name Yvonne. When I mentioned Len George, who lived in Brooklyn, Ms. Martinique said I could use their phone to call him.

A booming "hi" resounded from him through the plastic line. I hugged the phone to me.

"Len! This is Lola. I'm so happy to hear your voice."

"Lola? Hey, beautiful, what's going on?"

I explained my plight. The line went silent for a while, then, "Why don't you call Olga?"

"Olga? But she's in Maryland. I'm in New York, right here in Brooklyn, that's why I'm calling you. You live in Brooklyn, right?"

"Yeah, I live in Brooklyn. Look, you go on and call Olga, huh. If you can't reach her, call me tomorrow."

In the awkward silence that followed, I got the message. "I will call Olga. I only called you because you made a big case for me coming to America, telling me you'd give me room and board."

"I meant that, Lolo, I just want you to—"

"Please don't call me Lolo. Only a friend can call me that."

"Of course I'm your friend! Call me tomorrow evening, if you can't reach Olga. And Lolo?"

"What?"

"Stay beautiful."

I hung up. Ms. Martinique coughed. Mrs. Summers looked past my ear. Finally, I said, "I have the telephone number of someone who will help me. The only thing is, she's in Maryland, long distance."

"You can call her," Ms. Martinique said.

"Thank you."

For two hours, I kept trying, but there was no answer. The two women grew quiet, the respectful silence of mourners. In between calls, I cried. Without sounds, yet so hard I feared I would cry the baby out. Ms. Martinique and Mrs. Summer exchanged worried looks.

I dialed Olga's number once more.

No answer.

Ms. Martinique studied the ceiling. Mrs. Summer stared at the carpet.

At three p.m., I called again. Olga answered after the first ring.

"This is Olga."

"She's home!" I cried joyously to the women. "Hi, Olga! I've been trying to reach you all day."

"I had to get the kids from school." The high-pitched voices of her two youngest children could be heard squabbling in the background. "Who is this?"

"You'll never believe it. This is Lola."

"Lola?"

"Yes, Lola, from Dakar."

"Lola? Where are you calling from?"

"Right here in America. I'm in New York."

She was silent for a moment. "No, you're kidding, this is not Lola."

I panicked. I had expected anything but that she wouldn't recognize my voice.

"It's me, Olga. Lola."

"No, your voice sounds different. Come on, don't play games with me. Who *are* you?"

I fought for control. "This is Lola, it's me, Olga!"

"No, you're kidding. This is not Lola's voice. Yours sounds so hoarse."

"That's because I've been crying a lot."

"Oh yeah? No, you're putting me on. Cut the crap, you're not Lola."

"No, Olga, it's me! me! me!" Fresh tears started. I dared not look at the two women.

"Tell me, who are Mindy and Ted?"

MindyandTed, MindyandTed. Oh yes. "Your friends, mine, too. They were at your going-away party. Both work with USAID. They have two children. I think they returned to America too?"

"Hmmm, I still don't believe you. Tell me, what is that little song we used to sing?"

"What song?"

"The funny little song you taught us."

My heart was pounding so hard I was sure the women could hear it. *Treasure Island*. Yes. "Yes! I remember it."

"Sing it."

"Sing it?"

"Yeah, sing it. If you're Lola. Go on. Sing."

I looked up from the phone. Mrs. Summer and Ms. Martinique were staring, but I would have stripped naked if Olga had asked me to. I cleared my throat and sang hoarsely:

"Fifteen men on a dead man's chest,
Yo! Ho! Ho! And a bottle of rum!"

"Oh, Lola! You poor pussycat!"

I was bawling now, tears breaking free and flowing into my

mouth, down my chin, falling on my wrist, but I couldn't stop singing:

"Drink for the devil has done for the best,
Yo! Ho! Ho! And a bottle of rum!"

"Oh, Lola! Pussycat, pussycat."

I was tasting salt, sobbing out of control, holding on to the phone as if I were holding her.

"You poor pussycat, talk to me. What are you *doing* in New York?"

"I'm pregnant. I'm going to have a baby and I'm stranded."

"Oh gee, so what are you going to do?"

"I don't know."

"Can you get here?"

"Uh huh." I sniffled, wiped my eyes with the back of my hand. I would figure out a way to get there. She advised me to take the Amtrak train to Union Station in Washington, DC, and she would pick me up. I didn't know what Amtrak was, or where to find it, but I would die finding that train.

"I can't wait to see you, Lola."

I hung up the phone and turned to face the women. Mrs. Summer's face was a picture of incredulity.

"She says I can come and stay with her," I whispered. "I can take the Amtrak train to Washington."

Now that they were sure I'd soon be out of their hands, their kindness reached new heights. Ms. Martinique ran a bath for me and insisted I soak in it. It was pure bliss sliding my achy body into that warm water, closing my eyes with my head tilted back, feeling the ache seep out of my abdomen, my arms, my feet.

I slept for hours. When I woke up, darkness covered the windows. Ms. Martinique was hovering over me. A tall man with kind eyes stood next to her.

"Lola, this is my husband, Paul."

"Hello," he said. "I'll drive you to Maryland, if you'll pay for gas."

"I don't want to make trouble for you," I said.

"It's no trouble at all."

I asked about Jerry, the police officer, but Ms. Martinique said he'd gone to visit his father at the hospital. The father was in an intensive care unit battling heart disease. They didn't think he was going to survive the night. In New York, where Daniel had said no one gave a damn, Jerry had stretched out his hand to help me when his own father was dying. I couldn't speak. God's essence was indeed in heaven, and I prayed He would give Jerry strength.

Thick cotton balls of snow were falling from the leaden sky when Paul, his friend Guy, and I set off for Maryland. They tried to point out interesting sights to me, something about the Brooklyn Bridge, but my eyelids were too heavy.

We drove all through the night till we arrived at Olga's red-brick town house the next morning. Before I could get out, she was at the car door, flinging it open, hugging and kissing me, her throaty voice saying, "Pussycat, pussycat!" Her eyes were moist, and I felt the tightness in my throat again. This wasn't what we had dreamed of when we'd talked about reuniting one day: me pregnant with an unreachable fiancé. Her two youngest children, Katie and Scott, came out, jumping up and down like excited puppies. They dragged me up the narrow wooden stairs to see their rooms. They would have to get used to the fact that I couldn't run around with them anymore.

The smallness of their house surprised me. In Dakar, their sprawling bungalow had been airy, with marble floors. Each of the four bedrooms was en suite. Now they lived in this narrow town house with tiny bedrooms, a staircase for one person at a time, a small living room, and one bathroom upstairs for all. An upright piano crowded a wall, the space above it covered with African masks fringed with straw. Adjacent to the piano featured a wall with built-in, floor-to-ceiling bookcases flanking a television. A couch faced the television, with two antique rocking chairs and armchairs placed around. My jaw fell when they told me the house could buy two mansions in Dakar.

Barry, who had been in the backyard, thumped in. "Well, helloow, Lola!"

"Hello," I said.

"Pregnant, eh? It was that hefty marine, huh? The one in the picture you sent?"

"Yes, Armand."

"Boy." He stroked my back, shaking his head. "That Black American. I knew he was no good."

I moved away from his fingers, angry at him for echoing the prejudice from my family, from the world, it seemed. Within forty-eight hours, my world had somersaulted, my perspectives askew. I lacked the will to debate him. It was my first day as a guest in their home. I would take things one breath at a time.

Funtunfunefu Denkyɛmfunefu

Conjoined Crocodiles Share One Stomach

I slept deeply in the boxy but warm room next to the master bedroom. In the morning, Olga pressed her cheeks against mine and said I could call Armand. Then she rushed around making beds, something she never had to do in Dakar because she had maids. As I stood in the kitchen staring at the wall phone, anger burned in my heart. I didn't want to hear Armand's voice. So what if he was in the middle of one of those inspections where every marine had to do God knows what and barely had time to urinate? I didn't care. Why hadn't he come to the phone? I plopped down at the kitchen table.

Olga barged into my thoughts. "What did Armand say?"

"Nothing. I didn't call him."

"Why not?"

"Please. I don't want to talk right now."

She sighed, gave me a long look. "Okay. Let's talk later."

I carried my thoughts down to the basement that served as a

den, stumbling over plastic hampers brimming with clothes. I sat behind the huge wooden desk and rested my elbows on it, my head in both palms, staring at the concrete wall. I remembered how in Dakar, it saddened Armand to see street children, how he'd given them all the coins he had. Armand would never hurt a child, let alone his own. He didn't know where I was, so it was up to me to call him, but I couldn't bring myself to.

Spying a writing pad, I decided to write letters: a thank-you to Jerry's family, plus an update to Kwaku. I didn't want to write to my mother and cause her more pain, and if I wrote to Awurama, she would tell her. I had just finished Kwaku's letter when Olga clattered down the stairs.

She paced about, a cigarette in her hand. "You know, Mindy and Ted also live in Maryland. Mindy is at Yale finishing her PhD. When she gets back, we should all get together, eh?"

My smile didn't quite make it. She stubbed her cigarette and wrapped her arms around me, breathing tobacco over me.

For the next two days, I slept all day and woke up at night, still jet-lagged. Winter wasn't that dreadful for me, as I hibernated, and having all that fluid retention in late pregnancy provided a kind of insulation against the cold. Besides, my room was the warmest in the house, a tiny space with a full-size radiator.

The third day, the family drove me to sightsee in Georgetown. Snow covered the grass and the Potomac River was frozen. Because the trees had lost all their leaves, Olga could point out the mansions of the rich across the river, such as Jackie Onassis's house.

In Georgetown, we walked around, looking at the quaint shops and restaurants. I loved the narrow brick town houses. Olga had given me two pairs of socks, one dark brown and the other lime green. Wearing my red winter coat, purple pants, brown shoes, and green socks, I drew glances.

On our way back to Frederick, Barry started driving rather fast.

Olga looked daggers at her husband. "Don't you go tearing down the road like that!"

"I'm not driving fast," he snarled, increasing his speed. He looked into his rearview mirror. "Katie, do you think I'm driving fast?"

"No, Daddy."

"That's all you do, you always try to get the kids on your side," Olga said with a disapproving glance at Katie. Her voice went up an octave. "You're driving too fast, and you're going to get a ticket. The last time that happened, our insurance went up, and you used that as an excuse to give me less money for housekeeping."

Barry's neck turned rooster red. "You spend too much money, that's what!"

Just then, we rounded a curve and a police siren sounded.

"I knew it!" Olga said.

The policeman issued the ticket and we drove to Frederick in silence.

At home, Barry banged the door after him. "Stupid bitch," he muttered as he hung his jacket on the hall tree.

"You see what he does, Lola," Olga said, preceding me into the kitchen. "He calls me names, and then at night, he expects sex!"

"It's not as if I ever get any." Barry flopped onto the couch and switched on the television.

Olga marched back to the living room. "Look at him, he does nothing! He just sits in front of the television doing nothing! I don't know how people can live like that."

Katie and Scott slinked upstairs to their rooms and remained there until it was time for supper. That evening, there was plenty of snipping between husband and wife, sullen silences. After supper, the kids went upstairs again as we adults drifted into the living room. Barry picked up the remote for the TV. As if on cue, Olga started playing the piano.

"Jesus Christ!" Barry said. He threw the remote onto the center table, struggled into his coat, and banged the door after him. I took refuge in a book, wondering if Armand and I would ever quarrel like that. We shared a baby, like conjoined crocodiles who shared a stomach. Fighting each other would rip us both apart.

Olga played Mozart's Sonata in C major, which I recognized from past piano lessons, then she switched to a vigorous rendition of Gershwin, leaning her torso forward, her body jerking this way and that. Finally, she pounded out the last passage of the *Boléro*. Even without an orchestra accompanying her, she filled the whole house with defiance. When she finished, she sat for a few minutes, her head hanging down. Then she pulled the piano top down. She got up and gave me a dazzling smile, as though she had purged herself of the anger. She grabbed a packet of cigarettes on the center table, took out a long stick, lit it, and inhaled deeply, her head thrown back. I laid the book down, watching her expel smoke. She had one arm across her chest, supporting the arm holding the cigarette. She shook her head softly. "I don't know why I stay married to this man, Lola. If it weren't for the kids, I'd be out of here."

I didn't know what to say.

"Do you want to have some tea?" she asked suddenly.

I nodded.

"Yes, let's have some nice tea, eh?"

I followed her into the kitchen, where she put a kettle on the stove. I sat down and she took the chair facing me, her back to the white refrigerator.

"What about you, Lola?" She flicked a comma of ash into the ceramic ashtray. "What are you going to do?"

"What do you mean?"

"You haven't called Armand. Looks like you're avoiding him. You should file a paternity suit, you know. Then he'd have to pay you child support."

"A paternity suit? That's preposterous. Why do you assume we've broken up?"

"It's obvious, isn't it?" She tilted her head to one side. "You're far too trusting, Lola. The world isn't made up of wonderful people who just love to do the right thing."

I blinked at her. "Even if Armand and I broke up, I don't believe he would neglect his child. But again, why are you assuming it's over between us?"

"Look, he's Black and—let me finish—many Black men here father children and don't take care of them."

"How could you say that? Just because he's Black?"

"Blacks here aren't like Africans. They don't have the same sense of responsibility."

I was stung. That you're-different-from-Black-Americans attitude had the effect of someone attacking my family but excusing me. *Blacks are—no, we don't mean you.*

"Olga, how many Black families do you know?"

"Not many. It's not like Africa." She pointed her cigarette at me. "How many have *you* met here?"

"None, apart from Daniel and his Nora in New York. That's why I won't draw conclusions."

She shrugged and got up to pour hot water into two mugs. She dropped a sachet of tea into each cup and returned to the table, putting one in front of me. "You stay here long enough, you'll see."

"You know what? I'll call Armand right now."

She flashed me a wicked grin. "So that's what I needed to do, criticize him for you to call him." She stubbed the cigarette and rose to her feet. "I'm going upstairs to check on the kids. Give you some privacy."

I yanked the receiver off the hook and punched the American Embassy's number. Years went by while I twirled the cream spiral cord around my wrist

Armand's anxious voice came through. "Lola, you okay? I called Daniel but he's not picking up my calls."

"He dropped me at the Kings County Hospital and left."

"Shit! At that time of the night? Man, that must have been awful for you." He sighed. "Too bad you came with two hundred and fifty dollars, shit."

I grew hot with anger. "You might have warned me about how much money I'd need, to start with. You might have told me you were counting on me bringing all the money. That's why you decided to wait until my arrival before finding an apartment for me, isn't it?"

"I thought Daniel would keep you and—God, I'm so mad."

"*You're* mad?"

"Because you're there and I'm here and there's nothing I can do. You need to transfer the money to America immediately. We're going to need a lot of money."

I didn't answer.

"So why can't you send for money?"

"You know, you're so obsessed with money that you scare me.

If something happened and I lost all the money, I'd be afraid to tell you!" I wanted him to tell me I was wrong, that I was more important to him than money, that I could talk to him, that he loved me.

His voice rose. "You're right, I'm obsessed with money. I want to be rich."

"See what I mean? Money is everything to you, I can't confide in you."

"Yeah, money is important to me!"

"And your parents, they didn't want me, did they? But you never said a word!"

"My parents have their own life. They can decide what they want. They got nothing to do with us!"

"You should have told me!" I breathed deeply, then lowered my voice. "You should have told me." I could hear his heavy breathing. The seconds ticked, ticked away, each one widening the space between us.

"I get it," he said in a metallic voice, that of a stranger. "You want to keep all the money for yourself."

"What?! Is that what you think, that I want to keep the money? I lost it all, you bloody fool! I got cheated." I laughed bitterly. "To think I was afraid to disappoint you. You weren't worth my fear. You weren't worth my respect. You know what? I don't need you. I found my way to Maryland without a finger from you, I will survive without you."

"Sure, run to your mother."

"I'm not running to my mother."

We fell silent. Then he said, "Am I paying for this call? Because the day you arrived, Daniel called collect, that's very expensive."

"Oh God, you're unbelievable! No, my dear venom, Olga let me call direct."

"Venom. That's some nasty shit you're calling me." His voice had dropped. I could tell he wanted me to make him feel better, but I stayed mute. Finally, he said, "So, tell me, how are you going to cope with a baby?"

"What do you mean?"

"See, baby, you're on your own. You say you're through with me? You don't need me? Fine, then I don't want no baby, understand? Let's see you survive in America without me."

I put my hand to my forehead. "I don't even know who you are anymore. You know what? I will survive without you. I will." I breathed deeply. "You don't deserve me. Goodbye, Armand."

The phone fell out of my hand. A whirring began in my brain. The sound roared louder and louder till it drowned out everything else. I slid down on my back, knocking over a bowl on the floor. Olga ran downstairs.

"Lola? What's wrong? Oh my God, you're shaking!"

I opened my mouth, but no sound came out. It was a continuous inhale, a gathering of every breath from my toes, moving up.

Olga grabbed the receiver that was dangling freely. "You bastard! What did you say to her?" The dial tone of a dead call responded. "Son of a bitch!" Olga sat on the floor, gathering me into her arms, rocking me. "Pussycat, pussycat, pussycat. I'm so sorry, so sorry." My mouth remained open. She scrambled up and returned with a glass of water. She sat on the floor, urging me to sip. I pushed the glass away, spilling water. She wiped my face with her hands.

I pushed myself to my feet, tears of rage running down my face. I marched to the kitchen sink and began attacking the dishes. I picked up a glass, worked friction, suds from my hands to my elbows.

Olga hovered behind me. "I'm so sorry, Lola." I tuned her out.

Armand, who had scared me with his passion for kids. Six kids, he'd said. I washed and washed, clattering plates onto the rack.

I marched past a helpless Olga, up to my room, and grabbed a book, determined to be strong. Then the dam broke. Great sobs broke out of me. Then fear. Chills. Aches. Exhaustion. *Damn you, Armand Beaumont! Damn you to hell and back and back to hell!* I was crying again. All night, I wrestled with my pillows, crying one minute, damning Armand the next.

In the morning, I slipped downstairs to the basement. I wrote to my sister, Awurama, poured out everything onto paper, begging her not to tell our mother. A week later, a letter arrived from Armand saying how sorry he was. What he was sorry for was known only to him. I didn't care. In the envelope, though, was money. Crisp dollar notes, smelling as though freshly printed. Twenty hundred-dollar notes. I wanted to hurl them into the fire and watch them flame up, curl, and turn to ashes. But I had to be practical. I had no illusions about him sending any more money. But I would show him, oh, how I would show him. Anger blazed toward my mother too, the one who told me to go away, as if she was rejecting me. I would find work after the baby was born, save enough money, and return to a sunny life in Dakar or Ghana, save enough money to show all the doubters.

Mate Masie

What I've Heard, I've Hidden

My stomach ballooned. Olga and Barry, who disagreed on everything, agreed on one thing: I was in an impossible situation. How was I going to find a doctor and pay the medical bills? Before leaving Dakar, I had assumed that getting a work permit in America would be a simple matter of filling out forms.

"That's what your Len told me," I said to Olga, "that I could get a job just like that, save money to go back home and even open an orphanage if I wanted to." We were gathered in the sitting room, family-meeting style, me sitting on the couch, Olga pacing about, cigarette between her forefinger and middle finger, Barry in the rocking chair, holding the remote control as though ready to turn on the TV. The children were in school.

Barry tossed the remote onto the center table. "Len, eh? That guy is full of it. What does he know about immigration?"

Olga stood still, a frown on her face. "Come, on, Barry. No need to disparage him."

"Whatever, you're always defending him."

"Drop it, will you? This is about Lola." She bent to flick ash into an ashtray. "The thing is, it used to be true, once upon a long time ago, but there are new immigration laws now."

"Look who's talking. You never had to worry about that, did you? You married me before you came to America."

"Which is why I know more about immigration. New laws come up every day. Lola, we've got a friend who works with Immigration. I'm going to give him a call and see what he says."

She strode off to the kitchen. Barry and I sat in silence, him rolling his eyes as Olga shrieked hello before her voice dropped to a murmur. After talking for a while, she shouted, "Lola, could you come here? He wants to talk to you."

When I went into the kitchen, she passed me the phone. I held it against my ear, hopeful that the friend had enough clout to make things happen for me.

"I understand you're in a bit of a predicament," a male voice said. "Unfortunately, I don't have very good news. With the new immigration laws, you have no right to work in America."

"But my baby is going to be an American. Doesn't that give me the right to work?"

"I'm afraid not," he said with kindness. "You know, you could work things out with your fiancé and then he would sponsor you."

"I won't marry him," I said firmly.

He sighed. "All right. Well, you could go on welfare, but believe me, you don't want to do that. Applying for anything from Social Services would put you at a disadvantage if you were to apply for a resident permit in the future, because you'd be considered a public charge."

I certainly didn't want that. Welfare seemed akin to begging.

"I'm sorry I don't have better news. I'll tell you what. Let me think about it and get back to you."

I thanked him and hung up, feeling deflated.

"You know," Olga started, then shook her head, fumbling for another cigarette.

"What?"

She said nothing until she'd lit the cigarette, blowing her hair away from her face. "You could marry someone else, you know," she said with the tone of someone suggesting a walk to the market. I stared at her. She sucked in more nicotine, wagging her cigarette. "Someone on death row, for instance. I mean, if the guy is about to die, it won't matter anyway, right? We could pay him money to take care of any family he has. You'd get a work permit. He dies, you get your freedom."

"Olga!"

She cocked her head to the side, continuing as if I hadn't spoken. "Or you could divorce him after you get your green card."

"I don't believe what I'm hearing."

"Good grief, Olga," Barry said, walking into the kitchen. "You get the most cynical ideas!"

"I don't see what's so terrible about that. It's a matter of survival, you know."

"Jesus, Olga!" His fingers found my shoulders, kneading and squeezing.

Olga stubbed her cigarette. "People are so bloody sentimental. We're not talking about a real marriage here. We're talking about a paper marriage—don't you give me that look, Barry. *She's* got a baby to worry about."

"Don't pay attention to her, Lola. First things first. You bring the baby into the world, then we'll worry about work permits and green cards. In the meantime, I called the Department of Social Services and made an appointment for you to be interviewed for Medicaid."

"But I'm not eligible. I mean, I'm a foreigner and I'm not even a resident in this country. The immigration officer warned me against that."

Olga rolled her eyes. "Yeah, Barry, really nice idea." She patted me on the arm. "Don't mind him, Lola. You can stay here as long as you want to. Yes, Barry?"

"Of course she can, how could you even ask?" he said. "We can't buy you luxuries, but you're going to stay here for as long as you need to. Food is no problem. I think you should go to the appointment, anyway. Medicaid is different. It's for the American child, not for you. This is to ensure the baby's survival."

That made sense. The next morning, after the children sailed out the door for school, Barry drove me to my appointment, where I learned I could indeed receive prenatal care for the American baby. I also called Frederick Memorial Hospital to inquire about birth costs. Two thousand dollars, they said. I could deposit one hundred dollars and make monthly payments as low as twenty-five dollars. That small act gave me a sense of accomplishment, that I had taken some control over my life.

February 28, 1997

My dear Akua,

I am very, very sad to hear of what happened to you in America. Did I not warn against a long-distance marriage? Now see what you have got yourself into.

I cannot believe you are staying with friends when you

have family at home. I contacted the American Embassy in
Accra to petition them to repatriate you, but they said no.
Your visa hasn't expired. Moreover, they say you are over
eighteen years old, so you are an adult. An adult! Twenty-one
years old and you're adult. Is that the American life? What
is this world coming to when daughters can just ignore their
parents' wishes? See where your stubbornness has landed
you? I don't know what to say to you.

Your mother,
S. D.

Awurama. She couldn't hide what she'd heard from me? I
clutched at the letter, trembling. I felt the pull of home in every
cell within me. Mama wanted me home, but I couldn't bear her
disappointed eyes. People returned home from the West successful, with money to buy land and build houses. Not one woman I
knew returned with empty hands and a fatherless baby, bringing
shame to the family. Mama's silent condemnation would squash
my spirit and people would taunt her. Here in America, far away
from horrified eyes, I could have a fresh start, work for a couple of
years, save money, and then return home with confidence. Financial independence was the equalizer, it would empower me. No
one would dare shame me. That resolution concretized, I pushed
thoughts of home out of my mind. Now, what would I call my
child? I had once heard a Nigerian woman call her son Dele. She
said it was short for "Ayo dele." *Joy has come home.* Dele. A promise to hold on to.

Ɔdɔ Nyera Fie Kwan

Love Does Not Lose Its Way Home

I was curled up in bed reading a book when a dull pain grabbed my pelvis. I put the book down, rolled onto my back, and closed my eyes. As had happened on many nights in the two months that had passed since my arrival, Armand's limbs and face forced their way into my mind. Behind him, my mother's graceful body flowered. As I looked from one to the other, the ache intensified to a biting pain. *Stop it*, I told myself. *Think about the baby. Don't allow nostalgia to stir waves in your womb.* I half-turned onto my stomach and beat my pillow for comfort until sleep collapsed me.

Around nine a.m. I struggled awake. The ache was still there, but now it intensified and subsided with increasing frequency. I thought, Oh God, the baby.

Olga's shrill voice startled me. "Guess what, Lola, Katie got sick on me today." She was standing at my open door, dressed in black pants and a white sweater. Katie slouched in after her mother, pale and still wearing her ankle-length nightgown. Her dark eyes, slanted like her mother's, were heavy with sleep.

"Guess what, Olga," I said, "I think the baby will be here today."

Her eyes flashed. "Oh no. Are you in labor?" In two strides, her warm body was next to mine, her hand pressing my stomach.

"I don't know. I just have these cramps, but they seem rhythmical."

"Okay, Lola," Katie said, eyes opened wide, her own symptoms forgotten. "Let's time it." She was ten years old, going on twenty.

The cramps gripped me, five minutes apart.

"I'm going to call the hospital," Olga said, and scurried down the stairs.

Katie slid down next to me. "You're going to have your baby?"

I could only nod, for the pain had grabbed me again. Olga returned. "You have to go to the hospital. The nurse said to bring you in."

I pushed myself up, burying my head in my hands. She sat beside me and hugged me to her. As she rocked me from side to side, I leaned into her. I wanted to stay that way, listening to her voice calling me "Pussycat, pussycat." I started sniffling.

"Why is Lola crying?" Katie asked.

"It's not every day a woman has a baby. Oh, Lola, your life will never be the same again." I wiped my face, knowing she was right, that I was opening an unknown chapter of my life. I wished she'd just keep talking but she said, "You have to start packing."

I eased myself off the bed and began pulling things out of a drawer. I picked up a sweater, put it down. The overnight bag remained empty and clouds settled in my head.

"I can't find my things," I said. "Olga, I don't think the baby is coming. Maybe it's nothing."

"No, Lola." Her voice was firm. "We have to get you to the hospital."

I was leaving a life behind me. I would come back with a baby, forever changed. A sob rose within me.

"Poor Lola," she murmured, rocking me again while standing.

She helped me pack. Then she went downstairs with my bag. I wanted to lie down again but her voice told me to come on. I stepped out into the cold, then into the car, and we drove to Frederick Memorial Hospital.

The beautiful room with its television impressed me, all the more so because I didn't have to share it with anyone the way I would have had to in a government hospital back home. When I lay on my back, my stomach was so large I couldn't see my feet. Without her cigarette to calm her, Olga paced about like a restless panther, making me tense.

"Olga?"

She rushed to my side, brushing my hair away from my forehead.

"Could you please step outside?"

"What? I can't leave you alone and—"

I touched her arm. "Please."

Reluctantly, she straightened up. "Okay. But I will be right outside."

Nurses in white uniforms spoke to me in soothing tones, touching me as though I were a delicate flower. I practiced the slow breathing I'd once learned from a yoga book. Resembling a serene goddess, a nurse named Sophia installed herself in a chair beside my bed. I couldn't believe she was there just to attend to my needs. Her quiet confidence steadied my breathing. She seemed to sense my need for calm and turned down the lights, talking only when

I wanted to. This was in line with what Oforiwa had told me to expect, and yet the beautiful surroundings couldn't blot out the waves of homesickness that washed over me. I had a mother, a big sister, and cousins who would have gathered outside my room with Olga, fretting about me. Here I was by myself, *sans famille*, like Remi in Hector Malot's book of the same French title. Except Remi was a foundling sold by his foster father. I had chosen to leave my mother and family.

Unable to leave me alone, Olga rushed in, smelling of tobacco. She plunked into a chair by the wall, pulled a pad out of her purse, and started writing. She said she was writing to my baby about my "courage and beauty." When she put away her writing, she grew nervous again, torrents of words pouring out of her: "You can't be in labor. No. Just you wait till the pain hits you. When I was in labor, I screamed bloody murder . . ." I tuned her out.

At six p.m., the doctor decided I was dilated enough and sent a protesting Olga out.

Nurse Sophia pulled the bed apart and converted it into a delivery table. She put the side rails up, then put my feet in stirrups, which thrust my hips forward as when Armand plowed into me and I moaned my orgasm. Now I was in this air-conditioned bib and the cold penetrated my flesh. Ice for heat. Pain for pleasure.

Another nurse joined Sophia and they told me to grab the metal rails. I pushed with each contraction, but the baby refused to show up. They freed my feet. I walked. I squatted. I lay down again. I pushed. After one and half hours, the top of the baby's head became visible to all except me.

"He's got lots of hair!" the nurses said. I got caught up in the excitement. "Push! Push! Push!" was all I heard till I became intoxicated with it. *Push, Lola, push or die.* I grabbed the bars, teeth clenched, shut my eyes, and pushed with all my might until something exploded and everything went black.

Dimly, I heard a cheer. "His head is out! Good girl, Lola!" In spite of my semiconscious state, the rest of the body squeezed itself out. As though from far away, I heard, "It's a boy!" I opened my eyes and looked. There, still attached to the umbilical cord, was the ugliest blob of humanity I had ever seen.

"He's so ugly," I said. I didn't know all newborns looked like aliens when they were still covered with bloody, gooey substance. His eyes were as large as a frog's, and I was afraid to hold him.

Olga rushed in, crying. "Can I hold him? His name is Dele, yes? Dele, isn't he a darling!"

The nurses wanted his official name right away. In Ghana, no one would have troubled me to announce a name until the naming ceremony, when the baby was eight days old. The extended family would have gathered at sunrise to name the baby and follow the event with feasting and dancing. In America, there was no such ceremony and the nurses had to register his name right away. I called him Dele Kofi. Kofi for a male born on Friday. Oduro for my surname. There was no way I would give him Armand's name.

The new room they gave me sparkled. Mama would have approved of the gleaming beige floors and the television suspended from the ceiling that I could control from my bed. This time, I shared my room with one other person who happened to be Black, whose family crowded around her laughing that the baby had turned out to be a boy and not a girl as the ultrasound had previously indicated. The space around my bed stayed vacant when Olga went home to the kids.

I asked for food and, although the kitchen was closed, they

brought me a plate of sandwiches. Satiated, a sudden panic struck me: Where was my baby? I pushed the intercom and asked to see him. They made me wait so long I thought something had to be wrong with him. I pressed hard on the intercom and demanded to see him immediately. Finally, they wheeled him in.

My breath caught. He was asleep on his stomach, in a glass crib. I studied his tiny body, his knees propped up under him. Despite the puffy eyes, he looked decidedly different from the ugly, wiggling mass I had seen fresh from birth. His eyelashes curled up to his eyebrows. My heart lurched. He looked exactly like Armand. Never mind, he was mine. I reached out and touched him as if he were made of powder that might crumble. My heart swelled. I gathered him together and held him against my breasts. He was so warm, so soft and little, and he was mine. I, a mere mortal, had helped to create this precious life for whom I would gladly lay down my own.

If I'd had my way, he would have remained in my bed day and night, but the nurse said no. "You need to get a full night's rest." They'd bring him in twice in the middle of the night to eat. I was always awake, impatient to see him, and always, he was screaming at the top of his lungs. I found it upsetting, because in Ghana, they kept mother and baby together all the time.

After three days in the hospital, Olga drove us back to the house. Scott stood on the tips of his toes, trying to touch him. "He is little!" Katie's face shone with reverence. "Can I hold him, pleasepleaseplease?"

Olga shooed them off. "Give Lola room, for goodness' sake. Here, Lola, why don't you sit here?"

I installed myself in the rocking chair, Dele enveloped in a pale blue receiving blanket, his body fitted to mine. Katie and Scott hovered, pointing out his lashes, "so long!" and his fingernails, "so tiny, like a doll." One person didn't appear.

I looked up at Olga. "Where is Barry?"

She looked at the kids. "Hey, guys, why don't you go upstairs and make Lola a welcome card?" They pounded across the wooden floor. When the echo of their steps had faded, she sat down, reached into her pocket for her packet of cigarettes. She quickly put it back down, a rueful smile on her face. "I can't smoke with the baby around."

"Thanks for that, Olga."

A film of tears glimmered in her eyes. "I asked Barry to move out."

"You what?"

She bit her lower lip, shaking her head. "I couldn't stand it anymore. He bickers about every little thing. Now he's gone. I have my peace."

I gathered Dele carefully and moved up to sit beside her on the couch. With one arm, I cradled Dele's head and wrapped my other arm around her shoulder, giving her a playful smile. "I can't call you pussycat. How about big cat?"

"Some big cat."

I watched her carefully. She didn't seem to know what to do with her hands. "Are you hurting?"

"It does hurt. You don't get married expecting it to end."

"I'm sorry, Olga."

She gave me a brave smile. "Don't worry about me. This works out fine, you know. You can't sleep in that tiny room anymore. Now you can have the master."

"Oh no. Where will you sleep?"

"Don't worry. I'll take the couch. I never slept in that bed anyway, thanks to that goat."

"Oh, Olga. I don't know what would have happened to me if you hadn't taken me in. And now you're giving me your room. What can I do for you?"

"Can you sing to me?"

I burst out laughing. "No, you're not going to get me to sing that song again. It has awful memories for me now."

"Come on, I love that song. Go on, sing. Please."

I looked at her with all the love I could muster, then I leaned against her shoulder and sang "fifteen men on a dead man's chest." She leaned her head against mine as I sang, rocking from side to side with me, both of us knowing we were going to be all right.

April 2, 1997

Akua Olivia,

You didn't write when my grandchild was born. You wrote to your sister instead. How do you think I felt? And you gave him a name without consulting the family. A Nigerian name? You didn't name him after your father like tradition? I pray your son never turns his back on you, because I never want you to know what it feels like to have your child stomp on your heart like this and throw away your name.

If you must remain in America, I suggest you go stay with my cousin, your auntie Theodora. Do you remember her? She is also in Maryland, maybe not far from you. Look at

what you've got yourself into. At least your auntie Theodora
is family, and she has your number.
I hope you will listen to me.

Love,
Your mother

I wanted to tear at my cheeks. How didn't I understand the breach
I had committed by not consulting family about a name for Dele?
How could I have forgotten our tradition? In a short time, I had experienced what felt like a shipwreck in a strange land, so I had tried
to blot out home. Scenes rushed at me. How Awurama had moved
back home two months before my niece was born, leaving her husband behind. How, once the baby was born, her husband had moved
in as well. Awurama did little more than eat and feed her baby. For
the first three months, Mama took leave from the court. She bathed
the baby twice a day while Awurama watched. Sometimes the baby
just slept on Mama's lap. Although we had two maids, our cousins
also came to stay, holding the baby and helping with cooking. While
the baby was sleeping, Awurama had to sleep too. We took turns
keeping vigil while baby slept, in case she covered her face with the
sheet and suffocated. Husband and wife spent stress-free time at our
home until six months after the birth.

Now, in America, my arms ached all the time. Olga had taken
on a teaching job in Washington, so when her children were
at school, I was alone most weekdays. Sometimes, when I was
downstairs and Dele was asleep, I couldn't hear him crying. I'd go
upstairs to discover he'd been crying for a long time and my heart
would hurt. How I longed for my family. I wanted someone to sit
by my sleeping baby while I ate in the kitchen. When I needed to

use the bathroom, I wanted someone to hold him so I could sit on the toilet with free hands to tear the toilet paper. I wanted someone to take him from me when he cried and I couldn't get him to stop, someone to take him so that I wouldn't end up crying too.

While I was lucky to have Olga's help when she could, I worried about the financial strain on her. These thoughts intensified one day as I sat at the kitchen table, cutting beets for borscht, the Russian soup Olga was preparing. She was blowing into a ladle of broth and about to taste it when I said, "Olga, I have to move."

She dropped the ladle. She sat facing me. "What do you mean you have to move? You can stay here for as long as you want, I told you."

I reached over and touched her hand. "You can't support me. It's not fair to you. I'm here eating your food while you're separated from Barry. Do you even receive money from him?"

She freed her hand, reaching for a cigarette apologetically. "Dele is asleep upstairs, he's not going to get smoke into him." She cupped her fingers and rolled the lighter to a flame, inhaling deeply. "Yeah, Barry supports me because of the kids, nothing's changed. But I don't know if I'm going to get to keep them. He's suing for custody, the bastard."

"What? You never told me that."

"You've got enough to deal with."

I mulled things over for a moment. "Won't it hurt your case to have me staying with you?"

She shrugged, flicking ash into the tray. "I don't know."

"I can't stay here. I've got to go."

I watched the conflict on her face. She wanted me to stay but she knew I was right. She sighed, shaking her head. "Suppose you left. Where would you go?"

"Remember my mother's cousin in Silver Spring? I contacted her and she wants me to come live with her. She's family."

"I'm family too, damn it! Family isn't always blood."

"You *are* family. But I can't depend on you. It's not fair to you. Please don't try to stop me. My mind is already made up. Besides," I pointed out, "Frederick is such a small town. I imagine there are no jobs available. If I want to make it in America, I need to live in a bigger town."

She blinked from shimmering eyes. "Well, at least Silver Spring is still Maryland. It isn't too far." We held hands the way we both knew our bond would always hold.

Nsaa

Good Fabric

Dele was six weeks old when Auntie Theodora sent a car to pick us up. As we sped along the Beltway toward Silver Spring, I tried to remember what I knew of her. I had only seen a picture, taken when she visited Ghana years before. She was standing in front of a pink bougainvillea bush with her three children, two girls and a boy. The boy was about four years old, fair, with a bushy afro the way Michael Jackson used to wear his hair. The two girls were beautiful, about six and eight, their hair pulled back into two puffs each. They looked like an advert for Afro Sheen products. All three children were smiling, mother looking proud.

I had met her husband at a party. He'd talked about his wife, how proud he was of her, how, in his absence, she had gone into labor and driven herself to the hospital.

"Why are you living in Ghana and she in America?" I had asked.

"No Ghanaian wants to live permanently in America. Besides, we have student loans, and she is working to repay them." I was a teenager then and I remember asking, "Why aren't you there working to repay the loans too?" A gasp went around the room. He mumbled and walked away from me. Mama wagged a finger, telling me to mind my manners while I pouted at the injustice of it. I liked the sound of Auntie Theodora, strong and independent.

It was around four p.m. when we pulled into the cul-de-sac of her town house development. She opened the front door and flew out, her plump arms wide.

"Welcome!" Her eyes danced. She had a round face like a penny, and sprouted defiant hair below her chin. Her two girls ran out. I recognized them at once. Those wide almond eyes were impossible to miss. The older one, Mensima, gave me a reserved smile and went to the trunk to help with my things. Kuukuwa said hi in a high-pitched voice, her smile open like her mother's, her teeth white against dark gums.

An older girl emerged. A woman, really, but young, about nineteen. She peered at me out of intelligent eyes.

"This is my niece Mary," Auntie Theodora said.

"Hello." I waved at everybody. Auntie Theodora rushed to the backseat, where Dele was still in his car seat.

"Look how cute he is!" She unfastened the seat belt and got him out, pressing him against her chest.

In the sunny living room, I met her son. He was as handsome as his picture, but his face was more angular, his body thicker. He sat in an armchair in front of a Nintendo, playing Super Mario Brothers. The repetitive tune made me want to stuff my ears.

"Ekow," his mother said, "this is Sister Akua." When she asked him to take my suitcases upstairs, he flashed a smile, put the controls down, hefted my suitcases, and led the way up the hardwood staircase.

The room featured a sofa bed that had been pulled out and made with a yellow bedsheet and matching pillowcases. Sister Theodora had the master bedroom, across from mine. The three girls shared the third bedroom, at the end of the corridor.

"Where does Ekow sleep?" I asked.

"This is normally his room. Don't worry, he'll sleep on the couch downstairs." I was touched that he didn't seem to mind giving up his room for me. Auntie Theodora said she had raised her children the Ghanaian way. "When you have guests, you give them a room, and if there is no spare bedroom, then someone has to give up his room. Don't worry, Ekow is used to it."

Olga had given me her room too, I recalled.

The living room had just a couch and the armchair Ekow was using. The rest of the space was taken up by stuffed animals. A lot of them. Two adults could fit into the lap of a huge Dalmatian in a corner. Between its legs, assorted teddy bears sat, too many to count. When they needed to watch a movie or something, I imagined the girls sprawled on the hardwood floor cuddling a teddy bear. There was also a crib against the wall.

Auntie Theodora had cooked jollof rice with chicken. The smell of peppers and nutmeg transported me to Ghana. Kuukuwa kept smiling at me, asking me if I needed anything. Mensima said nothing, but I felt the weight of her eyes, as though she suspected me of something nefarious.

Dele thrilled Auntie Theodora. She held him. Kissed him. Tickled him. He smiled for her. In the morning, when I was nursing him, she knocked on the door, asking when I was going to give him a bath.

"I've never given him a bath."

"What?"

"I'm afraid the umbilical wound will get infected if water gets into it. I use a soapy wash cloth to rub him all over, and then I wipe him down with a moist towel." That is what I had been taught to do at the hospital.

She covered her mouth with her hand. "The water won't hurt him! You have never given him a bath?" Dele had stopped nursing to look at her. She crossed the room and sat beside me, giving him her finger to hold. "You poor baby, you need your bath. An African child wants his bath. If he were in Ghana, he would be bathed twice a day. Your mother or older women would take care of him. Let me bathe him for you."

Feeling foolish, I followed her into the master bathroom. She pulled out a plastic yellow baby bathtub with a slanted seat so Dele could lean back with his head elevated. I sat at the edge of the tub and watched as she lathered his hair with Johnson's Baby Shampoo. She cooed to him. "Yes, Dele. You want your bath, don't you? Yes, you do." Using a cup, she poured warm water on his shampooed hair, brushing it back to protect his face. Then she soaped the rest of his body. I watched carefully, learning and listening as she explained what she was doing. Before she finished, Dele was asleep. I tried pushing my nipple into his mouth, but his lips stayed shut. Auntie Theodora laid him on her bed. "Poor thing, he needed his bath."

I sank onto the floor, drained.

Auntie Theodora gazed fondly at him. "He's such a beautiful baby. Don't worry, one day Armand and his family will come asking you for forgiveness. Even if they don't, you don't need them. This is America. You can take care of your child by yourself. I'm sure you'll meet another man. I am proud of you, because at least you have a college education. Some women neglect their education, but you didn't. You know, you don't have to worry about a thing. I'll help you, we'll figure something out. In the meantime, don't worry about food or rent. I mean, if you want something special for your son, you can get it for him, but otherwise, feel free to help yourself to anything you want."

I lifted teary eyes to her. "I don't know how to thank you."

"No need to thank me. In this world, you never know when you'll be the one in need of help. Who knows, one day my child might need someone too. Besides, you are family."

Family. I had to return home one day. Every stage of our life in Ghana involved family: The naming ceremony. Circumcision. Outdooring of the baby at three months. Confirmation in church at fifteen regardless of personal belief. It was all about the gifts, new clothes, food, music, the feeling that you had arrived on the threshold of adulthood. I had taken it all for granted, but now I wanted my son to have that sense of community I could never have in America. However, I needed a job to save money before I could even consider going home.

"Look at Mary, for instance," Auntie Theodora said. "She's my niece but she's just like my younger sister. Her mother sent her to me when she was dying."

"She's very nice."

"Yes. I don't know what I'd do without her."

When Auntie Theodora left for work and the children huddled around the dining room to do their homework, I sat on the couch, scanning the help-wanted ads in *The Washington Post*. Dele was asleep in the crib downstairs. Mary slid in beside me.

"You need a state ID to get a job," she said. "A nondriver's license. It will never expire, unlike my driver's license that I have to renew."

"How do I get that?"

"We can go to the DMV, you know, the Department of Motor Vehicles."

"They will give me an ID just like that?"

"I think so."

"Hmmm. I don't know. I'm worried about going near any government offices. I don't want to get into trouble. Let me keep looking. Maybe some organization will sponsor me for a work visa."

A real estate firm wanted bilingual sales people, so I called for an interview. The next day, at Auntie Theodora's suggestion, I left Dele with Mary. Eight other people turned up for the interview. To my surprise, no one asked me questions. There were no forms to fill out. A grinning man in suit and tie ushered us into a small conference room and projected a video onto a large screen. As the documentary ran on, it became clear we were to sell lakeside properties in a remote area to the elderly. The land was beautiful, with rolling green meadows, but when Mr. Suit-and-Tie said we should tell customers that we ourselves owned property there even if we didn't, I pushed my chair back, rose to my feet, and departed. I wasn't about to dupe the elderly into buying fake anything.

Mary's idea to get me a state ID didn't work because of my visitor's visa. It was hard looking for a job without a work permit. I got turned down everywhere I went. Auntie Theodora told me not to fret. I told me not to fret. I fretted anyway.

"I'm thinking of getting a cat," Olga said on the phone, two months after I had left Frederick. "It gets too quiet when the kids visit Barry."

"Oh, sorry." It seemed a lame thing to say, but I didn't know how to comfort her. "How is everyone?"

"The kids are fine. Barry is still a goat, but what do you expect?"
I laughed.

"Guess what, Len George called—I know what you're going to say, he can be a jerk. But he's one damn sexy jerk." A throaty chuckle escaped her.

"Olga! In Dakar, did you and he ever . . ."

"No, I didn't. But he's coming down and wants to see me."

I snorted. "Sure he is."

"Come on, Lola, don't be so hard on him. How could he invite you to his house when you weren't friends with his wife?"

Reluctantly I had to agree she was right. He couldn't just have me over without his wife's approval.

"Now he's on his way to Divorceville, like me, so que sera sera." She laughed again. "Hey, do you remember Mindy and Ted?"

"Yes, how are they?"

"They're back in Maryland. Actually, that's why I called. Mindy just asked for your number. She wants to see you."

"I'd love to see them!"

"Good. I'd better hang up, she's waiting to call you."

Almost as soon as I hung up, the phone rang. I was so happy I shrieked into the phone. Mindy laughed softly, asking how I was doing.

"I'm doing well, I'm staying with family."

"That's wonderful. Would it be okay if I visited?"

"Yes, Auntie Theodora wouldn't mind, I'm sure."

"Of course, I wouldn't mind," Auntie Theodora said, walking into the kitchen.

I felt my ears grow hot. I covered the mouthpiece. "You heard me?"

"Yes. Any friend of yours is welcome here. You don't even have to ask."

Mindy's belly entered the house on a cool evening. The rest of her followed, unchanged. She had the same short blond waves, pale blue eyes, a big smile, and curvy legs.

"Mindy!" I said, thrilled to see her. "I had no idea you were pregnant."

She pressed me to her hard stomach and pulled back. "Look at you, you haven't gained an ounce."

I had forgotten how much I loved her smile, the way her lips spread wide and her eyes sparkled. She sat lotus-style on the living room floor, asking Auntie Theodora about the pharmacy, and the girls about their lives. When we were finally alone, she said quietly, "You're going to be all right, Lola. You've got good people around you. I'm also here now, in Rockville. If you ever need anything, I'm just a phone call away."

"Thank you," I said. "This means so much to me." When she was leaving, I clung to her neck. She was part of the world I had left behind, a Dakar that excluded a baby who demanded everything from me.

As a mother, I felt as though I needed two brains: one to dream about stories I wanted to write, a life I wanted to make, and another brain on the alert, trying to figure out what this little human wanted or needed every hour. He didn't come with an operating manual that said what to do, and as for the Dr. Spock book I tried to read, it felt as though he were talking about another baby, who wasn't Dele. There was no manual to tell me what to do when he was sick, like the day his stomach ran nonstop, three months after leaving Frederick.

Auntie Theodora had gone to work. No matter what I did, everything he ate ran out of his rear end. By evening, he was almost inert. His breath came out in quick, hot puffs. He lay in his rocker with sleepy eyes fixed on me, as if imploring me to help him. A cold fear gripped me. When Auntie Theodora got home from work, I wailed, "Dele won't move or do anything. His diarrhea won't stop."

Although her eyes narrowed, her voice was calm. "He's probably dehydrated. You need to give him Pedialyte. That will replace the fluids he's lost. Don't give him any more food, Pedialyte is what he needs."

She sent Kuukuwa to the store to pick up a bottle. I poured some into a sippy cup and held it to his mouth. His tongue came out, licking. Within half an hour, he was laughing and moving his arms. I wept with joy, pressing him to me.

"Thank you so much, Auntie!" I thought about how, in villages back home, such a simple fluid like Pedialyte could have saved babies who died of dehydration.

But death seemed determined to snatch my baby. That Saturday, Auntie Theodora had the day off. It was just before lunch. I nursed him and went upstairs to put him down for a nap because it was quieter there. I laid him on his back as I always did. He smiled, grabbed the front of my blouse with his right hand, and wouldn't let go.

"Go to sleep, darling." I uncurled his fingers from my blouse and turned to go back downstairs. I don't know what made me turn around when I got to the door. His mouth was open as if he was struggling to cry, but no sound came out. Then his nose and cheeks started twitching in the most dreadful manner. I could see milk in his mouth, as if he was drowning in it.

I screeched, "Help! Help! Something is happening to Dele!"

Mary's nimble legs got upstairs first. "Oh my God."

"He's choking!" Auntie Theodora said, right behind her. "Mary, suck his nose!" Mary put her mouth on Dele's nostrils and sucked.

He sneezed and let out a howl, milk running down the sides of his mouth. Death had lost its grip. Tears streamed down my face. I held him against my breasts, sobbing. "Thank you, Mary. Thank you!"

I was shaking. Would I ever get this parenting thing right? It was incredibly, overwhelmingly daunting to be responsible for a whole life, and I was so ignorant. As I watched his little chest rise and fall with sleep, I fell on my knees beside the bed and wept.

Dear Lord, please help me find a job. If Dele gets ill and needs a doctor, I want to be able to pay. I will take any position. Anything. Just help me get a job so I can take care of Dele. Please. Don't let me fail.

I owed Auntie Theodora my baby's life. In a way, I owed her my life, too. Though job searching proved discouraging, in her vibrant company it was easy to laugh. Mornings, we stretched with Jane Fonda on video and danced to Gloria Estefan. I especially loved Ricky Martin's "Maria" and would belt out *Un! Dos! Tres!*, fumbling with the rest of the lyrics. I would dance like mad and feel transported to Dakar. In the sanctuary of Auntie Theodora's house, I felt sheltered from hardship. When summer arrived and we could throw off our comforters and coats, there were trips to an amusement park called King's Dominion, where I failed to feel the pleasure in being turned upside down and almost heaving out my breakfast. Still, I was content to wheel Dele in his stroller and watch the rest of humanity shriek with mad joy as they got shackled into contraptions and swooped away.

Auntie Theodora always made the girls take the broom from me or snatch the vacuum cleaner whenever I tried to help with housework. When she was at work, I could arrange the stuffed animals in the living room and dust or hand-wash dishes in the sink. But I had never touched the dishwasher. One day, with Dele napping, the children at school and Mary out running errands, I decided to give it a try. I had observed Kuukuwa load the dishwasher and pour in detergent many times and it looked easy. I stacked the dishes, filling the compartment with Palmolive dishwashing soap. Water hissed into the machine. To my shock, soap suds foamed out, something that had never happened before. Suds frothed up and poured out of the front, the sides, everywhere. I stood gaping. It felt like an episode of *I Love Lucy* that Mary had shown me. Just then, the front door swung open and the girls stepped in. They stood at the kitchen entrance staring. There I was, standing in two inches of suds.

I wailed, "I don't know what happened. I was just trying to do the dishes."

Kuukuwa pulled off her shoes and stepped into the foam. She walked past me to the dishwasher and picked up the soap.

"Did you use this?"

"Yes."

She tittered, her hand over her mouth. "This is for when you're washing dishes by hand."

"You mean there's a different soap for the machine?"

She was shaking with laughter. "Uhm, yes!" She reached into the cabinet under the sink and produced a box of Cascade. We looked at each other and burst out laughing. Mensima snorted and stomped upstairs. Mensima had been reserved with me, but I could feel her eyes watching me often. It was as if she were holding something in, something that threatened to break out of her.

The following afternoon, a Saturday, I sat on Auntie Theodora's bed, telling her I wanted to wash my clothes. Olga had always added my laundry to hers, but this was a large household and I wanted to wash my own clothes.

"Don't worry about that," Auntie Theodora said. "Let me ask Mensima to do it for you. Mensimaaaa!"

I was immediately anxious. I didn't want to anger Mensima. "Just show me how to use the machine, I'm sure I can operate it."

She ignored me. "Mensimaaa! Hey, Mensimaaaa!"

"Yes, Mama," came the docile reply. "I'm coming."

Auntie Theodora's bosom heaved up. "That girl has no respect! You know, the problem with her is that she was spoiled by her grandmother. When she was nine months old, her father took her to Ghana and left her with his mother, who spoiled her. He didn't bring her back until she was three years old. By the time she returned, I was almost a stranger to her. You see how she has not come up yet? Mensimaaaa! You'd better come here if you know what is good for you!"

Mensima stood before her mother, a hint of defiance on her face. Her high cheekbones seemed pronounced because she'd tied her hair into a puff on top. Her tiger eyes held her mother's. "Look at her face! Look at the evil eye she is giving me, the witch! What took you so long?"

"I was helping Ekow with his lunch."

Auntie Theodora mimicked her with nasal sounds: "Feen feen feenfing feenfeen feen feen feen, I bet you were doing nothing of the sort!" Mensima did not blink. "Sister Akua has some laundry she needs to get done; I want you to do it for her." Anger flitted across Mensima's face that she quickly masked.

"Really, Auntie Theodora, I should wash my own clothes." It wasn't unusual for a younger person in Ghana to be asked to help with a guest's laundry, it was all part of the hospitality, but Auntie

Theodora's voice made me squirm. Mensima was growing up American and already resented me. I was sure she didn't want to wash my clothes.

"I'll do it," she said with tight lips.

"Of course she'll do it," Auntie Theodora said hotly, "how could you even suggest doing your own laundry? That's not how to treat a guest. That's not the Ghanaian way. Go on, Mensima, get on with it!"

I suspected it would go worse for Mensima if I didn't let her help me. I walked slowly to my room. She followed, wordless. I gave her the hamper of dirty clothes. Then she left my room to go downstairs. Suddenly, I heard a loud thump, like something smashing into the wall. When I rushed out, Mensima was already disappearing down the second flight of stairs. On the wall facing me was a black hole. She had punched the wall.

Auntie Theodora rushed out, still wearing just panties and bra. "What was that?"

"I don't know." I hoped she wouldn't see the damaged wall, but she did.

"Herrh! Mensimaaaa!" her voice thundered down the stairs. She didn't wait for a response but whirled around to face me. "What did I tell you?! That rebellious child!" She tore downstairs like a hurricane. I hurried after her, heart thumping. She rushed down to the basement and threw herself on Mensima. She slapped her hard across the face. Then she picked up a belt nearby and used it fast and furiously.

I tried to grab her hand. "Please, Auntie, stop it!"

She stopped for a moment, out of breath. "Don't feel sorry for her. She needs to be taught a lesson, the witch!" She rushed at her again. "You're lucky Sister Lola is here. I would have dealt with you good and proper. Now get up and do the laundry!" Mensima rose from the floor and staggered to the washing machine.

I wanted to punch my benefactress. Sure, I had grown up on Bible sayings like "Spare the rod and spoil the child." I myself had received a couple of slaps from my mother, and the occasional rod laid to my bottom for disrespect. But this rage over laundry that wasn't even Mensima's? And how come Ekow, the son, never had to lift a finger except to study and play video games? I bit my lip with fury. I needed to confide in someone.

Auntie Theodora followed me upstairs to my room, sweat running from her temples, armpits, and below her breasts. "I will not raise my children to become Americans who disrespect their elders. I wonder if I should just take off work and deal with her properly."

I injected as much sarcasm into my voice as I could muster. "Please go to work, you've done enough."

She threw me a sharp look, but I turned away from her.

After Auntie Theodora went to work and Dele was still napping, I went to find Mensima. She was lying on her stomach on the bed, her face turned toward the door, but she didn't look at me.

"May I come in?"

"Sure." Her voice was a harsh whisper.

"Is there anything I can do for you?"

"No."

"I'm sorry I made you angry. You don't ever have to do my laundry again"

She said nothing.

"And you can teach me how to use the dishwasher."

The parenthesis of smiles formed around her lips. "That was funny." She rolled onto her back and looked long at me. "You know French, don't you? Mama says you lived in Senegal."

"Yes, I speak French."

"I hate it. My teacher is so mean. She gives us work we can't do. I hate her!" She picked up the book and flung it across the room. It landed at my feet.

"What homework do you have?"

"Some stupid thing about culture. We have to present something to the class. It's so hard!"

I drew nearer and sat at the edge of her bed. "You know, the Senegalese are interesting. They eat local and French food. And they love to dance. I can teach you the merengue, and then maybe we can make crepes together. Would you like that?"

"Yes." She sat up, truly smiling this time.

We went downstairs and danced and danced. It was a dance of defiance. We shook our bottoms. We kicked the air. We were ripping off suffocating ties of culture from around our bodies, our will, our souls. Kuukuwa joined in. When were spent, we cooked together. The next day, Mensima took the crepes and music to school. After school, she burst into the house, shouting, "Sister Akua! Sister Akua! I got an A. I never got an A in French before!"

It was such a small thing to do for her, but I punched the air with victory. As for Auntie Theodora, my relationship with her had shifted somewhat and left me scrambled. How did a mother balance love and discipline? Auntie Theodora held Dele with gentleness, yet she slapped Mensima to make her respectful. I was sure she had cooed over Mensima when Mensima was a baby. In fact, she'd told me how she used to hold Mensima in her arms all night to make sure she felt safe. How did one know what was good parenting and what wasn't? Would I also get into a space where I felt such rage? I poured all my thoughts into a letter to my sister.

I was lying beside Dele, watching him sleep, when Auntie Theodora called out, "Akua Olivia."

Anxiety gripped me. My mother called me Akua Olivia only when she was displeased with me. Auntie Theodora had never called me Akua Olivia. Her door was open. She sat at the edge of the bed, an open letter in her hand, her eyes cold. "Is this how you repay me?"

I was breathing fast. "I, I don't understand."

"You wrote to people in Ghana about me being a bad mother?"

"What? No, no, no, I never said that! I only wrote about Mensima . . . about the laundry. I was sharing my own fears as a mother. I only wrote to my sister, no one else."

She stared at me, not blinking. "Don't you know how Ghana is? This," she jabbed at the letter, "this came from a friend. Your sister shared your letter with your cousin who talked to her mother, who talked to someone else, and on and on. It seems your mother is the only one who hasn't heard." She hit her forehead with her palm. "Now the story is that I'm about to kill my own daughter. How could you?"

"I never said that, I'm so sorry!"

She looked at the ceiling, at the carpet, at me. "Stories get repeated and changed, you know that. Now everyone is talking about me. I bring you into my home, ask my children to serve you, and this is how you pay me, destroying my reputation? Herrh!" She put her hand to her mouth. "Is that how you are?" The room spun. I couldn't speak. She threw the letter on the bed, staring at me. "I have nothing to say to you. You know, I have a very kind heart. You think you're a modern girl, so you know better, eh?"

"I'm so very sorry. I never said you were a bad mother. I was trying to understand motherhood. Sometimes, I've felt like shaking Dele."

"You wait and see if you'll be a better mother. I love Dele, so I won't throw you out just like that. But you'd better start looking for a place, you hear?" She pinched her lips, her hand under her chin.

Oh God, no. "I'm sorry, Auntie." She rose, marched to the bathroom, and shut the door.

Echoes of Mama's shut door hit me. How could I have been so stupid? I could have written a journal for myself. I could have written an essay to be shared with no one. But itchy-fingered me had to write to my sister. Or maybe I'd wanted the world to know and was just lying to myself. Now my relationship with Auntie Theodora was forever poisoned. I couldn't remain in her home.

Aya

The Flexible Fern

The phone call came on a Saturday evening. It was Kwaku, the son of Len's Ghanaian boss.

"Kwaku? Where are you calling from?"

"I'm right here in Virginia. I got your letter but I didn't reply because I was coming to America."

"Kwaku!" I shrieked joyously into the phone the Ghanaian way.

"Akua!" He wanted to know all about my adventures. When I poured my story into his ears, his voice choked. "Oh, my sister, I wish you had found me, I would have helped you." He told me he was working as a waiter because no one respected his education from a foreign country. "I don't care. I'm not here to impress anybody. I have my own restaurant at home. I'm just here to learn more, earn more money so I can go back and improve."

"Good for you, Kwaku."

"America is fine, but it's no place to live permanently."

"I feel the same way. No one understands the desire to work here with an eye on returning home."

"I know." He chuckled. "Most Americans don't get it. After all, everyone from areas of conflict wants to flee to America. Anyway, what about you, what about your writing?"

"That's what depresses me. Beyond keeping a diary, I haven't written a word since I got to America. I've been consumed with job-seeking and mothering. My baby is growing and I'm still not working. I don't know what to do." I left out the letter to Awurama, and Auntie Theodora asking me to move out.

He was silent for a moment. "I have an idea. Let me talk to someone and get back to you."

That simple statement was enough to set me dancing. Kwaku was not one to throw out words without already knowing the outcome. I decided to wait until he had finalized his plans before saying anything to Auntie Theodora.

Ever since that awful day when she'd confronted me with the letter, she responded politely to my greetings but without smiles. I tried to show her how sorry I was by rushing to meet her whenever her car pulled up in front of the town house. I'd try to take her bag and ask about her day but she would look past me as if I didn't exist. If the children noticed the chill between us, they said nothing. Only Mary knew. Nothing escaped her. She'd smile with sympathy and tell me I would find a job soon.

Now, with Dele crawling over me, I did sit-ups and pull-ups and pumped my muscles. I tossed him into the air and caught him. He shrieked, raising his hands for more. After dinner, I sat him on my lap and read to him while he chortled and drooled over me. When he fell asleep, I stroked his hair, noting how much he resembled his father. *Armand, you bastard. I'm going to make it. I am like the fern in dry land: flexible and strong. Resilient. Just you wait.*

A few days later, Kwaku called again. "How would you feel about working with someone else's papers?"

"What do you mean?"

"Those people you're staying with, is there someone who looks like you?"

I thought for a second. Mary was about my size and had my complexion. Indeed, many times people wondered if we were sisters. "Sure, there is this girl, Mary. We look a bit alike."

"Good. I know the Ghanaian manager at the restaurant where I work. I can arrange for him to interview you and give you a job as a waitress."

A waitress? I didn't have a clue how waitresses kept the different orders together, how they managed to look chirpy in the face of patrons who yelled at them, and the idea of working with someone else's identification card bothered me. Still, I wasn't about to reject the idea.

"Where is this restaurant?"

"In Alexandria, Virginia. You would have to move here, my sister."

"Would I stay with you?"

"How I wish you could, but it's not possible. You know, I live with my sister and her husband plus three children in a three-bedroom town house. But don't worry, I have a plan. A friend of mine, who is also from Ghana, lives close to the restaurant, just a block away. He's willing to let you stay with him for a couple of months until you can afford your own place. As for Dele, don't worry about him, my sister. The manager's mother-in-law is here and has offered to babysit him. She's from Sierra Leone, an African."

Everything was happening rather quickly. He said his friend was called Jacob.

"This Jacob person, is he single?"

"No, he's married."

"Oh good."

"Actually, his wife lives at another address and he visits her once in a while."

"That is strange."

"Well, he married her so he could get a work permit. He visits her to make the marriage seem legitimate, you know, in case immigration pays them a surprise visit. Her place is bigger."

I hesitated. "Are they consummating this marriage?"

"Oh yes. She's his girlfriend, actually."

Oh, so Jacob had a relationship. I didn't have to worry about him pursuing me or anything of the sort.

Jacob himself called me a few days later and soothed my concerns. "I'm helping you because I think it's important to help people. I know I will be rewarded in heaven. I'm sorry that I have just one bedroom, but it's not a big deal. If you like, you can sleep on the couch or I can sleep on it. You're my sister from Ghana. Kwaku is my brother. In this world, it's good to help people. You never know when you, too, will need somebody."

I hung up, stretching my arms out. Yes! This was going to work! It was a humble start, but a start nonetheless! I would start saving money for my victorious return home.

Auntie Theodora's reaction surprised me. She sat forward on her bed, her bare breasts hanging between her arms. "Why are you doing this? How do you know it will work out?"

"Kwaku is a good person. His father used to take me and Joana out to dinner, lunches. Anytime he came into town, we spent nights with him at his apartment. He was so proper that Joana even thought maybe he was gay."

"Fine, Kwaku is a saint. But what about this Jacob? It's not just your safety you're risking. It's Dele's, too. I asked you to leave, but I don't want Dele to come to harm."

"Jacob is in a relationship and more or less married. I'm doing this for Dele. He's going to need more in the future: clothes, food, money for doctors. I have to work." I knew good fabric from the fake.

"You don't have to leave, you know. You can stay here for as long as you need." Her voice was flat and she wasn't looking at me.

"Thank you, but I feel I should leave. I don't want to be a burden." She looked hurt. My words were coming out the wrong way. "I'm very grateful, Auntie. And I'm really sorry for writing the letter."

She sighed. "It's up to you. As I said, you don't have to leave." I knew she meant it. She would never throw me out, but the awkwardness and punishing silence had become unbearable.

It didn't get better. For the remaining week until Kwaku's day off when he came to pick me up, her eyes never met mine. They would light up at Dele and he would squeal with delight. She would pick him up, gushing, "Yes, my Dele! Yes, my pumpkin!" But if I asked how her day went, she wouldn't acknowledge my question, as if I were a lump of earth, something she neither saw nor heard. When Kwaku came to pick me up, she surprised me. She heaved herself off the bed and hugged me, holding me long against her soft body.

"Go with God. Take care of Dele. I'm going to miss him."

"Thank you so much for everything you've done for me. I'm forever grateful."

"It's okay. Just go."

Just go. That's what my mother said before I left her. Two little words, loaded with shifting meanings. Just go, you ingrate. Just go, I absolve you. Or, just go, I wash my hands off you. Just go. Two lumps in my throat.

Nyansa Pɔ

Wisdom Knot

Chi Chi's wasn't the type of restaurant I had expected in America. Spanish words flowed between the men wiping the tables in the empty hall, between the manager and them. Although we had driven straight from Silver Spring to Alexandria, we had missed the Ghanaian manager. This one scrutinizing Mary's driver's license and studying my face was a swarthy man with gray flecks in his beard, his skin the color of papaya. He pushed the papers toward me and said, "Okay, we can hire you, but I'm going to need to see your work permit, too. Can you bring it tomorrow?"

I cast an anxious glance at Kwaku, who blinked meaningfully at me. "Yes." My voice sounded croaky. I cleared my throat and said yes in a stronger voice. On my lap, Dele whimpered, making me wonder if I was holding him too tightly. I rubbed his hair, whispering, "It's okay, darling."

"All right then, Mary," the manager said. I almost corrected him that Mary wasn't my name. "Return tomorrow with your work permit and these documents, okay? The other manager will be here. If you have everything, you can start training the day after." He rose to his feet and shook hands with Kwaku, then me. Mary. Kwaku had urged me to remember. *If anyone calls you Mary, you mustn't forget, you hear?* Oh, God.

In the parking lot, Kwaku was buoyant, his teeth on full display. "What did I tell you? You've got the job! You just need to get Mary to give you her work permit. I'm working tomorrow, so I can't drive you, but you can take the bus. It's easy. You've got a job, my sister!"

My knees were shaking. He fastened Dele in his car seat and opened the door for me before sliding into the driver's seat. "Don't worry about a thing, okay? You're going to be fine." He patted me on the knees, then frowned a little. "You've lost weight, we need to do something about that. Lots of fruit, juices. Lots of urination and soon you'll be your fresh, beautiful self again. Not that you aren't beautiful. I'm just saying . . ."

What if I got caught and wound up in prison? Oh God, my mother would never recover. She, a judge, the upholder of the law, with an outlaw daughter. Yes, Ghanaians broke certain laws all the time, rules considered unreasonable. Like sitting at a red traffic light when not a soul was around. Or taking your own gold out of the country. But breaking the law in a foreign land that could land you in court? The shame would be greater than having a baby without marriage. People would taunt my mother, perhaps stop talking to her. She would suffer whispers and finger-pointing. And then there was Mary. Not only would I get into trouble, Mary would, too. And Auntie Theodora, she didn't know what we had done.

Kwaku switched on the ignition, snapping me out of my

thoughts. "Now I've got to give you some hard talk, Lola. You've led a very protected life. In America, a woman twenty-two, twenty-three years old is far more independent than Mama and Dadda's Ghanaian child. Americans your age have been driving since they were sixteen, working, doing all kinds of things on their own. They're savvy. You never had to work before your embassy job, you lived only a little over a year on your own in Senegal. Even then, you had guardians. Now, I'm here for you, but this isn't Dakar. You're going to have to grow up and do it fast—hey, don't look so sad. You're tougher than you think. You're going to make it. You just have to want it badly enough, okay?"

"Okay," I said, feeling anything but okay.

We arrived at a complex of red-brick buildings, each with two floors, labeled Garden Apartments. I carried Dele as we made our way up two flights of stairs, Kwaku lugging a suitcase in each hand. We knocked on a shiny black door on the second floor. A short, older man with balding hair and an angular chin opened.

He smiled politely. "Ah, you are looking for Jacob. Come in. He is in his room." East African, judging by his accent. That was my first thought. He was probably a guest. I stepped inside, taking in the large, well-furnished sitting room, wondering how Jacob could afford this. A woman with a close-shaven head sat on the couch, leafing through a magazine. When she saw us, she laid it down and hastened to greet us.

"What a cute baby!" she said. "This is going to be wonderful. We don't have children of our own, now I get to play with this little one. My name is Adimu, and this is my husband."

"You . . . you live here?" I was trying to quiet my heart. Before she could answer, the door in the left corner opened and a man I took to be Jacob slouched out. He was short, a bit on the round side, with small, spaced teeth that reminded me of a fish. He'd either just come in or was about to go out, judging from his striped green shirt tucked into his brown pants and his dress shoes.

He and Kwaku shook hands, snapping their fingers together the Ghanaian way.

"You are welcome," he said to me. "Meet Mr. and Mrs. Kamba, my landlord and his wife. They are from Kenya." His landlord? He lived with them? "My room is this way."

My mind whirled, unable to make sense. Mr. and Mrs. Kamba settled back onto the couch as Jacob led the way to his room, me following like a confused lamb.

In the room, I stood stiffly with Dele on my hip, the blood beating against my temples as Kwaku and Jacob stacked my suitcases against the wall. I threw an awkward glance at the double bed and the two chairs tucked into two corners. One chair almost touched the wall closet. The other was only about three feet from the opposite wall. The room was the size one would find in a modest hotel. Jacob bestowed on me more of his toothy smile. "Welcome. Make yourself at home." Then he went out and closed the door behind him. Kwaku patted me on the back, beaming.

I hissed, "Kwaku, I thought you said he had a one-bedroom apartment!"

"You misunderstood, I meant he had access to only one bedroom."

"What?"

"My sister, I don't know where you got the notion that he had his own apartment."

"He told me I could sleep on the couch. That's what he said when he called. Why would he say that when the sitting room wasn't his? Even if I got the wrong impression, he said nothing to correct me. I would never have agreed to this. What am I supposed to do now?" I swept away from him, staring at the stiff brown curtains, feeling trapped.

"Listen," he said confidently, "this is a good person. He is a churchgoer and a Christian. You have nothing to worry about." He planted his hands on my shoulders, urging me to look at him. "Just give it a try. One week. If you don't like it, we'll find something else, okay? Right now, you can't just turn around and go back. Just try." He smiled to reassure me. "You'll be fine. I promise."

He took off quickly after that.

Dele twisted around, his hands grabbing for the floor. I gave in and allowed him to crawl on the carpet. He touched it, then sat up to examine his hands, as if expecting the fluffy fibers to stick to him. I wondered if he was comparing it to the hardwood floors he had rolled on until now. I stood there, chin in my hands. Where were we going to sleep? We couldn't use the living room, since it belonged to the Kenyan couple. The floor was the best option. I could spread a blanket on it and we'd be comfortable. Normally, I slept naked, but with Jacob in the picture, I'd have to wear something.

I was about to change into a sea-blue gown Olga had given me when Jacob strode in. Without knocking. I stood in the middle of the room, staring at him. He went straight to the bed and stretched out on his back. He laced his hands behind his head and cast a benevolent smile at me. "You go ahead and get undressed." He wasn't going to lie there and gawk at me, was he? I forced a smile but remained standing. He didn't budge. The silence stretched between us, thick and challenging. He finally understood my unspoken words, because he said, "Oh, I see. You'd like me to leave."

I held his gaze. "Yes."

He heaved himself off the bed. When the door closed behind him, I tore off my pants and sweater with shaky fingers, yanked out the gown, shook my arms into its long sleeves, pulled it down to my ankles, and zipped it all the way up to its ruffled neck.

He returned and, right in front of me, he proceeded to unzip. Not wishing to see him naked, I looked away until he had on his dressing gown. A television in the corner was on, so I sat on the chair and watched the pictures, seeing nothing while Dele continued his exploration of the room. Jacob stretched himself once more on his back, gave me a benign smile, and patted the spot beside him. "You can come and lie down."

He had to be joking.

"No, thank you. I'll be sleeping on the floor." I grabbed Dele and held him on my lap.

His eyed me in consternation. "Oh no, I can't let you do that, there's hardly any room and it's not good for the baby." This man was from one of the northern tribes of Ghana where people were natural, I thought to myself. Perhaps I had misunderstood his motives.

"Why don't I put the baby next to you? Then I could sleep on the floor."

"Ah, how can I let you sleep on the floor?"

I couldn't ask him to give up his bed. We went back and forth.

Dele dropped to the floor, rubbing his eyes and whimpering. He was sleepy. I didn't know what to do. Finally, I compromised. I put Dele beside him and slid next to Dele, using a separate blanket for both of us. Soon, Dele was snoring gently, his body warm. I lay in the dark with my eyes open, trying not to fall off the edge. I listened to Jacob's breath until it grew heavy and fell into the steady rhythm of slumber. I slid onto the floor. How could Kwaku put me in such a situation? Maybe it was because he himself was a gentleman, I reasoned with myself. Safe memories of nights at his father's apartment, edged with laughter and the shut door he never breached, lulled me to sleep.

Early in the morning, Jacob disappeared under a cloud of after-shave, with a promise to be back on Friday. He planned to spend some weekdays with his green-card wife. Gone with him was the taste of discomfort. This was probably going to work out for the short term until I could figure out something better.

The Ghanaian manager stared at me from big round eyes. "You've got your driver's license and social security card, but where's your work permit?"

"I, erm, I left it in Maryland." I hoped my face didn't betray the lie. I added quickly, "I'll go get it this weekend."

"Okay," he said, his smile grim. "You're a fellow Ghanaian and I want to help you, but you must have it at the end of your training or you can't work here. If your paperwork isn't complete, it's my job on the line." He pointed with his pen. "You see all these people working here? Some are probably working with other people's pa-pers. Latinos, Blacks. We don't scrutinize the papers too closely, but we've got to have our files in order. We don't want any trouble with immigration. You understand what I'm saying?"

"Okay," I said in a small voice. I had hoped no one would re-member to ask for the work permit. I peeked at Kwaku, who had already changed into his uniform. I wondered if I'd ever feel that confident, smiling at fellow workers, walking to a table and saying "Hola" to that family with well-nourished children.

The manager slid a menu at me. "The first part of your training is to study the menu. You must know every ingredient in the different dishes. You have one day to study it. I'll test you. Two days, max. When you finish, you'll shadow one of the waiters and learn, okay?"

The restaurant was a hive of activity, unlike restaurants I had patronized in Dakar, and I couldn't believe I was in America in a restaurant chocked with the cadence of Spanish-inflected English, suffused with the smell of beans and cheese and toasted corn. The air buzzed with patrons, loud laughter, cutlery clinking against plates. You could see the cooks, Spanish voices calling out dishes I had to learn. I stared at the menu: Tacos, soft or hard shell, plus all the ingredients that went into them. Burritos. Chimichangas. I knew about tacos and burritos, but what in the world was a chimichanga? I had to learn about allergens, too, like MSG, whatever that was. My mind was taking snapshots of menus, memorizing foods and more foods. When I wasn't studying in the booth, I watched Kwaku whirl around, scribble on a pad, nod, smile, press buttons on a large screen, carry dishes on a tray. Repeat.

Around four p.m., after stuffing boxes of juices and food that Kwaku slipped me into my bag, I walked fifteen minutes to the babysitter's. Kwaku had walked me over to the town house earlier in the morning. Those were images I had wanted to forget: the Sierra Leonean old woman with a limp, who hobbled down the stairs to reveal a dank basement, whose brown carpet was stained darker and crusty in places, and smelled sour. Forget the cacophony of children climbing and jumping off cloth-covered couches, who banged/laughed/whimpered. There were at least twenty of them, some as young as six months and others as old as five. I'd wanted to forget how Dele clutched my arm tighter as I deposited the bag filled with diapers, jar food, and a plastic container of

Cheerios I had filched from the kitchen cabinet, God forgive me. Forget how I had covered my ears against Dele's yowls, the way he'd scrambled up my legs, the way I had torn myself from him and run up the stairs, tears streaming down my face, Kwaku telling me it was going to be okay.

Now I followed the old woman down the stairs. Everything seemed to pull her down, her downturned smile, her curved spine, her arms. In the basement, my hands flew to my cheeks. Dele sat in the middle of the din, dried gray streaks on his face, staring at air. When I rushed to pick him up, he buried his head in my neck and whimpered. His diaper felt squishy and smelled of urine. When I raised him to look, a dark patch revealed itself in his overalls between his legs, running almost to his knees.

I looked at the woman in consternation. "He's wet!"

"I just changed him," she wailed. But when I opened his diaper bag, only one diaper was missing. What's more, apart from the missing diaper, all his jar food was intact. Only the Cheerios looked half-eaten.

"Why is his food untouched?"

"But I just fed him, I just fed him!" She was trying to imply that I had miscounted the number of jars I'd put in there.

I tried prying Dele's head up to look at me. "Hello, darling," I whispered. He shut his eyes and burrowed deeper. I felt a cold dread in my core. He hadn't eaten, I was sure. As we walked to the apartment, he kept pulling at my chest, crying. As soon as we got to the house and I changed him, I let him have my breast. He latched on to my nipple, sucking with a rhythmic smack, so hard it hurt. All night he clung to me. The next day, as soon as we drew close to the babysitter's, he let out a howl, twisting away from her, clawing at me. With every will in me, I tore him off my body and deposited him into the arms of the older woman. *Oh God. Oh God.*

"Now listen and watch," said the waitress I was shadowing, a high school girl of about sixteen or seventeen. She said to call her Anita. She had developed her own shorthand for speed, she added. Kwaku was right about Americans knowing their way. This teenager was so confident and knowledgeable, I felt like an idiot. We walked to a table that sat a large family: parents, a grandmother, and four children. Latino people seemed a lot like Africans, doing things with the family.

"Hola, buenos días," said Anita. As they smiled and ordered, she scribbled rapidly on her notepad. The orders took forever, the kids changing their minds over soft or hard tacos, and they wanted chimichangas, which looked to me like some burrito of a different form. Even though I had managed to learn the menu and did passably well, I kept forgetting which was which.

She led me to a big screen and showed me how to enter the orders, when to tell the cook to fire them up. It was all so complicated. The many times I sat in a restaurant grumbling when food was slow coming, I had no idea what wit and alertness it took to keep track of different orders, remember who wanted refried beans, who didn't want cheese, who wanted extra cheese, who didn't want MSG. I fought hard. I needed this job. I memorized, took notes, dreaming of the future: a lovely home of my own in Ghana, a car and a housekeeper to help me with Dele, who wouldn't remember his earlier hardship with an incompetent babysitter.

"How did it go?" Mary asked on the phone. Something about the timbre of her voice troubled me.

"Not too bad. The manager isn't satisfied. He asked me to bring a work permit. Could I come and get it, please?"

She took a trifle too long to answer. "I told Auntie Theodora."

"What are you saying?"

"I'm sorry. We went somewhere and I needed to produce a photo ID but didn't have it. When she grilled me, I couldn't lie. She was very upset. She wants you to return it."

I had been terrified of using her papers, and yet now that she said I couldn't have them, I desperately wanted them. "Oh no, please, please, please, let me at least get this job. Just this one time."

I could hear her breathing, rolling my words around in her mind. "Please."

"I'm sorry. Auntie is very angry with me. You, too. I told her it was my idea but she wouldn't listen."

"Can't you hold her off for just one more day?"

"I'm sorry, I can't. I've got to go, she's coming downstairs."

The line went dead. Without her work permit, I couldn't get the job. I crossed my hands over my chest and told myself that if I squeezed myself harder and harder, maybe I'd stop shaking. *Remember Aya, the unbreakable fern.*

In the morning, I walked to the nearby post office and mailed Mary's ID back to her so I wouldn't have to pay for a bus ride, what with Kwaku working. I didn't return to Chi Chi's. If I was going to be fired anyway, I wouldn't subject Dele to the babysitter, who would probably sit nursing her leg, ignoring the din around her. I spent the rest of the morning cooped up with Dele.

I was sitting cross-legged on the floor, watching TV, when the door snapped open. I twisted around to find Jacob standing there, smiling, back from his visit with the green card wife. I greeted him and turned back to the television. Without any warning, he crossed the room, bent down, and pressed his lips against mine, probing with his tongue. I recoiled, pushed him away.

"Why?" he asked.

Why? "I have no wish to get involved with anyone. I have been through a lot."

"Oh, that's all right, you'll get over it soon." His mouth came down on mine more forcefully.

"Stop it, I mean it!"

He drew back, his eyes ablaze. "Oh yeah? I think I'd better talk to Kwaku about your attitude. He's not going to like it." What was he talking about? Was that the understanding, that I was going let him slide between my thighs? What was all that talk about his Christian virtues? He left without another word.

I darted to the phone and punched Kwaku's number. "That guy tried to force a kiss on me! I mean, I don't even know him!"

"So what did you do?"

"What do you think? I won't let him touch me!"

By the way he hesitated, I could feel his thoughts roaming. "Listen, I'm going to talk to you, my sister. Listen to me carefully. I didn't expect that from Jacob, but I tell you—" he sighed "—if you were my flesh-and-blood sister, I would ask you to do it."

"Do what?"

"Well, you know . . ."

"Sleep with him? No way! How could you—"

"What is so bad about sleeping with him so he can help you?"

"I'll never do that, Kwaku! How could you even ask?"

"Listen to me. Please, listen. What I am saying is—"

"No, I won't listen, I won't!"

"Hold on, hold on." He sighed again. "Okay. I'm coming over."

I lay on the floor and curled up.

When Kwaku arrived, Jacob was still gone. I scowled at him.

"My sister, my sister," he said, "don't be angry. I'm sorry." He sank onto the couch, looking miserable. "I told you to give in to him because I didn't know what to do. Your situation is desperate."

I folded my arms over my breasts. "I will never be that desperate, you hear? If I wanted to prostitute myself, I'd do it on Fourteenth Street in Washington, DC, where I've heard the prostitutes roam."

"I'm sorry, Lola," he said mournfully. "I thought that maybe you two could fall in love or something."

I eyed him with sarcasm. "Really?"

"Now, wait a minute." He sounded hurt. "I blasted Jacob when he called me. I told him he was wrong. I told him that if he liked you, he should try to win you with kindness, not thrust his tongue into your mouth. I had no idea he could be so crude."

"Well," I said, calming down a little, "he came home and left but didn't try to kiss me again."

"Okay, then. But why didn't you come into the restaurant today?"

I took a deep breath. "I don't have Mary's work permit."

He jerked forward. "What do you mean?"

"She won't give it to me. She told Auntie Theodora and they're all upset with me. I mailed her papers back to her."

"Lola! You don't get it, do you? This isn't Dakar! You've got to do what you need to do to survive. You should have pressed her harder!"

"You don't think I did? I can't force her if she doesn't want to help anymore."

He shook his head in frustration. "God, Lola. What are you going to do now? Do you want to run home to your mother?"

"You know I can't go back."

"Jesus, Lola. This is bad. I've got to think. And you won't let Jacob touch you."

"Never!" From the day the Gambian diplomat had tried to pry my legs apart, rage had filled me. To let Jacob into me when he didn't even pretend to like me was too dehumanizing. Kwaku mumbled something about needing to think and left.

I did my best to avoid Jacob, timing walks to the shopping center when I knew he would be returning home from work. I would pick up a copy of *The Washington Post*, searching the Help Wanted section, determined to find a job that would sponsor me for a green card. At night, I made sure to fall asleep on the floor before he came in. He left me alone. On Saturday, he was lying on his back napping when the phone rang. Dele was crawling around the floor. Not wanting Jacob to wake up, I dived for the phone. The crackle of static, coupled with the accent of the caller, indicated a long-distance call from Ghana. Figuring it was important, I called his name. He held out his hand, breathing heavily. As I leaned forward to hand it to him, he grabbed me by the wrist, tried to pull me on top of him.

"Let me go! Let me go!" I scratched with my free hand and kicked, but his arms felt like iron gripping my bone. I bared my teeth and clamped down on his arm. Hard.

"Bitch!" He let go of my arm and grabbed his. We were both panting. He looked at me, then at the telephone. He grabbed the phone and started talking. I picked up Dele, held him against my chest, and backed into the wall, my eyes on Jacob. When he finished speaking, he shot up and slammed the door after him.

I was shaking. Oh my God. What to do? It was dangerous to stay. Who to call, who to call? My mind felt fragmented. Olga was too far away and out of the question, with her custody battle. I couldn't return to Auntie Theodora. I put Dele down on the carpet and picked up *The Washington Post* I had bought earlier. Up till now, I had been searching for an office job. This time, I checked out Help Wanted Domestic. I had never scanned that section before, deeming it improbable because I had a baby, but I had to try. I wanted a position as a live-in babysitter with someone who wouldn't mind another baby. It would be like being a maid, but I was ready to do anything except sleep with Jacob. I didn't believe for a second that he'd be of much use even if I yielded.

A couple in Falls Church, Virginia, needed a caretaker for their baby. *Will sponsor*, the advertisement said. The pay was one hundred fifty dollars a week, plus room and board. I called the number, and a Nathalie O'Neal answered the phone. My voice was tremulous. She asked me questions, and I asked a few of my own, the vital one being whether it was true that they would sponsor.

"Yes," she said. "If we hire you, we will sponsor you."

"I have an eleven-month-old boy. Is that okay?"

She thought for a moment. "That's great, actually. The boys could play together. Do you have any references?"

"Yes, hold on, please." With trembling hands, I fished out my address book. Mindy! She was more composed than Olga and would sound more professional. I gave her Mindy's number. As soon as I hung up with her, I called Mindy.

"I'm sorry to call you in such a rush, but I just got interviewed for a job as a live-in babysitter. Could you please give me a reference?"

"Of course. Where is this?"

"Falls Church. Listen, the lady might be trying to call you. I'll tell you more later, please."

"Sure."

We hung up. I walked about, picking things up and putting them down again. Dele crawled after me.

Thirty minutes later, Nathalie called back.

"Could you start right away?"

Could I! "Just tell me when you want me to come."

"Why don't I come pick you up this evening? That way we can get acquainted."

Room and board, plus six hundred dollars a month! I would save as much as possible and be out of America within two years, with or without a green card. Preferably with a green card. The good thing about a resident permit was that if I needed to stay in America longer for any reason, I could get a better job and save even more money and return home victorious. Fear flew out of me. This was actually going to be wonderful.

Ɔwɔ a Ɔreforo Adɔbɛ

A Snake Climbing a Raffia Tree

The O'Neals ushered me into a den in the basement of their home. The husband, Dick, sank into an easy chair, his black-rimmed glasses and furry brows giving him the appearance of a humorless professor. He ran his hand up and down the back of a large dog who sat upright, its ears a pair of acute triangles jutting upward. I held Dele tighter on my lap.

"Don't be afraid," Nathalie said from her rocking chair, the baby in her arms.

"This is Loveliness," Dick said with pride. The dog's brown fur was nice enough, but its bunched-up black face was anything but lovely, as if someone had used a burning torch to ram it. A second dog, big and white, sniffed my toes and spread itself at my feet. Inside my boots, my toes curled in. Dick smiled. "White Fang is intelligent. He knows you aren't a threat." My toes remained curled.

Nathalie smiled nervously. "This is Buck." Buck leaned toward me as she bounced him on her lap, his eyes dark against his pink-

174

ish skin. "We just adopted him two weeks ago. I'm so happy—" she sounded weepy "—but I'm tired all the time. I took time off when he came. Now it's time to get back to work. I need someone to take care of him when I'm gone. Dick works at home selling insurance and needs quiet."

I smiled at Buck, a pleasant bundle of fat rolls, as pale as unbaked dough. I wanted to squish him against my chest, inhale him. "How old is he?"

"Three months. Would you like to hold him?"

"Yes, please."

She walked across the oriental carpet and placed him in my hands. He waved his arms about, studying my face. Dele was only too happy to slide to the floor. When White Fang licked his face, he squealed in delight and fast-crawled toward Loveliness, as if expecting licking from her as well. Loveliness hurled a frightful bark, bared her teeth, and was about to spring when Dick grabbed her by the collar. "Down, girl!"

Dele screamed and scurried back, clutching at my knees. I would have to keep him away from the beast.

Dick grunted. "Loveliness is not bright, I'm afraid. White Fang knows who's a visitor and who's an enemy. Loveliness doesn't." He bent over, cupped the dog's face. "They're going to stay here, kiddo. Don't bark at them." He looked up with a proud smile, still rubbing the dog's back. "This is *my* baby."

Loveliness for Dick, Buck for Nathalie. No wonder she looked scrambled, her brown hair stringy, her sweater a frumpy gray over caramel pants. She was alone in the adoption. I resolved to make myself so indispensable that they would keep me for the two years and sponsor me.

Nathalie beamed as Buck tried to eat my braids. "I think he

likes you. I want you to know Dele will get free healthcare. I'm a doctor." She confirmed the pay of six hundred dollars a month. "You don't have to worry about food or anything. I think this is going to be fabulous, Buck will have a big brother to play with."

After putting Buck to sleep, she drove Dele and me back to the apartment to pick up our luggage. I noted with relief that Jacob was gone. Of the two thousand dollars Armand sent me, two hundred remained, so I left a hundred-dollar bill on Jacob's bed as rent money. After all, he didn't get what he'd hoped for. Fair was fair. I just wished I hadn't decided to use most of it to pay Frederick Memorial Hospital.

Back at the O'Neals', Nathalie led me into the bedroom Dele and I would share, next to the basement den. The warm tones of the bedding, walls, and drapes made me feel sleepy. What's more, a space heater had toasted the air to perfection. Dick had shut the ugly Loveliness inside another room in the basement, Nathalie explained with a tight smile that delighted me. I wasn't the only one who didn't love that dog.

"Dick's upstairs in his office," she said. "He used to work for the government, but he quit because he wants to make more money." She showed me the kitchen upstairs featuring two skylights, then the nursery. "Nice, isn't it? It needs pictures on the wall or something, but I'm getting there. Right now, Buck sleeps in our bed. It's just easier to get him when he wakes at night."

To my surprise, the master bedroom had no bed, only a king-size mattress on the floor, oak dressers against the wall, and oak everything. I wondered how they could sleep on moonlit nights when the skylight revealed the bed, whether their bodies slapped against each other under celestial eyes.

Dele and I slept deeply under the blanket Nathalie called a duvet that was filled with feathers. In the morning, after breakfast, Dick retreated to his office. I rejoiced that Loveliness remained locked in the basement while White Fang played outside. As Nathalie and I stacked dishes in the dishwasher, she said, "I don't want you to cook or do laundry. The kitchen is the most important. Just run the dishwasher, keep the counters clean, and vacuum. That's what I meant by light housework. We'll cook together when I come home from work. I want you to focus on Buck."

"I don't mind cooking."

"Just take care of Buck." She closed the dishwater, setting it hissing. She leaned against the counter, her head low. "You know, I went into menopause at thirty, which means I can't have babies. Dick didn't want to adopt, but he gave in because I always wanted to be a mom."

Thirty seemed too young for menopause. I peered at her for evidence of moodiness but couldn't tell. The divide between husband and wife troubled me. I worried they might quarrel like Olga and Barry had and it might touch me somehow.

Later that afternoon, she drove me to the mall, both kids in their car seats in the back. She bought a high chair and walker for Dele to use, things Buck would inherit later. "Or," she said, "we can just buy another set if they both need them."

It thrilled me that she was investing in our future together. Perhaps we would become close, like Olga and me. By the end of two years, I would have about ten thousand dollars sitting in the bank, if I saved a lot. That would be enough transition money to help me resettle in Ghana. I was so giddy with joy that my tongue flapped loose. On the drive back, I found myself talking about Armand. Nathalie nodded with sympathy, saying that things would get better. "They always do."

The first time I changed Buck's diaper, I put him on the changing table and set to work. I removed the diaper and stared in shock at his naked bottom. I had no idea that the white skin was so transparent. There was a network of blue and purple veins everywhere. It felt like a violation, as if I had entered his skin. As I hovered, a warm squirt hit my chest. I jumped back, smiling ruefully, remembering the time Dele squirted me. Buck was the cutest, cuddliest little baby. He smelled of powder and milk when I pressed him to my chest. How could Dick not love this baby?

Two days after I started working for them, Dick marched into the kitchen, wearing a frown behind his glasses. Dele was exercising his vocal cords, he chattered all the time.

"Lola," he said with a disapproving glance at Dele. "Please keep him quiet. It's very difficult for me to talk to clients on the phone with baby noises in the background. I just can't work that way."

"Sorry. I'll do my best."

"I think it would be best if you kept him down in the basement, in your room."

"Downstairs? Without supervision?"

"Yes. This is not subject to a discussion."

"Why?"

"I just told you why."

His eyes challenged me. As they said back home, when your hand is inside someone's mouth, you don't hit him on the head lest he bites down. "Okay," I said in a small voice.

When I took Dele downstairs and turned to leave, he grabbed my leg. I pried his arms away and quickly shut the door. He let out a howl that slashed my heart. I kept going downstairs to hold and kiss him, trying to persuade him it was a game of peek-a-boo.

Dick refused to touch Buck, even when Buck was crying. I had to go to the master bedroom and pick him up, sometimes Dick wearing nothing but briefs. He'd grunt his exasperation that I had to enter his room. And yet it irritated him if I waited until he was dressed. "Can't you keep that baby quiet!"

One day, Buck didn't box the air as usual. A series of gas noises kept rattling from his bottom. I worried he might be getting ill the way Dele had at Auntie Theodora's. That night, I snapped awake to loud voices bursting through the floorboards above.

Dick's voice cut like a knife. "You shouldn't have spent all that money buying a fucking walker and high chair."

Nathalie sounded weepy and angry. "Don't you say that to me!" It was like listening to Olga and Barry arguing. I shut my eyes and prayed.

The next day, Buck's nose ran and he felt warm to the touch.

"Make sure you burp him when you give him his bottle," Nathalie told me before leaving for work. "Every two ounces, you know, to prevent gas." She held Buck as though reluctant to part with him, stroking his bald head. I waited patiently for her to hand him over to me. "I wish I didn't have to leave you," she added.

I prayed his stomach would settle. Within two days, he was back to boxing the air, pulling my braids, and gurgling when I talked to him. My first weekend off, I got Dele ready to visit Mindy and Ted. Dick had decided to drop us off at the West Falls Church metro station and pick us up on Sunday evening. I slung the diaper bag over my shoulder and was about to pick up Dele from the bed when Dick rapped on my door. Pleats formed between his brows.

"Lola, we don't think this is going to work. We'd like you to leave today. Here's a check for one hundred fifty dollars. For the week."

"What? What did I do wrong?"

"Nothing. It's just that you with a baby and all, we don't have enough room. There are always baby noises in the background when I'm trying to work."

"But you told me to leave Dele downstairs and I've been doing just that."

"I know, but it's very uncomfortable with two babies. We just feel it's not going to work out. Besides, we've found someone else who will be starting on Monday."

"I don't believe you. You bring me to your house and you don't give me any notice at all and you want me to leave?" I wished my voice wouldn't quiver so.

"We were just trying you out for a while. We had already contacted a nanny agency."

I felt myself growing angry. "You didn't tell me that before you hired me. You could have told me something, and now I have nowhere to go. I think you should give me some notice." I stared him down.

He stood looking at me. Clearly, he had not foreseen I would put up a fight. "Let me go talk to Nathalie."

Yeah, talk to Nathalie. How convenient for her to hide behind her husband, not talking to me when she was the one who hired me. I sat on the bed and tried to slow my breathing. Unable to calm down, I called Mindy's house. Ted picked up the phone.

"Hi, Lola, Mindy's out. What's wrong?"

A torrent of words poured out of me. After I was spent, he asked to speak with Dick. When I went up to the office, Nathalie refused to meet my eyes. She kept her gaze on Buck, her lashes pressed down.

Fine, then, I thought to myself, turning to Dick. "My friend's husband wants to talk to you." I returned downstairs.

They talked for a long time, then Dick shouted for me to pick up the receiver.

Ted's laughter was derisive. "These people are really something else. Anyway, I convinced him to give you a week's notice. That will give Mindy and me time to prepare a place for you. You're coming to stay with us, okay? In the meantime, go on and come over for the weekend."

I teared up. "Thank you so much, Ted."

Nathalie remained invisible. Dick was placid as he drove me to the metro. "Call me on Sunday when you get back. I'll pick you up," he said. I thanked him.

I spent a relaxed weekend with Mindy, Ted, and their two children, who fought over Dele as though he were a prize. On Sunday, Dick picked me up from the metro, as polite as ever, but as soon as I stepped into my room, I knew something was wrong. The space heater was gone. The soap in the bathroom was gone. The check for one hundred fifty dollars I'd left on my dresser had disappeared. Someone had also rifled through my clothes. It had to be Nathalie. She had given me some clothes when I moved in and had helped me put them in the dresser. I didn't like them but had accepted them out of politeness. Only she would know what was hers and what was mine. All the sweaters and turtlenecks had disappeared from my drawers. She had even been through my underwear. If she wanted what she'd given me, all she had to do was ask and I would have gladly given them back to her.

I put Dele to sleep and covered him with the comforter. I sat on the bed, contemplating what to do. I needed the space heater. It was so chilly. After pulling myself together, I went upstairs, where Nathalie sat in the kitchen pretending to read a paper.

"May I have the space heater, please?"

She rose without a word and went to the linen closet in the hallway. She dragged out the space heater and pushed it toward me, muttering, "Space heaters cost money. We have what we have because we work hard. We work hard for what we have." Grateful that Dele was not going to be cold, I didn't tell her how unfair it was to suggest I wanted a free ride when I worked for her.

Morning came. Both Nathalie and Dick had left when I ventured upstairs to make breakfast for Dele before tackling my tasks. I opened my door and turned rigid. Loveliness was sprawled across a step. The horrid dog had been left there to prevent me from going upstairs. I gripped the banister, heart pounding. Dele was hungry. I had to go up to the kitchen. The beast and I locked eyes. I hoped she couldn't hear my heart, because I could. I had tossed her a bone once, I hoped she remembered. I inched forward, one step at a time, legs trembling, never taking my eyes off the dog. I was three steps away from it.

"Hi, Loveliness," I whispered. She growled but didn't move. I crept closer. "Hi, Loveliness," I said softly, my heart hammering out of my chest. I pictured those powerful jaws clamping down on my legs. She still didn't move. I had no choice now. I stepped past her, forcing myself not to run. I tucked my heart back into my chest and strode into the kitchen. I made breakfast for Dele and me. I also washed the dishes and cleaned the kitchen. I was living in their home, so I felt I should continue to work. The only thing was Nathalie had taken Buck with her to work. I missed his warm rolls of fat. With all my heart, I would have cared for him. He was an innocent baby who had nothing to do with his parents' behavior. I took a piece of meat and tossed it in Loveliness's direction. She leaped for it and settled down to chew on the step, sticking her black nose up.

White Fang trotted into the kitchen and stood by the door, wagging his tail, waiting to go outside. I twisted the door handle but it wouldn't budge. Dick had never explained how the electronic security system worked. Now he had locked me inside the house. I felt reduced to nothingness. What if there was a fire? Dele and I would be trapped inside with the furniture.

When I heard them open the front door, I remained downstairs, but I heard them saying how surprised they were that I had continued to work. The next day, the soap reappeared in the bathroom. Loveliness wasn't on the stairs. White Fang was outside, and the doors were unlocked. I breathed. I cleaned the whole house, polishing the floor as well. For the rest of the week, I stayed away from them but worked diligently. At the end of the work week, I packed out, heading for the home of Mindy and Ted, feeling like a snake climbing up a raffia tree, sliding and sliding down the smooth bark.

Hye Wonhye

Burn Not Burn

As the Red Line train to Rockville creaked and rocked, and the trees whizzed by, I felt as if I were roasting in flames. America had become fire. I had once heard a pastor say it was necessary for people to burn in life's crucible so we'd come out purer versions of ourselves. It was all part of a divine plan. Mama also said God had a plan for our lives. Did He really? It seemed to me humans were rather like marbles poured onto a table, rolling randomly into one another, forced to change direction. If there was a plan, I failed to see it.

A frenzied mass of people swarmed in and out of the train, but I was unmoved by their jostling. Dele bounced on my lap and charmed everyone with his smiles, and they said, "Aww, he's so precious!" *Precious.* The precious one had been confined to a basement. I wished I had tears left to cry. The train screeched in the tunnels and begged me to join my screams to its own. I felt like a rock, dead.

Slowly, Dele and I emerged from the bowels of the earth. Ted was waiting at the tunnel's mouth, a big grin on his face. He wrapped his arms around me, his breath warm.

"It's so good to see you," he said. I wished I could say, *Me, too*, but my tongue refused to move. He put Dele into the car seat, cooing. "Look at this cutie!"

Ted. How soothing his gentleness in Dakar, getting me a drink when Len asked me to mopez le floor, how he'd always paid attention to anything I had to say. Dear, dear, Ted. Why couldn't I tell him how happy I was to see him?

When we entered their living room, I stopped. High on the back wall, a banner greeted me: Welcome, Lola and Dele! The words nearly succeeded in making me feel again. The children, Val and Bob, rushed to Dele, hugging him, touching his hair, his cheeks. They dragged me down steep wooden steps to show me how they had labored for our coming. A curtain wrapped around a corner enclosed a cozy bed. An antique lamp cast a warm glow over the night table. A welcome card stood near it. They had even placed a few books in a small bookcase for me. A lump formed in my throat.

Olga called from Frederick, her voice loud and shrill. "Those bastards! What could you possibly have done wrong? You know, Lola, just come back here and stay with me. You don't have to put up with that crap." She lectured some more but I felt separated from the person that used to be me. I thanked her and hung up, promising to call her again soon, knowing I wouldn't.

I cut onions for Mindy, helping her prepare black beans for dinner. My eyes watered. I looked at her placid back as she washed the beans at the sink. She raised her head and stared through the window. "You know, Lola, have you considered going back to Dakar?"

My tongue unglued itself. "There's nothing left for me in Dakar.

I quit my job, Joana's gone, I have no apartment. No money to buy a plane ticket and rent an apartment. And you know how tough it is to find work there, people with graduate degrees walking around for two years without employment. I could always count on diplomat friends to tell me about vacant positions that were never advertised, but now all my friends have left Dakar. Did you know how it felt for the Senegalese to see people like me get the precious jobs they couldn't? How they resented foreigners, even fellow Africans, taking over their country?"

"Huh, I never thought about it that way. What about Ghana, your family?"

"I'm too ashamed." I sighed. Something nagged me. Why didn't Americans tell the truth about how hard life was in America? In Dakar, they lived with servants in big houses, and yet complained about Africa, so we assumed they lived in even bigger mansions in America. American movies reinforced that feeling. In the cinema, Joana and I had watched Harrison Ford and other heroes defend a country so precious one must die for it. America sold itself that way: it was the richest, most magnificent place next to heaven. That's why people the world over lined up around American embassies for visas. To emigrants, America was this magical place where all you needed was a willingness to work hard for your fortunes to change. Just like that. You could remain in America or, like me, save money for a triumphant return home. No one told you America could crush your bones, grind you into dust. And yet, even as reduced as I felt now, I believed the American magic existed. It was just so bloody hard to find it.

Mindy turned to me. "Why are you so quiet?"

"I was just thinking. Do you know, in Dakar, even poor Americans I met told tales about their wealth in America. And, when

Africans return from America, they don't tell the truth. Either they crave admiration in the eyes of those who've never traveled or they're ashamed. No one wants to go home empty-handed, with broken dreams. I could return and tell the truth, but no one would believe me, a penniless woman with a fatherless child. They'll insist I'm saying that only because I couldn't make it."

Mindy's voice took on a slightly stern tone, as though I had reminded her of something. "You told Nathalie you had just arrived from Africa." She shook her head in annoyance and disbelief. "You shouldn't have. You don't understand how people here are, Lola."

"Why does it matter where I came from?"

Her tone softened. She seemed embarrassed. "I don't know how to say this. You see, they were worried about AIDS because . . . well, people believe it started in Africa. And you told them Armand was Black. They were worried about drug use, you know? Heroin. Needles. The sort of thing that spreads AIDS. Their baby got sick in your care. For all they knew, you could have contracted AIDS from Africa or even Armand, and passed it to their baby."

I couldn't have been more stunned if she had punched me. "What? They came to *that* conclusion because I came from Senegal? Or Ghana? Are you playing?"

"I'm serious, Lola. Be careful what you say to people. Don't tell them about your relationship with Armand. Americans are funny that way. You never know what they might be thinking. We know you. We've lived in Dakar, so we understand."

"Why didn't they say anything to me?"

"People are more likely to watch it than say anything."

In the silence that followed, what little reserve of energy that held me dissolved. Armand had served this country, and yet the very mention of him sent people into a racist paroxysm. Was that the future that lay ahead for Dele, my Black son? "I am tired. How could people be so prejudiced?" My despair had no place to go. "Why am I even asking? I'd gladly work for a Black family so I don't have to deal with this, but it's not as if I found one looking for a live-in babysitter. I've been in America for a year and am no closer to finding a job. It's, it's as if I'm stumbling through a dark maze. Each time, each bloody time I think I've found the way out, the light proves to be a mirage. Now people are rejecting me because of something I can't control? I am so bloody, damn tired." My body felt so heavy I didn't know what to do with it. I just wanted to sink down. "Have you ever wanted a cloud to lift you up into the skies? Or press you down into a grave? Because that's how I feel." My voice dropped to a whisper. "That's what I feel." I placed my palms on the table and laid down my cheek, my sorrow so hot it had dried up my tears and everything inside me.

"I'll finish cutting the onions." She wiped her hands and was about to pick up the cutting board when she stopped, her eyes scanning mine. "You haven't swallowed any pills, have you? You're not going to suddenly keel over or something, are you?"

I stared into space. The light blurred into tiny dots of red and gray chasing one another, the same pattern I saw when my eyes were closed.

"Lola? Ted, I need you!"

Ted strolled into the kitchen. I wondered how it was that he wore glasses similar to Dick's and yet looked cuddly while Dick's glance made me fumble and drop things.

"What's wrong?" he asked.

"Lola's depressed."

He looked at me and gave me a fatherly smile. "Aww, Lola. Come with me."

I didn't move. He pulled me up and I let him lead me into the dining room, with its wooden floors and rectangular area rug. Evenings at the table with Mama danced before me, painfully out of reach. A huge fault line had opened between my present life and my past. I wanted to hurtle down the fault; down, down, down until molten lava ate me into oblivion. Ted rested his elbows on the table, lacing his fingers together. I stared at the black hairs escaping from the wrist of his sweatshirt, the same color as Loveliness, the beast that had terrorized me.

"You're a brilliant girl, Lola. You have so much to offer. Heck, if I were in the market for an employee, I'd hire you at a glance." He looked at me thoughtfully. "You know, you could get a job in an embassy or something."

I didn't care. I wanted to swallow poison.

"You're the best chance for your son. No one will take care of him the way you would. Would you like him to live without a mother?"

My beautiful, happy Dele. It was unfair of Ted to bring him up but it worked. How could I leave him alone in the world? Who would be there when he woke up crying at night? That was the trap of motherhood. A love trap you couldn't, didn't want to free yourself from. I owed it to Dele to try. I reached out for the line Ted offered, and let him pull me to safety.

The next day, I called the French-speaking embassies in Washington to ask about vacant positions. If I were employed, they could authorize a visa for me, because I wouldn't be paid with American money. An embassy was like a little piece of that country, and I'd get a diplomatic visa. The embassy of Mali asked me to come in for an interview.

Leaving Dele with Mindy, who was on maternity leave, I took the metro to Washington. In the cold sunshine, I walked with the timidity of a trespasser, skulking along the walls of imposing buildings, my eyes straight ahead. When someone spoke to me, I jumped. If a man looked at me with admiration, my heart pounded with fear.

How I made an impression on the embassy remains a mystery, but they decided to try me for a month, after which they'd apply for a diplomatic visa for me. The first counselor, Monsieur Touré, explained in French, "We had a bilingual secretary who left a month ago. We're thinking of replacing her, but you know, it's not my decision. The ambassador is in Mali. When he returns, the final decision will be his."

"Merci beaucoup," I said, my eyes welling. The dream was still possible. I resolved to work so hard I'd become indispensable.

The only problem was the pay: seven hundred dollars a month. I could hardly afford to rent even a single room and pay for babysitting, compared with Dakar, where my six hundred dollars afforded me a studio apartment and a maid. How was I going to save? I had never appreciated my privilege in Dakar until now. In a country where graduate students hustled on streets for two years before getting a job, I had landed a relatively plush one because of my connections. Now I had quit the job and had nothing to go back to.

Mindy's baby was due in a couple of weeks, and she planned to return to work after four weeks. She made some calls, and help arrived in the form of Eugenia Hughes, an old British missionary with International Student Ministries, who drove from Virginia to see me. She regarded me with a kind face and twinkling brown eyes.

"Your hair is terrible!" was the first thing she said to me, but with the smile of a mother fussing over a daughter. "Are you a Christian?"

I knew what she meant. Was I a born-again Christian? Had I

spoken the oft-pronounced prayer: *Dear Jesus, I am a sinner, I am sorry for my sins. I am inviting you to come into my heart?* "No," I said. "I mean, I used to be a Christian, but now, I don't call myself one." In high school, I had whispered such a prayer, but had long since pushed out Jesus, assuming he had ever resided in my heart. The whole idea of Jesus as a resident in me seemed impossible.

"You *are* a Christian, then." Her feet were planted firmly on the hardwood floor. "Once you're God's child, you are always His, even if you go astray." She opened her hand and closed it in a fist.

Her words left me cracking my knuckles. Being labeled a Christian made me aware that I didn't resemble the church's idea of a child of God. I had welcomed a man between my legs, got pregnant without marriage. I had no intention of becoming anything other than what I was. I wanted to stay far away from this woman, but I couldn't afford to turn down her offer of help.

She studied me for a minute before speaking. "The International Student Fellowship is having an Easter Conference at Camp Joel in Pennsylvania this weekend. I'd like you to come with me. You'll meet all sorts of foreigners like yourself."

It became clear to me that this was the condition for her help. I hedged. "Doesn't it cost money? I can't afford to go."

She gave me a triumphant smile. "I already paid for you. You can bring your baby."

I had no choice but to say yes.

Late Friday afternoon, Eugenia Hughes nosed her car up a mountain road to a camp surrounded by trees. After settling in a dormitory with eight other women, we all trooped into the hall for a plenary session. A stout White man called Joe talked to us internationals about using deodorant, laughing as if he'd said something clever. I wondered if there was really any foreign student present who didn't know about deodorant. I shut my ears to the rest of his speech and looked around me. The audience comprised Asians, Africans, and a sprinkling of Caucasian students whose national origin I couldn't place. An Ethiopian man sitting next to me giggled. "I guess they want to make sure we know American ways." I giggled back.

After Mr. Joe had enumerated the virtues of living for Christ, he announced that we were going to be divided into small groups for workshops. I didn't care which group I joined. I couldn't feel God, but I felt at home in this international group where no one assumed I had been contaminated by a druggie carrying AIDS. Smiles flashed with nothing held back, no questions hidden behind them. I felt seen. I followed the Ethiopian and a couple of other Africans into a smaller room. I was about to slide into a chair when I froze.

I knew the workshop leader.

Those tight blond curls.

The kind smile from his blue eyes.

I could hardly hold myself still. The man from Virginia at the Dakar airport. The same man who bumped into me at the airport in New York, who gave me coins to call Daniel Roberts. He was standing before me. Rob. Rob Morrison. That was his name. As brief as our encounter had been, after he had left me to catch his flight, I felt as though I had lost a friend. Now here he was. Someone like Olga. Someone who knew my home. I wanted to rush across the room and grab his hand, but I held back, not wanting to draw attention to myself. Besides, what if he didn't remember me and I looked like an idiot?

He welcomed everyone. As he looked around the room, his eyes stopped on mine. I could see him struggling to remember, but then he moved on and delved into the treatise on faith. He spoke with such energy that I envied his belief in God. Somewhere along my journey, I had lost mine. As I listened, I felt myself cooling toward him. In Dakar, I had taken him for one of the expats doing some kind of NGO work. Now I could see he was probably a missionary, people I viewed with distrust. In high school history class, I had learned about how missionaries had softened up Africans and helped colonizers steal our land.

I watched him go on and on about living for God while I burned with questions. Afterward, I walked up to him, ready for a debate. He smiled uncertainly, his Bible under his arm. "We've met, haven't we?"

"The airport in Dakar," I said. "And in New York."

His caught his Bible as it slid down, "Oh my God! You're the pretty girl from JFK. Lola, right? Lola, you're safe!"

"Well. Yes. In a manner of speaking. So, you were a missionary in Dakar?"

He burst out laughing. "Trust me, I'm no missionary. I've never traveled outside to evangelize anybody. No, my church was involved in a housing development project over there, outside Dakar. I volunteered for a month. I come to this camp every year because I know how tough it is for foreigners. If faith can help the stranger in a foreign land, why not preach it? My God, I can't believe it, it's you!"

"You're an architect?"

"An accountant. I just love experiencing other cultures, I go abroad any chance I get. Africa is amazing. But you . . ." He shook his head in wonder. "What are the odds I'd find you here? I worried about you that night at JFK. You're not going to believe this, but after I'd raced all the way to my gate, I turned around and came looking for you."

I stared in disbelief. "You, you looked for me?"

He gave me a rascally smile. "Yeah, I missed my flight. It was a long way. What can I say? I was afraid for you. I even had you paged. When I couldn't find you, all I could do was pray. In the end, I had to trust God would take care of you. He did, obviously. You're here!"

I couldn't speak. In the city that Daniel said no one cared, this man had stopped to help a stranger and had even missed his flight. Or was it because he was a Christian? Then again, Jehovah's Witnesses had sheltered me, driven me all the way to Maryland in a snowstorm. Now here was this man with a cleft in his chin beaming at me. My God, how could such a beautiful man be a Jesus freak? I lifted my chin to him. "How do you know there's a God? How do you know there's a plan for our lives?"

He didn't flinch. "Don't ask me to prove to you that God exists. I can't. In every human being, that belief is born in the heart. You either believe it or you don't, it's that simple."

I had been prepared for an argument, not this honesty. No one had ever before admitted to an inability to prove God's existence. After all I'd endured, I had become numb to all things spiritual and given up praying like Mama always encouraged me to. Now I was full of questions and wasn't sure what to do with these new stirrings of vulnerability in me. "I don't think I'm good enough. You Jesus people are always going on about the evils of premarital sex. I don't regret it. To regret it is to regret my baby."

"Hold on. You have a baby?"

"You didn't realize I was pregnant? At the airport, I was nearly seven months pregnant."

He blinked, his mouth open. "Seven months? You didn't look it at all. You were so slim. You're still the same."

"Well, yes. And I'm not wedded, so I'm a fornicator. You said

God knew me before I was formed in my mother's womb. That goes for my son, right? So how can what I did to bring him into the world be wrong? Is he Satan's child? I can't even begin to count all the ways God would find me wanting."

He took my hand and looked at me for a while, as if he wanted to make sure he had my complete attention. "God loves you. Exactly as you are. It doesn't matter how others see you or how you got pregnant. His opinion is the only one that matters. He is perfect so that you don't have to be. You've got to trust that. You've got to trust Him again. Let me tell you, I question my faith all the time. If you knew the dark things in my heart, you'd be surprised."

I was transfixed, staring at him as if I were seeing him for the first time, the dark ring around his irises, the black flecks, the blond hairs on his veiny arm, the thick swell of his lower lip.

He squared his shoulders. "The thing is, perfection is false. I'm not perfect. I'm a sinner clinging to faith with all my muscles."

"It's hard sometimes," I whispered, feeling tears prickle my eyes.

"It sure is." He was still holding my hand and looking at me with intensity. Something was threatening to give way inside me. I needed to flee.

"Someone is waiting for me. I've got to go."

He smiled with regret. "Well, it was nice seeing you again. Perhaps we'll meet another time."

"Perhaps," I said, marching away. But something had unfastened within me. A puff of air could have lifted me above the trees, over the blue hills, into the sky. Faith had reentered my soul and stripped me of my burdens.

As Eugenia was driving us down from the mountain, I tried a

whispered prayer. I asked God to help me find a place to stay and a babysitter I could afford. We were pulling into Mindy and Ted's driveway when Eugenia said, "By the way, I forgot to tell you. A couple called Stuart and Molly Heineman have invited you and Dele to move in with them."

I turned to her, slowly. "Who are they?"

"A wonderful couple who live in Arlington. Simply wonderful. They have two adopted children, Josiah and Martha. Molly home-schools the kids, so she can babysit Dele while you work."

Unbelievably, a miracle had occurred. The tears broke free. "Thank you very, very much." I couldn't utter another word. The improbable had happened. God had anticipated the prayer of an imperfect person like me and answered before I had even asked. Until now, I had felt like a pebble on the beach, clinging to the sand as the tide washed over me and tried to drag me away. Now I felt steady. I knew I could keep holding on. I was about to begin a job at the Malian Embassy. I had a place to stay, with God's own people who would care for my baby. My dream of saving money to ultimately return home was alive! I wished Jesus was standing before me so I could fall on my knees and kiss his feet, wash them with my tears, and dry them with my hair the way the sinful Mary Magdalene did in the Bible. I turned to smile at Dele, whose chest rose and fell with sleep. His trust was a charge I had to keep.

Hwɛ Mu Dua

Measuring Stick

Molly Heineman radiated the warmth of freshly baked bread. Before Eugenia could introduce me, she'd taken me by the hand, her pink cheeks pushed high in a smile. "Hi, you must be Lola!"

Her husband, a bespectacled man with a friendly mustache, shook my hand and introduced himself as Stuart. With the exception of Olga's Barry, it seemed all the White men I had lived with so far wore glasses. Depending on the man, each pair gave him a different look. If Ted's kind eyes were magnified by his glasses, Stuart's displayed the countenance of a calm scholar.

Molly tried to present her children, eight-year-old Martha and six-year-old Josiah, but they were already crouched by Dele, asking to hold him. After Eugenia left, Molly led me up the green-carpeted stairs to show me my room, where a miniature crescent moon, surrounded by stars, glowed from the ceiling. When she switched on the light, the constellation disappeared to reveal a spacious room featuring a double bed, a dresser, and a large crib.

Our luggage deposited inside, we descended into the living room, which had matching green carpet and curtains.

"Where in Washington is your office?" Stuart asked in a strong, confident voice.

"At the Mali Embassy. Near Dupont Circle."

"Great. The metro is only a couple of blocks from here. I'll show you how to get there. What time do you get off work?"

"Five o'clock."

Molly said, "I guess you'll be home around six p.m. But he's a beautiful baby. Look at those eyelashes. Come on!"

Dele had a smile for her. Picking him up, Molly went to sit in the rocking chair and whispered things that made him touch her rosy cheeks and bouncy hair. I knew then that she would take good care of my baby. While he was taking a nap, she sat me down at the round kitchen table to go over the house rules.

"You have to get up early in the morning and get Dele dressed," she said, "so that I don't have to get up and get things for him."

"Okay," I said, surprised she'd tell me that. I found this frankness reassuring, a departure from Ghana, where we served soft words to guests only to grumble behind their backs.

"One thing I'll expect is that you clean up after yourself. If you use the kitchen and make a mess, you clean it up. Same as the bathroom. So, in general, you clean up after yourself. Otherwise," she added with an apologetic smile, "I am the one who has to do it." I resolved not to give her any added responsibility. "Now, I know from what Eugenia tells me that you've been through some trying times."

"Yes," I whispered. "It hasn't been easy." I hoped she wouldn't ask me any more questions.

"I don't envy you at all, and I wish we could do more to help.

We believe that the Lord gave us this house to share with others, but we can't have anyone live permanently with us." That made sense, but her words sparked anxiety in me. "We have people who visit us often and stay for short periods. In six weeks, we have a family of five coming to stay for a week. The room you're occupying is actually Martha's, but we figured we'd let you use it because the guest room is too small to put a crib in. So you can live with us for a month, but"—the apologetic smile again—"at the end of the month we'd like to have it back."

One month to find a place, something I hadn't expected. Here I was, thinking I had found a more stable situation that would give me space, about three months to figure things out. Now I had to worry again so soon. Those were questions I should have asked but didn't because I was so sure God had answered my prayers. After all this time in America, why didn't I know better? Still, I could tell these were good people who were doing the best they could. There was nothing I could do except agree.

"I'm sure we'll become close friends by the end of a month," she added with a laugh, "and then we won't want you to leave!" I didn't dare hope that would happen.

Eugenia had told me what a wonderful church the Heinemans attended, but she didn't think it would be a good church for an African. That had made little sense to me. If we were all one spiritual family, why did it matter that I was African? Surely we would have just one human culture where the common goal would be to love our neighbors as ourselves and do no harm to anyone? At any rate, that Wednesday, Molly said to me in a voice that brooked no refusal: "We're having a prayer meeting at the pastor's house, and we'd like you to come with us."

At the prayer meeting, a creamy-white population gravitated to my chocolate-chip self. Everyone wanted a taste of me. The redhead with green eyes fixed on me was the wife of a colonel.

"Where are you from?"

"Ghana."

"Oh, Guyana! I've heard of it!"

"It's Gha-na, not Gu-ya-na. Guyana is in South America."

She raised her brows, her smile waning. She shrugged as if it to say it hardly mattered, before turning to chirp at another woman, "Oh, hi! How *are* you?" I wished I were sipping something stronger than apple juice. For someone who was the wife of a colonel, it seemed incongruous that she wouldn't know that Ghana existed, that Ghana was a world-leading producer of cocoa, the same cocoa used to make the Hershey's Kisses that she tucked into her cheeks, or stirred into the hot chocolate she probably sipped. Then again, how often did foreigners make unfair and ignorant assumptions about Americans? I imagined myself in Ghana, defending America to those who didn't understand. Perhaps I would become an ambassador one day, I thought with a smile.

A pudgy, middle-aged man walked up to me, ice clinking in his glass. "Where did you learn to speak English?"

"In Ghana, West Africa." *Better add the continent from now on.*

"Don't they speak French in Africa?"

"No, Ghana is an English-speaking country."

"Oh, all right. But I mean, where did you *learn* to speak like that? I mean, where did you receive your education?"

"Oh, I attended university in Ghana."

His brows shot up. "Hum! I never would've thought that."

"Why?"

A faint pink colored his cheeks. "Well, you know, coming from Africa and all, you know . . ."

"I don't know," I said in a voice terser than I had intended. "I got all of my education from Ghana."

He threw his head back, laughing. "Oh well, what do I know? By the way, have you met Eric Green?" He pointed at a dark-haired guy passing drinks to a group of younger adults. "He's single, you know."

The singleness didn't interest me, but Eric seemed friendly, and the group presented a lively change from the older people interrogating me. I was walking toward them when someone tapped on my shoulder. I whirled around and almost dropped my apple juice. There he was, Rob, in jeans and T-shirt, looking younger.

"Hi, Lola." His eyes danced with mischief, a departure from the sober workshop leader. "Are you stalking me or something?"

"I don't believe it." I glanced around, pointing. "This is your church?"

"It sure is. What are you doing here?"

"Molly and Stuart brought me. I just moved in with them."

"The Heinemans? You're staying with them? They're good people. So, where's your baby?"

"Over there." I pointed to where Dele wiggled on Martha's lap, surrounded by five cooing little girls.

"Cute fellow," he said thoughtfully, folding his arms. I could tell he was circling around something he wanted to ask. Finally, he said, "I take it things didn't work out between you and his father. Was he the reason you came to America?"

"Yes," I said, tensing up.

"Well, he's a cad for letting you go." It was a statement, devoid of flirtation.

"I'm sorry, but I don't want to talk about him."

He grinned, his arms loose. "Fine by me! Do you want to sit by the fire?"

It was an April evening, quite chilly. We sat on a boulder, obscured by the singles chattering near us. I found myself babbling like a typical mother. I told him how Dele had turned one the month before.

"You had a party for him?"

"Sort of, if you can call it a party. I was in Maryland with my friends. They baked him a cake and we had a special dinner."

I was looking at the fire, the way it gave people an orange glow, but I could feel Rob studying me. When he spoke, it was with compassion. "I'm sorry things have been difficult. If there's anything you need at all, just let me know."

I turned to him. "You don't have a wife?"

He laughed as if it were an impossibility. "Oh no. I'm the leader of the singles group. Bachelor Rob, that's me. Hey, we're ice-skating this weekend. You want to come?"

Ice-skating? I had only watched figure skating on TV and couldn't fathom how they slid on those thin blades much less jump and land. Besides, there was Dele. "I don't know. It sounds dangerous and awfully cold. Don't they have to keep the place cold so that the ice doesn't melt?"

He was amused. "You're not used to the cold, huh? I thought it would be a great way for you to connect with the other singles, you know. We do a lot of activities together. You just put on your coat and some sweatpants and you'll be okay. I'll teach you how to skate. Once you get going, you'll warm up and forget the cold."

"Hmmm. What about Dele? The Heinemans take care of him during the week, so on weekends, I don't want to burden them."

"Bring him. We'll take care of him together, okay? Come on, Lolo, say yes!"

I stared at him. "Did you just call me Lolo? My best friend in Dakar, she called me Lolo when she wanted me to do something!"

"Well, what do you know? I just might replace her." He was smiling at me and I wondered why I hadn't noticed how white his teeth were until now. And his scent. He smelled of something woody and masculine. My body was reacting in a familiar, treacherous way. It was a relief when we were interrupted by Molly, accompanied by an Asian woman.

"There you are," Molly said. "I've been wanting you to meet someone."

"Hi, I'm Celestine," the woman said in an accent that told me she didn't grow up in America. She was so small that from far away she could have passed for a twelve-year-old. As she turned to greet Rob, Molly whispered that she was a deaconess. "The only female among the deacons. She's a single parent, just like you, but she's one of the most godly, respected women in the church."

"Are you Chinese?" I asked Celestine.

"No, I'm from the Philippines."

I had never met anyone from the Philippines and would have loved to find out more about her, but someone shouted, "Ate Celestine!"

"We'll talk later," she said with a smile, and drifted toward the voice, Molly in tow.

"I think I'd better go with Molly," I mumbled to Rob, and fled.

In the car back to the house, I found myself thinking of him, how weird it was I had met him at the airport in Dakar, then in

New York, then the retreat, and now here. He was not just physically close, he threatened to enter my essence. I shook him out of my mind and asked Molly about Eric Green, wondering why the pudgy man had mentioned him to me.

"Eric's such a nice guy," she said, "always helping people."

"Unfortunately, he suffers from epilepsy," Stuart said. Molly hushed him. I knew nothing about epilepsy except what I had read in a history book about the great Julius Caesar. I wondered why, of the guys present, that man had singled Eric out to me.

That night, I beat my pillows but found no rest. Rob's nearness crept into my mind. My body was alive with a kind of nervous energy that caused me to undulate like a serpent. I may have shut the door to emotional entanglements, but desire now charged my body. My finger probed my wetness until I shook and fell into satiated sleep.

The Saturday afternoon following the prayer meeting, Rob arrived to pick us up in a red Mustang with the top down, Molly and Stuart exchanging discreet smiles. He belted Dele into the backseat and opened the door for me. Dele and I were both bundled into winter jackets.

At the Fairfax Ice Arena, the other singles were already there, getting their skates on or rubbing their hands together or sipping hot chocolate.

"Hey, Lola," Eric Green said. "Hey, little man!"

"Hi," I said, wondering how they felt about me showing up with a child. I needn't have worried. They said hey, high-fived him, tickled him, rubbed his woolen cap. It was so easy to be around people my age who didn't ask where I got my education. They gripped their way to the rink and away they went. The relaxing flutes of music played and people glided in a circle, all following the same direction. There were kids, too, some holding their mother's or father's hand. Once in a while, a girl would break away into a corner and spin a little, not like the professionals but still wonderful to watch.

Rob took my elbow and led me to the counter. "We'd like to rent two pairs, please. One for her and one for me."

"What about Dele?" I asked.

"Sorry," the ponytailed girl behind the counter said, "we don't have skates for someone that little."

"Don't worry," Rob said. "I'll carry him, he'll be fine."

I was excited at the prospect of a new experience. Rob sat me on a bench and knelt at my feet. "We just have to keep the socks on." He helped me push my feet into the skates and laced them for me. It seemed intimate, sensual. "Are they too tight?" he asked, a worried expression on his face.

"No, they feel fine."

We had to put our sneakers in a pigeonhole. I thought how American I had become, already wearing the sneakers Molly had given me. He scooped up Dele with one hand and took me by the other.

"I've got you, I won't let you fall," he said, holding my hand and hoisting Dele up with his other arm. I took gripping steps until I got to the rail. Rob led me to where a man was giving first-timers a lesson. Nothing the man said made sense to me. He said to treat it like *in-line skating*, but I had no idea what that was. Eventually, he told us to push off, Rob telling me it was going to be okay. As long as he was holding my hand, I managed to stay upright, hunched forward, my other hand out like a blind woman grabbing at air. At some point, I got confident.

"I think I'd like to try without you holding my hand."

He gave me an appreciative grin. "All right!" As soon as he let go, I landed on my bottom. The ice was hard. Cold. He reached out and pulled me up. I tried to glide away again only to hit the ice once more.

"Listen," I said. "Just lead me to the rail and I'll be fine. You skate with Dele."

I gripped the rail and crept around the rink like a toddler learning to walk. Everyone flew past me, gliding, twisting, spinning to the music. Dele perched on Rob's shoulders, laughing maniacally, Rob waving and smiling at me. Later, we stood around the rink sipping hot chocolate, the sweetness warming me. As I watched Rob wipe Dele's smudged face, it became obvious that he wanted more than friendship, and Dele enjoyed him. More than Dele's need was my own softening feelings toward this well-traveled, educated man who caused me wet nights. But what was the point? I didn't want to live permanently in America.

Living with the Heinemans was like getting rid of something pressing on my chest. When Martha saw me use a cloth to tie Dele on my back, she asked, "Could you teach me how to do that?" She took to carrying him on her back while she did her chores. Dele often scurried into Josiah's room and upset his trains, but Josiah just laughed with indulgence. He and his sister pulled Dele around the neighborhood in a red wagon. Each day after I returned from work, they shared stories about the wonderful things they had done with him, like taking him to McDonald's, where he'd stuffed his face with fries and smeared ketchup on his cheeks. Or taking him to the playground where he shrieked with joy while going down the slide. Even when I was at home, Dele often sat on Molly's lap and his face would light up as she taught him to play "patty-cake." I was so thankful for this wonderful family's devotion, and I showed it by helping to clean and cook, Molly bravely tackling her shrimp when, unaware that shrimp in America was usually peeled, I had fried them in their shells à l'Africaine.

Sundays, we drove to church, where we congregated in the cafeteria of an elementary school. Tables got pushed to one side. Young men in shirts and ties arranged the plastic chairs with chrome legs into makeshift pews. Children raced about the wide hall: girls in pretty frocks and delicate bows, boys with clip-on ties, daddy replicas. Rob would corner me for a chat that was getting increasingly difficult to shorten. He'd hold my hand, help me with Dele's diaper bag, and sit behind me at church, since I always sat with the Heinemans. After church, the Heinemans and I would go out to lunch, followed by a walk around the neighborhood, people staring at this odd family: a White couple with two Southeast Asian children, a Black woman pushing a laughing or sleeping baby in an umbrella stroller. Nights, my fingers would please my open body and I would sink into deepest slumber, spared from contemplating my impending move.

At the end of my one-month trial period, the ambassador from Mali returned to Washington to determine my fate. After a brief executive meeting, Mr. Touré, the first counselor, who had hired me, called me into his office. He sat behind his mahogany desk with neat rows of papers stacked on it.

"Bonjour, mademoiselle," he said with unusual courtesy. "Sit down."

I sat in the chair facing his desk so that I looked directly into his eyes, admiring his smooth face, the chiseled body under his suit that belied his forty years.

"Comment allez-vous, mademoiselle?"

"Je vais bien, merci."

"Et votre fils, il va bien?"

"Oui, monsieur." Why was he being so solicitous, even asking about my son when normally he seldom nodded at me?

"I'm sorry, I have some bad news for you."

Oh no. I waited, my stomach roiling.

He shuffled papers, cleared his throat. "The ambassador has decided that it will be too much trouble to apply for a diplomatic visa for you." His eyes held mine, pausing for my reaction. I gave him none. Shifting his eyes, he put the papers down and interlaced his manicured fingers. I noted how the pearly nails contrasted with his coffee skin. "What I'm trying to say is that since we can't obtain a visa for you, we can't allow you to continue without a work permit."

Can't, can't, can't.

The chair squeaked under his shifting weight. "You may not believe it, but I really feel for you. You're an African daughter, and I know you have a child to raise. But this is the ambassador's decision."

"That's all right. I understand." I didn't.

"I really wish you the best of luck." His voice was ever so gentle. I wanted to tell him to stop pretending he cared, tell him he was just laying the guilt on the ambassador because he didn't have the guts to fight for me. *I need this job, you heartless man!* My brain said it wasn't his fault but my heart beat the drums of anger.

He picked up a white envelope that held my paycheck and held it out to me. The envelope weighed a pound in my hand. I rose on noodle legs and wobbled down the narrow wooden steps to break the news to Mouna from Mali, the other secretary who worked with me.

"That's not fair!" She slapped her desk. "I can't do all the work by myself! How could they do this?" She pecked furiously at her typewriter, threatening to resign, but I knew she wouldn't. An irregular immigrant herself, she could no more resign than refuse to eat.

A Ghanaian proverb says: If you have something to tell God, tell the wind. I wanted to scream at the wind and say, How could you do this to me? What kind of love is this? I thought about the day a woman from Sierra Leone wandered into the embassy seeking shelter. She had a fifteen-year-old son in tow. Their skin was grimy, their clothes torn. With the complicity of the security guard, Mouna and I had allowed them to sleep inside the embassy that night. In the morning, when we found the teenager, I recoiled. He lay folded up into a frog on the floor beside the toilet bowl, sucking his thumb, his eyes closed. A fifteen-year-old boy sucking his thumb on a bathroom floor. What hardship had turned him into an animal? Was his mother a woman like me when she arrived in America, full of hope for a great future for her son? *No! No!* I vowed. It would not happen to Dele.

I was jobless. I had seven hundred dollars to my name. The Heinemans expected me to move out of their home within a week. Although we'd become close as Molly had predicted, I had to respect the terms she had given me. That night after dinner, while she rinsed the dirty plates and I stacked them in the dishwasher, I told her about losing my job. The plate she was rinsing clattered into the sink. "Oh no, Lola! What are you going to do?"

"I don't know, but I'm sure I'll find something. See, I've come to understand that life offers no certainties. Wealth is not the measuring stick for goodness. I used to think if you believed in God, nothing bad would happen to you. That's not true. If it were, hunger wouldn't bite anyone's stomach. Innocent people wouldn't get blown up in wars. No one would rot with cancer. I'm young and don't know enough, but I think what God gives is strength to fight, or maybe fighting is all we have. I'll fight, never give up."

Molly's eyes grew misty. Her hands went up and down as if she didn't know what to do with them. She wrapped her arms around me, holding her wet hands away from my blouse.

PART TWO

✕✕✕✕

Bese Saka

Sack of Kola Nuts

Celestine seemed to be waiting for something from me beyond my initial hello. Here was this Filipina deaconess from church whom I had longed to know, and yet, now that I was alone with her, I couldn't say a word. All I could think of was how long before I'd have to move. I had rented a room from a woman who tended a bar, who spent days lying around drinking and smoking while her kids howled, whose husband was in jail for trying to sell cocaine to an undercover policeman, who kicked me out after one month when I couldn't make the rent. Then I showed up for church and Celestine offered me her basement. Apparently, Molly had discussed my situation with her.

"Let me show you around," she said with an energetic smile.

I followed her, Dele holding my hand. Celestine's hardwood floors and well-used furniture reminded me of my mother's childhood home in Bonsu, a small, leafy town. When I saw the basement, which included two bedrooms, a living room furnished with a flowered green couch with matching love seat, and a small television, I broke into a big smile.

"Thank you so much," I said. "I think we'll need just one bedroom. I don't want Dele to wake up scared in a new house."

"That's okay."

In the morning, we breakfasted in the dining room upstairs overlooking a huge backyard with lush grass. The only sounds came from birds chirping in the trees beyond the lawn and the rustle of wind through the leaves. The large windows made me feel as if I were one with the butterflies. Dele and I would love throwing stones into the small stream that snaked under shrubs.

I liked everything about Celestine, from her small face, slanted eyes, round nose, and short, fringed hair to her cinnamon skin. Everything about her was doll-like. She sat at the head of the table, sipping coffee from her steaming mug, telling me how cute Dele was, when I wanted to tell her how cute she was. Dele was strapped in his high chair, making a mess of his oatmeal because he'd slapped my hand away from his spoon. Thank God for the newspaper Celestine had thought to spread under his high chair.

"I know you've had a lot of trials, but don't lose hope," she said.

"It's the moving which troubles me," I whispered in a cracked voice.

"You can live here until you get a job and can support yourself." I studied her face and realized she meant every word. "And call me Ate Celestine. That is how it's done in the Philippines. I'm old enough to be your mother, so you call me Ate, a mark of respect. This way, it establishes a relationship between us, like you are my niece, family." In America, I had become accustomed to calling older people by their first names, but Celestine showed me that there were elements in our native cultures we needed to keep.

I tried it out, rolling it around my tongue like toffee. "Ate Celestine."

She told me how, as a young woman, she'd left the Philippines with her son rather than stay in an unhealthy marriage. First, she'd moved to the island of Guam and put herself through college. Then she moved to mainland America. Now her only son had graduated from Yale and was living with his own family in Oregon. If I chose to remain in America, that could be Dele one day. She attributed her success to her faith in God. She had helped bring her parents and most of her siblings to America. She had never remarried and had no regrets. I marveled. Had she remained celibate all these years, considering she was now about fifty?

"Do you mind if I ask you a rather personal question?"

"Go ahead. Ask me anything you want." She was smiling with indulgence, her teeth short and white, a teeny gap between the two front teeth.

"I know that, according to the Bible, you're not supposed to have sex outside marriage. How do you cope with that?"

Her face didn't alter. "You want to know how I do without sex?"

"Yes."

"Well, I don't watch programs on TV that will arouse me. I try to nourish my mind with good things like *Wheel of Fortune* and *Jeopardy* and the Bible." It made sense. Even so, she had to feel a tingling under her nightgown sometimes? I wanted to ask her if she touched herself at night and whether she would consider that a sin, but I decided not to. The truth was that I missed sexual moments. The burning attraction. The hot tip of a penis against my slippery labia, pushing them apart. The slow entry, the urgent friction until relief. Sex was a necessary meal. I regarded her purity with awe. At any rate, if a single parent like her could succeed in

America, I stood a chance of getting a job and reaching my goal. Sex would have to wait.

Monday, she babysat Dele while I went to Washington to place my résumé with various embassies. I picked only those within walking distance of metro stations. I had just left the embassy of Côte d'Ivoire and had almost reached the sidewalk when I heard fast steps closing in on me and a man's voice calling, "Mademoiselle! Mademoiselle!" I turned around to find a man in a white shirt and tie striding toward me.

"Oui?" I said, shading my eyes with my hand.

When he drew closer, he looked at the street and the cars, as though unsure what to say. At length, he said, "Ça va?"

"Ça va bien. Did I leave something behind?"

"No. I just wanted to . . . say hello . . . make your acquaintance."

"Oh, okay."

"I'm Jacques. What's your name?"

"Lola."

"Enchanté, Lola. Where are you from? I'm Beninois."

"I'm Ghanaian. I thought you were Ivorian."

"No, I just work here."

"Oh, that's wonderful!" Benin was only an hour and a half's drive from Ghana's eastern border. Our people shared ethnic groups. We spoke the same cultural language. Now we were both an ocean away from home. Under normal circumstances, I would extricate myself politely and walk away, but a rare meeting with someone from my part of the world had created an immediate sense of kinship. I lingered, smiling up at him. "Well, I just dropped my résumé. I'm looking for a job."

"I noticed that. I don't think there are any vacancies here, but I've got a friend from Mali. Her name is Fanta. She works at the embassy of the Central African Republic. I think she's about to quit her job to do her masters. If you like, I can introduce you to her. It's okay with you?"

"Oh yes, please. Thank you!"

"Okay. I can drive you now. I'm on my lunch break."

It was so much like Dakar, men dropping everything to play the gallant. "Super, thank you so much!"

We walked to his car, a white Toyota Corolla parked on the curb. He opened the door for me before sliding into the driver's seat. A white cross swayed from the rosary looped on the rearview mirror. I could see his shoulder muscle moving beneath his shirt, and I loved the powerful way he shifted gears. Oh God, here was another man, too, causing my skin to prickle.

"So, what's a Beninois doing at the Côte d'Ivoire embassy?" I asked.

"I was like you," he said with a glance at the rearview mirror. "I was looking for a job and they hired me. I've only been in America for two years."

Two years in America and he had a car. Wonderful. I could do it too.

He maneuvered the car through a series of one-way streets until we pulled onto a quiet street near Dupont Circle. I was surprised to see the Malian Embassy on the adjacent street, its flag flapping. I tried to still my heart as we entered the white town house with lime-green shutters. At the large reception, a man with protruding eyes stopped typing and greeted us.

"We're here to see Fanta," Jacques said.

The man indicated a couch, told us to sit down, and picked up the phone. After that, his fingers raced over the keyboard as he squinted at the screen of a desktop computer. Soon a clatter of black pumps made its way down the stairs, expanding to reveal a plump girl with a big smile.

"Jacques!" She kissed him on both cheeks. "What's up with you? It's been a long time."

"Not much," Jacques said. "This is my friend Lola. She's looking for a job, so I wanted her to meet you, since you said you might be leaving. Lola, this is Fanta."

She glanced at the man behind the desk. His fingers had stopped pecking on the keyboard and he was staring. "Let's step outside."

She closed the big door behind us and we made our way to Jacques's car. She leaned her back against it, Jacques and I facing her. "You have experience as a secretary?"

"Yes," I said, admiring her inch-high, unpermed hair. "I worked for the embassy of Mali."

She smiled with satisfaction. "That's very good. Francophone embassies are all the same. If you've worked at one, you can work at another. It's true that I'm leaving to do my masters at Georgetown."

"This is great!" Jacques said. "She can apply, no?"

My armpits prickled with excitement. Fanta waved her hands at me. "You don't have to. I'll recommend you. The ambassador trusts me. Just today, he was grumbling about my leaving him without a replacement."

I wanted to dance right there on the sidewalk. "Thank you, thank you so much, both of you!"

"It's nothing," she said with a flick of her wrist. "You're my African sister. Besides, Georgetown is too far from here. I can get a job over there if I need to make extra money."

My eyes filled with tears. "This is unbelievably kind. You have no idea what you've done. I don't even know what to say."

She gave me a reassuring smile. "Don't mention it. Mind you, the embassy doesn't pay that well, and you have to deal with diplomats and their ego. Not to mention the wives who call you to find out if their husbands truly had that reception last night and why they weren't invited. But if you can hang in there for a year, you can apply for a job at the World Bank or the IMF. They are the two organizations that can hire you without a green card."

I squealed. World Bank? IMF? Jacques was grinning at me, looking proud.

Fanta asked me to return the next day to meet the ambassador. I hugged them both and even kissed Jacques on the cheek. I couldn't wait to share the news with Ate Celestine. Fanta said the metro was just a block and a half away, which was the same Dupont Circle station I had used when I worked at the Malian Embassy. Jacques offered to drop me, but I wanted to walk. I said bye to them and sauntered off with the confidence of the soon-to-be-employed. Wasn't life just wonderful? See what happened when one didn't give up? I waved at my reflection in the glass windows, smiled at the hot dog vendor, smiled at a man entering Bagel House, skipped down the escalator, and hummed to myself as the train rocked me to the Pentagon, where I hopped on a bus for Fairfax.

Ate Celestine was thrilled. "What are you going to wear? Praise the Lord!"

I asked her not to tell Molly, just in case something changed.

The next day, I wore my best dress, a tailored sea-green with white polka dots. The receptionist called Fanta and she clattered down to get me. We mounted a flight of stairs, turning right into a narrow walkway. She pointed to an open office at the end and said, "That will be your office. Only you and the ambassador will share this floor. The rest of the staff is upstairs on the floor above." An office of my own! I tingled with excitement, praying to impress the ambassador. We stopped at a dark carved door to our left and she rapped with her knuckles, my heart thumping.

"Entrez," an authoritative male voice said.

We entered an office bigger than Ate Celestine's living room. It had cathedral high ceilings, red carpeting, a large mahogany desk, a leather couch, and velvet floor-to-ceiling drapes the color of curry. Behind the desk sat the ambassador, an elegant gentleman graying at the temples, flanked on either side by the U.S. flag and the Central African Republic flag.

Fanta said, "Excellence, j'ai l'honneur de vous présenter Mademoiselle Lola Oduro."

His Excellency nodded for us to sit down as he studied me with expectant eyes. Fanta reminded him of their previous conversation. She said she knew me and wanted to ensure he was in good hands after her departure. "She has worked at the Thai Embassy in Dakar and also the Malian Embassy right here."

He leaned back in his chair, speaking in the soft tones of a refined man. "How long have you been in America?"

"About a year and half," I said.

He beamed. "Mais vous parlez très bien le français, j'en suis ravi."

I was delighted too, I said, and ready to do my utmost for him.

"Mais c'est fantastique. We don't need to search for a new executive assistant." He leaned forward, his hands on the table. "You will start at the beginning of next month, d'accord?"

"Merci beaucoup, Excellence," I said, trying to contain myself.

When we closed the door behind us, I clenched both fists in glee, eyes closed. My cheeks hurt from smiling. I threw my arms around Fanta. "Merci, merci, merci!"

She laughed with pleasure. "It's nothing." As we were going down the stairs, she said with a naughty smile, "You know, Jacques likes you. He told me. He wants to go out with you, but he's too shy to ask you himself."

I sighed. "I'm sorry, I don't want to go out with anybody. I'm just not ready for the whole falling-in-love thing."

Understanding shone in her eyes. "I can imagine. You don't have to be his girl, you know. You could have him as a friend. This is a tough city, and it's nice to have a friend."

"I suppose you're right," I said, smiling. "I mean, he helped me get a job."

"There you go."

It was such a relief to laugh, something I hadn't been doing much of lately.

At home, Dele grabbed my legs and tried to climb me. I scooped him up, squealing to Ate Celestine, "I got the job!"

She clasped her hands together. Maternal pride shone in her face. "Praise the Lord! See, God always takes care of His own."

Molly whooped on the phone. "This is fantastic! You need a lot of professional clothes. The First Baptist Church of Clarendon has a clothing drive every Saturday. They get some really nice stuff, lots of rich people donate to them. Most of the clothes are practically new. I'll take you."

That Saturday, she picked me up to search for clothes. I felt glamorous in my new dress suits, skirts, and blazers. I even found pretty but practical shoes to match my outfits. Later that afternoon, Olga picked me up from the Shady Grove metro station in Maryland, laughing and crying at the same time. "Lola, pussycat, you got a job. I'm over the moon!"

We gathered at Olga's house: Dele and I, Mindy with her kids, and Olga with hers. It was an evening of clinking wineglasses, raucous laughter, and children falling asleep on couches or wherever space was available. By the end of the evening, we adults had converged at the kitchen table, our tongues loose.

Mindy, her newborn asleep on her lap, raised a glass, "To Lola, the biggest survivor!"

"Hear, hear!" said Olga, squeezing my arm.

"Here we are," I said, "Dakar right here in America. I could use a nap on the sand right now."

"Or swimming braless on the beach!" Olga said. "Let's plan a trip back soon, eh?" She reached for another bottle of Bordeaux, refilled our glasses, and raised hers, her eyes flashing. "To your no longer being illegal, free to fly in and out of the country!"

"Yes." I gulped my wine. "Can you believe it? The embassy is getting me an A2 diplomatic visa."

"Isn't that something?" Mindy said. "How much are they going to pay you?"

"One thousand dollars a month."

They exchanged cautionary looks. Olga said, "That's kind of low, isn't it?"

I laughed. "Hey, it's the most I've ever earned since stepping on American soil. Now, if someone asks me, 'What do you do?' I'll be able to lift my chin and say, 'I'm the interpreter and executive assistant to His Excellency Extraordinary and Plenipotentiary Ambassador of the Central African Republic.'"

Mindy howled with laughter. "Extraordinary and Plenipotentiary, that's something!".

I tilted my head at her. "I work, therefore I am."

"It's about time you got laid, extraordinarily and plentypotently!" That was from Olga, her eyes mad with mischief.

I put my glass down. "Olga, I'm not ready."

"Come on, don't give me that. It's been well over a year now since you came to America. Time to fuck your brains out."

"Olga's got a point," Mindy said.

"Can we stop talking about this? As I said, I'm not ready for emotional entanglements."

Olga reached for her packet of cigarettes, looked at Mindy's baby, and laid it down. "You're just scared of being hurt. Besides, what's there to be ready for? Sex is food for the body, and you're starving."

I smiled wickedly. "Well, I'm not completely starving, I help myself at night. It's not the best, I know, but it will have to do for now."

"You know, you could join the choir or something," Mindy said. "Get to know some hot tenor."

I snorted. "The choir? We don't even have one. We have a band with five people." I didn't mention Rob because I knew they would jump all over that and not let it go. "Look, can we stop talking about this?" I pointed at Olga. "Last I heard, you weren't doing so well yourself."

"Says who? Have you forgotten my date with Len George?"

My eyes grew wide. "You didn't!"

"I fucking did. And let me tell you, that man can fuck. No kinky stuff. Just straight, honest-to-goodness fucking." She laughed deliciously, rolling her eyes in her head.

Mindy patted my arm. "You just concentrate on the Extraordinary and Plenipotentiary while we get it on."

We were supposed to be celebrating and now I was being reminded of what was missing in my life. Perhaps Olga was right. It was easier for me to shut the door to romance than risk being hurt. I needed to learn to trust again. She reached for the bottle and refilled her glass. "Don't feel bad, Lola. You know, there's something to be said for not sleeping with just anybody. If you think about it, any man you fuck could be the father of your baby. Ugh."

"I'll say," Mindy said.

Olga lifted her glass, a naughty gleam in her eyes. "Here's to being horny."

Mindy's baby uttered a cry. She bent down and kissed her. "I love you, baby, oh I do, I do, I do!"

I shot up with my glass, a sudden burst of energy in my limbs. "And I love life. I do, I do, I do!"

Olga pinched my breast. "Like I said, it's time you fucked someone."

"Olga!"

My dear Mama,

I know it has been a long time since I wrote. Please forgive me. How are you? How is Awurama and the family? I hope all is well.

Things have not been easy here. I've had to move a lot, and getting a job has been a challenge. But now, I'm happy to tell you I'm the personal assistant, or as they call it here, the executive assistant, to the ambassador of the Central African Republic. You'll also be happy to know I've found myself a church. I am living with Ate Celestine, who is like family. She's from the Philippines, so "Ate" is the equivalent of "Auntie." I also have Molly and her family who invite me to dinners. So, you see, I'm not alone. Still, I miss you very much.

When I receive my paycheck, I will send you some

money. I know you don't need anything from me, but I haven't forgotten our tradition. I want to give you my first paycheck of one thousand dollars, a token of my gratitude to you for raising me to be the woman I am today.

Your loving daughter,
Akua

May 14, 1999

My dear Akua,

    Thank you for your long-awaited letter which was not dated, as usual. Perhaps you do that so that I will not know how long it takes you to write. That way you can blame the post for taking too long.

    I am happy you have now found employment, but I see that you are not doing well financially. Don't send me any money. You earn only one thousand dollars a month? I'm not so ignorant that I don't know it's next to nothing in that country. It's a pity you didn't listen to me before you got yourself pregnant and ran off to America. Now look at you with your miserable thousand dollars a month. I suppose it's better than nothing.

    I'm glad you have found a church that is like a family. It's odd to think of it that way because here, we go to church, do Bible studies, and the once-a-year or so church picnic or harvest. But family remains family. Family is like the back of your teeth, that's what you lick. If you don't like the taste, you brush it.

I pray for God's protection over you. If all else has failed, you can always humble yourself and come home. It won't be easy, but eventually people will forget.

Your loving mother,
S. D.

I had wanted my mother to be proud that I had a respectable job, instead I felt mocked. A thousand dollars wasn't much, but it was my sack of kola nuts, worth its weight in ancient times. But that was okay, I vowed to myself. I would prove to her that I was right to remain in America. When I returned home in triumph, with enough money for a home and a car of my own, everyone would respect me. *She* would respect me.

Nsoroma

Children of the Sky

Sunday, standing between Ate Celestine and Molly, I joined in singing, clapping and swaying to the songs as the band led us. I was uncomfortable with the hand-waving thing, but I made up for it with enthusiastic belting of "Our God Reigns." After praise and worship, Pastor Drake mounted the pulpit. He was tall, tall, tall, with a nose so fine I was sure it could slice bread. With graying blond hair that fell over his shoulders, he resembled an aging White Jesus.

Words of exhortation flew out of his mustached mouth. "I don't preach pretty sermons, folks. I'm not here to tickle your ears. I'm here to tell you hard truths. You're the sheep, and the sheep's job is to eat when the shepherd leads you to pasture, which is what I do. I provide the pasture, you eat. Yes, I'm not here to tickle your ears, folks, because hell sure isn't a picnic." He cast his eyes around the congregation, and I imagined they lingered longer on my face. Something in me revolted against the thought of me as a sheep guided by a shepherd. The disparity in assigned intelligence made me squirm. "Now, some of you are still drinking formula from bottles like babies, when you should be eating solid food."

Glancing around my spiritual brethren, I concluded I was that newborn on formula.

"The Lord is good indeed, even when we're not. I'm going to give you a few minutes. If you have a testimony to share, now is your chance." He paused, an expectant smile on his face.

Ate Celestine nudged me. "Aren't you going to share about your job?"

"No," I hissed. "I don't want people staring at me."

Her hand shot up.

"Yes, my sister?" Pastor Drake said.

She rose to her feet, beaming at me before turning to him. "I just want to thank the Lord. Lola got a job with the embassy of the Central African Republic."

Someone shouted, "Hallelujah!" A chorus of Amens, Glorys, and Congratulatons! followed, accompanied by smiles and buzz words like *Thanks be to God* and *God is great!* I gave them a weak smile, wishing they would stop looking at me.

"It's indeed good news, Lola," Pastor Drake said. He beamed at the congregation. "You see what happens when you turn your life around? Beloved, it's not easy to be a single parent. God never intended for us to be single. He said it's not good for man to be alone, that's why he created woman to be his helpmate. We're grateful that the Lord has provided for our beloved Lola. God is a husband to the husbandless and father to the fatherless. Now, I want you all to stand up and thank God for the mate God gave you."

People shared testimonies, quoting confidently from the Bible:

Isaiah 44, verses 9 to 12, says . . . Ezekiel tells us . . . In the book of Micah, chapter . . . For the hundredth time, I stared, dumbfounded. These people were so spiritual. It wasn't as if those spouting off scriptures were just old people. There was Paige, barely twenty-five, scriptures rolling off her tongue like her daily language, her even teeth sparkling with goodness. She balanced a chubby baby in her arms while her lean, muscular husband leaned over her with devotion. He could have passed for a film star the way he chewed gum and his black hair rippled over his white collar. Her older sister, too, recited scriptures as she leaned against her stocky blond husband. These were the building blocks of Christ's church: the young, newly married couples who rubbed each other's back during the sermon, and the middle-aged couples who still held hands. I was the only single parent. Ate Celestine didn't count since her child was an adult and long gone from home. Plus, she was a deaconess, therefore removed from judgment.

After the testimonies, Pastor Drake said, "Brother Benjamin, will you pray for the offering we are about to receive?" I followed his gaze to a big, tall man, one half of the only Black couple I'd seen in the church. He took his time gathering his long legs and rising to his feet, as if nothing was ever a bother. His wife, a tiny, fair-skinned woman who looked more like his daughter, gazed up at him with adoration. When he uttered, "Let's pray," I was astounded by his velvety bass voice, a voice I could have listened to forever. "Father, thank you for blessing us and allowing us the privilege to give. May we always be thankful. Amen."

Pastor Drake said, "That's Benjamin for you, a man of few words. But he's deep. Very deep."

Someone behind me whispered, "Such a beautiful, godly family."

The statement bothered me, but I couldn't figure out what

it was. As I walked out of the hall toward the toddler Sunday school class, Rob shouted from behind me, "Hold up, Lola! Are you going to pick up Dele?"

I gave him a reserved smile. "Yes, I'd better get him before he runs off on his own."

"I'll come with you."

It puzzled me that he was so persistent. He was easily the most handsome man in the singles group: tall and muscular, with his unusually tight blond curls. I had seen the single girls give him encouraging smiles and chat him up. And yet he sought me out all the time to join their activities. He served me barbecued chicken and fed Dele, who loved to sit on his lap and touch his face. However, I had never accepted invitations to dine alone with him.

The back of my head felt heavy with the weight of the eyes on us as we wove our way through the corridor, waves of conversations dying before us and rising again after us. Rob never seemed to notice.

"How old is Dele now?"

"Eighteen months."

"I love hanging out with him," he said quietly, taking my hand. "So, what is it, Lola? Why won't you go out with me?"

"Listen, I have to get Dele. I can't do this right now."

He followed me. We walked into a din of children banging toys, squealing, teachers shouting for them to remain inside. Dele was chasing a boy who looked at least a year older than he, laughing so hard he was drooling. The last-born of the Black family, his mouth was rectangular with fear, his eyes wide open.

"Stop, Dele," I said. "Stop! The poor boy."

Rob chuckled. "That's Harry, he's shy. Probably doesn't know what to make of this hyper kid determined to play with him."

He placed himself in Dele's path and caught him, tossing him into the air. "Hey, kiddo!"

Dele cackled and promptly forgot his friend, who flew into his mother's arms. When Rob put him down, Dele grabbed at the air, shouting, "Up! Up!" Rob laughed and tossed him in the air again. As soon as Rob put him down, Dele begged to be tossed up again. Rob obliged, then hoisted him onto his shoulder. As usual, Dele became riveted with the blond curls and proceeded to sift them through his fingers. Harry, seeing us advance, gripped his mother's hand.

"Have you met Penelope Washington?" Rob asked.

"Not formally. Hello, Mrs. Washington."

"Hello, Lola," she said in a low, melodious voice. "Please, call me Penelope." I wondered if she had ever expressed anger in her life. With her frock gathered at her tiny waist and a bow in her hair, she was a walking daisy. "Actually, I've been meaning to talk to you. Benjamin and I have been talking. We want to invite you to our home one of these days. Will next Saturday do?"

I placed my hand on my chest, surprised. "You want to invite me into your home?"

"Yes, we'd like that very much."

"Yes," I said, stammering. "Saturday will be fine."

"Wonderful. I can't wait to have you. Take care now."

As we watched her disappear into the hallway clutching her son's hand, Rob said, "Such a nice woman, isn't she? A truly godly family."

That word again, *godly*. Everyone in the church seemed godly to me, so why did people single out the Washingtons?

When we walked outside to the parking lot, an older couple turned around to smile at us, the man pointing and chuckling at Dele bouncing on Rob's shoulders. I had never seen them before.

"Hi, Lola," the woman said, her round cheeks dimpling.

"Hi, Mom," Rob said.

I looked from Rob to them. The woman sported the same tight curls as her son, but the blond color came from his father. The latter waved, then held the door open for his wife. She heaved herself in before he walked around and slid in beside her. I was surprised they didn't give me a second look before pulling away.

"They've been in California settling my grandfather's estate, that's why you've never met them. So, you're going home with Ate Celestine?" Rob asked.

"Yes."

The shadow of disappointment darkened his face. "I'd have loved to drive you home." Then he brightened up. "Congratulations on your job, by the way. Wow. In DC, eh?"

"Yes, thanks."

"So how are you going to get to work?"

"Ate Celestine says I can ride with her to Washington. We found a babysitter not too far out of the way. I can't ride back with her, though. She closes at five while the embassy locks up at four p.m. But we checked the bus routes from the babysitter's, so I'm going to be fine."

A smile tugged at his lips. "I could help, you know. I told you, I work for the federal government. I've got flex hours, so I can get off at three thirty and pick you up. Then we can get Dele from the sitter."

"You will do that?"

"Yeah. This way, I get to spend more time with you." His voice was soft and teasing. "There may be days when I have a meeting or something, in which case, I'll arrange it with the single guys. Believe me, someone will always pick you up."

For a moment, I didn't know what to say except blink at this man who seemed to be everywhere in my life. "Why are you so unbelievably kind to me?"

His eyes twinkled. "What man would miss an opportunity to spend time with a beautiful . . . why are you looking at me like that?"

I shook my head quickly. "It's nothing." It wasn't nothing. I'd had a sudden urge to flatten myself against him right there in church, rub my face in his shirt and smell him. His smile lingered on me for a little longer and I found my cheeks heating up. "Thank you very much," I said, and pushed out of the door. He followed, Dele still on his shoulders.

Ate Celestine stood a short distance away by her car, chatting with Molly, obviously waiting for me. I held my arms up to Dele. "Come down, darling."

"Nooo! Nooo!" He wrapped his arms around Rob's neck. Rob chuckled and tried to pry Dele's arms away. Dele locked his legs together, throwing himself backward. "NO!" When Rob managed to wrestle him down, Dele rushed at me, his hurt as deep as if someone had gutted him.

Rob squatted, cooing, "Don't cry, buddy, it's okay." But Dele continued to howl. Rob turned to me. "Why don't I put him in his car seat?"

It was useless to argue. Dele's howls had attracted curious looks from people and I knew they'd soon converge on me, asking questions. As soon as Rob picked him up, Dele gave me a triumphant smile, his head in the space between Rob's jaw and shoulder.

"What's the matter?" Ate Celestine asked when we got to the car.

"He won't let Rob put him down," I said, my face heavy with embarrassment.

Molly gurgled at Rob, "I guess you've got yourself a little man."

They laughed. My ears were hot and I wanted Rob gone. Dele clapped his hands as Rob belted him into the car seat.

"Thank you," I said in a gruff voice.

"My pleasure. Bye, buddy!"

"Bye!" Dele said, his little hand waving.

Ate Celestine kept smiling and looking at me, but she didn't say a word on the way home. Neither did I.

At work, the ambassador called me "Madame Lola," which made me feel important, and when he and the ambassador from Togo were walking past my office, he pointed in my direction. "She works very well and is elegant."

The other staff members nicknamed me the magician. They didn't realize that compared with what I had experienced, a small thing like tracing a bank check was as easy as sticking clothes in a washing machine and pushing a button. I didn't mind answering the phone, since no other support staff spoke English well enough to solve a crisis like this one:

Me: Embassy of the Central African Republic, how may I help you?

Caller: Hi, I'm calling to find out about getting a visa for Burkina Faso.

Me: Sorry, ma'am, this is the embassy of the Central African Republic. Please call the Burkina Faso embassy.

Caller: But I thought this was the African embassy.

Me: This *is* an African embassy, but we represent only the Central African Republic, not all of Africa.

Caller: But aren't you the African embassy? That's the number information gave me.

Me: Ma'am, there's no such thing as the African embassy. Africa is not a country. It is a continent, like Europe.

Caller: But I called information, and this is what they gave me! You represent Africa, don't you?

Me: No, ma'am. We represent only one country in Africa. It's like calling the French embassy to inquire about a visa for Portugal.

Caller: I just don't understand this; they said—

Me: Ma'am, why don't you hold on? I'll look up the number and give it to you.

Sometimes I was busy and couldn't stop to look up numbers. It would end with the person yelling, "I want to talk to your supervisor!" or "You're the most incompetent person I've ever dealt with!" Sometimes the person hung up on me or I hung up, muttering, *Idiot.*

The embassy possessed a skeleton staff, and it wasn't fraternizing material. There was the general secretary, who rolled in and remained screwed to his desk downstairs at reception; the first counselor, who puffed on cigars and asked me to order him wine from the duty-free shop; the elegant Madame Chevalier, economic counselor, who slipped dollars into my hands to "buy something for Dele"; the accountant who moonlighted at CVS after work; and, of course, His Excellency Extraordinary and Plenipotentiary, my boss. They were all married and lived across the river in Maryland, which left the church as my main social milieu. Maybe I needed to relax and allow Rob to take me out.

"Was it a hard day?" Rob glanced sideways at me, a sympathetic smile on his face. I had been working at the embassy for six months. We were sitting in the parking lot of the babysitter's apartment building. "You didn't say much on the drive here."

"It was a bit tough. I mean, the work is okay. It's the ignorance of callers that gets to me."

He leaned back and laid an arm on the top of my seat. I was aware of his clean, light blue cuff, the dusting of blond hair on his hand, the way his fingers tapered toward me. He gave me a warm smile. "I can imagine. Listen, how about we get Dele and get a bite to eat before I drop you home?"

"You don't mind? You wouldn't rather get home early?"

He snorted. "Yeah, early to my empty apartment. Come on, let's get the little man and do something fun."

I broke into a smile. "Wait here, please. I'll be right back." I didn't want eyes questioning my showing up with a man to pick up Dele.

Mrs. Shaw, the plump, middle-aged sitter, had the children gathered at her feet and was reading them a story.

"Mummy!" Dele scrambled to his feet and leaped at me.

Mrs. Shaw set the giant book against the wall and pushed to her feet. "Dele, don't forget your jacket."

"Thanks, Mrs. Shaw." I helped him into his jacket and zipped it up before grabbing his bag. "Say bye, Dele."

"Bye, Mrs. Shaw!" I noted with satisfaction that he gave her a hug, which meant he was comfortable with her.

Outside, as soon as he spied Rob, Dele broke away from me and ran to the car. "Rwob! Rwob!"

Rob opened the door and lifted him high. "Hey, buddy!" Dele shrieked with laughter. When he was belted into the backseat, and we were all seated, Rob eased the car back onto the street and headed toward I-95 North, back toward Washington instead of south toward Fairfax.

I turned to him. "Where are we going?"

He glanced sideways at me. "Ever been to the waterfront in Old Town, Alexandria?" I shook my head. He grinned with pleasure. "Good, I get to be the first to show it to you. You'll love it. So will Dele."

He parked the car on King Street and we found ourselves strolling along the sidewalk, looking at quaint stores. Old Town looked like Georgetown, where I had walked with Olga. I loved the trees, the narrow red-brick houses with curved façades. We walked, Dele between us, holding my hand and Rob's. When he tried to run, we held on to him and raised him high so he could swing and squeal with glee.

When we passed a window with mannequins wearing what looked like stage costumes, I turned to Rob. "Can we go in?"

"Let's!"

I tried on a wig with long black hair like an Indian's, and held out my hands. "What do you think?"

He smiled with pride. "You look like Pocahontas."

"Poca-who?"

He reached out and touched the hair. "An Indian princess." His eyes traveled around the room, then he walked to a shelf. "Hey, would you look at that!" He was fingering a three-corner hat with a feather glued to it. He put it on his head, then doffed it at me. "Mademoiselle." I laughed. He swiveled around and caught Dele on his toes, poking at a redheaded doll with hair standing straight and bulging eyes. "Hey, buddy, you like that troll?"

Dele grinned and darted around the store. I looked at the shop assistant, who smiled. She was a young lady in a long sweater over a pair of leggings. "Don't worry about him. There's nothing he can destroy here."

Rob turned to me, striking a pose, his arms folded across his chest and a stern expression on his face. "How do I look?"

I laughed. "You look like a mayor or a sheriff, monsieur."

"Yeah, baby!" He put the hat down and slipped a goofy mask on his face. It had black brows the size of toothbrushes and a big pink nose. I threw a ball at him, helpless with laughter. He caught it, grinning like a little boy.

We climbed a spiral staircase to an upstairs gallery and admired paintings and weird sculptures. I had to keep Dele from touching them. Then we walked until we spied a restaurant called Fish Market. It had a narrow outdoor seating area upstairs. I loved the red-and-white checkered awning and matching red-and-white tablecloths. "That looks so cheerful."

Rob looked at me. "Why don't we get a bite from there?"

I found my cheeks warming. "Yes, let's. You're so kind."

He picked up Dele and held him to his chest. "It's not kindness. I'd rather be doing this than a mac-and-cheese sandwich in front of the TV in my apartment."

He ordered a fish burger and fries for Dele. We adults went for the fish fillet with grilled potatoes. Rob ordered a bottle of white wine. By the end of the evening, I was chattering.

"Do you know the first counselor asked me to go fishing with him over the weekend?"

Rob's smile vanished. "Are you going?"

"No way. I don't find it appropriate to go fishing with my superior. Nor do I want to find myself alone with a married man in some strange waters."

"What about me?" He was looking at me with an unreadable expression in his blue eyes "Would you go to the movies with me?"

I took a big bite of my potato and chewed for a minute before answering with a naughty smile. "I just might."

"Whoa, you're saying yes? You'll go out with me?"

"I said *might*, not *will*."

He reached for my hand. "Hey, I'll take might. Let's do it soon. We can also do lots of things with the little man here. Right, Dele?"

Dele gave him a smile full of ketchup. Rob picked up his napkin and gently cleaned the ketchup from his face. That small gesture brought a lump to my throat. If Armand hadn't been such a bastard, he should have been doing that.

After dinner, we walked along the waterfront, looking at the shimmering water. Couples nuzzled each other on benches and rocks. A deep longing assailed me. I remembered the first time I skipped over rocks at the beach on Gorée Island, Armand toddling behind me. I pulled my jacket tighter around me, letting go of Dele's hand for a minute. I looked up to find Rob studying me.

"Why are you so quiet suddenly?"

I swallowed. "This place. It reminds me of Dakar."

"Do you want to leave?"

"No, let's walk a little while. I want to remember what it's like to see the moon shimmering on the water, and hear the night birds." When he put his arm around my waist, I let it remain.

Dear Awurama,

How could you even think I've forgotten you? Believe me, my life consists of just work and more work. Okay, that's not entirely true.

There's this man, Rob. I met him at church. He's nice. He picks me up from work nearly every day and helps me with Dele. He has become an important part of me, ssh! Don't tell Mama! I mean, regardless of where we come from, we're all stars, children of heaven, aren't we?

A Black couple, Penelope and Benjamin Washington, invited me to dinner at their home. You know something funny? When I cracked my chicken bones to suck the marrow, Penelope looked at me with pity and said, "You don't have to do that here. There's plenty of chicken." Can you believe it, Americans don't chew bones! I had a difficult time persuading her I actually loved the bones.

I really miss you, but it's hard thinking about home and Mama's disappointment. I'm just trying my best here.

Lots of love,
Akua

Penelope floated to me after church one day. "How are you?"

"I'm okay." My voice sounded curter than I intended it to be. After all, she had hosted Dele and me in her home.

"You must be overwhelmed by everything. Benjamin and I have been praying for you. Is there anything you need?"

"No, really. I'm doing okay."

"I brought you a bag of clothes." She was holding a large brown paper bag I hadn't noticed. Judging from her pinafores and drop-down-waist dresses, I knew I wouldn't want her clothes. But she looked so earnest I couldn't refuse. Her husband stood a few feet away, his blue-gray eyes muted with respect.

I accepted the bag. "Thank you so much."

"There's a loaf of bread inside too. I baked it for you."

"Oh, how wonderful! I love homemade bread. I haven't had any since I came to America. Thank you, thank you. I can't wait to eat it!" I raised the bag to my nose. It smelled of honey. My mouth watered.

She gurgled with obvious delight. "I'm so glad. Now that I know you love it, I'll bring you a loaf anytime I bake."

I thanked her and watched her join her husband. Their four children were now gathered to them: three boys in shirts and ties, and a girl dressed exactly like her mother. As they walked away, I realized how little I knew of individuals at the church, how they could flip over and show me another side.

Akoma Ntoaso

Continuity of Hearts

Pastor Drake was winding down his exhortations when I slipped in from my truancy in the sun. Not wishing to turn ears to the crunch of my shoes, I sat on a chair in the row nearest to the door, next to a young woman whose shoulder was encircled by a hairy hand, presumably her husband's.

She gave me a shy smile, her brown eyes flecked with gold. "Hi, I'm Debbie," she said. Her husband leaned forward to look at me and glanced away, his mustached mouth serene, as if satisfied I was no threat.

Their baby, about four months old, was having none of Pastor Drake's sermon. He lay in his rocker on the floor, boxing the air with fat arms like sausage links. He was snuffling, his quick breath puffing out. Judging from his mottled face and rectangular mouth, he was about to let out a howl. Debbie bent down and set the rocker in motion, but that only provoked pre-howling sounds from him. Eager to relieve a fellow mother the way a Ghanaian at church would, I bent down and picked him up.

"It's okay, darling," I said, and pressed him to my bosom. He quieted down for a moment. Then he began howling in earnest, so I stepped out into the hallway and started walking up and down, patting him on the back.

Debbie's husband rushed out. "Here, I'll take him," he said, and peeled his baby off me, giving me a sense that I had done something I shouldn't have.

When I crept back inside, Debbie gave me an apologetic smile, but said nothing. We exchanged no more words until a few days later at a house fellowship lunch hosted by Ate Celestine. Dele was stomping around with other toddlers, squealing his joy as people tickled or picked him up. I was trying to keep up with him when Debbie walked over to me, a shy smile on her face.

"I heard you were looking for a room to rent," she said.

"Yes, it's true. I've been living here for three months. Ate Celestine is wonderful, but I'm ready to find my own place. Something cheap so I can afford a babysitter."

Her voice was respectful. "I found something near us. There's a family that wants to rent out a room in a town house. It's the master bedroom suite. There're only two girls living in the house. The owners live close by, and the wife says she'll babysit Dele for you. Would you like to look at it?"

I stared at her. This quiet woman had been looking for a place for me? She'd even thought of a babysitter? "I don't know what to say. Thank you very much."

"Okay, then. Can I pick you up tomorrow, around four?"

"Please do. Thank you!"

For the first time since coming to America, I had agency. I had taken a step to finding my own place as opposed to being forced to move for one reason or another. There was dignity in living independently, and dignity was salve for the soul.

Debbie arrived in a brown Toyota pickup truck. I marveled at the ease with which she manually shifted gears. She leaned forward, her eyes on the asphalt. "I forgot to tell you, the girls that live in the house also work in Washington. They have a car pool. They said you could join them for ten dollars a week."

I stared at her placid profile, auburn hair falling over her collared blouse, the bangs nearly reaching her brows. This quiet woman was steel, and she had thought of everything. "That's so nice of you. I don't know how to thank you."

She turned to me, her smile confident. "Oh, not at all. You're very nice yourself. You helped me with my baby when you didn't even know me. I know my husband was uncomfortable, but I used to live in Lebanon, so I know other cultures are different."

"You lived in Lebanon? How come?"

"My father was a missionary, so we moved there. Me and my brothers, all four of us, shared one room. The Lebanese people were so kind. They'd welcome us into their homes, just like that. I loved it there. I really get you, Lola."

I felt tears pricking my eyes because I didn't have to explain my every thought or motive to this kind woman.

She smiled and patted my arm. "Don't worry, Lola. You're going to make it. This is America."

Something warm like soup my mother used to make in my childhood spread through me.

The brick town house was on Darlington Court, and a darling neighborhood it was. Shaded by dogwood trees, the row of homes stood on a carpet of lawn, so green it seemed unreal. A playground with swings and slides beckoned.

In the house, we met Lydia Mercedes, a tall Native American woman. Up until now, I had seen Native Americans only in *Dances with Wolves,* Indians wielding bows and arrows, sleeping in tepees, speaking broken English or none, the same way Africans in movies lived in villages, clutched spears, and spoke no English. Apart from her cinnamon skin and shiny black hair, Lydia was like any American woman with an open smile. She walked us into a large, eat-in kitchen facing the street. The lace valance on the window allowed the sun to stream in. We followed her into the wide dining area, then on to the sunken living room with orange carpeting, furnished with a blue couch, love seat, and two armchairs. A large television stood in a corner.

"This is lovely," I said.

"It's the common area we'll share, but your room is upstairs." She led the way up the curved staircase to the master bedroom, which boasted a queen-size bed, a bathroom, and a closet I could walk into. Sunlight poured in through the glass patio doors and danced on the orange carpet, giving the room a glow like fire. A home of my own.

Leaving Ate Celestine's house was a simple affair, with hugs and a "we'll see you at church every Sunday, anyway." Every workday morning at six o'clock, I picked up Dele, whose breath was heavy with sleep, and eased him into his car seat, his head lolling to the side. Lydia drove us to the Mercedes family house, only five minutes away, where I transferred him into a crib and left him in the loving care of Lydia's mother. We climbed into the van driven by Lydia's father, who, like her, worked for the Bureau of Indian Affairs. They dropped me off near the State Department on C Street, and then I walked ten blocks to the embassy. I could have taken the metro from C Street to Dupont Circle, but I was counting my nickels. My rent was four hundred dollars a month. Babysitting cost seventy-five a week. What money remained went into buying diapers and groceries, so I walked to save money. It was beginning to dawn on me that, at this rate, accruing money was going to take longer than the two years I had envisioned. More than once, I wondered if it was worth it, but an intransigent stubbornness kept me going.

To battle the bone-piercing cold of winter, I wore leg warmers over pantyhose, with boots and double gloves. I wrapped my head with a woolen scarf so that only my eyes showed, as if I were an Arabian in the desert. Topping it off with a knitted hat, I strode past vendors selling scarves and baubles, and hot dog stands by the roadside. I loved the wide sidewalks, but the homeless men huddled in clumps made me tear up. I visited the First Baptist Church of Clarendon and collected blankets that I handed to the homeless. Sometimes I dropped quarters and nickels into their bowls or cups. Church people said not to give money to the homeless lest they use it for drugs, but I didn't care. I could have been huddled under a pole too. The difference was that I had been lucky to find people who extended a hand and pulled me inside a home, people who drove me to the store, and Rob, who drove me home after work every day and hoisted my son onto his shoulders.

In the dim glow of a French restaurant, Rob held my gaze. Christmas had come and gone. It was Valentine's Day. We were now in the year 2000, the year some computer glitch called Y2K was supposed to bring the world to a standstill, but nothing had happened. My stomach was filled with the salmon cooked in champagne. My fork raked the plate for remnant flakes of fish and mushrooms in the cream sauce, my braids brushing the table.

"I love your braids," Rob said, reaching over to finger the ones falling over my arm. He let his hand drop and graze my wrist. When he closed his hand around mine, my breath caught. He'd held my hand countless times to cross the street or help me over a rock, but never stroked it like this. A delicious warmth spread through me, and I laughed, as if someone had liberated me from a tight dress.

"It's so good to hear you laugh out loud like this. Do you realize how long it's been since I've been asking you out? Months. Now you're here. Phew!" He put his other hand over his heart as if to hold it in.

I looked down, running my finger along the rim of my wine-glass. "Yes, you've been very patient. But think about it. We've already gone past the getting-to-know-you stage."

"I'm sorry to bring this up, but . . . Dele's father, did you love him?"

"It took me a while, but I did."

"So, am I competing with him?"

I looked up at him, aghast. "No, you're not, trust me. I got over him fast after I decided he was shallow. You and I, we've known each other for some time now. You've become almost as familiar to me as my pillow. I've seen you move furniture, carry things for old people. You are the kindest man I've ever met in America. You aren't bad looking either." I gave him a flirtatious smile.

He rocked in his chair. "Whoa, whoa, I've never heard you put so many words together. This is awesome. Unbelievable."

"Actually, I talk a lot. Just not around church people."

"Well, color me lucky." He raised his glass, grinning like a boy. "Here's to moving on."

"To moving on."

"I've been waiting a long time for you to look at me this way."

"How am I looking at you?" I teased.

"Like you want this . . ." He raised himself, leaned over, and touched his lips to mine. My nipples hardened. When he pulled away, I wished he would kiss me again. Instead, he sank back into his chair and seemed to be brooding. "I suppose you've heard the rumors about me."

"What rumors?" I was rigid, arms folded across my breasts.

"You know my father is a deacon, right?"

"I didn't, but what of that?"

"Well, I haven't been baptized as an adult. Technically, that means I'm not a Christian because I haven't been"—he made air quotes with his hands—"born again."

"That makes no sense to me. You were the one at the retreat preaching about faith and trusting God."

"Yes. It's one thing to trust God, to know with absolute certainty that He is real. But here's the thing, I don't believe in the exclusivity of Christianity. I don't believe only Christians have a path to heaven. I think about people of other faiths: Jews, Muslims, Buddhists, what have you. They didn't choose where they were born, right? You know there's a common theme of loving your neighbor as yourself that runs through them, right? So how do we conclude they're going to hell?" He rolled the stem of his glass with thumb and finger. "I guess I don't want the kind of Christianity that comes across as superior or excludes others."

I jerked forward. "Oh my God, I feel the same way! In Dakar, many of my friends were Muslims, and they were the kindest people I knew. My friend Olga in Maryland, she's an atheist. And Mindy is Jewish. Both women have treated me with nothing but love. God is love, and love is the ultimate uniter. You know what I'm loving about you, right now? I've had men tell me I'm too bloody intellectual, but you? You never say that. I can talk to you."

He was looking at me intently. "I can't tell you how happy this makes me. When I talk like this to the single girls at church, they shrink away as if I've blasphemed. I don't even know why I'm still the leader of the singles group. I'm not their spiritual ideal."

"But think about it." I grabbed both of his hands. "The word *Christian* first appeared as a nickname for disciples who were behaving like Jesus Christ. Religious labels don't automatically imbue a person with virtue. Identity spirituality means nothing. What counts is practicing the higher ideals of that religion." I saw it clearly now: the Jehovah's Witness family in New York and all the wonderful people who had soothed me in one form or another. They personified love. So did Rob. He loved me, I was certain. It hit me then. I had found something precious: someone whose heart was like the continuation of mine, someone I could spend my life talking to. I pressed his palm to my cheek. "I don't care what you call yourself. You, Rob, love your neighbor as yourself, which is more than I can say for many people."

He was looking at me with astonishment. "Where did you come from?" Then his eyes shimmered with tears.

"What is it, Rob?"

He blinked fast. "You've no idea how alone I've felt. Hope this doesn't scare you, but you've been my one bright spot." He freed his hands from mine. "Sorry, I can't help it." He pressed his fingers over his eyes, as if forcing the tears back.

I was seeing him clearly. He had always seemed so confident that I had never recognized his vulnerability. I got up and walked around the table. I sat on his lap, putting my arms around his neck. Without thinking, I pressed my lips to his. He opened his eyes. We were exchanging warm breaths. I kissed his nose, smoothed his brows. He crushed me to him and I felt the shock of his tongue against mine. When we pulled apart, I laid my head on his chest, hearing the thumping of his heart. I had never before felt so close to another man. I knew his soul. We held each other for a long time, just breathing together. My heart was in real danger, I knew, but what a relief it was to let down the wall I had built around it. I had been lying to myself about not wanting emotional entanglements. This feeling of security was what I'd needed all along. When I looked up at him, my smile held nothing back.

"If you smile at me like that, I'm going to lose my head." Then, out of the blue, he said, "Will you marry me?"

"What?" I sat up.

"Will you marry me? You know how I feel about you. Do you feel the same?"

I had for a long time, long before I knew it. "I do."

"Then marry me, damn it, Lolo."

I gave him a playful push, laughing. "You heathen, did you just say 'damn it'?"

"Yes, damn it." He wasn't smiling.

"God. I don't even know what to say. You're joking, right?"

"I'm serious. I want to marry you."

"So quickly? I mean I'm used to that. In Ghana, we don't play around. When we find the one, we marry as soon as possible, but I can't marry you just like that. I've been planning to save money to go back home. This will turn my plans upside down."

"You want to go back to Ghana? Fine, I'll go with you. But could we start a life here?"

"Slow down, slow down." I put my hand to my forehead and closed my eyes. This man, whose breath warmed my face, spoke the language of my soul. I wanted to sleep and wake up with him. I wanted to laugh with him. I wanted him inside me. Ghanaians used to think only whores married White men, but things were now changing. Not that I cared what anyone thought. But what about his family? I opened my eyes. "What about your parents?"

"My parents?"

"Yes. They're not uncomfortable with my foreignness?"

"Not a chance. They couldn't care less."

I thought about them, Mr. and Mrs. Morrison, how they always smiled at me though they never engaged with Rob and me. They'd say, "Hi, Lola, how is Dele?" and scurry off but nothing much beyond that. Perhaps they simply respected their son's right to his friendships. Marrying Rob would mean shared laughter and bodies. Dele would love it. I could see it now, Dele bragging to other kids, "Rob took me camping, Rob is so strong!" He'd probably call him Daddy. *Slow down, slow down.* I needed to think. Any decision I made involved Dele's future.

"Ask me again in another month," I said. "If I feel as convinced as I do now, I'll marry you."

He took my hand, turned it over, and pressed his lips to the palm, making me wish he'd do that to my breasts. Olga, that sly fox, was right. I was ready to straddle him right there in the restaurant.

"Let's visit my parents. I want you to get to know them," he said, sitting up.

"Right now?"

"Yeah. They're only fifteen minutes away. It's not as if you're a stranger."

I felt confident enough to agree, and he waved to the waiter for the bill.

We sat around the circular table: Rob, Richard Morrison, and I. I was happy we were having tea together in the kitchen, a blue-and-pink checkered valance on the window, as opposed to a formal sit-down in the living room. Rob's mother, Barbara Morrison, bustled about in a loose blouse with a wide neck. She placed four mugs on the table and set a can of Danish cookies in front of me, saying, "Eat up. You need more meat on those bones."

"She's not too skinny," Rob said, squeezing my hand. "Prettiest girl I ever saw."

My armpits felt hot and itchy. I reached for a cookie crusted with sugar. Mr. Morrison laughed, slapped the table with his hand. "That's exactly how I felt about your mother."

I tried to picture him as a young romantic. Although everything about him sagged, from his ears and eyelids to his cheeks, his large eyes danced with the mischief of a teenager.

"I asked her to marry me, Dad," Rob blurted. My ears seared. I grabbed a tea bag from the box labeled Lemon Zinger and dropped it into my mug. Mrs. Morrison sank into the chair beside her husband, her elbows anchored on the table, hands interlaced, looking more surprised than displeased.

Mr. Morrison sipped slowly from his mug, then put it down before looking from me to Rob. "Already? You sure are in a hurry, son."

Mrs. Morrison said with a naughty smile, "The apple doesn't fall far from the tree. Your dad asked me to marry him three days after we met."

Rob's eyes widened. "You've never told me this before, Mom. And you said yes?"

She grinned. "He wouldn't take no for an answer."

"I did take no for an answer," Mr. Morrison said. "You said no, remember?"

"I said wait."

Mr. Morrison turned to grin at me. "She was wise."

"I don't know about that," Mrs. Morrison said. "We eloped a week later."

Rob laughed. "Whoa, whoa, I knew you guys eloped but I didn't know it was so soon after you met. Wow."

Mr. Morrison seemed to be mulling over something. "So, you guys want to get married. There's just one thing you must bear in mind, Lola. Rob here hasn't formally accepted Christ into his life, and you know what the Bible says—"

Rob rolled his eyes and made air quotes at me. " 'Be not unequally yoked with unbelievers.' That means, as a Christian, you may not marry me."

"But, Mr. Morrison, he is a Christian," I pointed out quietly. "I mean, isn't the word *Christian* just an adjective? Christ-like?"

Husband and wife looked at each other. "God help us, Barbara. She's just like him. Lola, you are missing the point about grace. When we accept Christ, we're forgiven and have assurance of eternal life. It's not about doing good works, though you do good works as a result of the Holy Spirit."

"So why is it like a test, a judgment against me if I haven't declared that?" Rob asked.

Barbara ignored him and turned to me. "We raised him to be a decent man. But the Bible is clear on this. He must accept Christ. We can't in good conscience let you marry someone who isn't walking with the Lord. Even if he's our son."

"As a deacon, my responsibility is to God, first and foremost." Richard delivered this with the finality of a sentence.

I was about to say something when Rob squeezed my hand. For the rest of the night, we ignored the issue. Would you like more cookies? No, thank you. This is very nice tea. Yes, we love tea and Danish cookies. Did you know Rob was a rascal as a kid? Haha.

In the car, as he drove me back home, Rob's jaws clenched. "I just didn't want to argue with them in front of you. I'm fucking tired of it. It's blackmail. Invite Jesus into your heart or we'll not give you our blessing." He shook his head, the headlights showing us the way. "Isn't it enough that I believe?"

I remained silent, my hand on his shoulder. I didn't want him to make pronouncements just to satisfy people. It was clear the church wouldn't break into hallelujahs for our marriage. Pastor Drake would not beam at us and pronounce us husband and wife. The way I saw it, at twenty-six, Rob was the one to chart his spiritual path. Whatever that was, it had produced this man whose life I wanted to share.

"Yes," I said.

Rob glanced at me. "Yes what?"

"I will marry you." A month wouldn't make a difference, I knew now. I hadn't wanted children, and yet I had kept Dele. Now, after shunning the idea of a relationship, I was leaping into marriage. But wasn't that life, to change one's mind when circumstances presented different perspectives? Why insist on being single when this man enriched my life? "I will marry you," I repeated softly.

"You will? I thought . . . Yes! Woo-hoo!" He pulled off the road, parking on the curb. He took my face in his hands, looked into my eyes, a reverent smile on his face. "Thank you," he said, before our lips met, before he slipped his hand inside my blouse, found my nipple, and squeezed.

"I've never made love in the backseat of a car before," I whispered, reaching to unbuckle him.

He put his hand over mine. "Not like this. I want to marry you first."

"Come on, I'm dying."

He groaned. "Me, too. But as Christians, we can't have premarital sex." He pulled me close, squeezing my bottom. "Hey, how about we elope, like my parents did?"

It felt delicious, subversive. I felt the same sense of agency as I had when I moved out of Ate Celestine's. I was taking control of my own life, doing what felt right to me and not the church, not society. "Let's," I said.

It was a Friday afternoon. I wore a cream satin dress with a scooped neckline. Dele's hand clutched my finger. Even he knew to be serious the day his mother got married. Rob's blue eyes searched mine. "Are you okay with this? Eloping like this?"

"I'm the one who should be asking you that. I have no family here. Are you sure your parents aren't going to flip tables over and grab you by the neck?"

"I can't imagine why. You heard them. They themselves eloped."

I sighed, a sudden knot in my stomach. "Just promise me one thing. Don't become obsessed with money, and whatever you do, don't die on me, you hear?"

He pressed me to him, laughing. "Not on your life."

At the justice of the peace, in a room blander than my office, the pomp and theater of my sister's wedding rose before me, Mama's face placid. I pictured her watching me now. I pushed her out of my mind and fixed a smile on my face. This simple ceremony without family or friends suited the person I now was.

The suited official, an open Bible in his hand, said, "Do you take this man to be your lawfully wedded husband?"

I said "I do," Rob said "I do," and we did.

Rob had already moved our belongings into his two-bedroom apartment in Fairfax. For the first time in his life, Dele had a room to himself and he didn't mind. He dived on his brand-new red car-bed, a big grin on his face.

Alone in the second bedroom, Rob handled me like a queen. With his tongue, he paid homage to my toes and the back of my legs, and set me on fire. I discovered the penis really did fill with blood. In a White man, you could see it. Blood against blood, separated by the thinnest of membranes. I dug my fingers into his buttocks and sucked him into me.

We lay facing each other, my leg over his, his arm around my shoulder.

"You said you wanted to write, right?" he asked. "So why won't you let me help you? I can support you while you write."

I traced the pink disk around his nipple. "I love you for thinking about my writing, but I can't be dependent in that way. What if something happened to you and I had no money of my own? Besides, I actually do love my work. Do you know they call me the magician? There's no problem I can't solve. Also, I don't want to be stuck here all day without adult conversation. I'd go crazy. I'll just have to find time to write."

He kissed my forehead. "Well, if you insist on working, then we'd better get on with applying for a green card for you. That way, you can even get a better-paying job. I'm gonna sponsor you, baby. Just give me a couple of months to straighten out my tax issues."

"What tax issues?"

He smiled. "Nothing for you to worry your beautiful head about."

He also had plans to buy a bigger place and had already been preapproved for a town house.

"And now, for the music with your parents."

"Not now," he said in a husky voice, and rolled on top of me. "One week of bliss before that."

A lifetime of this wouldn't be enough, I thought, opening for him.

Ɔtamfo Bɛbrɛ

The Enemy Will Suffer

"You what?" Mr. Morrison was on his feet, hands on his waist, bushy brows pleated. He looked at me as though seeing me for the first time, and turned to Rob. "Say that again."

Rob's arm felt heavy on my shoulders. Sweat formed under my red blazer. He took his time to answer, trying for a smile. "Lola and I got married. We went to the justice of the peace a week ago."

Mrs. Morrison's mouth quivered. She was seated in the armchair, rigid. I twiddled my fingers, grateful we had left Dele with Molly. Mr. Morrison sank into his chair, staring at Rob. "You eloped?" He turned to his wife. "They eloped?"

"How could you do this to us, Rob?" Mrs. Morrison was wailing. "You got married, just like that?" Her face was red now, disfigured with crying.

Rob drew his arm from my shoulder and sat forward. "Mom, I thought you of all people would understand. You eloped. You yourself told me."

She didn't appear to hear him. "How could you, Rob? And you, Lola? We trusted you. We welcomed you, and you do this to us? You married without a pastor?"

"Leave Lola out of this." Rob's chin was lifted, more angular than ever.

Mr. Morrison got up. He paced around, his hands brushing his gray hair back and forward. He stopped for a moment and looked at me, his hand over his mouth. "You agreed to this, Lola? You married an unsaved man?"

"Dad, please, don't talk to my wife like that."

"Your wife?" He looked at Mrs. Morrison, pointing at me. "His wife?" There was a special stress on "wife," as if it were a foreign word he was struggling to understand.

Mrs. Morrison moaned, "You robbed us of a wedding. How could you do this to us?"

Rob shook his head, incredulous. "But you eloped!"

"That doesn't make it right for you to do the same thing! I can't forgive you for this."

"Mom, you're acting as if we've committed a sacrilege. We married. We didn't kill someone. You went on about how romantic it was to elope. The vows were the same as in church: for better, for worse, in sickness and in health." His voice broke. "Please don't blame Lola. I begged her to marry me. Can you be happy for us?"

Mrs. Morrison struggled up, her curls mussed about her face. "I've got a headache. I've got to go lie down." She wobbled, holding on to the wooden bannister, her steps heavy on the stairs.

Mr. Morrison, too, got up. "I've got to go make sure your mother is okay, but mark my words. God is not mocked. Those who hate his words will suffer." He didn't look at me as he walked toward the stairs. He mounted them slowly, each step leaden.

Rob sat as though someone had punched him, his jaw tight. The veins on his temples stood out. Silence weighed on us, and I wondered if he wanted to go after his parents. His shoulders went up and a long sigh blew out of him. He pressed me to his side, searching my face. "Are you okay?"

"I'm fine. You're the one I'm worried about." I leaned my head on his shoulder, squeezing his arm up and down as if to massage the shock out of him.

Sunday, when Rob and I arrived for church, the cafeteria buzzed. People gathered in clumps, talking. As soon as we entered, the buzzing ceased. I could hear the distant humming of cars. Someone cleared his throat. In front of the pulpit, Rob's parents were surrounded by congregants. When Mr. Morrison saw us, his face closed up. Everyone turned to stare at us.

"I need to talk to them," Rob said. "You're going to be okay?"

"Yes. Go on. I'm going to walk Dele to Sunday school." Dele tore his hands from me and ran off. As I sped through the hallway after him, I noticed a group of people huddled against the wall, their backs to me. I was walking past them when a woman's voice said in a low voice, "You know how Black people are. She probably seduced him. They probably fornicated before marriage."

"Poor Rob, he might have accepted Christ. Now, I don't know. He probably won't."

"We need to pray for him."

"Yeah, pray for them both to repent."

The floor swayed before me. I steadied myself. Another woman might have ignored them, but I had always been too outspoken for my own good. "Fine morning to you, people of God," I said. They whipped around as if I had struck them. Faces turned into different shades of red.

The redhead gave me an awkward smile. "We hear you got married. Congratulations."

Another woman said, "That comment about Black people, we weren't talking about you."

I looked pointedly at them.

"No, truly." A nervous giggle. "We weren't talking about you."

"Actually, we were." This came from the man whose dark hair and swarthy body made me wonder if he was Greek, the same man who had asked where I'd learned to speak English, who wanted me to know Eric Green. "I'm going to give it to you straight. You've become unequally yoked with an unbeliever. That's a sin in and of itself. Then you compound it with marrying a White man. We don't approve of interracial marriage. The Bible says, 'Each animal shall reproduce according to its kind.'"

That undid me. "Funny you should say that, as if people of different races are entirely different creatures. When I first came to this church, didn't you hint that I date Eric Green? Is he not White? Or is it because he has epilepsy?" He folded his arms and tightened his lips, but I couldn't stop. "If I hadn't met Rob earlier, I might have liked Eric. He's a fine man, he deserves love like anyone else, but don't think I haven't noticed the girls don't date him. I guess it's all right for a Black woman to marry a White man who the White girls don't want. Isn't that so?"

"Now, wait a minute, young lady—"

"Deep down, you think disabled people are inferior, so are Black people. And you call yourself a Christian." He turned a deep red, whether from anger or shock, I didn't know. Not that I cared. I was tired of being so bloody polite all the time. I swept off.

From the end of the hallway, Debbie walked toward me, her baby in her arms.

"Hi, Lola." Her smile held a hint of defiance, as if she had guessed what had just happened and wanted to show me kindness. "I hear you and Rob got married. He's such a nice guy. Congratulations."

I swallowed the lump in my throat. "Thanks."

"I've got to change this guy's diaper, but I'll see you later."

At least, she was with me. I peeked into Dele's Sunday school class. He was standing with the children, a big smile on his face, his voice high as he joined the kids in singing with the teacher: *Jesus loves me, this I know, for the Bible tells me so. Little ones to Him belong . . .*

I turned around, bumping into Rob, tears of rage on my face.

He held me. "My God, you're shaking, what's wrong? You're crying."

I panted into his chest, my fists clenched. "I can't do this, Rob. People are so hurtful."

"Shh." He wrapped his arms tighter around me. "Come on, let's go outside."

He led me to a park behind the cafeteria, but I wouldn't stop crying, so he walked me across the street to the county park nearby. He sat on a swing, pulling me onto his lap. "Talk to me, baby, what happened?"

My bosom heaved with suppressed sobbing. "Such hypocrisy. People act all nice in church, but underneath the smiles, they discriminate. I'm so tired of it." I sniffled, flicking my nails together. "Penelope and Benjamin Washington. They have four perfect kids. I haven't been in America that long, but I have eyes. That family is the quintessential spotless Negro. They're exceptional. That's why people call them godly, isn't it? That's the kind of Black that makes some Whites say, *We're not racists. We have this*

263

wonderful Black family. But I get treated to *What do you expect from those people?* I heard them. They . . . they say I seduced you, probably fornicated before marriage."

Rob wiped my tears with his hands. "I'm so sorry, baby. God, this is messed up. You're not the only single parent in the church. There's Ate Celestine. She's a deaconess."

"Ate Celestine is acceptable. Never remarried, has probably never touched herself at night. People love Dele, but his mother is a sinner."

"I'm bummed. I never thought they'd behave like that. Ssh, don't cry. Don't listen to them."

We swung gently, my head on his shoulder. "If you don't mind, I'm in no mood to listen to Pastor Drake today. You can return to church if you want."

"And leave you here? No way. Let's go back and grab Dele and go to IHOP."

I smiled through my tears. "You know what? I'm not sorry I married you."

He traced his finger around my lower lip. "I could make love to you right this minute."

"Well," I smiled mischievously, sniffling, "remember what the Mother Superior said to Maria in *The Sound of Music*? The love between a man and woman is holy too. And anyway, we're at a park."

He raised his brow in a question.

For an answer, I raised my hips. I sank onto him, my skirt covering us. I closed my eyes, face lifted to the sun, my breasts tingling against his cupped hands, my whole body surrendering to the pounding waves of holiness, the rapture of it escaping out of us, unrestrained and pure.

Dear Mama,

I hope you and Awurama are well.

I have news, but first of all, please don't be angry. I got married to a man named Rob Morrison. I can imagine your shock, but I beg you, he's a good man. Please, please don't be angry. As I write this, I know I should have written more often. I should have let you know what was going on. It hurt too much to think of home and what a disappointment I've been. Please don't worry. Rob is intelligent and handsome, but most of all, he loves me and even wants to adopt Dele. I didn't marry out of desperation but out of genuine love and respect for this man. I pray you come to love him when I bring him to Ghana.

Rob even tried to get me to stop working so I could concentrate on my writing, but I refused. Look at what happened to Dadda, how you had to earn a living. I want to always have my own money. Rob works for the federal government as an accountant and also has a side business doing taxes for people. It's a once-a-year thing in America where people have to report their earnings and do some weird calculations I don't understand. It doesn't affect me because as an embassy employee, I don't pay taxes. I make little, for that matter.

I haven't changed my name to Mrs. Morrison and I am not going to. Awurama changed hers, but the way I see it, your family name will be lost if I change mine. We live in a two-bedroom apartment, so Dele sleeps in his own room, which I know will sound awful to you. In America, there's a strange habit of putting little children in a room by themselves, and it's considered a wonderful thing. I have to say Dele loves scattering his toys all over his room. Rob wants to buy a house soon.

Please stop worrying about me. I'm okay. Greet everyone for me.

Lots of love,
Akua

April 19, 2000

Akua Olivia,

Have you cracked your madness open? You are married? To another American? You married without even telling me anything? Is that how you reject your family, not even tell me you met someone much less marry him? San kɔ fa! Have you forgotten your roots?

No wonder our elders say childbirth equals pain. You might as well stab me in the stomach. I leave you to it, then. From now on, your life is your own.

Yours,
S. D.

Dear Akua,

Mama gave me the news. I don't believe it. How could you get married like that? I don't even know what to say to you. That Rob? You married a White man? Ah, Akua! Don't you remember what people say, that an African

266

woman marries a White man only when no Black man wants her? Oh, Akua. Yes, Mama taught us all humans are stars, children of the sky, but you can't stop people from thinking bad things about you. They'll think you're cheap or a prostitute. More disgrace to the family!

Anyway, you're already married, so I can't tell you to leave him. Besides, you say you love him and he is good to you. Well, as for me, I don't have a problem, but other people? Hmm. And Mama? I think you have pushed her too far this time.

I'm curious about something. Is the White man's penis as small as they say? You can tell me. I won't tell Mama, hee hee!

Will I see you again? I have a second child and you don't even know her. Are you lost to us? Anyway, greet my in-law for me.

Your sister,
Awurama

Sharp pains roiled my stomach. *Your life is your own.* I had pushed my mother too far, turned my back on our culture. Everything we did—child naming, baptism, confirmation, marriage—revolved around family. Nobody just married. Even when people outside Ghana got married, they got married by proxy in Ghana and made sure to perform the necessary rites. By marrying Rob the way I did, I had broken the branch that connected me to the family tree.

Salty water gushed from under my tongue and filled my mouth. I rushed to the bathroom and doubled over the toilet bowl. The spasms seized me from inside and I retched and retched, wishing Rob wasn't at work and I hadn't taken a rare day off.

Dele scurried in. "Mummy sick?" I nodded and flushed, sinking to the floor and pulling him to me.

"Wash hands," he protested, wiggling from my grasp.

I smiled weakly and rose to the sink. After washing and wiping my hands, I lifted him by the waist and he held his hands under the faucet, grinning. "Clean!" He wiped his hands and wiggled down. "Mama read!" He raced to the sitting room, grabbing *Pat the Bunny* from the floor. The demands of motherhood banished self-pity. I sat on the couch and he crawled into my lap.

"How big is Dele?"

He raised his hands to the ceiling. "Sooo big!"

I went through the motions with him, feeling like a marionette, wondering if, in addition to sadness, I had the flu. I had taken the day off because I had woken up tired and nauseated, unable to bear the smell of oatmeal . . . I sat up straight. I was pregnant. The symptoms were unmistakable. Dele tugged at me, asking me to read again. I continued as if in a dream, my thoughts jumbled.

When Dele went down for his nap, I crawled into bed and slept too. I felt better later and even took Dele for a walk, but the sour taste in my mouth persisted. We returned home to find Rob at the kitchen counter, cutting tomatoes, the smell of onions and beef steaming on the stove.

"Daddy!" Dele said, tearing away from me.

Rob scooped him up. "Hey, buddy, how're you doing?" Then he saw my face. "Are you okay?"

I nodded, but I was fighting tears. He set down Dele, who scurried to kneel by his orange truck. Soon he was crawling, pushing the truck. Rob put his arms around my waist and pulled me closer, searching my eyes. If I told him about my mother's letter, it would sadden him. He turned off the burner and led me to the bedroom.

"What's wrong, Lola?"

"I'm pregnant," I said in a flat voice.

"What?" He plunked himself on the bed. "We're having a baby?"

I nodded. "I haven't taken a test or anything, but the symptoms are clear. You're okay?"

"Are you kidding me? This is the best present of all. My swimmers are healthy!" He made a victory salute with his fist. I laughed. He bent over me and kissed me softly. "Hello, Mama."

That night in bed, Rob ran his hand over my thighs, his breath hot on my neck. "You're so beautiful."

He moved inside me as though I were as delicate as an egg until I protested, "You're not going to poke the baby."

"Oh, honey." He picked up his rhythm. Afterward, as I lay with my head on his lap, his arm encircling me, he whispered, "Thank you for marrying me."

I gave him a naughty smile. "What can I say? You're not too bad."

Every morning, we'd leave Dele in the capable hands of an older woman who came to watch him, then we drove to work together. After work, Rob was there to pick me up. He'd kiss me and say, "You know the best part of my day? This right here, you sitting beside me as we drive home." On the rare occasion he couldn't pick me up, he'd arrange with one of his friends to do so, but he was always home for dinner. We competed to see who was the better cook, Rob insisting he was as he fixed spaghetti, Dele's favorite. "Right, buddy?" he'd ask Dele, the two high-fiving each other. I would look from one to the other, thinking how lucky I was. Somehow, we had managed to create the nucleus of a family that now spelled home to me. Within a month, the nausea, or what people called morning sickness, had disappeared. Rob found an African supermarket in Alexandria where I could get ingredients to make fufu and goat meat soup. He loved to eat with his hands, licking his fingers like an African. I vowed I would take him to Ghana, beg my mother to forgive us, and show her how much we loved each other.

One day after work, five months into our marriage, I walked out of my office to an empty spot where Rob's car should have been. I was almost fourteen weeks pregnant. I waited a little, thinking he was caught in traffic. After a while, I ducked back into the building and phoned his office, upset with myself for insisting I didn't need the cell phone he had tried to buy me. There was no answer. I puzzled it out. There had never been a moment that I couldn't reach him or account for his whereabouts. If he was running late, he'd call before I left my desk and went downstairs. Was there an emergency meeting he'd forgotten to tell me about? I called again, but he didn't respond. I called the front desk, but they didn't know where he was. After pacing for half an hour, I decided to take the metro.

At home, Dele's chatter seemed far away. I kept calling Rob's cell phone. I put Dele to bed, him asking when Daddy would be home. In the empty bed, I twisted about, seized with worry. Around eleven p.m., the phone rang.

"Rob, what happened to you?"

"Baby—"

"Where are you? You scared me."

"Baby, listen to me." He sounded exhausted, but something frightening lay behind the fatigue. I hushed so he could talk. "Baby, I'm really sorry. I've got only a few minutes. The sheriff—"

"Sheriff? Sheriff! Where are you?" The picture on the wall seemed to be spinning.

"I'm in jail."

"Did something happen to a client?"

"No, honey. Please. I've only got a couple of minutes. I did something wrong. Short version: I cheated on taxes."

"What do you mean you cheated? You don't cheat, you're honest."

"Taxes are different. You know, people work hard for their money and they don't want Uncle Sam taking a chunk out, so I find ways to hide the money."

Taxes. "Are you saying you hid money that you were supposed to pay to the government?"

"Something like that. Remember in the Bible, when Ananias and his wife lied to the church about how much they had made?"

"What? Don't natter to me about bloody Ananias and his wife, who dropped down dead for cheating the church and lying about it. Stop playing with me, Rob. You're not a cheat and a liar."

He became silent.

"You're not a lawbreaker, come on. Why won't you talk? Answer me, Rob!" For sure, it was all a cruel joke we'd laugh at after I had thrown pillows at him.

"Listen," he said in a steady voice, "I don't want you getting your pretty head twisted about this. I've got a lawyer. I'm going to plead guilty. I was wrong, Lola."

I started crying. "No, Rob, you've led Bible workshops. You're a spiritual leader. You're honest."

"I'm sorry, Lola. I'm everything you say, but I'm no saint." He sighed. "They got me as I was leaving the office. There's so much going on in my mind right now. I'm so sorry, baby. I'm sorry I did this to us. Now I've got to go."

"No, Rob, tell me it's not true, please."

"I'm afraid it is, baby. I'm truly sorry. I have to go."

"Wait, please, don't go. Tell me where you are."

"Fairfax County Adult Detention Center." Someone shouted *Time's up*, and Rob whispered, "I've got to go, baby." The line died.

Please, God, no. I bent over as if someone had hurled a rock at me. Taxes. I had never understood the system. What had Rob done? Oh, God. I shivered. I crawled under the comforter, drawing the pillows next to me, sobbing, not caring if Dele woke up.

Because visiting was on Saturdays, five days passed before I was allowed to visit him. Debbie Winston drove me. We sat around a table, close to other inmates and their visitors. When Rob was led in, Dele flew at him and wouldn't let go of his neck.

"Daddy! Daddy!"

"Hey, buddy, how're you doing?" Rob said. "I've missed you."

His eyes puffed out in scary orbs. His chin and upper lip sprouted a blond stubble. This was my husband. In a prison blue uniform, looking so crumpled and broken. Was this a weird movie we'd been cast in? Whatever the case, we were a team. It was important that I showed strength for us. I pasted a smile on my face, blinking at him. "So how are they treating you?"

He failed at smiling. "Could be worse." Dele had both hands on his cheek, patting him and smiling, his eight teeth flashing white. Rob's eyes pierced me. "We need to talk."

The tightness around his lips increased my anxiety. I turned to Debbie. "Please, could you take Dele outside?"

Dele anchored his feet in Rob's chest and let out a howl.

"It's okay, baby," I said. Rob disengaged him firmly from his neck, his eyes shining.

Debbie took Dele by the hand. He scratched her hand, trying to pull his arm free, screaming as if betrayed. After they left, a cloud darkened Rob's features. He leaned forward on his elbows, his fingers interlaced. Instinctively, I folded my arms over my breasts, looking at him without blinking.

"Lola, please forgive me for what I'm about to say." His voice was loud because he had to speak above the voices of other inmates talking to their visitors.

"Tell me how you got here."

He hung his head as if filled with shame. Then he raised his head, his blue eyes brimming over. "I did some shady things with my taxes, other people's taxes, too. I'm going to plead guilty."

"Okay," I said, my stomach taut. What did this mean?

He took a deep breath. "Baby, I want to let you go."

My arms dropped. "What are you talking about?"

"I want you to divorce me—let me finish. You see, my lawyer has already done his homework. I'm going to jail. My account, my money, everything will be frozen. I'm going to be penniless. I *am* penniless. If you divorce me, then you can marry someone else."

My chest expanded with so much air I thought I'd explode. "Robert Morrison, how dare you!"

"It's for—"

"No, *you* listen to me." I was breathing fast, mouth quivering. "You don't get to tell me what to do. I am furious with you, but I'm not divorcing you, you hear?"

His eyes went dead, like glass. "I don't want you wasting your life waiting for me. When I get out, it won't be easy starting over. I won't be pitied."

I was crying now. "I will be here every damn Saturday!"

"Look who is swearing now," he said softly, leaning over to tuck my braids behind my ears. "I don't want you here. I don't want any of this to touch you. I don't want Dele here. Please listen. I will never allow you to visit me again. If you schedule a visit, I will refuse."

"Are you out of your mind?"

"I mean it, Lola."

"Fine, then, I will be waiting when you get out."

"Don't wait for me."

I pushed my chair back and shot up. "You know what you are? A cliché. A goddamn cliché! You want to be what, my savior? My gallant? I've survived a lot worse than this. I survived being abandoned in New York City. I survived working as a maid. You don't get to tell me what I can and can't do."

"Listen to me, listen, please. The lease on the apartment will expire in three months. Without my income, you won't be able to renew by yourself. Even if you could, how would you pay the rent? It's going to be tough, baby. I don't want this for you. Please. Look at me. Go to Ghana. Go back home. I will do my utmost for you when I get out. But it could be five years or more, if they throw the maximum at me. Please, listen to me."

"I won't leave you, you hear?"

"Time," a burly guard said, hovering over us.

I threw myself at Rob, imprinting my body on his. He pulled back, his face teary but determined. "Goodbye, Lola."

"See you later," I whispered as they pulled him away.

I crumbled onto the table, sobbing. After a while, I wiped my eyes, knowing I had to fix a smile on my face for Dele. Not just for Dele. I needed to straighten my back for the little one who had taken root inside me. "We're going to be okay," I said, my voice fierce.

PART THREE

Owuo Atwedeɛ

Death's Ladder

I watched the rise and fall of Dele's chest as he lay splayed like a star on his back. He wore nothing but his diaper. In a while he would be naked. I had no idea how he managed to peel off his diaper in his sleep every time. I closed the door softly and entered the living room. I shut my eyes, pushing back those words that refused to stop stabbing me, my hands on my abdomen.

Rob hung himself in his cell.

That's what they said.

Suicide.

How had he managed to do that? Where did he find the rope? Why hadn't anyone suspected something before then? Why hadn't he been on suicide watch?

No one had answers for me. He didn't even leave a note. He could find a rope but no paper? Or he didn't want to write? Oh, you rogue! Even in prison, you found a way around the law, you bastard! You cowardly bastard!

I fell into the armchair in the living room, dejected. I looked around the furnished one-bedroom apartment Debbie's father had rented to me, unable to believe Rob had left me. Nothing made sense. I felt disoriented in this apartment attached to the main house. The huge compound. A massive tree with a swing hanging from its branches shaded the front yard. Hanging. Rob hanging. How could I enjoy this flat with its beautiful kitchen while his body fed the maggots in the earth at Fairfax Memorial Park? A park. Bitter laughter burst out of me. A park with lush greenery and flowers, right off the road leading to George Mason University. What a world. They couldn't call it what it was, a cemetery housing a twisted neck and rotted dreams, whose gray tombstone I wanted to slash, whose concrete slab I wanted to bludgeon, whose coffin I wanted to pry open and slide in next to Rob? A park. I wanted to puke.

I hugged myself, rocking back and forth. My mother used to say everyone had to climb death's ladder, but why did Rob have to climb it now?

The baby kicked me in the abdomen, as if to remind me of its presence. I urged my body to relax, breathing slowly. I needed to be steady for the baby. For Dele, too. Oh, I was good at smiling, watching Dele devour his rice and chicken stew. Good at wiping his face, reading and singing to him before he slept, but once he was tucked in under the comforter, grief ground through me like a train. I held on to its poles, trying to remain upright, not fly out the window and spiral into a dark hole where the earth was moist and smelled of rotting flesh.

The baby kicked again. I wiped my face and pushed myself to my feet. I grabbed the three hundred dollars I had put on the center table, stumbled through the narrow corridor, into the kitchen, and pushed the screen door open. I crossed the few steps it took to reach the adjoining back entrance to the main house. Debbie's father, a sixtyish man with a flat tummy and toned arms, opened the door.

"Hello," he said in a gruff voice.

"Good afternoon, Mr. Newman, I've come to pay the rent." I held out the three hundred-dollar bills to him.

He folded his arms, tilting his head to one side. "Are you getting any money from Rob's parents?"

"No. I . . . I haven't asked them for help. They don't speak to me."

He stroked his stubbled chin for a minute, then shook his head. "I can't take your money."

"But we agreed. Three hundred a month."

"You keep your money." His looked down at his boots, rocking on his heels. "I could never take money from a woman alone with a child and another on the way." I didn't know what to say. He looked up, leveling his eyes with mine. "You can stay here for as long as you want. Don't worry about paying nothing. I don't know if Debbie told you this, I'm going through a divorce. I'm doing my best to hang on to this house, but my wife wants it sold so she can get her share of the equity. If the judge rules against me, I'll have to sell and move out. But as long as I'm here, you can continue to live here. You cheer up, young lady. You've got a difficult road ahead of you, but there's nothing God can't do."

I blinked down the tears.

"You go on and take care of them kids. Anything you need, you just holler."

"Thank you," I whispered.

Wiping my eyes with the back of my hands, I peeked in on Dele. His diaper was still on. I settled back into the armchair in the living room and closed my eyes, feeling Rob's muscular arms around me, trying to let them massage me.

In the morning, the sitter came in to stay with Dele. As I walked the two blocks to the Ballston metro station, I no longer saw the vendors or women who marched in the sneakers they would later unlace to replace with the high heels that hurt their ankles. Scenes from the funeral haunted me. The sanitized way we sat under two canopies on either side of the grave, the hole in the ground covered with a red velvet carpet, the lacquered brown casket balanced on silvery rods. Pastor Drake's voice resounded like a drum beating on my heart, saying something about how the Lord giveth and taketh. Or was it taketh and giveth? Rob's parents not sitting with me but on the opposite side, both in sunglasses, Barbara slumped against Richard, their only child gone. I had no one I wanted to lean on. Not Molly, not Ate Celestine, though they'd sat beside me in sympathy. My body had held rigid against the beating thoughts, the unvoiced accusations from church members, their furtive glances. Debbie cast sad looks my way, her husband holding her hand. How I wished Rob was there to hold mine. Flowers were laid over the casket and then they said to go home. I shouted no. How could I leave when the casket was still standing? *No, no*, Ate Celestine said, patting my hand. *They lower it after you leave so you don't feel too sad.* Sobs wrenched from me as I lunged forward. They had pinned me back. I didn't want to be spared. I deserved to watch Rob sink down the hole. I deserved to hear the coffin hit the earth, strike my soul with its finality. Oh, God!

A car horn blared, brakes screeched. A man stuck his head out of a red Mustang.

"Watch where you're going, lady!"

I jumped onto the curb. How had I ended up on the road?

I hugged myself, shaking as the driver tore off.

At work, I shut myself in my office, entering His Excellency's office only when he summoned me via the phone. He was a new ambassador with frog eyes and a cataract on one, like a piece of egg white stuck in a frying pan. He was nothing like the previous ambassador, who'd praised my intelligence and left me to do my work. My first day back after maternity leave, this new one had insisted on taking me to a Chinese restaurant for work. I felt respected sitting opposite him until he opened his mouth and poured his life on me.

"In every country I have been posted," he said as he wolfed down his fried rice, "I have made at least two babies. I have children all over Africa."

I laid my fork down.

He laughed with mischief. "I don't have a Ghanaian child, though."

I fantasized about turning my plate upside down on his head. I quickly changed the subject to health insurance for his family. It was difficult explaining to him that the insurance company couldn't cover all eighteen children living with him in and outside America.

In addition to seeing to health-care coverage, I had to enroll his younger children in school and accompany them to get their physicals because, like their father, they didn't speak English. I also had to accompany His Excellency to all his diplomatic functions, and find time to do paperwork at the office.

"Just delegate," he kept saying, but none of the secretaries spoke English. I even had to accompany him for a physical, remain in the room with him while he disrobed, my face turned so that I would not have to look at his underwear.

Evenings, I read to Dele while the baby kicked inside my belly. We had no radio or television, so I made up for it with a lot of singing. We also went for long walks and visited playgrounds. I got on the swings that made me dizzy. I was the only pregnant woman to be seen grappling with the monkey bars or going down the slide. Once, I got stuck in the elbow of a slide, and a man had to pull me out, but the smile on Dele's face said it was worth it. Underneath my activities, the feeling of not deserving itched persistently, like the plastic tag on a new dress. I deserved to be on my miserable way to hell. When, one Sunday after church, some women cornered me, I was open to suggestion.

"We were just thinking," the redhead said. "Have you considered giving up the baby for adoption?"

I stared numbly at her. Ate Celestine added her voice: "It's going to be tough for you raising two children on your own. You don't want to do that."

Their words rolled off me. I could do tough.

"Think about Rob's baby," Molly said. "Think about what's best. He or she deserves to be raised by two parents who will give him a better life than one with you."

When they fluttered off, I plastered my back against the wall, my heart sprinting. A better life for my baby. Maybe they were right. Somewhere in Rob's mind, perhaps the desire to give me a white-picket-fenced life had led him to cheat on taxes. Missing in the voices of church members urging me to give up my baby were Rob's parents'. They had left the church where their son had become unequally yoked with a foreign woman. I, witch, burn me at the stake. Put me in irons!

At home, the phone rang. It was Molly.

"There's a couple in the church that has a problem with you," she said. "It's Paige and Clifford Watson. Clifford asked me to talk to you. He says that you're a source of temptation to him and that it's difficult for him to sit near you in church."

"What? What have I done?"

"Well, it has to do with the clothes you wear. Last Sunday, your dress seemed to be falling off your shoulders."

Sometimes the maternity clothes from the First Baptist Church fit me like a skinny maid in her mistress's gown, but I didn't have money to buy new clothes. I tried to explain that to Molly. "I mean, I'm very pregnant and heavy, why would any man want to look at me?"

"It doesn't matter, it isn't decent. Last Sunday, we picked you up for church, and there you were in a dress with such a wide neck falling off your shoulder."

The following Sunday, the Watsons stayed far away from me. It was as though I were all the bad girls of the Bible rolled into one: Salome, whose dance cost John the Baptist his head; Delilah, whose seductiveness led Samson to his death; and Jezebel, the foreign woman who turned the king's head from the God of Israel, the temptress husbands fantasized about. A fierce stubbornness entered me. I would not be driven away. I would leave the church only when I was ready, dress falling off my shoulders and all.

After the service, one of the singles, who went by B.K., a tall girl with auburn hair, drove me home. When we arrived at the apartment, she turned to me, a thoughtful smile on her face. "Is there anything I can do for you?"

"I can't think of anything," I said, admiring her strong brows and chin.

"What do you do on weekends?"

"Nothing much. On Saturdays, I just clean the house and cook enough meals for the week."

"Then I'll come help you on Saturdays."

I blinked at her. "Why do you want to help me?"

"You seem like a nice girl. Besides, I don't like to see you isolated."

"I'm used to it. But thank you," I whispered, turning away so she couldn't see my tears.

She came every Saturday to help me clean the apartment and cook. Sometimes she drove Dele and me around Washington, DC, pointing out the notorious Watergate Building and the all-marble Kennedy Center. We visited Mount Vernon, where Dele hopped to the music of the fife players, and the Baltimore Aquarium, where he begged to jump in with the dolphins. Every Saturday, she thought of fun things for us to do, places to eat. Apart from her, some of the single guys offered me lifts, even babysitting sometimes.

At a church picnic, I wandered about with a plate of grapes, my eyes on Dele, who raced around with other children. I felt someone watching me and turned around. It was John Peters, a missionary newly arrived from Canada, observing me quietly. His wife, Zelda, stood by him, her stomach round with a baby. The two had done a presentation at church, so I knew they had visited Liberia in the past. Although that gave me some comfort, I'd stayed away from them because they seemed holy. As I held his gaze, he said something to Zelda and eased his lanky body toward me. She followed. When they got to me, I noticed his gentle hazel eyes.

John said hello, his tone reverent. I said hello back, puzzled.

"My wife and I have been talking. You're going to need someone to be with you in the delivery room when your baby is born. Rob can't be there, so I'd like to be with you, if that's all right with you."

Zelda's brown eyes were frank behind her glasses. "Yes, you're really going to need somebody."

I hesitated. It was true they had just returned from some kind of French-language training program in Quebec, but hadn't they heard about my sinfulness? John stood watching me, his eyes full of compassion.

"As you can tell, I'm also pregnant," Zelda smiled. "My baby is due about the same time as yours."

"Thank you so much," I said, still puzzled by their ease. However, I couldn't afford to turn down their offer. B.K. worked full-time. I didn't drive and, in the suburbs, there was no bus route to many places.

John drove me to my prenatal appointments. He'd stay in the room with me, his tall, lanky body leaning against the wall, his hazel eyes full of compassion. Zelda often took me grocery shopping and babysat Dele while I worked. Gradually, I learned to be comfortable around them.

When Debbie's father lost the fight to keep his house, I found an apartment I could afford. I fought the roaches that roamed over the telephone, the rats that bore holes under the sink and gnawed on my address book. I fought them with scrubbing, spraying, and disinfecting until I forgot they had once existed.

As my due date approached, a church woman slipped me a cassette tape by Dr. James Dobson, a Christian psychologist. While I was curled on my side on the couch, Dr. Dobson told me it was better for a child to have two parents than one. His guest, an adoptive mother, spoke in loving tones about how the Lord answered her family's desire to love a child and give it a home, how God filled her empty hands with a child who was now the happiest girl in the universe, how they thanked the brave mother who had done the right thing in giving up her child to loving parents. I cried and cried. The tape ended with Dr. Dobson saying, "If you're an unwed mother out there at the sound of my voice . . ."

Other congregants emailed me exhortations or poured them into my ears via telephone.

Rob was from such a good home, give his child the same.

You don't want to be selfish. Do the brave thing.

Give your baby the benefit of two loving parents.

The words pounded my brain, altered its shape and chemistry. After all, I didn't deserve to keep my baby. What I deserved was to have a knife twisted in my guts until I screamed. I would find a good family for my child and have an open adoption like the one described on Dr. Dobson's tape, where the adoptive parents sent pictures and birthday greetings to the birth mother. When I declared my intention, the church started a prayer chain in search of adoptive parents, and the prayers floated all the way to Lake Pleasant, New York. In less than a week, Ate Celestine called me. "My son knows of a couple in Lake Pleasant, Tilly and Pierce Livingston. They're wonderful Christians who want to adopt a child."

I agreed to meet them. Olga called from Frederick. Despite my long silences, she'd never given up on me. When I told her I was considering adoption, her shrill voice went higher than usual. "Lola! You'll never forgive yourself if you go through with it! I'll do anything to stop you. You can come here. I'll support you for two years, I promise, until you can get back on your feet. Just don't do it, Lola!"

I tried to explain why I was doing it.

"You're guilt-tripping yourself! It's your baby and you shouldn't give it up!"

I shut my ears and stopped answering her calls.

Fofo

The Plant Whose Petals Turn Black

"Why do you want to adopt my baby?" That was my first question for Pierce and Tilly Livingston when we sat down to dinner at my apartment. I had insisted on them coming to my turf, where they would be my guests instead of them taking me out. I had cooked jollof rice and chicken stew, to be followed by ice cream wrapped in crepes.

"Well, we can't have children," Pierce said, shaking his knees rhythmically, making his whole body vibrate. A smallish man with dark hair and a bushy moustache, he resembled a shaggy dog in glasses. "Low sperm count. I'm sterile."

"Yes, we just can't have children," Tilly said in a loud voice, and laid down her fork. "That's why we want to adopt." Everything about Tilly was loud, from her unusual height and size to her voice.

"Why not go through an adoption agency?" I still hadn't touched my plate.

"We've tried that, but there's a rather long wait," Pierce said, still shaking his legs under the table. He took a quick sip of his apple juice with shaky hands, and juice dribbled out the corner of his mouth. He grabbed his napkin.

"Yeah, the waiting period is unbelievable," Tilly shouted, and took a mouthful of jollof rice. I looked at these people. Why would they be better parents for my child than I? As if sensing my thoughts, she swallowed quickly. "We believe in college, Pierce and me." A nervous giggle burst out of her. "I don't know. Maybe it's because I am Asian. We Asians believe in college."

"We Africans believe in college, too."

"Yes," Tilly hastened to agree. "You're very well educated, I can see that."

"I want to be clear on one thing," I said. "The reason I wanted to meet you is so I can have peace that my baby will be in a good home. The other thing is, I want to keep in touch. I want to know that he or she is okay. Would you agree to keep in touch with me? Would you write and let me know that he or she is okay?"

Pierce's fork stopped midway to his mouth, but Tilly nodded rapidly. "Sure, that would be no problem whatsoever."

"And I would like the baby to know that he or she has a sibling."

"I think that would be all right," Pierce said. "If Tilly's okay with it."

"That would be just fine," Tilly said. Pierce's fork finally reached his mouth. Tilly turned to Dele and squeezed his hand. He lit up, prompting her to say to him, "We'd love to have you come and spend some holidays with us." Then she turned to me. "And you know, I'm sure we'll all become very close."

I didn't realize how hard I had held myself erect until then. My shoulders dropped into place.

"And don't worry about medical costs and legal fees and all that," Pierce said.

"We'll take care of everything," Tilly said.

They would pay for my legal fees? "All right, then," I said, picking up my fork. Tilly asked when my next prenatal appointment was. "In two days. Why do you want to know?"

"We wondered if you would mind if we came with you. We want to bond with the baby right away."

I bit my lip, and then I thought, if we were going to be one family, why not have her come with me? "Sure," I said.

That's how when John took me to visit the obstetrician at Arlington County Hospital, Tilly rode along on a bonding mission. She sat in the back of the car, sharing her thoughts in her booming voice.

"We have this foster child living with us! She's so excited, because she's getting a baby sister or brother!"

I felt my fists balling. A baby sister or brother for some girl I knew nothing about, a baby sibling who was really Dele's. I didn't care if Tilly was a saint opening her heart to receive my child. I wanted to sew her lips together.

At the clinic, when Dr. Oyono was ready to examine me, John withdrew outside. I expected Tilly to follow him, but no, she perched on the bed by me, smiling at me as though she were my husband, sucking up all the air so I couldn't breathe. She rubbed my legs, chuckling. "You've got very smooth legs. Do you shave?"

"No." My voice was curt. "I've never shaved, I just don't grow hair on my legs."

"That's very unusual, you're so smooth." Rub, rub. I wondered what would happen if I kicked her. I shook my head. On the other hand, was it a good idea to kick the future mother of my baby? The urge to kick intensified. I resisted. She babbled on. "By the way, I am going to buy a special pump for my breasts."

What was she nattering about?

"I've read that if you stimulate your breasts, they'll start producing milk. That way I can breastfeed the baby."

The image of her reddish brown nipple in my baby's mouth made me want to throw up. I wished she wouldn't sit there with plump cheeks glowing, telling me all the marvelous things she was going to do with my baby. *My* baby. And I didn't want her rubbing my legs. I caught her hand. "Do you mind?"

"Oh, sorry." She giggled. "It's just that your skin is so smooth." *Oh, God.*

John came in when Dr. Oyono had finished examining me. I grabbed his hands. He kissed me on the cheek. "Are you okay?"

"Oui, mais elle m'énèrve," I said in French, letting him know Tilly was annoying me.

"Ne t'inquiète pas," he soothed, and turned to talk to Dr. Oyono, who was scribbling in my file.

Tilly gave me a loving smile and wiggled closer, as if she weren't close enough. "You and John are . . . rather close, aren't you?"

I looked at her. *I hope you are not insinuating anything by that.* I itched to slap her, then she went on to prattle about more lovely things, such as how she intended to decorate the nursery. I gritted my teeth. I wanted to tell her the baby was mine, not hers, that she should go back to Pierce, go back to Lake Pleasant, go back to kingdom come and leave me alone. I didn't care if she was kinder than Mother Teresa. I was as bitter as the fofo plant.

Somehow, I managed to hold myself together for the rest of the doctor's visit. I was very relieved when she and Pierce returned to Lake Pleasant, making me promise to call them as soon as I went into labor so they could be there to witness the birth of our baby. It was all I could do not to screech at them.

I was a twisted knot of contradictions. Yes, it would be a good idea to give up my baby for adoption to these two apparently loving people who were better than single me. But still. Single women in Ghana raised children. Of course, they maybe weren't responsible for their husband's death.

Church people seemed to have a vested interest in my baby. My phone rang constantly from them wanting to know if I was in labor yet. I wanted to yank out my phone and hurl it across the room. Thank God for my little circle of friends. Zelda had delivered her baby three weeks before, but within a week, she was visiting me in my apartment. B.K. came over every day after work to help me cook or take care of Dele. John monitored my pregnancy, listening to the baby's heartbeat daily. He had taken a course in midwifery and delivered his own baby. He bought me a cell phone and asked me to call him if I went into labor, regardless of the time. He, Zelda, and B.K. formed a protective shield around me. Not a day went by without my seeing one or all of them.

One afternoon, the phone rang.

"This is Scott Roanoke," said a booming, cheerful voice.

"Yes?"

"Pierce and Tilly Livingston retained me to represent them in the adoption."

"Oh yes, of course. How are you?"

"I'm fine. Thanks for asking. Do you have an attorney I can contact?"

"Wait a minute, I thought you were going to be my lawyer."

"No. I can't represent you. You see," he explained patiently, "I represent Pierce and Tilly. You need your own attorney, and the baby needs one, too."

"But I don't have money to hire one! They said they would pay the legal fees. I thought that included mine, too, otherwise why would they have told me that?"

"It's a conflict of interest. You need your own attorney."

I wanted to cry. "I don't even know how to go about finding one."

He sounded concerned. "This isn't right, you not having a lawyer. I'll see what I can do." He hung up, promising to call within a few days.

My stomach cramped and I wondered if labor had started. I called John, who rushed to my apartment. "Maybe that's it," he said, settling beside me on the couch. "I'm going to stay with you, just in case."

"Thanks, John." I slouched on the couch, feeling gloomy.

"What's wrong, Lola?" he asked, squeezing my hand.

"I know this sounds weird, but I don't want the baby to come, because then I wouldn't have to give it up."

"I know," he said softly, and took both of my hands in his.

We waited and waited, but the cramping stopped. I looked at his placid face. Here he was, a new father, spending so much time with me. I wondered how Zelda could allow him to do that.

"John, I'm okay," I said. "Really, please. Go home to Zelda, she needs you." He agreed to go, but an hour later, he was back.

"Well," he said, shaking his head. "Zelda is worried about you. She doesn't want you to be alone, so she asked me to come back."

A lump formed in my throat. She and their kids were staying with her parents, so she wasn't alone. Even so, it was incredibly generous of her. In a church that saw me as the seductive witch, she trusted her husband to take care of me.

By ten p.m., the cramps had disappeared.

"False labor," John said. He returned home.

Four days later, he and B.K. were with me in my apartment around six in the evening when pain grabbed my abdomen. This time, the labor was real. Molly came to pick up Dele. John checked the baby's heartbeat every hour. I decided to do all my laundry before I had to go to the hospital. B.K. couldn't believe it. I was doing six loads of laundry while in labor. In between contractions, I taught her to do the merengue. I was a witch, after all.

She laughed. "Lola, you're crazy!"

John grinned. "Since you're so full of energy, why don't we go for a walk? That will help speed things up. B.K., do you mind staying behind in case Zelda arrives?"

"Sure," she said, plopping down in an armchair.

I grabbed a light jacket, and John and I stepped into the chilly night. The lampposts cast a soft glow over the landscape, turning the sidewalk gray. Conflicting feelings roiled inside me, the excitement of an impending life and the sharp sadness of Rob's absence. Suddenly, something warm spattered out of my panties onto the pavement.

"John?"

He knelt down and pressed his fingers into the fluid and examined them in the light. He frowned. "It's thick. I think you're leaking water, amniotic fluid."

I gasped. "Is the baby coming?"

He twisted his mouth to one side, thinking. "I don't think so. It's just a small amount. In my midwifery course, they said this wasn't unusual. Let's keep going."

About ten yards later it happened again. The third time, there was a thick brown substance in the middle.

He squatted to get a better look, then looked up at me. "That's meconium, a mucus-like substance that protects the baby. I think we need to head back. Better play it safe."

We returned to find Zelda settled on the couch, baby Rahab on her lap.

"She's leaking amniotic fluid," John said. "We better get ready for the baby. I'll boil the knives and instruments."

Zelda frowned. "I think she should go to the hospital, John."

"It's not necessary. I can deliver the baby myself. Didn't I deliver Rahab?"

I didn't know what to think. The idea of a home birth appealed to me because I didn't want strangers poking inside my body. I glanced at B.K., but she smiled and shrugged as if to say, *Your call.*

I looked at John. "If you want to deliver the baby, that's fine by me."

John turned to go to the kitchen.

"John, you don't know enough," Zelda said with increased anxiety. "If she's leaking amniotic fluid, you need to take her to the hospital. There may be a complication that you couldn't handle."

That's something I hadn't considered.

"What do you think, Lola?" John asked.

"I'm not sure. I hadn't thought about a possible complication." As I stood there, water fell from between my legs again.

Zelda raised her voice. "John, take her to the hospital!"

"Yeah." I laughed nervously. "I think I'll go."

It was ten p.m. when John and B.K. drove me to the hospital while Zelda returned home.

Nyamedua

God's Rod

The doctor on duty was a fresh-faced intern called Dr. Hernandez. An ultrasound showed very little amniotic fluid left around the baby.

"If your labor doesn't progress, you might have to have a cesarean," he said.

"I don't want a cesarean."

"Then let's hope the baby arrives soon."

He belted the monitor so tightly over my belly that I couldn't breathe properly. I told him so, but he said pompously, "That's how it's supposed to be."

"If I can't breathe properly, that might cut off oxygen to the baby."

His face registered surprise, then respect. "I understand you're giving up this baby for adoption."

"Yes, and what of that?"

"Nothing," he said, and left. John squeezed my hand.

"I can't breathe properly and he won't listen."

Ten minutes later, the doctor strode into my room. "The baby is showing signs of distress, I'm going to have to operate."

"A cesarean section? No way. I tell you it's the fetal monitor. The belt is too tight and I can't breathe."

He got upset. "You'd better consent to a C-section or you'll have to sign an affidavit releasing the hospital from any liability because of your stubbornness."

I felt my blood boil. "I'll do no such thing. You want to get off scot free if you do something wrong. Just loosen the belt over my tummy!"

"You're just being stubborn. You don't care about the baby, because you're giving it up."

I nearly choked with rage. "How dare you! How dare you!"

"If you cared, you'd agree to a C-section."

"Get out!" I panted. The muscles of my stomach clawed at my womb and squeezed. I moaned.

"You must sign the affidavit."

"I refuse!"

"Signez-le," John said in French.

"Non! Je refuse de signer!" The muscles of my womb started to let go. The doctor turned on his heel and stormed out of the room. He returned with an older female doctor.

"I'm Dr. Simmons. What seems to be the matter?" she asked with a smile.

"This doctor is very insulting," I panted as another contraction came on. "He wants to give me a C-section. I won't do it and he's pressuring me to sign papers!"

"Well," she said, "the monitor does show that the baby is in distress. If we don't do something soon, it could be fatal."

"Tell you what. You loosen the belt on my stomach and give me a couple of minutes. If there's no change, then I'll do the bloody C-section."

She agreed and loosened the belt. They both left and I was able to breathe. Five minutes later she came back alone.

"You know what," she said, "I can't explain it, but the baby is fine. Looking at the two readings, you'd think it was a different baby."

"I told him it was the belt but he wouldn't listen!"

"You have to understand," she said in a conspiratorial tone, "he's young and nervous. He's just afraid of making a mistake, you know. According to the reading, the baby was in serious distress."

I allowed myself to be mollified. John stroked my forehead and B.K. held my hand. She had remained quiet throughout my tirade. Just a solid wall of silence holding me up. I breathed evenly. A few minutes later, the labor became intense, one contraction following another. Dr. Simmons examined me and said, "She's a hundred percent dilated!" The delivery room was a different room on another floor, upstairs. I felt an urge to push. "Hold on!" the doctor said. "Hold on! Don't push!" Dr. Hernandez joined her.

The orderlies raced down the corridor with me on the bed, the doctors struggling into surgical gowns and masks while running to keep up. I caught sight of John and B.K. racing along with them.

"Hurry," I said. I felt an urge like a bowel movement, and I wanted desperately to push.

"Hold on, just hold on!" Dr. Simmons said. We got to the elevator but not everyone could fit in. The doctors got in with me, and the rest scrambled around for another elevator. I kept saying, "I've got to push, I've got to push."

They got me into the labor room just in time.

"Episiotomy!" Dr. Hernandez said.

"Forget that," Dr. Simmons said. "Just go on and push."

I pushed and the baby's head came out. After a second, she asked me to push again and the baby came out so fast that, according to John, they almost dropped her.

She turned blue right away because she had swallowed a lot of meconium. They raced to a counter and placed her under a machine. They pumped the mucus out of her, and she howled her first breath. Dr. Hernandez leaned over me and asked if I wanted to see her. Yes, I said.

He frowned. "I thought that because you were giving her up—"

"I want to see my baby!"

I had chosen the name Kemi if she was a girl. It was an optimistic name that meant "Pamper me with wealth." I hoped she would grow up to have not just material wealth, but a wealth of wisdom, character, and love. When the nurse placed her in my arms and I looked into her almond eyes, at her silky hair and tapering fingers, I thought she was the most beautiful thing I had ever laid eyes on. She was alert, casting her eyes in all directions. I cradled her to me as to life itself. Because I was going to give her up and didn't want her to miss my nipple, a nurse brought me a bottle I gave to her. I insisted they put her crib in my room for the three days we would spend in the hospital.

Molly Heineman called Pierce and Tilly, and they drove down from Lake Pleasant that very morning. Tilly burst into my room, glowing with joy. She planted a big kiss on both of my cheeks with a resounding smack. Try as I did, I couldn't warm up to her. This woman was going to take my baby from me, even if she was doing it with my permission.

"What a wonderful thing!" she gushed. "She's so beautiful!" John shot me a sympathetic smile.

The Heinemans also came, bringing Dele with them. He was unusually quiet, his eyes downcast.

"Come here, Dele," I said softly. "See the baby? That's your sister."

"Baby," he said, and patted her forehead. I cast my eyes at the Heinemans to thank them, but my tongue wouldn't move. Pierce and Tilly were staying with them. Not only were those two taking my baby, they were stealing my friends as well. Ate Celestine and Zelda arrived separately. So did Pastor Drake and his wife. Scott Roanoke, the attorney, also came, which surprised me.

"Lola, it's nice to meet you," he said in his strong voice, which seemed out of place with his soft brown eyes. "What a beautiful baby you have there!" I liked him at once.

For three days, Kemi slept on my stomach both day and night. I wanted to spend every last, precious minute with her. Dr. Hernandez kept coming to see us. He spoke to me in soft tones and even looked sad sometimes. Once, he asked, "Are you really going to give up your baby?"

"Yes," I said. A look of sorrow clouded his face and he left quickly.

John and I had talked about how I would hand Kemi over to the Livingstons. I had come to the conclusion that I couldn't trust anybody with my baby, so I had decided to have a dedication ceremony in the hospital chapel before giving her up.

I invited only those I felt really cared: John and Zelda Peters, B.K., Ate Celestine, Stuart and Molly Heineman, Philip and Debbie Winston. I also invited Scott Roanoke. I had invited Penelope and Benjamin Washington, the Black couple at our church, but they had refused to come because they were against the adoption. Rob's parents remained invisible.

The morning I was to be discharged, we gathered inside the small hospital chapel. Pastor Drake preached a short sermon about Hannah, who gave up her son Samuel for the service of the Lord. There was no use pointing out that Samuel had remained her son; even if he had lived at the church with Eli, the priest, that she visited him once a year. I sat there numb, like someone observing some strange ritual that had nothing to do with me. There was praying and singing. Kemi nestled in my arms, fast asleep in her white sweater, her silky hair sheathed in a hood, her tiny feet in bootees. John got up and sang in his beautiful tenor: "Go forth, Jacob, do not be afraid. Go to the land I have chosen for thee . . ."

Dele rested his head on my shoulder. He was unusually quiet. Tears rolled down my cheeks. When the dedication was over, people came up to me and said sympathetic things, but I heard nothing. John stood next to me, holding my hand. I tried to speak, but I had difficulty getting the words out. He bent down so that I could whisper in his ear. "Could you ask the Livingstons to step outside, please, I need some time alone."

The sanctuary emptied except for John and B.K. She knelt beside my wheelchair, eyes brimming over.

"Oh, Lola," she sobbed, "more than anything, I wanted you to keep this baby." She had been a rock throughout. Now I gripped her hand, unable to speak, stroking her hair. She took Kemi's hand then bent over and kissed her forehead. She stood up and looked down at us, then she turned around and walked outside.

John knelt by me. We were alone with my children. I lifted my pained eyes to his. "So, John," I whispered, my voice hoarse, "do we give her up?" The tears poured out. He let me cry, saying nothing. Then he took out a handkerchief and wiped my eyes before wiping his. I felt paralyzed. There was no way I could physically hand my baby over to the Livingstons. Somehow, if someone I trusted took her, it would feel as if I wasn't giving her up to strangers. "I can't do this, John. Could you help me? Could you give them Kemi?" He nodded. I pressed her against me one last time and touched my lips to her warm cheeks. Gently, he eased her from my arms and wrapped her carefully in her beautiful white shawl, a gift from a Panamanian friend. He walked out slowly. An intense pain cut through me. I doubled up. "Oh, God! Oh, my God!"

B.K. rushed in and knelt by me. "Lola, oh, Lola, I'm so sorry. Please!" I couldn't stop crying, and neither could she. We were there for a long time. Finally, she wiped her face and asked me, "Are you ready to go out? You have to say goodbye."

I nodded like a zombie. My eyelids were so swollen I could barely see. When she wheeled me outside, I was relieved to note that most of our guests had left. Pierce and Tilly's car was parked out there with the right back door open. A car seat awaited. Tilly was holding Kemi, who was still sleeping.

"We'll take good care of her," she promised.

I nodded while the tears continued to flow past my cheeks onto my purple pinafore. Then they went to their car and put her in the car seat. How do you say goodbye to your own flesh? I felt as if someone had punched my stomach open, grabbed and pulled until all of my insides got ripped out. I wanted to shriek, claw my skin. Kemi was still asleep. I reached my hands out, grabbing at air. They drove off. I sat there for a long time looking at the vanishing New York State license plates until my vision blurred.

Wo Nsa Da Mu A

If Your Hand Is in the Dish

I had assumed the Livingstons would call to thank me when they got to New York, but my phone stayed silent. All through the night, I wrestled with my pillows, sleeping in fits and starts. I kept jerking awake because I thought I could hear Kemi crying for me. In the morning, I woke up with a start. Something was terribly wrong. Something . . . Kemi, oh God. Fresh tears started. Dele huddled in a corner watching me with somber eyes. I made him breakfast, but I didn't talk to him. Afterward, I curled into a ball on the couch.

John arrived with a meal from Zelda. Other people sent meals, but my throat seemed closed off. All day long, I kept hoping the Livingstons would call me, but they didn't. Finally, in the evening, I called them. Pierce answered the phone.

"Hello," he said coolly to my hello. Didn't he recognize my voice?

"It's Lola."

"Yes. Can I help you?"

Can you help me? You have my baby and you ask if you can help me?

"I called to see how Kemi was doing."

"She's doing fine," he said matter-of-factly.

Silence.

"Well, let me know how things go."

"Okay," he said.

I hung up and fell onto the couch, shaking with anger. Is this how they proposed to keep in touch, this coldness from them? I called Scott Roanoke.

"I'm very upset," I said.

"What's wrong?"

"The Livingstons went to Lake Pleasant and didn't even call to tell me they'd arrived safely or even to say thank you! Then, when I called them just now, Pierce got on the phone and said, 'Can I help you?' Can he help me? What is that supposed to mean? I don't think they'll keep their promise to keep in touch."

He calmed me down with promises to call them. Pierce called me a few minutes later. "Lola, I'm sorry if I upset you, but I didn't know what to say when you called."

"You could have said a warm hello the way you did before you got my baby!"

"I'm sorry, but I'm not very good with people and I didn't mean anything by that. Look, I give you my word, and I'm a man of my word. I give you my word that we'll keep in touch with you."

Tilly got on the phone with her happy voice. "If you like, we can have Scott Roanoke draw up a clause in the adoption papers that we'll keep in touch with you."

"I'd like you to send me pictures."

"How often?"

I hadn't thought it through. "Send me a picture every month."

"Okay, we can do that for the first year, and then twice during the second year and then maybe once a year after that."

I was looking for any strings that would allow me to hold on to my daughter. I wanted to have her pictures, arrange them before me as she grew, using my imagination to view her life as in a film.

Two days later, I woke up to find my breasts the size of watermelons. They were so engorged, I thought they would burst with milk. My nipples burned. By evening, I was running a fever. Zelda came over with baby Rahab.

"Sit down, Lola," she said. I sat on the love seat. "Let's try to get you to nurse Rahab. That should relieve you of some milk."

She put Rahab on my lap. Rahab smiled at me and tugged at my chest. I eased my nipple into her mouth. She licked it lazily for a moment, then pushed it out with her tongue and turned her head away.

"Come on, Rahab, go to work," Zelda urged. She took Rahab's head in her hands and directed her mouth toward my nipple. Rahab shook her head and turned away. How did wet nurses do it? After several tries, Zelda gave up and put Rahab in her car seat. She looked at me anxiously. "Are you in a lot of pain?"

"Yes," I said. My breasts throbbed, felt hot. I let out a howl. "I want my baby! I want my baby!"

Poor Zelda didn't know what to do. Then she got an idea.

"Why don't we go into the bathroom? I think if we put warm water on your breasts, maybe we can squeeze some of the milk out."

Leaving Rahab in the living room, she led me into the bathroom. I tried to stop the heaving in my chest. She eyed the shower. "We'd better get out of our clothes or we'll get wet."

We peeled off our clothes and hung them on a chair in the dining area. Then we returned to the bathroom and stepped into the tub together. She drew the plastic shower curtain before turning on the shower, checking the water to make sure it was hot enough. "Why don't you get under the shower?"

The hot water ran over my breasts and steamed around us. She grabbed my right breast in both hands and pressed toward the nipple. I leaned back against the pink tiles, planting my feet firmly so I wouldn't slip. She squeezed and squeezed, but not a drop came out. The steam turned foggy, like a sauna. Here we were, I thought to myself, two naked women in a tub, one trying to squeeze milk out of the other's breasts. A giggle escaped me.

She laughed too and said, "If only we had a breast pump."

"What's that?"

"It's something that pumps milk out of a woman's breast."

"I've never heard of it. In Ghana, when a woman gets too much breast milk, they get a child to suck the milk out."

"Really?" She stopped squeezing, her eyes wide open. A film of water covered her skin, her boyish black hair matted.

"Yes."

"Well, I could give it a try? Because we're not getting anywhere with this."

I hesitated. "You don't mind?"

"No. You might get an infection if we don't get rid of some of the milk."

"Okay."

As if it were the most natural thing in the world, she lowered her head, put her mouth to my nipple, and sucked. The relief was instant. "Yeech!" She spat out. "This stuff tastes awful! I can't believe babies eat this." I giggled. She spat again and bravely filled her mouth before spitting out the milk. "Yeech!" She wiped her mouth with the back of her hand. "This stuff is ghastly!" I laughed as she sucked and sucked my breasts until the pressure and pain eased. We laughed until our tears mingled with the water on our faces.

We were so noisy we didn't hear B.K. arrive. Since the apartment door was unlocked, she had let herself in. She was sitting in the armchair facing the hallway when we stumbled out naked and dripping. She blinked at us. I stopped in my tracks and crossed my arms over my breasts.

"Hi, B.K.," Zelda said casually, and got a towel out of the linen closet.

"It's not what you think," I said.

"Oh, Lola," B.K. choked out, laughing, "life is never dull around you!"

When Zelda and I got dressed and joined B.K. in the sitting room, Zelda kept muttering, "That stuff tastes terrible," a look of disgust on her face as she cradled Rahab.

"What stuff?" B.K. asked.

"Shall I tell her?" I asked Zelda. She nodded, and I turned to B.K. "Zelda sucked the milk out of my breasts because they were hurting."

"She what?" B.K.'s eyes were saucers. We dissolved into laughter.

She agreed to go buy a breast pump, and returned as Zelda was nursing Rahab. She took a plastic cylindrical pump out of the box and read the instructions.

"Well, Lola," she said, "should we try this?"

I nodded. She grabbed a chair from the dining area and sat opposite me as I removed my blouse and bra. She fastened the mouth of the pump onto my nipple and began pumping. My nipple stretched into the tube, looking absurdly long.

"Well, Lola," she said, "I have to thank you for this unique experience. Never in my wildest imagination did I think I'd be sitting here pumping another woman's breast."

We giggled. The device grabbed and sucked my nipple until milk filled the chamber. She transferred the milk into a feeding bottle, but I refused to pour the milk down the drain. I put it in the refrigerator and stared at it. Colostrum, which is mainly fat, rose to the top. Rich yellow colostrum, which the doctors said was good for babies and provided precious antibodies. Here was good milk for my baby and she wasn't here to suckle it. I swallowed hard.

It was now only Dele and me at the apartment for the three-month maternity leave the embassy had given me. I fixed sandwiches for him, curled up on the couch, and stared at the small black-and-white TV the Winstons had given me. When I wasn't staring at the television screen, I listened to music from a small Sony radio, a gift from Benjamin and Penelope Washington. Dele kept the beat by drumming on the wooden arm of the couch with his crayons, yet his silent eyes followed my every move. John visited me every day, sometimes with Zelda, sometimes by himself. B.K., too, came by every evening after work. I would forget my pain for a while and laugh with them, but the moment they left, the searing heartache would return and I would take to the couch. I slept in the bedroom only when Dele had a nightmare.

I had learned to use the breast pump, twice a day, filling jars with my milk that I continued to store. But one day, I made myself pour the milk down the drain. Then I clutched my abdomen and sobbed. That night, it felt as if my mind were cracking itself into two.

I reached for the phone and dialed the number of Jacques, that kind gentleman who had helped me get a job at the embassy. He had taken me to dinner once, his hopeful eyes dimmed by my refusal. Then he'd seen me pregnant, on the metro.

"I gave up my baby," I sobbed into the phone. "I gave up my baby for adoption."

He gasped. "C'est pas possible! That could drive you over the edge."

"Could you come over?"

"Bien sûr!" he said, and within half an hour, he was at my door. I threw myself in his arms, crying.

"Stay the night," I implored.

He got into bed with me and held me while I wept. He stroked by back. I twisted myself around to face him, took his face in my hands, and kissed him. Then I was tugging at his shirt, pulling it off him, pulling his zipper down, the hole in me so deep I needed him to plug it. I tore off my sweater and offered him my breast.

"*Oh, God,*" he said, sucking on my nipple. He raised his head, surprised pleasure on his face. "Milk. You've got milk."

The breast couldn't distinguish between a baby's mouth and a man's. I thought of the starving man in *The Grapes of Wrath*, how Rose Sharon, whose baby was stillborn, had offered him her breast to save his life. This time I was the one with a desperate, different kind of hunger. I pushed my breast at him. "Eat it. Eat it all." He did, oh, how he did. He gulped and moved below me. All he did was touch his tongue to me and I was climaxing. I tugged at him, urging him inside me. "Plug me!" I was seeking to plug a void inside my soul and failing. He tried to slow down, but I pulled him in deep. Everything in him poured out as I muscled him in deeper until he'd shrunken from engorgement into a reduced, limp stillness that slid out, me spasming to hold on, wanting to never feel this empty again. Utterly spent, I fell into deepest slumber.

In the morning, he fixed me breakfast, cold cereal. I sat across from him, unable to meet his eyes.

"I love you, Lola, you know that. I'm in love with you."

Oh no, I groaned inwardly. I was so empty. I had nothing to give him. "I'm sorry, Jacques."

He winced. "Je comprends." He obviously didn't comprehend. I looked at his lean, handsome face, guilt washing over me. He didn't say another word to me.

As he was leaving, I touched his arm. "Maybe one day . . ."

"Sure." He didn't smile.

I had just returned from the bathroom when a knock sounded on my door. I opened it to find Scott Roanoke standing there, his stocky body encased in a suit, a briefcase in hand.

"Hi, Lola," he said. I stood there blinking at him, wondering what he was doing at my door. "I called yesterday, remember? I brought the adoption papers."

"Oh, sorry, I forgot. I haven't been myself lately. Please come in."

He stepped over Dele's fire truck and walked to the dining table, placing his briefcase on it. Dele stopped banging on a can and grabbed the truck, pushing it around. Scott sat down, flicked his briefcase open, and drew out a stack of papers.

"Here they are," he said. "You want to read carefully before you sign."

I took the papers with trembling hands, not sitting down. I read with a sense of finality until I saw "termination of parental rights."

My head jerked up. "What does this mean, termination of parental rights?"

"When an adoption becomes final, the court terminates your parental rights. In other words, you're no longer Kemi's mother."

"No longer MY daughter's mother? I *am* her mother. I will always be her mother. Besides, the Livingstons agreed to keep in touch."

"That's one thing you need to understand. Once your rights are terminated, you have no rights at all. The Livingstons can choose not to communicate with you, and there's nothing you can do about it. The state will issue them a new birth certificate with their names on it."

"What!"

"And they can move anywhere in the world with your child. If they choose, they can disappear and never keep in touch with you."

"But they gave me their word."

"Yes, but you'd only be depending on their goodwill. Legally, once the adoption is final, they don't have to honor their promise to you."

A roaring began in my ear. I had never heard of termination of parental rights. I plopped myself onto the couch, gripping the paper, the full weight of adoption hitting me.

"Look," Scott said, rising to his feet. "I think you need to think carefully about it. If you're not sure about this adoption, then don't sign the papers." He looked steadily at me. "I'll tell you what, I'll hang on to these papers and tell them you're not ready to sign. Legally, you have six months to make up your mind. I can't in good conscience let you sign anything unless you're absolutely sure of what you're doing. Because once you sign the papers, it's almost impossible to get your baby back."

"Thank you so much. I can't thank you enough for your integrity."

We shook hands and he left. I sat again, stunned. How many girls in my position had been pressured into signing papers when they were not ready? As a single woman without a job, I stood no chance against a wealthy, two-parent family.

After Christmas, I returned to work. Near the end of January, around lunchtime, I was at my desk when His Excellency buzzed me on the intercom to come into his office. Grabbing my notepad as usual, I opened the door and sat at the edge of the couch. He was sitting behind his massive desk, light flooding in through the bay window behind him. I placed my notepad on my lap and clutched my pen in the ready position for note-taking. He smiled and rose from his desk. "Comment vas-tu, mademoiselle?"

"Très bien, merci," I responded, eyeing him. In all our interactions, he had never before come out from behind his desk. My eyes followed him as he walked toward me, his pillowy stomach leading him, until he sat down next to me on the couch. I shifted to create space between us.

"I am very sorry your husband died."

I swallowed to ease the burning in my throat, staring at his cataract eyes. "Merci beaucoup, Excellence."

"You must be really lonely, you poor girl. A beautiful thing like you." He inched closer, his breath hot on my cheek, his smile oily, displaying his jigsaw teeth. I leaned away from him and ended up on my back. "You know, you didn't even give me a Christmas present."

"Excuse me?"

He laid a callused hand on my knee, grinning like a hyena. "Well, it's not too late, you know. I have to collect my Christmas present today. We will comfort each other over your poor, deceased husband."

He squeezed my thigh. My mind froze. Everything unfolded in slow motion. I watched me lie there, mute. Unmoving. Watched as he rose up. Watched his hands go to the buckle of his belt and loosen it. Watched as the brown belt snaked through the beige straps and fell down. Watched as he unzipped his trousers and let them fall to his ankles, revealing discolored long johns. Watched. He stepped out of his trousers. Watched. He drew out his distended organ from the long johns. Watched. He moved forward and above me. Watched. He raised my skirt, feeling the dryness between my legs. He wet his finger with his saliva. My mind snapped. My fist landed in his soft abdomen. He yelped and stumbled backward, his eyes round. All the rage in me collected in my fists. I sprang up and landed a blow to his cheek. He went sprawling on the wine-colored carpet. His glasses flew off. I kicked the turgid flesh between his legs. He groaned and folded up. I grabbed the door handle and was out of his office, running down the stairs, running all the way to the metro.

I sat on the train, heart pounding. His Non-Excellence's long johns and organ kept rising before me. I fought the urge to throw up. At home, I held myself together, but as soon as Dele fell asleep, I started shaking. In the night, the ambassador came at me with his hyena smile, his organ in my face. I bit him and jerked awake, shaking, my heart sprinting. The next day, John and Zelda huddled together on the love seat, looking at me.

"Were you wearing makeup?" Zelda wanted to know.

"What's that supposed to mean?"

"Your makeup makes you look inviting."

"I can't believe you'd say that to me."

John said gruffly, "Come on, Zelda. Would I try to rape a woman because of her makeup?"

She ignored him. "What I mean is, you want to attract men with your character, not your looks. You're already beautiful. Makeup is seductive. I never wear any."

"True," John said. "I mean, Zelda wasn't much to look at when I met her, but I was bowled over by her personality."

They went on and on. I didn't trust myself to speak. They noticed my silence and stopped talking. After they left, I grabbed the phone and called the desk officer for the Central African Republic at the State Department. I had spoken to the lady countless times and we had solved problems together. That was one person who would know how to advise me.

"I'm sorry this happened to you," she said quietly.

"What can I do to him?"

She hesitated. "Well, you could report him and start a case against him. But you know," she added in a conspirator's voice, her voice lowered, "there were no witnesses, from what you said. It will be your word and against his. If you go to court, they'll dig into your background. Trust me, most women end up being shamed and portrayed as sluts who asked for it. It happened to a friend of mine. Believe me, you don't want that. Not my official advice, just a personal opinion. It's up to you if you want to pursue this, but he has diplomatic immunity. You don't, you're an A2 diplomat. They won't put him in jail. Are you sure you want to pursue this?"

I hung up the phone, laughing hysterically. America was no different from Ghana or Dakar after all! All that talk about women's equality. In Africa, I had known the score. A man forcing himself on me was banal. Almost every woman I knew had experienced that. We tucked sexual assault into the cupboards of our minds and locked them up because no one would listen anyway. Now an American woman official was advising me not to bother. I already knew how to seal it and forget. It wasn't my fault, I knew that. I would not let his Non-Excellence steal more from me by branding me a slut and destroying my reputation.

I remained at home. The economic counselor called me, wondering where I was. She said the ambassador was in the hospital. I narrated what happened. "I can't work there anymore."

"Oh, mon Dieu. What will you do for money?"

I had no answer, but I knew I would never give up fighting to find a job. I had succeeded once and would do it again.

"Don't resign right away. I would advise you to look for another job quietly, then resign. In the meantime, you just have to stay out of his way. I'll do what I can to protect you."

"I can't come, madam. What will happen when he returns from the hospital? He will probably fire me."

She paused for a moment. "Okay. Your visa is valid for another year. I'll talk to the first counselor not to cancel it. That way, you'll remain legal and get another job, okay? I'm sorry about this. So sorry. This is terrible."

I thanked her and hung up. That night, when Dele was sleeping, I called Jacques. I just wanted to talk to him.

He was curt. "I don't want to be the drug you reach for when you want to numb yourself, okay?"

"I'm sorry," I mumbled.

His voice softened. "Look, I said I love you and I meant it. If you want to talk, fine, but I won't stay over."

"I'm sorry I called. It's not fair to you."

"Lola, I—"

I hung up. He was right. I threw myself on the couch, howling, punching the cushions until I was drained. Dele whimpered in his sleep. Dele. He was still here. He needed me. I attended to his physical needs but I was emotionally absent because I couldn't stop thinking about Kemi. I was so tired of life taking from me. Why did I have to add to my punishment? Why give up my baby? What madness was that? I would never have the energy to move on and pursue a career when I *knew* she was out there, not knowing how she was, not being able to hold her. The pain jagged at me over and over again.

The Livingstons had sent me a picture of her at one month and at two months, but rather than make me feel better, it made me want to bang my head against the wall. Tilly had included a typed note using abbreviations like "pics" for pictures and without signing her letter. Also, she'd typed a Bible verse from Ecclesiastes and taped it to the top: "Two is better than one. If one falls down, his friend can help him up." I took it as a jibe at my status as a single parent. Then they sent me a copy of the home studies done by the Department of Social Services. Tilly described herself as a lazy housewife, and addicted to bingo nights. Moreover, she said that her side of the family was racist toward Black people but was prepared to accept Kemi. Tilly's redeeming quality was that she liked to read. Pierce described himself as lively, practical, someone who loved to garden in his free time. To save money, their house was kept at fifty-five degrees Fahrenheit throughout the winter of upstate New York. But he said that Kemi's room was set at sixty degrees. What did these people have that I didn't have, except a steady income, a large, cold house, and each boring other? These people were going to raise my baby? I complained bitterly to Scott Roanoke on the phone. He said, "You're just not ready to give up your baby. Like I said, you just say the word, and we'll have your baby back in your arms."

My phone rang constantly. Debbie was upset. "I don't get you. It's your baby. It's an easy thing. God gave you that child. Just take her back." I hung up on her, unwilling to talk.

Penelope Washington said in her sweet voice, "That little girl is yours. We will not harass you, but our family is praying and we know you will take your baby back. I'll bring you more bread on Sunday."

Molly admonished me. "Think about this carefully. If you take her back, just know that for the next eighteen years, you're going to be locked up in parenthood. How do you expect to take care of two children when you don't have a job? Don't be selfish."

Ate Celestine implored me. "I raised one son and it wasn't easy. Think of what it will take to raise two children."

Olga yelled from Frederick. "Take her back! I'm hurt you didn't take my offer of support. It still stands, you take your baby back, you hear?"

I stopped answering my phone. John and Zelda continued to visit, holding their tongues. "It's not for us to tell you what to do. We love you, that's all," John said.

For weeks, I swung back and forth above a vacuum of indecision. The Livingstons must have bonded with her, I thought. I remembered how I wanted to die when the New York license plates carrying her disappeared from view. I pictured Tilly's face swollen with tears, Pierce's mouth quivering, destroyed because of me.

One day in bed, I found myself reading the book of Romans "It is God who justifies. Who is he that condemns?" *I am the one condemning me.* "I am convinced that neither death nor life, neither angels nor demons, neither the present nor the future, nor any powers, neither height nor depth, nor anything else in all creation, will be able to separate us from the love of God." *Yes, yes, yes!*

I didn't need to flagellate myself and give up my baby to atone for Rob's death. I was one with God Nisi, the Warrior; God Shalom, Peace; God Jireh, Provider. I was the Little Engine That Could. I could pull two kids along. As for Pierce and Tilly, they could bear the pain of loss too. They would have to find a way to pull themselves along.

Sunday, after the sermon, I stood up and announced, "I'm taking my baby back."

You could hear every pulse in the silence that followed, every breath, the whir of butterfly wings outside. Then Pastor Drake smiled. "Good for you. I never thought you should do it."

Ate Celestine looked composed. Molly Heineman's mouth settled into a line. Debbie Winston shot me a victorious smile. B.K.'s eyes misted. John and Zelda hugged me.

That night, I sat down and penned the Livingstons a long letter. I thanked them for loving and taking care of my baby and asked them to forgive me for hurting them. I asked when would be a good time to pick her up. I sent a copy to Scott and made copies for myself.

Then I waited. A week passed, and there was no response from them.

"You haven't signed any papers," Scott pointed out over the phone. "All they have is a power of attorney that gives them the authority to take Kemi to the hospital, nothing else. If they give you any trouble, we can just call the sheriff, and they'll pick up your baby for you."

Penelope Washington called. "If they won't respond to your letter, don't wait for them. Benjamin and I have talked it over, and he'll drive you to Lake Pleasant."

"Really?"

"Yes, Lola, we'll get your baby back."

Benjamin called me to confirm that he would pick me up the next day at seven in the morning. I wrestled with the sheets all night long and was up by four a.m. When Benjamin knocked on my door precisely at seven, Dele and I were ready. Benjamin's twelve-year-old son sat in front. Dele and I sat in the backseat for the drive, seven hours and thirty minutes from Arlington, Virginia, to Lake Pleasant, New York. The journey was long, much too long. I was so feverish with excitement that I could hardly contain myself. Kemi had been with the Livingstons for four very long months.

After forever, we pulled up in front of the big pink building. It was sunny, and the trees had just started adorning themselves with the yellowish green leaves of spring. We parked under a tree. Benjamin told me to wait. He got out of the car and went to the door. Someone opened it, but I couldn't see who it was through the storm door. The person disappeared, and Benjamin strolled back toward our car. I wished he didn't look so calm. My heart beat wildly. I felt dizzy. What if they refused to give her up? What if there was a standoff? Sweat trickled down my sides. Benjamin leaned in through my half-open window.

"Pierce says you should please wait," he said. "They'll bring her out to us."

Every minute seemed like a year. I shifted, touched my hair, scratched my throat, pulled my coat. My head was beginning to hurt. Eternity passed before Pierce opened the door and came out. He was holding Kemi in the crook of his right arm. A diaper bag hung over his left shoulder. I noticed his faded blue jeans and plaid shirt. My temples throbbed. Benjamin began to walk toward him, but Pierce motioned for him to wait. Pierce bowed his head, his lips moving rapidly. He was praying. Then he raised his head and nodded to Benjamin. Benjamin strolled up to him and eased Kemi from his hands. Pierce turned quickly and went inside the house. Benjamin walked to the back of the car. I jumped out and grabbed Kemi, hugging her, crying. I buried my nose in her neck and inhaled her baby scent. I sat down and held her in my lap. She smiled. I couldn't speak.

Dele looked at her, turned a look of wonder on me, and said, "Baby!" It was as though I had given him a present. He kept touching her fingers. Kemi gurgled.

"We've got to get going now," Benjamin said. I nodded, my throat tight. He put her in the car seat next to me, and we took off for Virginia.

The trip home seemed shorter. When we pulled up in front of our apartment building, Benjamin helped me carry my bags while I carried Kemi. Dele skipped excitedly and clapped his hands. "My baby, my baby!"

"Here's an Easter present for you, Lola," Benjamin said in his quiet voice. He held out a check to me. It was for three hundred dollars.

"Thank you so much, Benjamin," I said. "And please, thank Penelope, too. I'll never forget your kindness, never!"

Dɛnkyɛm

The Crocodile; It Breathes on Land and Water

I sat at the dining table, in front of the computer John and Zelda had bequeathed to me before leaving America. Kemi lay on her back on the couch, waving her arms about as Dele made faces at her. Each time he said *my baby*, she gurgled. I had dressed and fed them both. I didn't know why people said it would be hard caring for two children. Getting Kemi back had infused me with energy. I no longer woke up wishing I could go back to sleep.

After Rob's death, my life had frozen, like a movie paused in the middle. I hadn't thought any more about what I wanted to do with the rest of my life. I had cast aside my original goal of wanting to go back home, especially after my mother's last letter. Now I needed to refocus. My immediate goal was to find a job. Now, more than ever, I couldn't conceive of going home empty-handed, with two children to provide for. Now I realized how ridiculous my two-year goal was. It was going to take time to save enough money to start over in Ghana.

Rob hadn't started working on my green card before passing away. We'd always assumed we'd have time enough after the baby was born. Now I needed to find a job that would provide sponsorship. B.K. had printed out applications for me so I could apply for a job at the World Bank and International Monetary Fund, both headquartered in Washington, DC, the only entities I knew that could hire me and apply for a special permit for me. Both organizations had scheduled me for translation and office skills tests. Using the keyboarding manual Molly gave me, I turned to a page and started practicing. I pecked for half an hour, checking my speed, trying to improve on my accuracy.

At eight, I got up and joined the kids on the couch. I smiled at Dele. "Are you happy your sister is home?"

"Yes," he said, jumping around in his gray OshKosh B'gosh overalls.

Kemi waved her arms vigorously, smiling. I picked her up and pressed her against my bosom. "How are you, darling? Yes. You're okay, aren't you." I strapped her into the umbrella stroller and turned to Dele. "Come on, sweetie. It's time for camp." I had enrolled him in the free county summer camp program.

We walked along the road, me pushing the stroller and Dele skipping beside me. We walked four blocks until we got to the rust-brick building. Dele raced into the open door. "Bye, kiddo," I shouted after him, smiling at his teacher, a tall brunette.

After returning to the apartment, I sat on the couch with Kemi on my lap and read to her. She watched me with wonder, gurgling whenever I looked at her. My heart swelled. After a while, I put her on a blanket on the floor. "Yes, my darling, you just sit here next to Mummy while Mummy types, okay? Mummy is going to get a better job." She laughed, reaching for her rattle.

Heaving a happy sigh, I sat in front of the computer again and began typing. I did a timed test, checked my results, and took a break to lie beside my daughter, touching her hair, talking to her. At noon, I put her in the stroller again and went to pick up Dele from camp. I made a tuna sandwich for Dele and me and spooned sweet potato from a jar into Kemi's mouth. Then I gave her a bottle and she fell asleep in my arms while Dele dozed against my shoulder. I put Kemi in her crib and Dele on my bed, then attacked the keyboard again. I was now at forty-five words. I needed to type fifty words per minute in order to pass the typing test.

If I passed the typing, translation, reading, and comprehension tests in French, I could get a foot in the door as a bilingual administration assistant. They would apply for a working visa for me and I would continue to be legal in America. Even better than a resident permit, both the World Bank and IMF offered foreign workers paid leave to visit their home countries every other year. Now I had options. I could stay longer in America, piling dollars in the bank, and be able to visit home every two years until I had saved enough to start life over in Ghana. I needed my children to grow up in a community of Ghanaians, while benefiting from our frequent travels. They would enjoy the best of America and Africa. Those thoughts energized me. Every day, for four hours, I practiced speed tests. Soon, I attained fifty words a minute, but I aimed for eighty.

On a sunny day in June, I sat in an office of the World Bank, in a blue skirt with matching blazer, across the desk from a smiling woman with frosted short blond spikes and large brown eyes.

"You are such an attractive candidate," she said, flipping through my file. "Your translations are accurate, typing speed wonderful. And you've worked in several embassies. You'd be a wonderful asset." She stopped and looked up at me. "Can you merge documents?"

"Yes." How hard could it be to learn it?

"Footnotes?"

"I can learn anything I need to know."

She smiled some more, nodding. "Yes, it's not such a big deal. As I said, you're a very attractive candidate. We'd like to hire you."

I felt buoyant. "Thank you very much."

"I just need one more person to interview you, and that would be it, but I tell you, you're such an attractive candidate. Why don't you come with me?"

Her high heels clicked-clacked as she walked me to the office of a colleague, an African-American lady. "This is Lola," she said, and left, closing the door behind her.

The woman wore a scarf knotted at her neck, her face blank. I smiled hard and sat down, admiring the sheen of her wavy black hair. She flipped quickly through my chart, closed it, and leaned on her elbows, hands clasped under her chin.

"You are indeed an attractive candidate, but I want to know more about you."

I shifted, my hands clasped tightly in my lap.

"Why are you leaving the embassy?"

I tried for humor, chuckling. "The money isn't good."

She smiled a little. "I understand. How much notice would you need to give before leaving?"

"Oh, I already quit, so I can start anytime you want me to."

Her smile faded. "You quit?"

"Yes."

"When was this?"

"Two months ago."

"I'm afraid the bank can't hire you. You don't have a valid visa."

"But my visa is valid for at least eight months!"

"No, it isn't. You were issued a diplomatic visa to work in an embassy. The visa expired automatically when you quit. You had a month to switch visas, however, you quit two months ago."

"But they know why I quit. They said they would leave my visa open so I could get another job. They didn't notify the State Department."

"Whether they notified the State Department or not, I know you quit two months ago. I'm sorry, but you're ineligible to work here at the bank."

"Please!" I was fighting the tears, my body rigid. "I need this job. I have two children to feed. I'm a hard worker. You can call Madame Chevalier at the embassy. They call me the magician. I solve problems. Please, give me a chance. No one told me my visa would be invalid if I quit my job. The stamp in my passport hasn't expired. Please."

"Sorry, we can't hire you. We will keep your application open for a year. If you can get your papers in order, we will hire you, no questions asked. For now, your application is denied. I'm sorry." She pushed my file to one side, an indication that the interview was over.

I swallowed, rising on wobbly feet. I walked slowly to the door, then turned to look at her, pleading with my eyes. Her face remained closed. At the sidewalk, I leaned against a tree, sobbing. To have come so far! It was like surviving starvation and finally being invited to a bountiful meal, and then, just when I was about to take a bite, my plate was snatched from me. I was shoved outside, back into the hunger. If only I had known, I would have lied that I was still with the embassy. Apart from

His Non-Excellency, any one of the staff members would have covered for me if I had asked them to, I was certain. I raged against the ambassador. *You bastard! You tried to take my body, and now I've lost a great job.*

I have little memory of how I got home, however, after moping for a day, I geared up for battle again. Motherhood meant providing. Children ate the house, ate diapers, ate clothes, ate laundry detergent. They also ate my energy: they needed me to read, sing, play, and dance with them. I did it all with the busyness of an ant: marching forward, turning this way and that, scurrying down to the Giant supermarket, parks, laundry room, scurrying, scurrying. I babysat a neighbor's child for extra money. In the midst of all this, I made time to keep up with my typing speed, because the IMF, too, had scheduled me for tests. It was my last chance at a dream occupation, complete with visa and work permit. This time, I would lie about quitting the CAR embassy.

Two weeks later, I sat at the IMF for tests. For reasons I couldn't fathom, though I aced the language skills tests and typed eighty words a minute in French, I couldn't type fifty words a minute in English.

The Latina examiner, a plump woman with dark hair piled on top of her head, smiled kindly. "You get to have three tries. Go home and practice for a month and come back. This is a great opportunity, don't blow it." She told me about how she'd come from Venezuela, how she'd typed her way into a great job at the IMF, which let her visit home every other year. "Just keep trying. Back home, where we come from, we have nothing. It's better to stay in America, then you can help your family."

I appreciated the kinship, the sympathy she felt for me as a fellow immigrant, even if our circumstances differed. Mine was a story of disgrace to the family and what I took to be my mother's rejection. I envied the way this woman held herself erect, her confident smile and the assurance of esteem within her family. I wasn't about to jeopardize my hiring by telling her my ultimate goal was to return home. I prayed that one day my mother would forgive me and fold me back into the family. I just needed to save.

Another month of intense typing went by, but I failed the test again. The examiner remained compassionate, urging me to keep trying. On the third and final try, I was so nervous that sweat dampened my armpits. My hands shook. I started, but had to backspace to erase mistakes. It was an exercise in stops and starts. I wanted it so badly I couldn't fight the panic. When it was over, the examiner printed out my results and sighed. "I'm afraid you just can't make it. I'm sorry. It's over."

I ran out to the elevator, blinded by tears. I punched the button and when the elevator doors opened, I dashed inside, sobbing. How could I fail at something as simple as typing? Now the doors to the only two organizations I knew could hire me were shut.

Back home, I paid off the babysitter and went straight into mummy mode. Shut the emotions; function, function and smile. I was as adaptable as a crocodile on land and in water. I changed into a strapless dress and strapped Kemi to her stroller.

"Go for a walk, Mummy?" Dele asked, jumping up and down.

"Yes," I said in a robotic voice.

He raced ahead, pointing. "A butterfly!" Kemi gurgled and ended up asleep, her head lolling to one side. After our walk, I put them down for their nap. I cleaned the apartment and washed the dishes. Chores had a way of creating order amid chaos. The more I busied myself, the calmer I got. Finally, it came to me: I could find another embassy job, preferably with a country like Canada that would pay more. I would give it one more push, but if I failed, then I would return to Ghana to grovel at my mother's feet. If I succeeded, I would still go home and grovel, but, unlike the proverbial prodigal, I would be assured of financial independence. Now that I was a mother of two, I got it. No matter how angry she got, a mother could never throw her child away. That was what my sister meant about the hen treading on her chicks but not killing them.

When the kids woke up, I fed them apple sauce. Dele tried to spoon some sauce into his sister's mouth. She cooed at him, clapping her hands, her face gooey. Later, I read *The Little Wild Ducklings* to them, followed by *The Little Engine That Could*. Dele vocalized the words from memory, grinning with pleasure. Kemi said daa daa daa, and her smile, so like my mother's, made my heart lurch.

The phone rang.

"Hello, Lola. Barbara Morrison here."

Rob's mother. On the phone. Talking to me. How did she know my number?

"Is this a bad time to call?" Her solicitous voice did nothing to stop the agitation inside me.

"No. The children are sleeping."

I heard her sigh. "I don't know how to say this, so I'll just get on with it. Richard and I are very, very sorry for the way we've treated you." She paused for a moment as though she were waiting for me to respond. My mind whirled. After the funeral, they had left the church, shunned me completely, and now here they were. I had nothing to say to them. "I hope you can find it in your heart to forgive us. We want to be there for you, and not just for Kemi, but Dele, too. We want to be proper grandparents to your children."

A long silence followed before I could answer. "I don't know what to say."

Mr. Morrison's voice came on. "Listen, Lola, we'd like to visit. Could we do that?"

Whatever my anger, they were Rob's parents. I swallowed hard. "Yes. You can come anytime you want."

"Is tomorrow too soon?"

"Tomorrow will be fine."

I hung up in disbelief. Dele tugged at my arm. "Story!"

"Yes, darling." I settled down in a daze, staring until he tugged at my arm again.

The Morrisons arrived, bearing flowers, a gallon of milk, eggs, cheese, jar foods, and Huggies diapers. Another bag was filled with shorts and T-shirts for Dele, as well as a toy ambulance. Dele grabbed the ambulance and knelt on the floor, rolling it around. They sat side by side in blue jeans and matching plaid shirts. I balanced Kemi against my hip.

"Can I hold her?" asked Mrs. Morrison. I said yes and allowed Kemi to go to her. Kemi studied her with wide eyes.

Mrs. Morrison started weeping, one hand hooked around Kemi and the other dabbing at her eyes with a handkerchief. Mr. Morrison gave Kemi his finger and she promptly took it in her fist, trying to eat it.

"Oh, she's so precious," Mrs. Morrison said, sniffling.

"Look at them curls," Richard said, "just look at that."

"She looks so much like Rob. She's got his forehead."

"Yes, but that smile is her mother's."

Barbara turned her face to me, her eyes teary. "Thank you so much for letting us see her. We want to have a relationship with her. Watch her grow up. Rob would have been over the moon for her." She pressed Kemi to her bosom. "Oh, you precious thing. Oh, you gorgeous baby."

She sat at the dining table with us while I scooped mashed string beans into Kemi's eager mouth. Richard crawled on the floor beside Dele, explaining how the siren worked. Dele squealed at the sound. "Mummy, look, ambulance!" When Kemi finished eating, I got a bottle of formula ready for her. Barbara gave me an expectant look.

"Would you like to give her the bottle?" I asked.

"Yes!"

I placed Kemi in her arms and watched her guide the nipple. Kemi sucked while I busied myself cleaning up.

"Thanks for letting me feed her," she said, gazing fondly at her granddaughter.

"You're welcome."

"So, what are your plans for the future?" Mr. Morrison asked.

"I think I will return to Ghana." I don't know why I blurted it that way. My plans were still shaky. The Morrisons looked at each other with worry. I shrugged. "My ultimate goal was always to return home anyway. I want the kids to know my family and their heritage."

Mrs. Morrison bit her lip but said nothing. Kemi lay on her lap, sucking contentedly until her eyelids drooped and her breath deepened, the milk oozing out of the corner of her still mouth. Mrs. Morrison was delighted when I said she could put Kemi down for a nap. She stood over the crib, rubbing Kemi's back. Dele sat on the carpet rubbing his eyes, so I put him down on my bed, allowing him to keep the ambulance in his hand.

Mr. and Mrs. Morrison thanked and thanked me, hugging me. When they got home, they called to thank me again, asking me to forgive them. While my voice was friendly, I was careful not to be too warm. I didn't want to get hurt from their door slamming in my face again.

A few weeks later, Debbie knocked on my door. In her arms was her baby, Kendall, born five weeks before Kemi. Bald and plump, Kendall glided around on her toes, holding on to the wall. Kemi was still not crawling, preferring to scoot on her bottom. Debbie sat on the love seat, while I settled into the settee so that we faced each other.

"So, how's it going?" she asked, her brown eyes soft.

"I'm okay," I said with false bravado.

She looked around the room before meeting my eyes again. "It's not good for you to live alone with the kids."

I pulled on my braids. "I manage."

"Philip and I want you to come live with us. We've talked about it."

I stopped fingering my braids, staring at a spot on the green carpet.

"It can't be easy for you to keep paying rent for this place."

I said nothing, though I knew she was right. I had little savings, just enough to pay for the following month's six-hundred-dollar rent. Even so, I wanted to cling to the apartment for as long as I could. I loved the freedom of being alone with my thoughts, walking around in my underwear when I felt like it.

"I know you hate moving," she said quietly, "but believe me, you won't have to worry about that. You can stay with us for as long as you like. We'll find out from Immigration if there's anything we can do for you, you know, sponsor you for a green card—anything you need."

The word *sponsor* made me raise my eyes from the spot on the carpet. This was what I longed for, the stability a green card would afford. From the way she'd found me the room to rent with the Indian family, I knew she meant it.

"I don't know how to thank you," I said. "This is too much."

She gave me a reassuring smile. "I'd be honored to have Rob's child in my home. I really liked him. When Philip and I got married, Rob was tireless, helping Philip with his tux, et cetera. Rob was a good guy who made mistakes. Don't let the thing with the taxes bother you."

"I don't think about that. He loved me. Whatever he did, I've forgiven him."

"Good. Come live with us, Lola, we'd really love to have you.

I broke into a smile. "Okay."

The next day, we hauled my things into the Toyota truck and drove to their split-level subdivision home in Burke. The fear of moving, pinpricks that had kept me tossing at night, disappeared. It was freeing to have regular conversations with another adult, something I had missed. My language had been reduced to preschool vocabulary. I loved cooking with another woman, eating on a blanket under the blue skies, and watching our children play on the lawn.

Dele and Kemi blossomed like fresh plants in spring. Philip and Debbie's two children, Daniel and Kendall, formed pairs with mine: Daniel and Dele, Kemi and Kendall; DD and KK, as we referred to them. KK spoke gibberish to each other, creeping around the house, pulling things out of the kitchen cabinets, twisting the knobs on Philip's stereo. DD rode big wheelers in the driveway and scuffled over toys.

Living with the Winstons aroused even sharper pangs of nostalgia for my family. I had now been in America for nearly four years. Kemi was learning to talk and walk and yet, like Dele, she didn't know her grandmother. After my mother's last letter, I had stopped writing home. When I thought of how my sister, Awurama, and I used to sleep in the same bed, how Mama and I read together, her jazz records playing in the background, I wanted to weep.

Again, I took to looking at the pictures I had brought with me to America. There was a particular picture I loved, Mama spooning soup from a bowl at a banquet. I was ten years old. I remembered how I had insisted on accompanying her and she had let me. Wiping my face with the back of my hands, I felt lucky to have survived. The children were healthy and happy.

After I called and informed Rob's parents about my move, they began to visit daily. Initially, I was thrilled the kids had grandparents, but the Morrisons took to dropping in at odd times, even when the children were sleeping. They'd insist on me waking Kemi up so they could play with her. They'd arrive early in the morning, taking over the kitchen, stirring a pot of oatmeal, watching it bubble over, then settling Kemi in her high chair to spoon oatmeal into her mouth.

One morning, after staying for three hours feeding and playing with Kemi, they asked if they could stay for the day, until nighttime. It was a Saturday, after all, and they had a free weekend.

"Have you considered inviting Lola into your home?" Philip said, trying to smile but failing. "Wouldn't it be simpler?"

Mr. and Mrs. Morrison looked at each other. "Are we in the way?" Mrs. Morrison asked.

"I wouldn't put it that way," Debbie said, "but it would be great if you called before coming, you know."

I suppressed a smile just as Mrs. Morrison turned to look at me.

She stood up, her lips pinched together. "I think we'll run along now. See you all later."

"Yeah, see you later," I said, embarrassed.

They didn't visit again, they didn't call. Three months later, the sheriff's car rolled into the driveway. I watched through the window screen as he got out and marched up the concrete steps to the front door in his well-ironed khaki uniform.

"Miss Oduro, please," he said, touching the brim of his olive hat. The gold star on the front of his hat matched the one on the side of his car.

"I'm the one," I said.

"Here, you've been served." He placed a white business envelope in my hand, turned around, walked back to his car, and drove off. I stood at the top of the stairs staring at the envelope.

"What is it, Lola?" Debbie asked, pushing out the screen door to join me.

"The sheriff gave me this," I said, showing her the envelope.

"Oh, dear. Open it and see."

I opened it and began reading. "What? I don't believe this. Rob's parents are suing me. For custody of Kemi." My heart hammered. They had never shown any interest in even seeing Kemi until recently. And now they were suing me. Suing *me* for custody? Of all the gall! All because they couldn't visit anytime they wanted? I marched into the kitchen and called Scott Roanoke.

"How can they do this when they're not the parents?"

"I'm afraid they can. As grandparents, they can sue as interested parties, especially with Rob gone. I'm sorry."

"Could you represent me? I don't have money now, but I will pay in installments in the future, I promise."

"Don't worry. Just let me know when."

On the day of the custody case, three months after the sheriff had served me, Philip babysat the kids while Debbie accompanied me to court. Scott Roanoke and I had talked several times on the phone. I had the truth on my side. Surely, the judge would listen to me and tell Rob's parents to go tend flowers or something.

Mr. and Mrs. Morrison arrived, he in a fine suit and tie, she in a pink-and-blue flowery frock with puffed sleeves and no waist. I was as aroused as a spitting cobra. As we entered the courtroom, their lawyer, a red-faced man with dark, wavy hair, gave me a smug smile. My fists balled.

"The plaintiff calls Barbara Morrison to the stand," the lawyer said.

She put her hand on the Bible and swore to tell the truth, the whole truth, so help her God. Then she told His Honor in a pitiful voice how she yearned to be part of her granddaughter's life.

"We have so much to give our granddaughter. Our son is gone. His daughter's alone, save for Lola. Lola won't let us see her whenever we want. She doesn't have a home of her own. She lives with people who restrict us." She dabbed at her eyes. A tremor began in her voice. "We have so much love to give Kemi. And stability."

His Honor, a thin, elderly man with graying hair and thick glasses, nodded sympathetically. They were not wanting in relatives either. "We have sisters and brothers, cousins. She'd get love from so many people. Loads of great-uncles and great-aunts." She was whimpering now. "Lola is an immigrant and she wants to leave the country. If she leaves, we won't get to see our granddaughter grow. Our Rob is gone, Kemi's all we have." She was crying softly, rocking forward and backward.

"Where did she say she would move to?" asked their lawyer in a compassionate voice, "someplace in . . . Africa, was it?" He placed special emphasis on *Africa* and looked meaningfully at the judge.

"She's from Ghana."

His Honor frowned and shifted in his seat. I wanted to slap the lawyer. Barbara, too. How dare they suggest that my country of origin was something distasteful?

Scott chose not to cross-examine Barbara. After she stumbled to her seat and laid her head on her husband's shoulder, the lawyer called Mr. Morrison to the stand. He took his time about it, wiping his wife's tears with his palms, squeezing her hand, murmuring to her. They looked so pitiful.

Mr. Morrison sat in the witness box and talked about his long career as an engineer with the army, something I didn't remember. "I've got investments, stocks and all. I'm retired. We'll have all the time in the world for our granddaughter." Then he turned to look in my direction. "We're not saying Lola here is a bad person. She's quite sweet, but let's face it, she's in no position to raise two children. She's welcome to visit anytime she wants. We just feel we should do what our son would want." The way he said it, it wasn't his fault they hadn't seen much of Kemi until recently, because, well, you see, I had chosen to give up the baby for adoption. "Lola doesn't have a job, and she lives with the Winstons. That precious little Kemi has to share a room with Debbie's daughter." Never mind that KK shared fits of laughter every morning. It was all I could do not to jump up and shout at him. "In our house," he intoned, "she'd have her own room."

With a flourish, the lawyer went to his table and produced Plaintiff's Exhibit A: pictures of Casa Morrison, with the gleaming grand piano and a neatly decorated room with frilly curtains where Kemi would sleep.

The lawyer swiveled on his heels and turned to Scott. "Your witness."

Scott, muscles bulging like a boxer ready to knock him off, marched up to the witness box.

"Mr. Morrison, when Lola was considering adoption, did you offer to adopt the baby?"

Mr. Morrison bit his lip, adjusted his glasses. A sheen of sweat glistened on his forehead. "No."

"No? And why is that?"

"Well." He pushed his glasses up. "The truth is, we were mad with grief. We couldn't think straight."

"So you never offered Lola any help whatsoever. Didn't you leave the church?"

"Yes," he whispered.

"You abandoned your daughter-in-law. Did you not think she was"—he made air quotes—"mad with grief?"

Mr. Morrison sighed, giving me a look full of sorrow. "I know she was grieving, we felt for her. But Rob was our only son. She eloped with him, they married quickly, and then he died." His voice broke into sobs. He removed his glasses and took the tissues the bailiff offered. I felt his sorrow, but where was his compassion for mine?

"Mr. Morrison, how much do you give Lola in child support?"

Mr. Morrison looked around, blinking. "Child support? We didn't think we had to."

"What?" the judge said.

"You say she didn't have a job and you loved your granddaughter, so why didn't you support her?"

"She was working at the embassy. She had her own apartment. We just didn't realize . . . she never asked for help . . . we would've . . ."

"Yes, Mr. Morrison, she was a dedicated employee until she was forced to quit because the ambassador sexually harassed her. She—"

"Objection!" Their lawyer was on his feet, red-faced. "This has no bearing on the case!"

"Overruled."

"But you never asked, did you? While you were busy feeling sorry for yourselves, she was busy surviving, against all odds. Your Honor, I have no further use for this witness." Scott marched back to his seat and squeezed my hand.

When the plaintiff rested, Scott put me on the stand. I told His Honor about walks with the kids, the reading and the singing, how the Winston children related to mine, how, despite my initial frosty relationship with the Morrisons, I had welcomed them into our lives.

"They're Rob's parents and I wanted them to know her, but they suffocated me. They showed up before breakfast and stayed all day long. Every single day. It's not as if they were contributing to Kemi's upkeep. The first time, they brought gifts, but that was it. They never supported me."

After what I believed to be searing testimony from me, the Morrisons' lawyer rose for his cross-examination. He walked toward me, a look of concern on his face.

"Miss Oduro, do you have a job?" he asked.

"No, but I'm looking."

He frowned for His Honor's benefit. "How do you propose to look after your daughter?"

"Well, I—"

"You don't have any idea."

"Well, it's not easy because of immigration—"

"That is neither here nor there. The fact is, you don't have a job and you're not in a position to provide for your daughter. Isn't that right?"

"It's not as simple as that, I don't have a green card and—"

"Just answer yes or no!"

My heart pounded. "Yes."

He let that sink in. "Miss Oduro," he resumed in a quiet voice, almost solicitous. "Would you say Kemi was a well-adjusted child?"

"Yes," I said proudly, "she's very well adjusted."

"Then why can't she visit with her grandparents?"

"I—she can, but—"

He whirled around to face the judge, forefinger wagging in my direction. "Your Honor, we attest that the defendant's actions have been not just inappropriate but downright irresponsible!"

Scott shot up. "Objection!"

"We want custody." The lawyer pointed at me. "She herself says the child is well adjusted."

"Objection, Your Honor!"

"Sustained," said the judge.

I gripped the sides of my chair, waiting for the room to stop spinning. Scott sat down. The lawyer dismissed me. I stumbled to my seat.

The judge's words came to me as if emitted from space. "Mr. and Mrs. Morrison may have visitation with their granddaughter every other weekend. I am awarding custody to the mother. I am also instructing social services to conduct home studies of both the Winstons' and the grandparents' homes and to report to me in three months, at which time I'll render my final decision. Furthermore, neither the mother nor the grandparents may take the child out of the country without prior permission from the court."

He banged his gavel, and court was adjourned.

I shot into the hallway. The blood pounded against my temples. I rushed to the Morrisons, who were walking with their lawyer. They avoided my eyes and increased their stride. I followed them. "I hate you, you hear? I hate you!"

Debbie hissed through gritted teeth, "How could they do that to you? They could have invited you to live with them!"

"They've never forgiven me for Rob. They can't get over that he married me without telling them. They probably blame me for his death."

It was so unfair. They said they themselves eloped and yet, when Rob and I did the same, they'd treated me like an infestation. I had forgiven them. But not this time. I would comply with the court's rulings and allow visitation, but I would never again let their smiles blot out the past.

Mpua Nnum

Five Tufts of Hair

Hatred for the Morrisons became my sustenance. I ate it, drank it into me. I pictured them losing all their money in a stock market crash. I prayed a heart attack on them. I prayed them into a plane crash. I didn't trust that after the home studies the judge would let me keep Kemi. Every day, I snapped awake at three in the morning, a searing in my stomach. My heart pounded as if I were having the heart attack that I willed on the Morrisons. I lay awake until morning when the kids woke up. Debbie kept at me to get a grip.

While the kids were napping, I sank onto the carpeted floor, brooding. Debbie slid down to face me, a glass of water in her hand, her back against the sofa.

"Lola," she said thoughtfully, "I talked to Philip. If you want to go back home, we can help you with a ticket, you know. Unfortunately, we can't include Kemi, I'm sorry. We can't break the law."

"I understand," I said, trying not to sound bitter. "Do you know that when you left for the store yesterday, I even contacted Catholic

Relief Services? I found out about an organization that helps repatriate immigrants who want to return home." I swallowed, fighting tears. "They, too, can't help me. The minute I mentioned the order barring me from taking Kemi out of the country, they turned chilly. No one wants to be an accessory to a felony, which is what I will commit if I take my own daughter out of America. I'll get put on the FBI wanted list. That means I can never step foot in America again, nor in any country with an extradition agreement with the United States. For the rest of my life, I would live in fear, and, if somehow they managed to snatch Kemi from me, I would never see her again."

Debbie set her glass down. "I'm so sorry, Lola. What are you going to do?"

"I am not leaving without my daughter, that's for sure. I will remain in America. God, my visa has expired, I can't get a work permit, and yet, I can't leave the country with my own baby! Family law doesn't care about immigration law. Immigration law doesn't care about family law. It's like walking on fire, no matter where I put my foot, I get burned."

Debbie's eyes shone with tears. "I don't know, I just don't know. There has to be a way for you to get a job."

I was amazed at how ignorant the average American was about immigration. Americans don't have to deal with immigration except when they marry a foreigner or adopt a foreign baby, where there is a path to permanent residence and citizenship. For the likes of me, there was no path, only blind alleys and walls. Someone would call me saying, "I've found a job for you. They say you can come and work. I talked to them about your situation. They understand." I'd show up only to discover the employers couldn't hire me. Then the person who tried to help would complain, "But

I don't understand it, aren't you a citizen because your husband was an American? Didn't you become a citizen when your baby was born?" It exasperated me. They couldn't grasp that an American child had to be eighteen to sponsor a parent. Until then, the parent had no rights.

I was weary of hurling myself against the wall of work permits. If I couldn't take my baby out of the country, then there was only one thing to do, break the law and find a job at all costs. Working without a permit was a lesser crime than kidnapping. I was a lioness, ready to hunt for my cubs, ready to tear to pieces any obstacle in my path.

While working at the CAR Embassy, I had obtained a social security card for banking purposes. A notice printed below my name said: "Not Valid for Employment." I ignored it.

When I went to Blood of Jesus Academy to fill out an application for a job, no one asked to see my social security card or work permit, and I didn't volunteer any information. They were desperate for a French teacher, so I was hired on the spot. Debbie offered to babysit Kemi, and Dele would attend preschool. One half of me wanted to run down the street shouting my news, but the other half of me kept cool, fearful someone would eventually figure out I had no right to work. At home, I closed my eyes and conjured the drumbeat for adowa in my head and I danced, oh, how I danced.

On my first day in an American classroom, I quivered with nervousness. It was one thing to have knowledge in one's head, quite another to transfer that knowledge to someone else's head. What's more, I had heard American students didn't respect teachers the way kids did back home. When I entered the classroom, they didn't rise to their feet and say a collective "Good morning, madam." Instead, students stood in groups, chatting in loud voices. Those sitting just slouched in their seats, ears plugged with wires connected to a device in their hand.

"Good morning, class," I said.

A few answered.

"Please take your seats." I stood waiting silently until they settled in their seats.

"My name is Miss Oduro," I said, and wrote it boldly on the board. "I shall be taking you for French One." Surprisingly, they didn't have a problem pronouncing my name, unlike people who went into a series of paroxysms only to come up with "Oh-dahrow" or "Odd Dawroe."

I noticed whispering and tittering in a corner. I decided I might as well face whatever was brewing head on. A boy with freckles like oat bran raised his hand.

"Yes?" I said.

He gave me an insolent stare. "When you were in Africa, ha, did you like, wear a ring in your nose, and like, wear a grass skirt and, you know, jump around?"

There were hoots and chortles. The boy behind him clapped him on the shoulder.

"You know," I answered with a smile, "if I were you, I wouldn't air my ignorance in public."

Shouts of "Ooooh, she got you, man!" went around the room. His face turned red and I felt sorry for rising to the bait.

"What's your name?" I asked him.

"Peter," he murmured.

"Well, Peter, I'm sure I've asked a few questions of Americans I probably shouldn't have. What do you say we treat all people with respect and dignity? Obviously, I don't have holes in my nose where a ring would go, and I'm sure you can tell I didn't grow up wearing grass skirts."

He nodded.

"Let's focus on this class and what you can get out of it." I told them a bit about my history and learning to embrace new things, such as playing tennis.

A Black girl piped up. "You don't talk at all like a Black person."

"How is a Black person supposed to talk?"

"I mean, you talk about playing tennis and us being doctors and all that."

"What is not Black about that?"

"Well, Black people don't talk like that, we don't have those kinds of expectations."

"And why not?"

"I don't know." She shrugged in a way that said, what's the point?

I launched into a lecture: "There is no predetermined way for a race to think or talk. You just talk and think like a human being. You can do anything you set your mind to do. Don't let anything limit you. To suggest you are limited by race is to imply that your race is inferior and thus you have less potential."

"But they don't give you a chance," one boy said, shaking his head.

"Who doesn't give you a chance?"

"White folks."

"There you go again. You act as if Whites have the right to give or not give you a chance. It's up to you to decide what you want out of life and to do whatever you need to do to achieve it."

Everybody started talking at once.

"You just don't get it," one voice shouted above the din. "If you're Black, you've got to work twice as hard as a White person!"

I raised my hand, and they became quiet. "If it's true, well, then, work twice as hard, whatever it takes. But set goals for yourself, and then strive to achieve them. Don't give anyone the power to reduce you." Somewhere at the back of my mind, a nagging feeling pricked me that I was ignorant about the long-term effects of slavery. I made a mental note to read more literary works by American Blacks and listen more. Perhaps this was what Len George meant when he said I didn't understand, as a Black person, what it was like to have to prove oneself. I couldn't imagine what stories African-American parents had shared with their children for generations. Outside history books, no horrifying personal stories about slavery had ever touched my ears. Even when we'd visited slave castles, though I'd viewed them with fury, I saw the stories as something that happened to others, not to my great-grandfather or grandmother or mother. In America, I had been so absorbed with my need for survival I hadn't thought enough about my place or role as a Black person. If I could now roam around freely in America, it was thanks to the freedoms won by American Blacks. Didn't they volunteer to join the struggle when Ethiopians fought the Italians a long time ago? Didn't they agitate for the release of Nelson Mandela? I needed to open my eyes and heart to learning. To do that, I needed to listen to the voices of my fellow Blacks in literature.

I was so caught up in my musings that it took a moment for me to realize the class had become agitated. A fly had entered the room, looping around.

"Over there, Ms. Oduro!"

The chase began. I was determined to win. I yanked off my

cardigan, darted through rows, whipping the air with it. The kids cheered me on, some swishing with books. When it flew toward the ceiling, I climbed onto an empty desk, snapping the cardigan wildly. I jumped from desk to desk, the kids howling. Swish! I smacked the fly and it tumbled to the ground. Students jumped up, pumping their fists. "Yay! You got it!" Suddenly, the class fell silent. Everyone scurried to their desk. My hand was on my waist, my cardigan raised high in a victory pose, a huge grin on my face, but the kids looked past me. I turned to find Dr. McCray, the grim-faced principal, standing in the open doorway, her knuckles white on the knob.

"Ms. Oduro, may I see you for a moment?" she said in clipped tones.

I climbed down and stepped into the hallway, still high from my victory.

She stared me down until my smile faded. "You do know your class is right next to my office?"

"I'm very sorry, I forgot."

"I'm glad your class is lively, but keep it down or I'm going to have to move you to a trailer outside." A slow smile brightened her face briefly.

"Yes, ma'am," I said, trying to keep a straight face.

She marched off, her shoes clopping on the ceramic tiles.

When I reentered the class, the students giggled, wanting to know if I was in trouble. I put my finger to my lips for them to be quiet. They obeyed, darting me looks of solidarity.

It wouldn't be the last time I'd receive a reprimand at Blood of Jesus. One day, we sprinkled water on the floor in the hallway to see how coalescence worked, the theory being that smaller droplets would coalesce to form larger droplets, that molecules in any liquid would stick together. It didn't matter that we had no other liquid for comparison. When we poured water on the floor, it ran as one mass, into the crevices between tiles. You could also see how the floor was uneven by the way the water puddled in places. One kid took off his sneakers and socks and glided in the puddle. Before I could send for a mop, Dr. McCray caught us.

"Mrs. Oduro, could you keep the creativity under control?"

It was true that coalescence wasn't part of language instruction, but as far as I was concerned, all subjects were related, and every question deserved an answer with a demonstration where possible. After a couple more escapades, Dr. McCray roped me into teaching life science.

She didn't know, but it was a fitting punishment, for I had no desire to know how a frog caught flies with its tongue or how a worm digested its food. Apart from dogs, I never wanted to touch anything that didn't walk on two feet. I befriended the biology teacher, who performed all the dissections with my students while I tucked a copy of Frederick Douglass's biography into my teacher's manual and read. Our potted plants withered. The biotic community we set up for fish suffered. The water temperature was either too high and a fish steamed to death or the water was too cold and some fish froze. The water turned milky from too much fish food. Nearly every day, students gathered in the bathroom to conduct a funeral and flush a fish to its watery grave while I kept watch at the door for Dr. McCray. When there were no goldfish left in the aquarium, the students wrote papers explaining our failed experiments and the importance of protecting the natural environment.

On days when the sun shone and we could cast off our jackets, I conducted classes under the trees, where we could act out French skits the students wrote. I also took them to the playground. I laughed to see them pushing along on big wheelers, their feet on the ground, or playing house in the giant dollhouses, until we were ordered to stay away.

As much as I enjoyed teaching, I wished I earned more. After the school deducted tuition costs for Dele, I earned seven hundred and sixty-two dollars a month, which would later increase to one thousand. By their creative accounting, I earned thirty thousand dollars a year, if one factored in the free tuition. Never mind the book fees we paid, books they collected at the end of the year so they could reassign them. The fault lay with church leaders who made financial decisions. The senior pastor used words as a bandage to stem our bleeding wallets. At staff meetings, he extolled the special place we occupied in the Lord's heart for taking on the labor of training His little ones. He said God was preparing a special place in heaven for us and blah blah blah and the laborer was worthy of his hire and blah blah blah. I knew it was exploitation, but without a green card, I had little chance of getting another job. I earned only enough for my little family to rent the basement of a town house about five minutes' drive from the Winstons, a place smaller than the pastor's office. Thanks to my students' recommendation, I was now listed on the Who's Who of the Best Teachers in America, which earned me, at last, a credit card. I would not touch it, though. I would save it for use only when I absolutely had to.

Ɛpa

Handcuffs

"Mummy, are we going to the store?" Kemi asked, her head alive with the rainbow colors of the plastic barrettes I had clipped at the end of her braids. At five years old, life was an adventure for her. Months had turned into almost eight years in America. We were now in 2005. America had endured attacks on the twin towers of New York as well as the Pentagon, and we had survived. As an individual, I had been battered, but was still here and now twenty-eight years old. I felt forty. Kemi tugged at my dress.

"Yes, darling," I said. "We're going to Safeway." It was a beautiful Saturday. Birds tweeted and fluttered in the dogwood trees. Flowers swayed in the breeze.

Dele dropped his book on the floor and rushed to the red shopping cart I had bought because I didn't have a car. He gripped the edge of the cart, jumping up and down while Kemi tried to climb.

"Wait until we get outside, guys."

Dele held the door open while I bumped the cart down the

front steps. I slung my handbag over my shoulders, lifted Kemi, and put her in the cart. She said "Yay" and hooked her fingers into the rectangular holes, her braids bouncing around her head. I had been awarded full custody, provided I didn't take her out of the United States, which set me up for chilly but polite exchanges when the Morrisons picked her up and returned her on alternate weekends. Over time my anger had abated, but I still didn't trust them.

Dele raised his arms and I put him inside too, wondering how he got to be thigh-high and so heavy. I pushed them across the road, onto the sidewalk and up the rise, singing a song I made up, "Up the hill, up the hill, up the hill we go, oh, and down the hill! Down the hill! Down the hill we run!" We careened down, the kids laughing so hard they drooled as drivers rubbernecked us.

"You know what, guys?" They looked up at me, their eyes shining. I bent down to rub noses with each child. "You are so special."

Kemi clapped her hands, then shouted, "Look, Mummy, a butterfly!"

I stopped the cart, looking at the blue-and-yellow butterfly fluttering over a shrub. "It's beautiful, isn't it? That's afafrantɔ. Say aa!"

"Aa!" they said.

"Fa-fra."

"Faafra!"

"n-tɔ."

"n-tɔɔɔ!"

They put it together, Kemi smiling and saying, "I love afafrantɔ!" I was proud of them both for having such good ears for sounds. Kemi in particular loved new words, testing them, rolling them about her mouth, using them any chance she got.

"I see a squirrel!" Dele pointed to the bushy tail scurrying up a tree.

"That's opuro, in Twi. Can you say it?"

"Opuro!" They said.

I resumed pushing, smiling at them. "When I was growing up, we used to sing a song that goes like this:

Opuro ɛnya nabɛn,
okusie repɛ adwe,
kraman repɛ dompe,
na wo pɛ adesua anaa?"

They wanted to know what each word meant, so I explained. "The squirrel has got its palm nut, the bush rat is searching for nuts, the dog is looking for a bone; are you searching for knowledge?"

"What is knowledge, Mummy?" Dele asked.

"Hmm, let me see. It's the things you learn when you read about animals and trucks and tools."

"Books?" Kemi asked. She loved books so much she had to have one in her hand when she sat on the potty.

"Yes, books, too."

"Mummy," Dele said, "when are we going to Ghana to see Grandma and Auntie Rama?"

"Soon, darling. Someday soon. Now, let's sing." I sang the song over and over again and soon they had learned it. We sang as I pushed, singing in rounds, oblivious to the stares of drivers. At the store, they got down. They helped me pick out vegetables, asking, "Is this one good, Mummy?" smiling with delight when I said yes, and learning which tomato was too ripe, which banana was bruised, which celery was limp. I taught them to look for blemishes and crispness. On our way back, groceries carefully arranged around their feet, we sang again, breaking into a run when the road dipped, laughing and laughing and laughing.

When we returned from the store, we ate lunch and they went down for a nap, Dele climbing the ladder to the top of the white bunk bed while Kemi slept on the bottom bunk. I went upstairs to the dining room, where I sat writing down a folktale from Ghana I planned to read to them. It was a good day.

There were many such days when I taught them to gyrate to the adowa dance beat and waltz to Bach cassettes. There were also heavier and darker days when I hid in the bathroom and punched the walls, crying bitterly, days when I raised my voice and told them to pick up toys or leave me alone. But they were thriving. That was all that mattered. They had piano lessons, and Kemi studied ballet. Dele played basketball. They starred in school and church plays. And still, like a lioness, I lay low in the grass, waiting for my chance to spring upon the elusive green card. When Debbie recommended an immigration officer who worked magic, I gave him a call and he proposed a visit to my home.

He dragged in his barrel body, reminding me of Santa Claus. He had beefy red cheeks, a furry mustache and beard, except his hair was brown and spare. The top of his head gleamed pink where the hair refused to grow. What hair remained stuck to the nape of his neck in an oily mat. He swiveled around on the orange carpet, sniffing the air.

"Do I smell fried plantains?"

"Yes." I had just finished frying plantains for lunch and was about to call the kids inside.

"I haven't had plantains in a long time." He put his briefcase down, a happy smile on his face, rubbing his palms together.

"Wow, you eat plantains?"

"Yes, deeelicious! I had them in Ghana."

My eyes opened wide. "You've been to Ghana?"

"Yes, wonderful people!" He put his thumb against the forefinger to make an O for emphasis. "Won-derful people. Hos-pitable."

I beamed, thrilled he knew my country. "Would you like some?"

"Oh yes, please."

I served him. He sat down in an armchair and gobbled enough fried plantains and beans for three. After dabbing at his mouth with a paper napkin, he opened his briefcase and took out a legal pad. He asked me for my immigration history, scribbling as I narrated. When I finished, his eyes twinkled at me. "Now, I'm going to need an advance of one thousand dollars from you to start with."

"One thousand?" I swallowed. I had been babysitting to supplement my income and had some savings, but still. "What will you do for me?"

"I have a plan, but I have to do a little research. Don't worry about a thing. I do this all the time. I'm going to plan a strategy, and I'll call you. We'll take it from there." He scribbled and tore out a paper. "Here's my number. You can call me anytime, but I'll call you before you call me."

I supported my cheek with my fist, thinking. Debbie had never failed me. She'd found me a room to rent and an apartment. She and her husband had sheltered me in their home. She'd stood by me through my custody case. She'd remained in our lives, driving Dele to basketball when I couldn't, driving or picking up Kemi from ballet. If she recommended this man, he had to be legitimate. She would never allow anyone to take advantage of me. Breathing deeply, I wrote out a check for the requisite one thousand dollars. He tucked it into his briefcase and waved goodbye.

A week went by with no news, so I called. A female voice chirped, "Mr. Blake is not available."

"When will he be back?"

"I don't know, ma'am. This is an answering service."

"What do you mean?"

"I just take his calls and pass on messages to him."

"Wait a minute, there's no direct number I can call?"

"That's right. I mean, I'm sure he has a phone number, but I don't have it."

"Do you have an address for him?"

"No, I can only pass on messages."

I wanted to scream. "Well, then, please tell him Lola called. Tell him to call me back."

I sank into the rocking chair and buried my face in my palms. The children crashed inside, laughing. I raised my head, an instant smile plastered on my face. They threw themselves at me. Dele pressed both hands on my cheeks. "Mummy, are you crying?"

"No, sweetie, I just got a little dust in my eyes."

Kemi stood on her tiptoes, brushing her brother's hand away. "I'm going to kiss your eyes and make the pain go away." She pecked my eye, laughing. "I got your eyelashes, Mummy. It tastes like salt."

I hugged her tightly, not responding.

"Do you feel better?" Dele asked.

"Yes, thanks, sweetie. Let's get you some plantains. There aren't enough, but I'll fry some more as you eat."

"Yay!" Kemi said. "I love plantains." They raced to the bathroom to wash their hands, squabbling over who got there first.

All evening, I eyed the phone, but it didn't ring. When the children were sleeping, I flipped the phone open to dial 911. I touched

9, then 1. My heart pounded. What was I doing? This was not an emergency and I didn't have the nonemergency number. Besides, if I got the police on the phone, what would I tell them? That I was illegal? They'd probably handcuff me, throw me into a van, and cart me off to heaven knew where. I closed the phone and sat in the dark, staring at the patio fence, its spikes ashy, stark.

"I know a good lawyer," said a Sierra Leonean teacher at Blood of Jesus Academy. She'd just joined the school and I had confided in her. We were alone in the staff room, preparing for class.

"Who is this lawyer?" I asked in a weary voice.

She leaned forward, her mug in her hand. "Trust me, this one is good."

"So was the last one who made off with my thousand dollars."

"No, this one is different."

I threw her a look full of cynicism.

She grabbed my wrist. "I promise you, she's good. I used her myself. Her name is Rita Roche. My husband and I went to see her when we were applying for citizenship." As I pulled my hand away and folded my arms, she spoke with energy. "Rita is dynamite, I tell you! Look, just try. She will give you a free consultation the first time, then you can decide for yourself."

I was unconvinced, but I had no options left. What did I have to lose by calling Rita? That afternoon after school, I called. Her voice was strong and reassuring. "Why don't you come to my office? I'll give you a free consultation, and we'll take it from there."

I had never heard of a lawyer giving a free consultation. Now driving, thanks to Debbie's husband, Philip, who had taught me how, I jumped into my battered blue Mustang and zipped to Rita's office in Vienna, in an affluent neighborhood lined with trees and lush lawns.

"Sit down," Rita said, waving at me energetically, indicating the chair opposite her desk. She looked like just the kind of person I'd want to muscle me through the unyielding path of immigration. She sat behind a large desk, peering at me over a pair of narrow black-rimmed glasses perched low on her nose. I sat down carefully before this awe-inspiring woman.

"Now, let's see." She had a yellow legal pad in front of her, pen poised on it. "Why don't you tell me everything from the beginning?"

I told her my story while she scribbled. When I finished, she leaned forward on her elbows, her voice lowered to the gravity of a sermon's punch line. "I don't take on a case I can't win. I've got a hundred percent success rate." Her confidence said nobody dared deny her anything, and she was on my side. Her energy infected me and I straightened my spine. She showed me a newspaper clipping featuring her picture, where she was quoted as saying immigrants were survivors. She evidently sympathized with foreigners. That persuaded me. She spoke so fast, I had to hold my breath to catch every word. "We can get you an H visa, which is a professional visa, if your school agrees to sponsor you. Foreign-language skill is a necessary one. After working for three years, you'll become eligible for a green card."

Her fee was a flat two thousand dollars. I felt deflated. "I have only five hundred dollars. I don't know how I can afford you."

"That's okay," she said with sympathy. "I know many irregular immigrants get exploited and earn little. You can pay the five hundred as a retainer, then pay the rest in installments. Can you do one hundred a month?"

"Yes, that will be fine." It would be tight, but I would manage somehow. I whipped out my checkbook and tore out a check for her. This was it, I was going to make it, at last! On my way home, I fiddled with the radio and turned to an oldies station playing a song I loved. I cranked up the volume, singing loudly: Do you love me? Do you love me? N-o-w, that I . . . can da-a-a-a-ance?

I could just picture myself with a job that came with what I had up to this point only imagined: health insurance and whatever pension my employer could contribute to. I'd be free to go to Ghana, visit Mama anytime I wanted, move back to Ghana without fear of the law.

At home, I hugged the children tight. Hands held in a circle, we swung our arms up and down to the rhythm of my childhood nursery rhyme. I chanted a line, they responded:

> Dele Maame eeee rice wataaa!
> Yaaay yaaay, rice wataaa
> Kemi Maaame eeee rice wataa!
> Yaaay yaaa, rice wataaa!

Then I went mad on the chorus, and they shrieked with laughter, jumping around, still holding hands.

> Ɛyɛ dɛ asikyire wom
> Yaaaa yaaa yee asikyire wom, oya!
> Ɛyɛ dɛ asikyire wom
> Yaaaa yaaa yee asikyire wom, oya!

We were delirious with joy because Dele and Kemi's mummy's rice water porridge was sweetened with sugar and was so delicious. Oh, the future was going to be sweet, just like rice water! I fell onto the carpet and they fell on me, drooling with laughter. Yes, Rita was going to get me that H visa and all was finally, finally going to be well.

Rita turned into a ghost.

Each time I called, her oh-so-lovely secretary, a Hispanic lady with frosted blond hair, told me Rita wasn't there but would call me back. But Rita never did. For four months, like the desperate soul I was, I continued to send her a check that never failed to get cashed. I reminded myself how busy she was, how her reception room was always packed. Remember the newspaper articles, I admonished myself.

One night, after I had herded the kids to bed, depression flattened me on my bed. I pounded the wooden paneling with my fists. I felt handcuffed. All I needed was a green card so I could get a better job, so I could be free. A simple little green card that wasn't even green; I had seen one, it was pink. Why, why, why? Why couldn't I get the bloody damn card?

Nine years now. Nine bloody years in America. Dele and Kemi were now eight and six years old and had never met their grandmother and auntie. I wished they knew what it was like to hear Mama read. I wanted to see them dance with her, laugh out loud. They didn't know what it was like to have cousins. What would I tell them one day? What had I achieved by being so stubborn?

I sat up and dragged out an old album I had brought with me to America. The first pictures were those of Joana and me at Ngor Island. In one, we stood, dressed in pant-court, which Americans called capri pants, and sweaters, our faces lit by a bonfire. She had just told me how much she missed her father, and I leaned my head on her shoulder. The picture had nothing to do with Mama, yet it was enough to make my eyes burn with tears. A drop splashed on the plastic covering. Wiping my eyes,

I turned to look at Mama's picture. I traced her long neck and curved smile. A sudden weakness in my hands caused the album to slide off my thighs. I fell back against my pillows, sobbing. At some point, my hand fell on the house phone. On an impulse, I picked up the handset and dialed Rita's office, not expecting anyone to answer at that time of the night. To my amazement, a female voice answered the phone. And it wasn't the secretary. I sat up, grabbing the phone with both hands. "Who are you?"

"This is Grace Logan. What can I do for you?"

Even though I didn't expect her to do anything, I poured my frustrations into her ears.

"I'm desperate," I said. "Each time I call, I'm told Rita is not available. I don't know what to do. I want to take both kids home to see my mother. She's getting old. I don't want to go home after she's dead and gone."

"I'm sorry about that. I'm a paralegal with the firm. I tell you what. Let me search for your file. I'll look into it and call you back tomorrow."

"Promise?"

She laughed. "Promise."

True to her word, she called the next day. "I found your file. Could you come into the office to see me tomorrow afternoon?"

"Absolutely."

The reception area was crowded as usual with immigrants, their eyes hungry and hopeful. The secretary smiled at me from pearly pink lips. I smiled back, knowing she was not responsible for Rita ignoring me.

A tall woman in a striped dress twirled down the spiral staircase and walked toward me, arching her brows. "Lola?"

"Yes! Hi, Grace."

"Why don't we sit outside? It's a nice day." She led the way to a picnic bench and table under the shade of a dogwood tree.

It was a nice day indeed. A lazy breeze blew her shoulder-length blond hair. She was nearly six feet tall, which made me feel rather small. I loved her smell and was tempted to hug and inhale her.

"You smell good," I said. "What scent is that?"

She gave me a shy smile. "Victoria's Secret, English Rose." We sat across from each other, the file between us. She flipped through it, then she placed both hands down and breathed deeply. "Okay. I want you to know that your school can't sponsor you for an H visa."

My stomach dipped. "Why not?"

She smiled apologetically. "Well, there are complications because of a statute of limitation."

"What do you mean?"

"It's just that the law has changed and it looks as if the time for you to file for an H visa has more or less elapsed. But don't despair. I've been discussing your case with another lawyer here. There's another way to make you legal. A rather risky one, I'm afraid, but you have a strong case."

I regarded her with caution. "What can you do for me?"

"We can apply for suspension of deportation."

Deportation?

She hastened to explain: "An immigrant who has stayed in the country illegally for five years can file for suspension of deportation. Basically, you've broken the law and should be deported. What we'll do is turn you in to immigration officials, and they'll begin deportation proceedings against you."

"Turn me in? I don't want to be locked up!"

"Oh no, it's nothing of the sort. You'd just be charged with violation of immigration law. No one will lock you up. You'd be free to go about your business. In fact, they'll give you a temporary work permit and a court date. Then you'll go before the judge. Now, if we can show that you've been a good citizen and that there were circumstances that forced you to break the law, the judge can suspend your deportation and grant you permanent residence. You told me you wanted to go back to Ghana, right?"

"Yes." I was bouncing my heels, biting my lips. "You said it was risky."

"Yes. If they deny your petition, you'd be deported. But you say you wouldn't mind if they sent you back."

My heart stopped and started again. "Yes, but what about my children? The judge says I can't take my daughter out of the country without an order."

She smiled confidently. "We'll work out something. By the way, don't worry about the monthly payments. We'll do this pro bono."

"Pro bono? I don't have to pay anything?"

"That's correct."

"Okay." I sagged with relief.

"Now, do I have your permission to go ahead?" She was looking at me with caution.

I took a deep breath and said "Yes."

"Okay, then. The first order of things is to turn you in to immigration."

The very notion churned my stomach, but as I looked into her solemn eyes, a strange calm settled on me. Whatever lay ahead, I would face it.

Dwan Ne Mmɛn

Ram's Horns

I was taking a nap in my bedroom when the phone rang.

"Hi, Lola," said a voice as rich as wine. "I'm Phoebe Gordon. I work with Rita Roche."

I sprang up, sitting on my heels. "Oh, hi!"

"Grace has been discussing your case with me."

"Yes, she told me."

"Yours is a fascinating one, and I'd like to represent you. I'm sorry about all you've had to go through. Can you come to the office tomorrow at around one?"

It was a good thing the children were outside playing, because I was doing the very thing I had told them not to do: jumping up and down on my bed.

Phoebe looked more like a college student than a lawyer. She wore faded, sawed-off jeans that revealed her slim legs. Her shirt was knotted at the waist. Her vibrant auburn hair cascaded almost to her waist. I loved her green eyes, which smiled above an upturned nose. We exchanged pleasantries and she asked me to come into her office. It felt like a promotion. No one had ever invited me upstairs before.

I followed her at a brisk pace up the spiral staircase to a tiny office. Files crammed every available space, except for her desk. She strode around it, sat down, and picked up my file. I sat opposite her. Her smile was full of compassion.

She shook her head slowly. "You've been through a lot. It's a wonder you didn't just pack your bags and fly home."

"You have no idea."

"Don't get me wrong. As an immigration lawyer, my passion is helping immigrants settle here. I'm just curious as to why you've stayed this long in America."

I sighed, cracking my fingers, looking out the window. "You know, this is a question I get asked often. Each time, my answer is different, but they are all true. I never wanted to come to America in the first place. I was young and foolish. By the time I decided I wanted to return, I was stuck in a job that paid a pittance, and nobody and no organization wanted to be an accessory to a felony by helping me."

Phoebe's brows shot up.

"Because of the court order barring me from taking my daughter out of the country."

"Oh yes, that must have been harrowing."

"I had wanted to leave with my daughter, regardless, but a plane ticket costs over a thousand dollars for one person. There were three of us. Even if the children paid half a ticket, that was still money I couldn't come up with. Apart from plane tickets, I needed some transition money, maybe a thousand dollars, at least. Where could I find even fifty dollars a month to save? Until recently, I made less than eight hundred dollars a month. Even now, I make only a thousand." I wiped my eyes with my sleeve. "Every month, I play games with the electricity company. Phone. Gas. I wait until they're about to cut off my service before paying. This is how many of us immigrants get trapped. You meet people who have been here for twenty years, who are saving money to return home but never seem to get there. Trapped. Ramming my horns against closed doors." I shifted in my seat. "And here's the thing, I couldn't afford not to pay for my children's piano lessons and sports, things I enjoyed as a child. Living in America, I wanted my children to be like the middle-class kids in our neighborhood, even if I was destitute."

Phoebe nodded with understanding.

"They attended the school where I taught, and while they enjoyed free tuition, I had to pay book fees, books the Christian school took back at the end of the year."

"What? That's not right."

I nodded. "Yes. When I couldn't pay, they sent bill collectors after me. When I appealed to the pastor, the chancellor of the school, he urged me get a second job or go on welfare." I laughed derisively. "This from the same pastor who urged congregants to vote against social programs, who said the poor were the church's responsibility and not the state's. This, when besides teaching full-time, I tutored students after school and even babysat."

Phoebe sat still, staring at me with round eyes.

"Sorry," I said. "I got carried away."

"No, this is fascinating."

"I tried. I starved myself, but there was little money left at the end of the month. Anyway, I made the best of it. Even if I was struggling, I knew it would be different for my kids in the end. They are

Americans, after all, entitled to its promises. This is why I stayed. But now I've had enough of living on the fringe. I want the freedom to travel in and out of America. I want to see my family and have my children know them. I want to have a choice as to where to live. That's true freedom, isn't it? Freedom to choose to remain or return to Ghana or live partially in both countries. Freedom. That's what I crave. That's what every human deserves."

She stared at me for a long time, then she handed me a tissue, blowing her nose. "Wow. I take my hat off to you. What a strong woman you are."

"Thank you." I broke into a sad smile. "I didn't have a choice, really."

"Oh yes, you did. You could have succumbed to madness. But you're here, and you know what, you have a very strong case." She began leafing through papers.

"Thank you."

"I know Grace has already explained suspension of deportation to you, but I'd like to go over it." She spoke succinctly, repeating almost word for word what Grace had told me. "Here's the risk: if your case is denied, you'd be deported. You'd never be able to reenter the U.S."

I uncrossed my legs and crossed them again. "My children—"

"That will be part of our strategy. We'll petition the court to allow you to leave with her. You have custody, after all. Right?"

"For now, yes."

"It's true the grandparents would be deprived of a relationship with their granddaughter. But, even if they fight, I believe we can move forward with this. Now, I have to ask you, is deportation a risk you're willing to take?"

"Yes." My voice was firm.

"Okay, then. Let's go for it. Just one thing. I'm not a partner here, so Rita would be the one to turn you in to immigration. But don't worry, I will prepare the files myself and make sure everything is in order."

On the appointed day, my heart raced as I walked from the metro to Immigration in Alexandria. The prospect of entering the brick building and turning myself in as an illegal immigrant made me tremble. Rita had instructed me to meet her outside the building but she wasn't there. I waited, sweat rolling down my temples despite the cool weather. She showed up thirty minutes late.

"Morning!" she said with her brash confidence.

I stared. Black smudges stained the skin around her eyes, and specks of mascara swayed on her lashes. Her lipstick was faded, except in the red vertical creases of her lips. Her hair stuck out in different directions. She looked as though she'd got up after an eventful night, jumped into her car, and driven over. How was this specter going to represent me? Who would take her seriously?

I remembered to return her "good morning," before following her quick steps to the elevator.

We sat shoulder to shoulder in the small waiting room, separated from the main office by a glass window atop a wooden frame. I hadn't seen her since my initial consultation with her but no apology dropped from her mouth.

"I need to ask you a few questions," she said, taking a spiral notebook and pen out of her bag. "When did you first come to America?"

My mouth opened. "Don't you have my file?"

"No, I didn't have time to stop by the office before coming."

My mind scattered. I wasn't a lawyer, but when you have someone's life in your hand, when the person is facing a critical situation, how could you not have time to collect a file and review it? Why didn't she take it home the previous night? And even if she had left it, hadn't she ever read it?

"So, tell me about this White man who brought you to America," she said. "The one who died."

"The one who brought me was Black, from Haiti." My voice was sharper than I had intended it to be. "And he didn't die, we broke up."

She smiled with confidence anyway. "Oh, I see. And your husband, the one who died in jail, he was Black, right?"

"No, he was White."

"I thought he was Black."

"He was White."

The smile left her face. "I had no idea."

"Why would you think he was Black?"

She shook her head, looking stumped. This woman was going to represent me? She asked a few more useless questions until they called my name, by which time I felt as trussed up as a live turkey.

We sat side by side again, this time, in front of a Black immigration officer in suit and tie. I was shaking with fear, but I had to trust that Rita wouldn't let them lock me up. The man took down my history. She spoke for me, and several times, I had to correct the answers she gave. I might as well have been there by myself. At some point, the officer leaned forward and asked, "If your application for suspension of deportation is denied, where would you want to be deported to?" His pen was poised over his pad, ready to write.

"Venezuela," Rita said.

The officer dropped his pen. He sat back, frowning. I turned to stare at Rita. Venezuela? Why would I want to go there?

"But she's from Ghana," the officer said.

"That's right," she said, staring him down. "We want her deported to Venezuela."

My eyes begged her to look at me, but all I got was her stubborn profile.

"What if the Venezuelans don't want her?"

"That's not for you to worry about. We want her deported to Venezuela."

It dawned on me that it was a strategy. If the Venezuelans didn't want me, then I belonged nowhere, and it would be up to the Americans to figure out what to do with me. It was some kind of delaying tactic. If Rita had studied my file, she would have noted that I didn't mind being deported to Ghana. And she might have discussed her strategy with me before making such a pronouncement. My tears were close to breaking out and I had a desire to slap her.

The officer shrugged, shaking his head. "Well, if that's what you want, then that's what I'll put down." He scribbled a little, gave me a curious look, and scribbled again. He asked me about my marriage, why I didn't get my husband to sponsor me.

"He died before he could do it."

"I'm sorry, ma'am." He pushed to his feet. "Please come with me for fingerprinting." Fingerprints? I looked at Rita. She wasn't looking at me. "I'm afraid you have to do this alone," the man said.

The last time I had been fingerprinted was in Dakar, when the police had stopped Joana and me, together with our friends, simply because we didn't know to carry our personal identification with us everywhere. It had ended with us spending the night behind the counter. Now here was this immigration officer talking about fingerprinting. I followed him through a narrow corridor into a small room where a fingerprint technician was bent over another culprit. He had to tell me to be steady as he took his time rolling each finger on the cool black pad before pressing it on the glass plate. I heaved a sigh when he said, "It's okay, you can go now."

I slid my body next to Rita, who patted my arm with affection.

"You're to appear in court three months from today," the officer said, thrusting a paper at Rita.

She stood up and smiled confidently. "We'll be there," she said, scrawling quickly on her pad. I stumbled down the stairs after her. At the curb she stuck out her hand. "I've got to get back to the office, but don't worry, everything will be just fine."

With an effort, I raised my hand from where it was glued to my skirt. She shook it vigorously and took off. When I pictured her representing me, I bent over and threw up everything inside me until I was dry-heaving onto the grass.

As soon as I got home, I punched Grace's number. "She's awful! She didn't even read my file! How can she defend me?"

"Don't worry," she said in a calm voice. "I'll make sure Phoebe represents you in court. There's just one thing. You see, Phoebe is leaving the firm. Legally, she can't steal you away from Rita, because you're Rita's client. But I have it all worked out. Trust me, Phoebe will represent you. What you have to do is fire Rita."

"Gladly. All that woman ever did for me was relieve me of my money."

"I understand. But we have to be careful. If you fire her, she could refuse to hand over your file to you."

"What?"

"The files belong to her, because all the work we did was for the firm, and she owns it."

I felt deflated.

"So here's what we'll do. We have to get the file out of the office before you fire her."

"How do we do that?"

"Come to my office tomorrow. We'll have a pretend consultation upstairs, then I'll give you the file."

"Okay."

That night, I wrestled with my sheets. What if Rita discovered our plan and demanded to have the files? I threw off my cover, pulled it over myself again.

The winds of fall were dying down, and winter was just around the corner. For the covert operation, I wore pants and a thick yellow jacket that grabbed my hips. At Rita's office, I smiled at the secretary and climbed up the spiral stairs to Grace's office and closed the door. She had the file ready on her desk, about three inches thick.

"I'm also leaving Rita," she said. "I've already given my notice. I'm going to another firm. That's why we have to get the file out of here today. I won't be here to help you."

I could only shake my head in amazement. "Thanks, Grace."

"Don't mention it. I really believe in your case." She picked up the file and stood. "Wait a minute, you brought only a small handbag? You can't hide a file in that."

"Sorry, I didn't think about it." I thought for a minute. "How about I hide it in my jacket?"

"Yeah," she said with a wry smile. "I guess that will have to do." She walked around her desk and came to where I was standing. I giggled. I was stealing what rightfully belonged to me. She held the file in place on my chest while I zipped up the jacket. Thanks to all that walking, I was still a size four, so when I zipped up the coat, the file was indiscernible.

"This is like espionage." I laughed. We looked at each other and hugged. "Thank you so much, Grace."

She smiled like a fellow conspirator.

I crept down the spiral staircase in full view of the secretary, as if I held a raw egg between my thighs. The fitting at the end of my jacket wasn't tight, so I knew the file could fall out if I made a sudden move. I put my hand on my stomach and rubbed it casually, whistling softly as if I was just happy. When I was all the way down, I hugged my stomach, smiling at the secretary. "It's so cold," I said. She smiled back before turning to talk to a client. I didn't look at the other people in the lobby. I kept my body straight, heart thumping, and waddled out of the office. I knew the secretary could see the parking lot through the window, so I resisted the urge to run. I opened the door to my car and sat down without removing the file. Then I switched on the ignition. As soon as I backed out of the parking lot, I floored the accelerator.

Phoebe's new office nestled in a red-brick building in Arlington, close to Debbie's father's house, where I had lived with Dele. The reception area was as large as all of Rita's first floor. White letters on the glass door stated, "Stevens, Laroche and Gordon." The office gleamed with the muted tones of polished mahogany. Wearing a blue jacket over a white shirt, the receptionist sat behind a counter talking to someone on the phone.

"I'm here to see Phoebe Gordon," I said when she put down the receiver. "My name is Lola."

She smiled, rising to her feet. "Right this way, Lola. She's expecting you."

She led me through a corridor with wood paneling. When I saw Phoebe standing behind her desk in a sleeveless black dress, her hair held back, I wanted to hug her.

"Hi, Phoebe. I have the file." I held it out to her.

"Great, you brought it!" She took it and plunked down. I sat opposite her in a comfortable chair and looked around with admiration. Her office had proper file cabinets, no files on the floor. Two people could walk around her desk without touching each other. A couple of framed certificates hung on the wall. House plants greened a corner.

She handed me a pen with a letter she had already prepared. "This is a letter for you to sign. It says you no longer require the services of Rita Roche."

I had never been so happy to scrawl my signature on a paper.

She continued, "I'll have it delivered to her, and you'll never have to worry about dealing with her again. Now, your case. We'll fight it to the death." Her rich voice was emphatic. "We'll take this as far as we need to. Congress, even to the Supreme Court."

I didn't know if she would be successful, but of all the people I had interacted with over immigration, she and Grace had dealt most professionally with me. She was representing me free of charge. Whatever the outcome, I had faith she would do her utmost.

Sesa Wo Suban

Transform Your Life

May 2007

After the trial, I'll either live legally in America or be deported back to Ghana within six months. I'm wearing a skirt suit. It's silky gray, with tiny herringbone stripes. I've even got on panty-hose, something I don't like to wear. My hair is parted on the side, slicked back and held by a black bow.

Phoebe. What an attorney. She has prepared the case as well as she can. Aside from subpoenas, she has obtained written affidavits from my ex-father-in-law, the principal of the high school where I teach, my roommate—anyone connected to me. Last night, over the phone, her voice wavered with maternal fretting:

Make sure you dress the children nicely.

That little girl of yours is something else, so pretty. Make sure it shows.

Remember to be yourself. Let your emotions show.

Speak clearly.

Dele has on a black suit with a blue shirt and a diagonally striped clip-on tie. He's a miniature executive with a half-dimpled smile, the smile that has pumped me with adrenaline every morning. And Kemi. Look at her. Look at her dress, so pretty, the way it swirls around her ankles. Fruit, vegetables, and leaves bloom against a background of yellow, gathering at her flower-stalk waist, a big bow at her back. White lace trims the wrists, the baby collar, and the scalloped hemline. It's her favorite spring dress and, though it's unseasonably chilly, I know she'll be warm. As I take in the black tendrils gathered on her head, a few curling around her temples and nape, my throat tightens. Her smile is pure trust. I dare not fail her. I dare not fail them.

I pick up my purse and sling it over my shoulder.

"Let's go." I hope my smile is reassuring.

Kemi wraps her arms around my thighs. "It's okay, Mummy." Her big almond eyes make my chest tight. Dele looks at my face intently. He doesn't smile. I haven't fooled him. He takes my hand and we walk to the car.

We meet Phoebe in the lobby of the courthouse in Arlington. The giant building reminds me how small I am, how my future is in the hands of a man whose face I've yet to see. To him, I am just one of countless illegal immigrants America wants to root out.

"Hi, Dele, you look wonderful," Phoebe says. Her eyes flash with confidence. Gone is the tremor in her voice from last night. Dele's smile is brief. "Kemi, what a pretty dress!"

Kemi lights up and my heart flips. Phoebe fixes her big brown eyes on me. "Well, Lola, this is it."

I swallow. She squeezes my hand.

We take the longest elevator ride to the courtroom. An elderly gentleman with silver hair stands beside us. I'm grateful that, beyond a polite "good morning," he doesn't talk. Every minute is a year. I can feel the little pings of my pulse. My hands are cold. The children are unusually quiet. Normally, they love to read the numbers of the floors and fuss about who is going to push the button. The elevator screeches and whines into the silence.

"I didn't sleep last night," Phoebe says. "I kept going over every aspect of the case in my mind, wondering if there was anything I had overlooked."

"You've done everything you could possibly do for me," I say. "No matter what happens, I want you to know I'm grateful. I'll never forget your kindness."

The doors part open. It's clear the gentleman wants to get out. So does Dele.

"Allow the gentleman to go before you," I say. He hangs back. The gentleman brushes past and turns left into the hallway. We turn right to find our courtroom.

The flapping birds are still inside me.

Our witnesses arrive in bunches: fellow teachers; Ted, who talked to me the night I wanted to die; Mr. and Mrs. Morrison (to ensure I remain in America); the ever loyal Washingtons, the Winstons, Pastor Drake, B.K., Ate Celestine. They are here to tell the court why I shouldn't be deported. Each time people arrive, Phoebe points them to a witness room. More than twenty people are here, men and women I've met along my journey. I am overwhelmed at this manifestation of love.

"Lola," Phoebe says, "the judge will be here soon. The children, too, have to go into the witness room."

I tremble. She looks at my face and takes them herself. B.K. or any of the others will take care of them.

The prosecutor has arrived. It's a different person from the one we met three months ago. I can tell she's the prosecutor by the smoothness of her gait, the black suit and briefcase. She is a slim woman with a Middle Eastern complexion. Her curly hair is lustrous, unhindered by hair spray. She's heading in our direction. A burning sensation begins in my chest and rises to my throat.

"Phoebe Gordon?" she asks.

"Yes," Phoebe says.

They smile, shake hands, and say lawyerly things. The ease of the prosecutor's smile generates sweat in my palms. She must be sure of victory. In front of my skirt, my palms are glued together. I'm praying.

"Why don't we step aside and talk?" the prosecutor says. Her quiet voice increases the sweating and I fight to control my breathing. Phoebe doesn't move, so they talk in front of me. My heart stops. I don't understand, don't believe what I'm hearing, what she's saying to Phoebe. "I've read your brief. It's a compelling case. I'm going to recommend to the judge that she be granted permanent residence." It's as if she's talking about someone else, because I'm standing in front of her, but she's not looking at me.

Phoebe nearly drops her briefcase. She is shaking her head, breathing fast. "Are you sure? Because we're prepared. We've got witnesses. We're ready"

"It's not necessary," the prosecutor says with a nice smile. "You have a compelling case. The judge will agree."

I'm in a daze. I don't trust her words.

"All rise!" the bailiff says. "Court is in session. The Honorable Judge Franklin Shaunessy presiding."

We stand before our chairs, waiting for the robed judge to take his seat. I gasp, because he is none other than the gentleman who shared the elevator with us. A funereal hush hangs in the air. The courtroom is now empty of spectators. Only a few of us remain: the court reporter, Phoebe, one of her new partners who has just arrived, the prosecutor, and me. The judge takes the bench, and the case of the government of the United States of America versus Olivia Akua Lola Oduro begins. I'm fighting the urge to flee.

The prosecutor stands up for her opening. "Your Honor, the government feels this is a compelling case. We move that the defendant be granted permission to stay in the United States of America."

My heart is going krrpoom krrpoom krrpoom. The judge is not smiling. He leans forward, his eyes on the thick file open before him. He looks up. His face is solemn. My chest is so tight I can't breathe.

His lips move. "I agree." My eyes pop. I don't know if I am hearing his voice or something my ears are making up. But his mouth is still moving so I know he's speaking. "I, too, have read the brief, and this is a compelling case. I'm glad you've seen the wisdom in not wasting the court's time with this."

Phoebe stands up, drops her pen, scrambles to pick it up before it rolls. She straightens her skirt. "Your Honor, I would like to put on a case just for the record." Her voice is anxious but firm. She, too, must not believe it's that simple. The prosecutor does not object. "I'd like to call Ms. Oduro to the stand."

I know what to do. I walk with dignity, stand, put my right hand up, and swear to tell the truth, the whole truth, so help me God. Phoebe stands in front of me. There's love in her eyes. Her voice reverberates with confidence. I state my full name for the record. Then I tell His Honor about my journey. My voice wants to break, so I try breathing slowly, but I can tell I'm failing.

"And what are your hopes for your children?" Phoebe asks.

I tell the court about Dele and Kemi. The tears have broken through and my voice won't obey my admonition to be firm. But I have to speak for them, for those precious lives who depend on my ability to provide. When I finish speaking, I look up at the judge. His eyes are shining. My tears are warm streams on my cheeks. Phoebe's eyes are pools. She's looking at me as if she has only just met me.

When she speaks, her voice is hushed reverence. "The defense rests." She locks eyes with me. I blink and nod. Her work is finished.

The prosecutor leans back in her chair, a pen in one hand. My knees are shaking.

"Have you ever committed any crime?"

"No, ma'am."

"Are you wanted for any criminal offense in any country?"

"No, ma'am."

"If you lie to us and we uncover anything, you'll be prosecuted and deported."

"Yes, ma'am."

"Would you like to change your answer?"

"No, ma'am."

She turns to the judge. "The government rests, Your Honor."

Our collective eyes are trained on the judge. Both his palms are flat on the table. The seconds tick, tick, tick. I'm still in the witness box, trembling. Then he opens his mouth and his words are unlike anything I imagined.

"You are hereby granted permanent residence. Welcome to the United States of America."

For a moment, I'm a statue. Then Phoebe tears up, hugging the other partner from her firm. The prosecutor's eyes are wet too. My body sags into the chair and I bury my head in my hands. I am shaking from the sobs. I can still hear the judge's voice, but I can't look at him.

"I congratulate you for finding yourself a fine attorney. Most cases appear before me and I have no idea what they're all about. But your attorney prepared an excellent brief, well documented and annotated, with a table of contents."

I wipe my face and sit up, yet the tears won't stop flowing. Phoebe gives the judge a respectful smile. She and the prosecutor shake hands. The judge wants to see the witnesses. Phoebe runs out to fetch them. The prosecutor smiles at me.

The witnesses crowd in and the judge says, "I want to thank you all for coming here today to do your civic duty. I know you took time out of your busy schedule to get here. However, this is a special case and I feel compelled to grant the defense's request. Therefore, your testimonies are no longer needed, but I thank you for honoring the call to testify. I want you to know the court respects your time and hopes that, in the future, should you be called upon to testify in any case, you will honor it. Thank you very much and I wish you all a good day. Miss Oduro, good luck to you. I wish you a prosperous future in the United States of America."

He bangs his gavel and rises. We wait for him to enter his chambers before letting out the hoots. I'm weightless, laughing and hugging everyone. Phoebe and I hold each other.

"Phoebe, how can I ever thank you?"

"Be successful. Be happy." She's sniffing and smiling through her tears.

"I will never forget your kindness. You and Grace. Never."

Ted grabs me and hugs me. "Darn it," he says, grinning. "I was looking forward to my day in court. I've never been subpoenaed before!"

"Thank you, Ted. Thank you for everything. For saving my life that night when I wanted to die. Do you remember?"

He waves me off, "Nah, that was nothing. I just helped you see what was inside you. I know Mindy will be thrilled." Because of a business trip, she is not in court today. I'll call her when she gets back.

The children race around the room. I catch Dele, then Kemi, and I hug them. I can hear everyone saying, *Awww, just look at them.*

Phoebe tells me she has to go to the office, so we hug one more time and make a date to celebrate with Grace who is out of the country.

Everything looks different. The sidewalk. The streets. The houses. I belong. Fear has flown out of my heart. I will never tremble if a policeman stops me in traffic. If a lawyer defrauds or cheats me, I can sue, report them to the bar. I can pick up *The Washington Post*'s employment section and apply for any job that takes my fancy. With no objection from the Morrisons, I can travel to any destination I want with the children. And what I want is to go back home. I no longer care how others may perceive me. My mother's last letter, written despite my silence, has haunted me, hinting at her aging: *I am afraid you may never see me again.* I don't want to wait to make enough money only to go weep over her corpse. If there's a lesson I've learned, it is that life holds no promises for anyone, no allegiance to anyone's plans. I will touch her now, while life still throbs in her veins.

I've been trapped in the cage of immigration, and now I've broken free. It's May. The long summer break from school is around the corner. What I need is to go back to Ghana, to mend the broken bridge between me and my family. It's time to use the credit card. I need space to figure out what I want to do for the next stage of my life. Now I can leave, thanks to Phoebe, and Grace, who stayed up and talked to me that night when I was sad. I'll board a plane and return, like the San kɔ fa swan, to pick up what I left behind.

Mpatapɔ

The Knot of Pacification

When I stepped off the plane into the air at Kotoka International Airport at five thirty a.m., I felt as a baby must feel inside her mother's womb.

Fresh from sleep, the children stayed mute. My limbs were coiled springs, waiting to bounce off the plane. As we descended the stairs to board a bus to the terminal, my whole body tingled. A diffusion of milk bush, mango, fried beans, diesel, and humid clothes welcomed me. I closed my eyes and inhaled, wanting to hold the air inside me forever, surrendering to its caress on my arms and neck. I was one with the wisps of white chiffon mist that draped the shrubs and trees.

Immigration, customs, and welcome to Ghana.

A sea of faces jostled over a barricade, waiting to receive travelers. The children clung to me as we made our way out. There, waving madly, was my sister, a little rounder but her smile was just as lively. I stopped moving, drinking her in.

"Akua! Is that you?" She broke free. I ran and threw my arms around her.

I looked around wildly, expecting to see my mother, but she wasn't there. She had received the news that I was coming home with what I thought was joy. Was she just being polite? I tried to still my heart. "Where is Mama?"

"She's at home, she is not feeling well, but she said to bring you straight to Kumasi."

I felt deflated. Kumasi. Four hours away by road after a nine-hour flight from New York. Three and half, if we didn't stop for a meal on the way. But after ten years of not seeing my mother, four hours was nothing. I cast my eyes around for Awurama's husband. "Where is my in-law? And the kids?"

She laughed. "You think I was going to share this moment with them? No, no. But come on. Mr. Poku, can you take her things?"

A man I assumed was Mr. Poku stepped out from behind her and pushed my cart through the crowd. It had to be her current chauffeur.

It was a long drive through the city and finally along the road to Kumasi. The vegetation turned from small shrubs to giant trees. We drove through towns with churches on hills, through villages with a blend of mud and concrete houses, thatched and slate roofs. People stood or sat by the roadside selling plantains, tomatoes, pineapples, oranges. Sometimes a hunter would hold up some slaughtered animal, a grasscutter or antelope whose meat I remembered was delicious. I was home. I wanted to leap out of the car and hug every person. The children pointed and laughed. Soon we pulled into Kumasi, driving past Kwame Nkrumah University of Science and Technology with its magnificent bridge shaped like a traditional stool, where the road curved beautifully in divergent arcs. We wove through a din of honking cars and drivers shouting. The town was bigger and busier than I'd left it ten years before.

"You know Mama is retired, right?"

I hadn't known that, but she was past retirement age. I felt gripped by sadness. I had missed so much.

We arrived at Mama's new house around noon. The brick bungalow, smaller than her official residence, sat on the outskirts of the city, snuggling under tall trees. But to me, it was almost as grand as a palace because Mama had managed to step into royal history: Even from the gate, I could see a balustrade designed with her favorite Adinkra symbols wrapped around the front veranda, the way it was done before colonization. I had never before pondered the word Adinkra itself, which means to take leave or say goodbye. In one sense, the symbols represented instructions left behind after one exited the world. Incorporated into the design of houses, they provided symmetry and balance, both physical and spiritual. Balance. That was what Mama had tried to teach me all along. Now I was on the trajectory to achieving that in my own life. Balance between independence and family, new norms and tradition.

A houseboy pulled open the wooden gate to let us in. The veranda with its red polished floor welcomed us. I saw Mama through the screen door. She was sitting in an armchair in the living room. Was she as nervous to see me as I was to see her? My stomach tightened at the thought that she might have aged, that she wouldn't look like herself, that I would cry.

I opened the door and stood in front of her. She sat there looking at me, a joyous smile on her face.

"Hello, Mama," I said softly.

"Welcome, Akua." She stood up and I rushed into her arms,

nearly knocking her over. I inhaled her powder and Ponds cream. My fingers crept over her face. I rubbed my cheeks against hers, which were still firm. I touched her hair pulled on top of her head in large puffs. Gray streaks twirled through them. Her face was lined slightly but her eyes displayed the same fearlessness. And they were smiling at me, tears pooling in them. Dele tugged at my arm. "Grandma?"

I nodded, unable to speak. I pulled back and the kids flew at her. She hugged them both. She looked down at Kemi, who had wrapped herself around her legs. "Let me look at you." I held my breath. If she said the wrong thing about her being half-White, my heart would break. "What a well-mannered child," she said. "And so beautiful." I exhaled. Dele was grinning, not displaying his customary reserve. "And you are Dele." She looked at me. "They are wonderful."

What a contrast from my last visit with her, when a canyon opened between us and we couldn't cross over to each other's side. Now no space hung between us. On the wall above a cupboard, the San kɔ fa swan held her egg over her back, both feet on the ground. Below the swan stood a framed picture I had mailed to Awurama: me in the middle, my children on either side of me. Mama smiled slowly, sandwiching my hand between both of hers. "I never stopped believing you would come back home, my daughter."

My tears broke freely.

There was so much to say to her, but that would be for later.

After a delicious lunch of fried plantain and beans, Awurama went home to fetch her husband and children. Mama took us for a walk around the neighborhood. Each time we met people, she said, "This is my daughter come home from America. These are her children." She wanted everyone to know me and welcome me into the community.

We sat on a large rock, watching Dele and Kemi race off to look at plants that grew along the path.

"Oliv—" Mama stopped herself. "You don't like it when I call you Olivia."

I touched her gently on the wrist. "It's okay, Mama, call me Olivia if you like. I know it was your best friend's name."

"I'm happy. You see, I always nourished the hope that from a formless little person, you would eventually transform into a woman who could stand beside me in fellowship. Olivia is my reminder that you are an individual. Olivia is from olive, the symbol people use for peace."

I looked at her in wonder. The universe seemed to bathe her in light and I was seeing her for the first time. Her smile was relaxed, as if there was nothing else she needed to do with her life. All this time, I had no idea what the name meant to her. "I called myself Lola because it means 'the child is wealth.' It made me feel precious."

"Lola," she said, as if trying out the name. Her face remained calm. For a moment, I wondered if I had caused her pain. "It's a beautiful name. You *are* wealth to me."

"But I will always be Olivia, because you named me for a purpose." I was always precious. I didn't need to get another name to prove that.

She gave me a dazzling smile. We sat in a peaceful silence. Then she nodded in the direction of Dele and Kemi, who were crouched beside a sunflower, touching its petals. "You have raised them well."

My heart swelled like the symphony at the end of a great movie.

"I did my best."

"You did well, my daughter."

And just like that, we were one. I hooked my arm to hers, thinking of mpatapɔ, the adinkra knot of pacification. Maybe that was Twi for Olivia. In Western societies, when you've had a conflict with a parent, you both sit down to hash things out. It may end in a screaming match, but you say what is in your heart. Sometimes, a parent might even apologize. But such a discussion presupposes an egalitarian relationship. That's not the Ghanaian way. Children are not the equals of their parents. And parents seldom say I love you, but they feel it no less. By her simple statement, *You did well*, Mama was also saying that she might have been wrong about some things. However, she would never articulate it. That was fine by me. It was enough that she received me as an honored guest. It was enough that she said I had done well. That was an apology and forgiveness.

And it was enough that I sat beside her, touching her arm now and again, stroking her hair and smiling at her. That was forgiveness. And an apology.

ACKNOWLEDGMENTS

A writer is nothing without a village. Huge thanks to my editor, Rakesh Satyal, for loving this story and bringing it to the world. This book wouldn't be here without the entire HarperVia team: Deputy Publisher Tara Parsons, Ryan Amato, and a host of others I haven't had the pleasure of interacting with directly. I know you all have my back. *Merci infiniment* to my publicists extraordinaire, Alison Cerri and Paul Olsewski. You make magic. My agent, Sharon Bowers, believed from the start and pulled more out of me than I thought possible. Receive your flowers.

Many thanks to my readers, especially Jeffrey Lin, Elizabeth Johnson, Roxanne Bougsin Koffi, Nii Teiko Evans-Anform, and Yvonne Serwa Dzormeku.

I've always been able to count on Writers Project of Ghana, especially Dr. Martin Eblewogbe and Elizabeth Johnson. Thank you!

My cousin Kofi Sika donated his IT skills and kept me laughing. Kofi, your *alatani* loves and thanks you. My dearest "Erot," Jemima Oware, is a very present help in trouble. You make the impossible possible. My cousin and Twi expert, Dr. Kobina Ofosu-Donkor, ensured accurate translation of Adinkra symbols and lavished love. It's returned tenfold.

To all the angels in my life, Apple Bob and Yezmin Ulfers, Carol Kramer-Leblanc, Vladmira Raftlova, Mark Newman, Liliah Parekh, Nanay and Tatay of blessed memory, Jim and Anne Newman, James and Joni Dubbs, Ana Rosa Pena, Dave May, Naomi Ortega, Anthony and Corinne Carr, Robyn Webb, Bill Bourland of blessed memory, and Kimberly Claire Burzio: may the universe shower you with blessings. Bob and Yezmin. Bob and Yezmin. Bob and Yezmin. That's all I can say.

Sheila Starkey Hahn and Terry Mannigan. There are not enough ways to thank you for those two life-changing phone calls. You are the best of the best, and I will always be in your debt.

Special gratitude and love to Rebecca Hayford of blessed memory. We'll carry on the torch of fearlessness, honesty, and loyalty. In my heart, your light will never dim.

Chimeka Garricks, Ayesha Harruna Atta, Mariel Abenser-Mould, and Shika Kwenin, thank you for anchoring me and never tiring. Lola Shoneyin, *ose gon, modupe*! Maaza Mengiste, I can't thank you enough; many thanks to Zukiswa Wanner for bringing us together.

Suzanne Peggy Amanor-Wilks, my sassy, funny, sister-friend, inspired the character of Joana. She always has my back. Love always.

Baffour family of Ghana, my faithful friends through life, I love you all. Thank you, Papa Andoh, for teaching me all about waiters. Thank you, Paul and Pauline Simmons for always being there. Charles and Simonetta Kusi, I couldn't have done that video at the last minute without your patient help. Sending you hugs and kisses.

My love and eternal gratitude to my big brother and lifesaver, Professor Kenneth Adjepon-Yamoah—oh, how I love you—and the entire Adjepon-Yamoah family. May we always know the way home.

ABOUT THE AUTHOR

Bisi Adjapon is the author of the critically acclaimed novel *The Teller of Secrets*. Her work has appeared in *McSweeney's Quarterly, The Washington Post, Ms.* magazine, *Aljazeera, New York Times,* and *The Guardian.* She has won the Foreign Service Award for Human Relations and an Excellence in Teaching Award. She divides her time between Ghana and America.

A NOTE ON THE COVER

This cover design focuses on the experience of inhabiting New York's dizzying landscape through a lens of Ghanaian tradition. The adinkra symbols on the cover include the conjoined crocodiles, the knot of pacification, and the emblem of cooperation and interdependence.

—Jim Tierney

Here ends Bisi Adjapon's
Daughter in Exile.

The first edition of this book was printed and
bound at Lakeside Book Company
in Harrisonburg, Virginia, February 2023.

A NOTE ON THE TYPE

The text of this novel was set in Times New Roman, a serif
typeface designed by Stanley Morison and Victor Lardent in
1931 as a commission for the British newspaper *The Times.*
Inspired by 18th-century printing traditions and early Baroque
printing, Times New Roman is a high-contrast, robust design
that moved away from the old-style model. It has become one
of the most popular typefaces of all time.

HARPERVIA

An imprint dedicated to publishing international voices,
offering readers a chance to encounter other lives and other
points of view via the language of the imagination.